Acclaim for
THE STORY PEDDLER

"Lindsay A. Franklin is a fearless storyteller. She weaves a colorful fantasy of light, darkness, and the many adventures in between. *The Story Peddler* is a perfect blend of humor, heartache, and healing."

—Nadine Brandes, author of *Fawkes* and *A Time to Die*

The Story Peddler is like nothing I've ever read. Lindsay A. Franklin weaves a magical and one-of-a-kind tale packed with danger, treason, and forbidden stories. A girl who wants to escape her mundane life. A king who harbors dark secrets. A princess in search of truth. *The Story Peddler* has it all.

Filled to the brim with mystery and intrigue, this stunning debut will transport readers to a realm from whence they'll ne'er desire to return. Save a spot on your TBR list for this beauty! *The Story Peddler* is a binge-worthy read sure to be treasured by peasants and kings alike.

—Sara Ella, award-winning author of the Unblemished trilogy

"Pirates, rebels, and the most original [illegible] I've seen since Patrick Carr's *A Cast of Stones* make [illegible] A. Hawkins's *The Sw*[illegible] *Peddler* a unique and engrossing debut. I read through the book in two days. Did not want to put it down."

—JILL WILLIAMSON, Christy Award-winning author of *By Darkness Hid* and *King's Folly*

The Story Peddler

The Story Peddler

THE WEAVER TRILOGY

BOOK 1

LINDSAY A. FRANKLIN

an imprint of
GILEAD PUBLISHING

Published by Enclave, an imprint of Gilead Publishing,
Wheaton, Illinois, USA

www.enclavepublishing.com

ISBN: 978-1-68370-136-1 (print)
ISBN: 978-1-68370-137-8 (eBook)

The Story Peddler

Edited by Steve Laube
Cover design by Kirk DouPonce
Interior design/typesetting by Beth Shagene

Printed in the United States of America

For Dave.
Always.

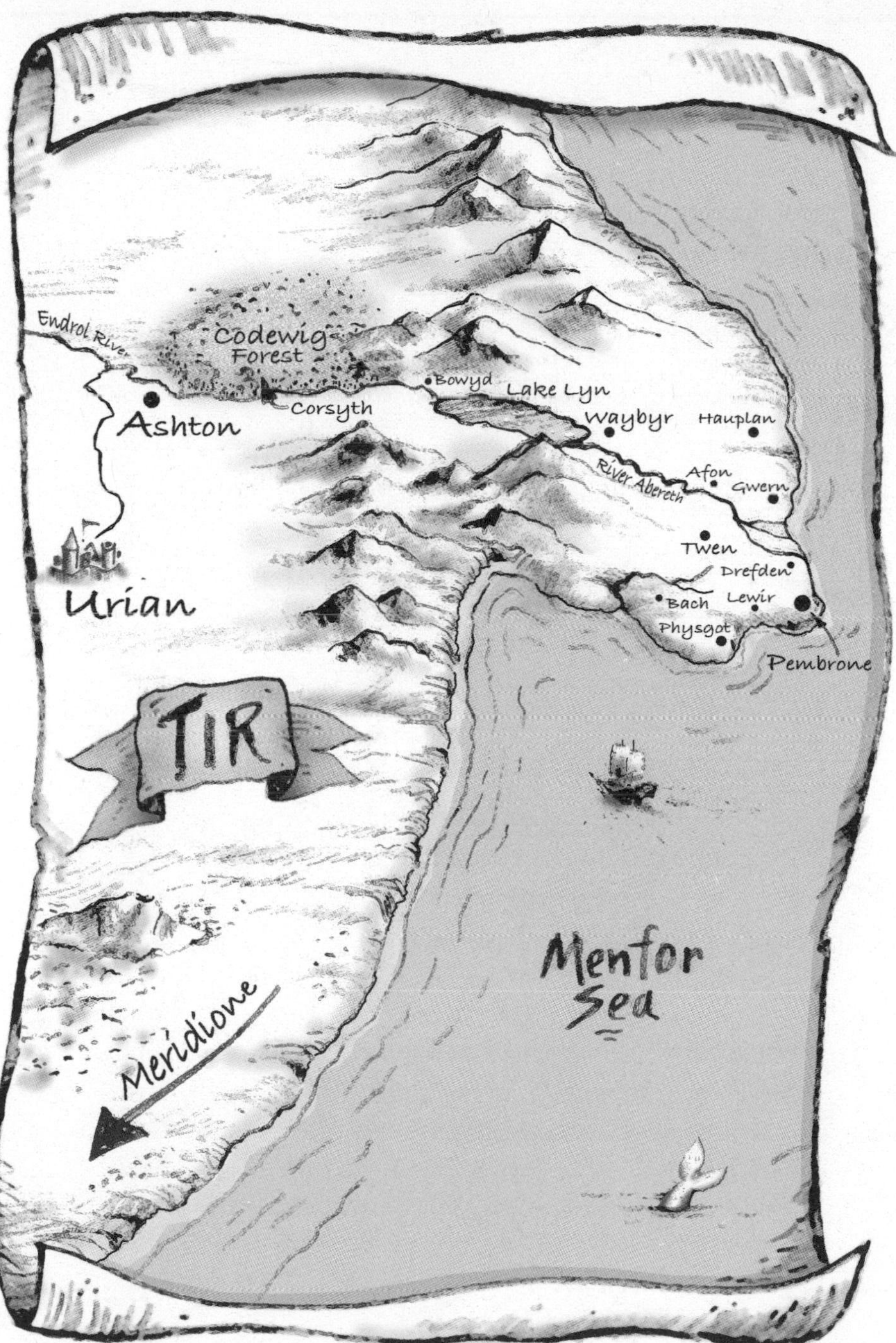

Endrol River
Codewig Forest
Ashton
Corsyth
Bowyd
Lake Lyn
Waybyr
Hauplan
River Abereth
Afon
Gwern
Twen
Drefden
Bach
Lewir
Physgot
Pembrone
Urian
TIR
Mentor Sea
Meridione

CHAPTER 1
TANWEN

Colored ribbons of light poured from my fingers. One strand broke free and soared above the crowd's head, glowing golden in the afternoon sun.

A child in the crowd gasped. "Look, Mam!"

I swallowed my smile and pushed all my focus back to my words—practiced over and over until I could say each phrase in fancy, schooled Tirian. Couldn't let any common village speak bleed into the stories all Tirians know so well. My storytelling mentor, Riwor, loomed near the edge of the crowd, eyes narrowed and watching my every breath. She'd make me pay for it if my practiced peddler words slipped into my usual lowborn drawl.

Again.

But when I opened my mouth, my best storytelling voice carried on the breeze through the village square, just like it was supposed to. "The orphan princess, Cariad the Stone, now forced to rule Tir in the wake of her parents' untimely deaths, vowed ever to be strong and noble for her people."

The swirling story strand hardened from glowing light into a swathe of matte gray fabric, then wove itself into a braid. It cinched tighter as I told the old tale.

"Cariad, though she was so very young, held fast to her vow."

I circled my fingers, and the braided fabric followed my command. It coiled around itself like a snake in the garden, until it looked less like fabric and more like a tiny stone tower from a fairy-story castle.

"Countless suitors from the best families of the realm courted her hand to no avail. She did not wish a husband's ambitions to direct the course of her people, whom she had sworn to protect."

The tiny tower stacked higher.

"But when the Stone Princess grew older, she fell deeply in love with her most trusted friend—her cupbearer, poor and unhandsome, but wise and loyal."

From one finger on my right hand, a grass-green story strand unraveled and wove through the stones of Cariad's tower.

"Cariad tried to convince herself that an alliance with her cupbearer would be disastrous, but as the years ticked by, her love for him only grew."

I glanced up. Every gaze was fixed on the story I was building. Perfect. With a flick of my fingers, the grassy vine that was meant to show Cariad's cup-bearing lover burst into bloom. Tiny red velvet-petals sprang forth all over. The children squealed, and several women gasped.

Good. I'd likely sell this one. Riwor would be pleased as a pickle.

"Cariad found herself unable to displace the loyal cupbearer from her heart, but she saw no reason to break her vow to the Tirian kingdom. So she bestowed the rule of her people and the title of king to her chief advisor, an honest and brave man whose line would rule Tir for two centuries."

I made a swirling bit of yellow light in one palm, then lifted my hand so it looked rather like the sun rising behind my stone tower—it was supposed to be the dawn of a new life for Cariad.

"And so Cariad and her cupbearer left the palace and lived simply and happily in the country for the rest of their days."

This was it. The end of the story. Time to change those fluid strands of idea into something solid—something to sell.

"The lesson of Cariad's story is . . ." I peeked sideways at Riwor.

She stared at me, face darkening by the heartbeat. It was always as if her disapproval chiseled out the creases around her mouth so they were deeper each day. She placed a gnarled old hand on one hip and glared her worst at me.

My voice wavered. "The lesson is . . ."

But I hated this ending. Giving up the palace? Trading fine gowns for peasant rags? That was addlebrained, if a body wanted my opinion.

Which no one did.

My story quivered before me, seemingly waiting for my next words.

But maybe I didn't have to shovel out the old, tired ending I hated. Maybe I could tell an ending all my own.

"Cariad and the cupbearer were happy—until they realized what she'd given up."

A smooth, black strand ribboned from my hand. It danced around the tower in a slow circle. A strand to represent Cariad's ambitions—a strand I could actually relate to.

Out of the corner of my eye, I saw Riwor's arms waving away.

Guess she doesn't like my new ending.

A couple villagers around the edge of the crowd stared at her, flapping like an old blackbird caught in a snare. But most of the crowd stuck fast to me and the new strands oozing from my hands.

"So Cariad unscrambled her brains long enough to raise an army." The rolling hum of my storyteller voice flitted away, and words that proved my peasanthood gushed out instead. "A big army, with swords and bows and arrows and suchlike!" I hopped off my wooden stool and shot a strand of glowing red light into the air.

"Tanwen!" Riwor's hiss reached my ears, but my new ideas had carried my mind too far away to care.

"It was an army full of peasants wanting to live in the palace, too!"

Story strands volleyed everywhere. Different colors, materials, textures—they wheeled every which direction, all over the blooming place.

"And they took the palace back so Cariad could be princess again—no, queen! No, empress!"

Then the strands froze like time had stopped. The tower with the red velvet-petals and my rogue, made-up strands stayed fixed in midair, gaping at me, if such a thing were possible.

Then, like a dropped glass, it all shattered to pieces. Before the story shards could fly into the crowd of wee ones, I swept my hand over the bits and they dissolved into light. I blinked, and the entire mess vanished.

I was left staring at an empty space where this week's supper money had been sitting.

Hovering around the back of the throng, the men of the village erupted into laughter.

"Nice try there, lassie." One man tipped his floppy farmer's hat in my direction. "Had us going for a moment, you did."

"Waste of time, this is," said another, grabbing a woman by the arm and leading her away.

Three older women brushed the dirt from their skirts as they stood.

One stared down at me and flashed a frosty smile. "We'd best be off. Some of us have real work to do, eh?"

They all chuckled and turned to leave. I made a face at their backs.

A young farmer grinned at me. "It wasn't all bad. I liked when you made the flowers come out, and I liked that the ending was different than I've heard before." He shuffled his feet in the dirt. "Say, what's your name?"

I forced a smile so as to be friendly to the customers, even if I felt like sinking into the dust. "Tanwen."

He smiled. "Have a drink with me at the tavern, will you, Tanwen?"

It took me a heartbeat to eye his shabby clothes and calloused hands. "I don't think so. But stop by next time we're in town. I'll sell you a story."

His smile collapsed. He nodded once, then trudged off.

I grabbed my stool and muttered to myself. "Sorry, but if I had a drink with every smitten farm boy in every village's scummy tavern, I'd never see the light of day again."

Still. He didn't seem like a bad fellow. A bit of guilt pricked me. Didn't help that the lad looked forcibly like Brac.

I sighed and turned to help Riwor load up the donkey cart. Figured I might as well face her wrath sooner than later. Except it found me first.

Sound and pressure exploded over my ear as she boxed me on the side of the head.

"Foolish girl!" Fire blazed in her eyes. "You were right at the end! What's the matter with you? Can't you just stick to the stories, like I've taught you?"

I rubbed my ear and stole a look around. The crowd was gone, except a few stragglers.

Good. I didn't need the whole village of Lewir watching me get torn to bits by a toothless crone—master story peddler or not.

"I'm sorry, Riwor. I just wanted to try something new."

"Something new?" She boxed my ear again. "There's something new for you to try, eh?"

Except Riwor boxing my ears wasn't anything new.

"Aye. Thanks," I grumbled, mostly to myself.

She snatched the wooden stool from me and shoved it onto the wagon with force. The lazy donkey picked up his hooves and brayed a mournful note. "And anyway, I told you to ask me before you tried to sell the Cariad story again. It wasn't on the latest list of crowned stories, and the last thing we need is one of the king's guardsmen taking offense."

My shoulders drooped. "I forgot."

She tossed a tarp over the donkey cart. "Fool thing to forget, Tanwen, unless you're looking to land in the dungeon. Stick to the crown-approved stories, or that's where you'll end up. And I don't mean to follow you there."

I sighed out my breath in a long huff that sounded like defeat. "Suppose it's just as well the blasted thing blew up. I don't get that Cariad story anyway. It's hard to tell it and sell it if I don't get it."

"Get it?" Riwor looked at me like I'd sprouted another head.

"I mean, I don't understand it. Why would anybody give up being a princess in the castle? It don't make sense."

"*Doesn't* make sense." Riwor grunted. "You ignorant child."

Ignorant? My speech was getting better all the time, and I was one of the few peasants I knew who could actually read. Just because I'd never had a tutor. . . . But I bit down hard on my annoyance and didn't backtalk Riwor. Never helped anyway.

"It doesn't make sense," I corrected myself. "Why would Cariad leave the palace?"

Riwor pressed her palm to her forehead like I was too dumb to breathe. "That's the whole point of the story, Tanwen. The lesson is that no price is too high to pay for true love." She yanked on the donkey's reins. "Standard romance thread, fool girl. Think you can sell it?"

She didn't give me a chance to answer. Didn't really want me to, of course. Always had to have the last word, the hairy old monster. She busied herself about the donkey, and I contented myself with feeling miserable while I waited.

"I thought it was nice 'fore it blew up."

I turned to the sound of a small voice. A wee lass, no more than six years old, stood behind me. A gap showed where she was missing two teeth in front.

I knelt down and smiled at her. "Thank you, lassie. Want me to tell you a story?"

Her eyes lit up, and she plopped down cross-legged in the dirt.

I scooted next to her. "Once, there was a little girl."

A strand of blue light curled from two of my fingers. It glittered as it swirled before us.

The child giggled. "It's same as your eyes."

"Shh." I winked at her. "This little girl was very poor. Her mother was dead and her father . . ." I frowned, and my story strand almost disappeared while I tried to rope in the right words. "Her father was gone too." I smiled at the lass again. "So it was up to her to find a way to take care of herself."

"Did she?" The lass's eyes brightened with the question.

"She did. She took care of herself when she was just a wee lass, like you. But she kept her dearest dream safe inside, where no one could touch it."

A pale golden light unfurled from my palm and swallowed up the blue ribbon. "She would have liked nothing so much as to live in the palace like Cariad once did."

I directed the light strands until they swirled into a circle and three points formed along the front of the ring. "And that's exactly what she aimed to do."

At my last words, the ring of light turned solid—into a golden crown, just the proper size for the lass. Sunlight glittered through the crown, delicate and clear, like crystallized stories were supposed to be. It dropped into my lap with a soft *plink*.

I picked it up and handed it to the lass. "There. That's for you."

Her smile dimmed. "Oh. I ain't got money."

"Don't worry about that. You can have—"

"Fenir!" A man's voice cut into my words. "What are you doing with that story peddler?"

"Papa, I—"

"It's all right, sir." I flashed a smile at the red-faced man. Smiles never hurt in trying to soothe men, at least in my experience. "I was just telling her a story."

"And trying to filch a few coins from her pocket, doubtless." He dragged the girl to her feet by her arm.

She cringed at his tug, and I leaned away from his breath. Smelled like he'd spent the last of their coins at the tavern. "No, it was a gift. No charge."

He snorted. "Oh, sure. A free gift. Ain't no such thing in Tir, everybody knows." He wrenched his daughter's arm again. "You can't trust these people, Fenir. Give me that." He snatched the crystallized story from her hands and chucked it to the ground. It splintered to bits against the hard-packed dirt road.

"Hey!" I jumped to my feet. "That was for her!"

His eyes lit up like the drunks' eyes back home did when there was about to be a brawl. "Aye? So's this!" He slapped the little girl full across her face. She cried out and crumpled to the ground.

I lunged for her out of instinct, but she held up her hand. "It ain't no trouble, miss. I'm all right."

Like blazes she was.

The man waved me away. "Get out of here, you. I told my lass you people was dangerous. Take your storytelling rubbish and leave our village be." He took a few lurching steps away. "Come on, Fenir."

Fenir scrambled to her feet. She watched her father go for a moment, then spoke quickly to me. "He don't mean it. Harvest was bad this year, so he can't pay the king's taxes. Mam says he's turned to the ale because he don't know what else to do."

"We all have it hard under the taxes." I brushed my hand across her red-streaked cheek. "It doesn't mean he should hit you."

She nodded to Riwor. "She hits you."

I paused. Clever little lass had a point. "Still. He's your daddy and it's not right."

"I gotta go." She smiled sadly. "Thank you, Peddler."

"Bye, Fenir." I watched the little lass disappear down the road after her father.

Maybe she was right. I scoffed to think of my early hopes when Riwor had first sought me out as her apprentice. I'd thought she could fill that empty, echoing space in my heart—that place the love of family was supposed to fill. I'd hoped maybe she would be like a granny to me. Fool idea that had lasted all of an hour, until the first time she struck me. A full six moons ago that was. Yet here I was, still standing beside her.

I tried to remind myself why I put up with Riwor. Was it because she taught me how to peddle and not just tell stories? Because she was the one to show me how to sharpen my gift and kept me using it in a way that wouldn't land me in the king's dungeon? Or maybe because she was my pathway into the unknown villages of the Eastern Peninsula?

Truly, it was because I had no other choice.

"Tanwen!" Riwor's voice ripped me from my thoughts. "Unless you'd like to relieve the donkey of his duties and pull the cart yourself, I suggest you get over here. Now!"

I sighed. "Coming."

CHAPTER 2

TANWEN

I WIPED THE SWEAT FROM MY FOREHEAD WITH THE BACK OF MY arm and looked up at my mentor, seated on the wagon and holding the donkey's reins. "Riwor, you said it was to be two silver bits."

Riwor pressed a single silver piece into my palm and sneered at me. "That was assuming you'd do something worthwhile."

I fought to keep my voice even. "I sold one today."

"And flubbed another in front of the whole village. We'll need to wait weeks before we return to Lewir, and you're lucky there wasn't a guardsman about."

I adjusted the pack on my shoulder and stroked the donkey's nose, stalling for a minute. Was the extra piece of silver worth the fight with Riwor?

Yes, I decided. It was. If I wanted to eat anyhow.

"It won't matter if we can't go back to Lewir for a while. We're headed across the river for two weeks anyway."

A scowl deepened the creases in her face. She seemed to be scouring her mind for some sort of argument. Finally, she grunted and flicked another piece of silver down to me. "Here, take it, selfish brat. If I don't have my supper tonight, it's your fault."

My gaze wandered to her bulging coin purse, tied to a belt I could barely see beneath her overhanging gut.

Aye, sure, she'd be skipping a meal.

I plastered on a grateful smile. "Thanks, Riwor. I'll meet you here tomorrow morning, just after sunrise."

"And don't be late." She adjusted the reins in her hands, and the donkey picked up his feet and plodded down the king's road. "If you can manage it," she called back to me.

I watched her continue on the road to Drefden, where she kept a small cottage. I tried my hardest not to despise her. I was lucky she'd agreed to take me under her wing as a peddler, even though I hadn't technically come of age yet. I'd be in big trouble without her help.

Leastways, that was what I kept telling myself. When she was out of sight, I spun around and faced the road to Pembrone. The road home—dusty, poky, ordinary, just like the town itself.

My leather-clad feet tramped down the dirt path. I tried not to despise Pembrone too. At least we had the ocean. Along the southern border of the town, below the rocky cliffs, the Menfor Sea tossed and rolled. And it was downright pretty if a girl ever got to break away from her work long enough to go look at it.

I passed Farmer Rhys's plot on my left. Way out in the south field, his eldest daughter Celyn waved to me. "Ho, Tanwen!"

I waved back but couldn't risk shouting hello to her. Riwor would slap me into the next moon if I lost my voice before our two-week tour. Getting on Riwor's bad side before our tour had even begun was definitely not my goal. In fact, I was hoping to be let off the leash a little this time. Maybe even venture into a village or two by myself.

Dirt became cobblestone as I reached the main thoroughfare of Pembrone. I didn't even glance up when I heard footsteps pounding the stones beside me. I didn't need to. Already knew who it was.

"Ho, Tannie."

I smiled. "Evening, Brac." I shielded my eyes against the setting sun and looked up at him, a head taller than I and lanky as a scarecrow of late. "What are you up to?"

"Waiting for you, of course." He pinched my arm and handed me a small jug of water. "Same as always."

And he wasn't kidding. Brac watched for me to come home every day Riwor and I ventured any farther than the central lane of Pembrone. He'd be leaning against the wall of one of the outlying buildings until Riwor's donkey carried me near, though how his father could spare him from the farm while he waited for me, I didn't know. And he always had cool water, knowing I was hot and tired from the dusty road.

I pinched him back. "You forgot your hat today. Again. Your face is all burned."

He shrugged and brushed a straw-colored shock of hair from his eyes. "It don't hurt."

I could hear Riwor correcting his words in my mind, but I didn't say anything. He didn't much like my "hoity-toity peddler talk," as he called it.

I nodded to the tavern up ahead. "I have to stop for food."

"I know." He strode to the tavern door and held it open for me.

The barmaid looked up from the counter she was scrubbing. She pushed her graying hair off her forehead. "Ho, Tanwen." She narrowed her eyes at Brac. "Brac Bo-Bradwir, you owe me a copper for that mug of ale yesterday."

He frowned at her, then at me. "You know I don't have it right now, Blodwyn. The blasted tax took every spare copper from my pockets."

Blodwyn's gaze struck hard as flint. "Then you shouldn't be taking ale from my pockets, young sir."

I plunked down on one of the three-legged stools. "Pockets are an odd place to store your ale, Blodwyn."

She glared at me and then rounded on Brac. "And does it stop at ale, Bo-Bradwir? If I go upstairs and ask my girls, will they tell me you owe something else to my account?"

Brac's ears reddened. "I don't go in for that, Blodwyn. You know I don't."

I stared at the bar top and silently hoped that was true. It'd make him about the only lad in town who didn't.

Brac slid onto the stool next to me. "I'll have the copper for you by week's end."

Blodwyn nodded once. "Fine." Then she turned to me and smiled, as if that whole conversation hadn't just happened in my hearing. "What can I get you, love?"

"Supper for two, please. What do you have?"

She turned to a giant pot dangling over the fire and used her rag to lift off the lid. "Grazer stew with watta root."

The smell tickled my nose and made my stomach growl. My lunch of hard rolls and sweaty cheese was a distant memory. "How much?"

"Four coppers buys enough for two." She scowled at Brac. "Lucky you have Tanwen to look out for you, lad, but it should be the other way around, if you ask me." Then her gaze settled back on me. "Just be careful who you're binding yourself to, Tanwen. That's all I'll say."

The awkwardness stuck in my throat. If she only knew the battles we'd had about this . . .

Brac's scowl could have started a thunderstorm. "I wonder what it'd be like to have tavern-keepers who minded their own onions."

Blodwyn flipped her towel over her shoulder and seemed to be biting hard on a smile. "I wonder what it'd be like to have farmers' boys who paid for their ale."

I cleared my throat loudly before Brac could fire off another sharp remark. "Here you are, Blodwyn." I pushed one of my silver bits across the counter.

She handed back some coppers and two hollowed-out rounds of dry bread filled with grazer stew. "Mind, it's hot."

Brac eyed my change as I slipped it into my pouch. "Tannie, could I borrow—"

"Not a chance." I took one of the bowls and nodded to the other.

Brac took it and reached behind the counter to swipe one of Blodwyn's spoons. "I'll bring it back later."

She sighed. "Aye, you better."

He pushed the front door open for me with his backside. "You could've spared me *one* copper, don't you think?"

I lifted my chin and glided past him. "I don't spend my life peddling stories to pay for your ale, Brac Bo-Bradwir."

"Hey, now, that ain't what I—"

"Never you mind, Brac. I'm not worried. We're not bound, whatever Blodwyn and the rest of Pembrone thinks."

He coughed on a mouthful of stew, then grimaced. "Aye, about that . . ."

I stopped and sighed. Why had I brought that up? Think first, then speak, Tanwen. When would I learn?

Too late now.

But I faked a cheerful smile. "About what?"

He rolled his eyes. "About what Blodwyn said. Binding ourselves together and all." He shoveled another spoonful of stew into his mouth and seemed to be waiting for me to say something.

But I wasn't taking that bait.

He scanned the surrounding farmland, doing a terrible job pretending it was interesting. "Just wondered if you'd given half a thought to what we talked about before."

His words made my feet feel like they were hewn of stone. Truly, *we* hadn't done a lot of talking before. There'd been his confession of undying love, tears, some shouting, and more tears. Seemed to Brac no earthly reason why we shouldn't be married by now.

It was getting harder and harder for me to find those earthly reasons.

I forced my voice to sound light. "I don't know when you got the hogswoggled idea in your sunbaked brain that I'd make a good wife for any lad, Brac. I'm too young."

"Too young? Near eighteen, last I checked."

"Half a year till that happens."

He pretended not to hear. "And I a year older than you." He tucked Blodwyn's spoon into his trouser pocket and took to devouring his bread bowl. "Be straight with me, Tannie. Age has got nothing to do with it, does it? You don't love me, do you?"

A searing-hot brand pressed into my heart. "Don't say that. That's not what I'm driving at."

I did love Brac, in a manner of speaking. Deeper and stronger than a brother. He was my truest friend.

But marriage . . .

The idea froze in my mind—homemaking, raising babies, tending the farm. That's what Brac was asking. And story peddling wasn't part of that picture. How could I give up my dream before I'd even begun?

"Brac, I know seventeen isn't too young for most people, but it's different for me. You know it is. I just started peddling with Riwor. I need more time."

He polished off the last of his bread. "But if we marry, you won't need to sell stories and travel around anymore. I'll take care of you, and we'll live with my folks. Or we'll live at your place. Just the two of us." He brushed a strand of hair off my face.

I pulled away from his touch. I didn't really like to. Brac felt like family when no one else did. Brac was safety and affection and comfort. But surely I didn't need to encourage him. "Brac, I don't know how else to say it so you understand, but I *want* to sell stories and travel around."

"And work your way up to Urian." His face darkened.

Urian. The capital city. It unnerved me how he put such a fine point on things I'd never quite come out and said.

But he was right. If I could work my way to Urian, get someone from the king's court to notice me, then maybe . . .

"Tannie, did you hear me?"

I stopped walking. "What?"

Brac sighed and stopped beside me. A few villagers milled about, but no one seemed to pay us much mind. "I said we could build a good life here. I know it's only Pembrone, but this is where our family is. Haven't Mam and Dad taken care of you all these years?"

My temper ignited. "Oh, and marrying their son is the price I have to pay, is it? Your parents take me in as an orphan for a while and now I have to give myself to their boy?"

Brac put a hand over my mouth. "Sakes, Tannie, calm down. I didn't mean it like that. Just meant they'd help us get started. You're getting loud. People will start staring." Suddenly, he grinned in that impish way he had. "If you think I ain't handsome enough to marry, just say so."

I shoved him as best I could with a bowl of hot soup in my hands. "You're not handsome enough."

A blatant lie on a fine spring evening. I tried not to notice his twinkling brown eyes, the straw-colored hair falling over his forehead, or the sharp cut of his jaw. If I did, I couldn't say he was unhandsome with a straight face.

But caring for him, thinking he was a handsome lad, wasn't the same as being in love with him. Was it? I stared at my food. Sometimes my feelings seemed more mixed up than a bowl of grazer stew.

Brac nudged me. "Well, it ain't the first time you said I was ugly."

"Now who's making up stories? I never said anything like it."

"Aye, you did! When I was fourteen and I tried to kiss you while you were milking the grazers for Mam." He laughed. "You told me I was the ugliest brute you ever had the misfortune of seeing. Ain't that right, Tannie?"

It did ring a bell. And I'd quite meant it at the time. "Oh, come off it. See me to my cottage like a gentleman, will you?"

We stepped off the cobblestones and onto a packed-earth lane to the right. It led to both our homesteads.

"Speaking of grazer milk, Mam saved some for you. Come to our barn and we'll get it."

I glanced up at Brac. The tips of his ears reddened—just like I suspected they might.

"Brac Bo-Bradwir, don't you lie to me."

"Don't know what you mean, Tannie." But he stared off in the other direction and wouldn't meet my gaze.

"The grazers haven't been producing well lately, and we both know it. Farmer Bradwir and your mam are good to me. They would share if they had extra, but I know they don't. That milk's your share, isn't it?"

"Well, I . . . It ain't quite the way you framed it, I don't reckon . . ."

I stopped walking and waited until he would look me full in the face.

He sighed. "Aye, Tannie. It was meant to be mine. But no need to go on about it. A lass needs milk, too, even if she's all of seventeen.

Mam says so. Besides, you share with me." He nodded to my bowl of stew. "Family always shares."

A dagger of guilt pricked me. Brac looked out for me and always had. Always would. We looked out for each other. I probably should take him seriously as a suitor. My head must be emptier than the discarded shell of a huskbeetle.

The offer of a secure life on a good farm was everything most country lasses longed for. A kind husband who truly cared for them was more than many lasses got. Maybe I hadn't a right to wish for more than my life in Pembrone. Maybe my hopes of Urian were as selfish and wrong-headed as Brac made them out to be.

"So will you take it?"

I jumped at Brac's question. "What?"

"Stars' sakes, Tannie. You and your daydreams. I asked if you'd take the grazer milk. It's only fair. You bought me stew."

I smiled. "Aye, all right. Let me just set this down." I put my stew on the low stone wall surrounding my cottage. "It'll give this a chance to cool anyway. I don't know how you swallowed yours down."

Brac shrugged. "Needed to finish it in time for supper."

I didn't bother addressing his insatiable appetite. All the farmers' boys had a tough time finding enough food to keep going around tax time. It's why I didn't mind sparing the two coppers for his stew. That was different than ale.

We took off down the dirt path in the other direction toward the Bradwir stead. In the distance, waves crashed below the cliffs that butted up to the backside of my cottage. The lonely sound was my only company at night.

We passed a field of shriveled grain on the left. I frowned. "Will your dad be able to pay the harvest tax this year? The crops look bad."

I braced for the fit of cussing that might follow my question.

Brac's eyes clouded. "Goddesses know. I can't even keep all the blasted taxes straight, forget trying to pay them all. There's the planting tax we paid early spring, the reaping tax we'll be expected to pay early autumn, then the 'Harvest of Gareth the Handsome's Thirteenth Year Tax.' Fried if I know the difference between a reaping tax and a harvest tax. Between them and the 'taxes' the rotten king's guard demands and the offerings the temple demands, it's a wonder anyone in Pembrone has a crumb to put in his mouth at supper."

He kicked a rock and sent it careening into his father's fields. "And that ain't even considering when the trees get salt burn and the marshes flood ocean onto our grain. The king doesn't give a blaze about low yield. Taxes due, just the same." He picked up another rock and threw it this time.

"You shouldn't get so angry."

He looked at me like I'd dropped out of the sky. "Don't it make you angry?"

"Of course it does. But you need to keep your head down, especially with the king's guard about. If you're looking to survive, it's got to be done."

He stopped walking and rounded on me. "Keep my head down while they steal food out of my mouth and that of my kin? Keep my head down while they march around here like they own the place, just because they got the king's seal on their filthy armor?"

I folded my arms across my chest and stared at him. Best to just let him get it all out.

"It's the blooming king's guard that makes it so hard for a body to get anywhere around here. Them and the priests. Mam says we ought to make more offerings to the goddesses to help the harvest. Dad says we oughtn't make so many. Blasted if I know what to do about it."

Then my breath caught. Behind Brac, a horse picked silently through the shriveled grain field. The mounted guardsman was well within earshot. My body stiffened, eyes widened, but Brac didn't seem to notice.

"And you know what else?"

I shook my head a little, hoping he'd read the signs.

Shut up, Brac Bo-Bradwir!

But he kept right on rambling. "Those soldiers that like to squeeze us under their thumbs answer to the king, so I don't suppose he's any better than the lot of them. Probably have his blessing to go on kicking us whenever they feel like it."

The intruding horseman dismounted from his sleek beast with a clank of armor and a cold smirk. "Treason, if I ever heard it. Bo-Bradwir, isn't it? The farmer's son?"

The color drained from Brac's face as he turned to the sound of the guardsman's voice. Brac looked like he might be trying to keep down that bowl of stew.

"You're Farmer Bradwir's son, aren't you?" the soldier repeated.

"Aye."

The guardsman snorted. "'Yes, sir,' you fool. Address your superiors properly."

Brac's lips squeezed together until they turned white against his over-sunned skin. The knight would have to draw his sword to get Brac to say anything of the sort.

"Complaining about the tax, are we?" The soldier removed his helmet and smoothed his wheat-colored hair back into its tail. "I could have you hanged for that."

"Aye, *sir*."

The knight's cold blue eyes flicked over to me, then back to Brac. "You ought to be thinking of ways to earn my forgiveness, both for your treasonous rumblings and your blatant sarcasm."

"You want me to polish that piece of metal that covers your backside, Your Majesty?"

The guardsman's calm finally shattered. "You insolent—"

I stepped between the two of them and curtsied low. "Sir, please, forgive Farmer Bradwir's son. The harvest's been poor, and he's hungry. Growing lads with no food are often temperamental." I ignored the look of utter indignation darkening Brac's already red face. "We're just simple country folk."

The guardsman's lip curled. "Your lass here is smarter than you are, Bo-Bradwir." Before I knew what was happening, his dagger was unsheathed in one hand and he had me around the waist with the other. The steel of his blade tingled cold against my skin. "Maybe you'll learn to show some respect if your lass's life depends upon it."

Brac's face froze. His work-hardened muscles flexed, but there wasn't a thing he could do, and we all three knew it.

The soldier laughed. "Not so tough as you were a moment ago, eh, Bo-Bradwir?" He slipped a gloved finger across my neck and under the leather cord I always wore.

My hand instinctively flew to the necklace, and I nearly sliced my fingers on the man's blade. "Please, sir! It's not worth anything."

The guardsman snorted. "Yes, I see that." He studied the little knot of wrought silver that served as a charm. Then he turned back to Brac. "Do you not have anything else sharp to say, now that my dagger's at your lass's pretty throat?"

"I'm not his lass, sir."

The soldier glanced down at me. "Oh?"

"No, sir."

"Not yet, maybe," Brac interjected. The frown he fired at me couldn't have been any deeper or more annoyed.

The guardsman's grip on me slackened, and I turned to face him. My eyes grazed over his face. Though he knew Brac's name, I didn't think I'd seen him around here before, so maybe he was from the capital. Only one way to find out. "Are you from Urian, sir?"

"Urian?" His face screwed up in apparent confusion. "No. I'm from Afon."

I tried not to let my disappointment show. Afon was a town not far across the river. Not even off the Peninsula.

"But have you been to Urian?" I pressed.

"Once." He sheathed his dagger. Apparently, the game was only fun if Brac and I were afraid, and I didn't aim to be. "When I was commissioned for the guard. But I had a tutor who lived in the palace for a time."

My mind sorted through his statement. If he had a tutor once, it meant he came from a wealthy family. I supposed his appointment to the guard was enough proof of that anyway. But if he'd only been to Urian once, it wasn't likely—

Brac's harsh voice interrupted my musings. "Why don't you leave us be now?"

The guardsman laughed. "I'm in fine humor today, so I'll let your impudence slide." He swung a leg up over his horse and clanked back into place. He winked at me before replacing his helmet and directing his horse to nearly trample Brac as he left us. "Mind yourself, Bo-Bradwir, lest you cross me on a less agreeable day."

When the hoofbeats became too distant to be heard, I slapped Brac on the arm. "What's gotten into you?"

His mouth dropped open. "Me? What's gotten into *me*?"

"Are you trying to get yourself hanged?" I shook my head and stomped toward Farmer Bradwir's house.

"And what about you?" He grabbed my arm and forced me back around. "He pulls his knife on you, then you act like you're not bothered? You were almost flirting with him!" Steam might start pouring from his ears any moment. "You trying to land a king's guard husband or something? Is that what's wrong with me? I don't wear enough metal for you?"

I rolled my eyes. "I was trying to get him to settle down—and it worked, didn't it?"

But inside, I knew he had a right to be irritated. I'd never let a country boy treat me the way that soldier had. And Brac had witnessed me suffer more than a few leers and advances from the guardsmen after they'd been at their ale.

But Brac didn't understand. Getting close to a soldier—or a knight, better yet—might be the quickest way to the capital. The quickest way for me to gain an audience with King Gareth, and that's what I needed. How would I ever manage that if I didn't have connections in His Majesty's court?

"Tannie!" Brac was nearly shouting. "You listening? I thought you was a different kind of girl than that. I don't think there's much you wouldn't let those louts do, if they'd only get you to Urian."

My temper flared again. "Oh, ho! I'm not virtuous enough for you now? Says the boy who kissed Celyn En-Rhys when he thought I wasn't looking." I brushed past him. "And you're wrong, you know.

Just because I have plans and ideas about what I want to do and where I want to go, it doesn't mean . . . Oh, forget it. You wouldn't understand."

And he didn't. Brac could live the rest of his life in Pembrone, farming and wiling away his extra hours at the tavern and be content.

But not me.

And that was why I couldn't marry him. That was one part of Princess Cariad's tale I could grab hold of. I didn't want a husband dictating my course, either.

"Tannie." I could hear Brac's footsteps pounding the road as he ran to catch me at the end of the lane leading to his house. He caught up and planted himself in front of me. "I'm sorry." He plucked a stalk of straw and twisted it between his fingers. "All right? I'm sorry. I shouldn't have said that about the guardsmen." He made like he might touch my hair again, but I ducked out of his way.

And this time, I felt no regret for it.

I donned my most arrogant smile and pretended I was a fine lady at King Gareth's court. "Very well, peasant. You're forgiven. But I have a suggestion for you."

Brac cocked an eyebrow as he chewed his stalk of straw. "Aye?"

"I think you should join the king's guard. It could brighten your prospects." I patted his cheek, then stepped through the front door of his house to greet his mother.

Just before the door closed, his retort came flying in to me. "I'd rather kiss a mountainbeast!"

CHAPTER 3

TANWEN

It wasn't easy to open the front door of my cottage with a bread bowl of stew in my hands and a jug of milk under one arm. But I managed. Then I pushed the door closed behind me with a bump of my rear.

I set my stew on the scrubbed-wood table, put the jug of milk in the cold pantry, and dropped my leather sack by the river-stone hearth. "I'm home."

The expected silence answered me.

The fire had dwindled to a couple of glowing embers while I'd been gone. At least it was into the second moon of spring now. The cottage was a perfect ice block in wintertime. Maybe that was why my parents didn't seem to have made it their permanent home.

I stoked the fire until it hopped back into flame. The glow warmed my face and cast orange light through the room—clean but shabby these days.

The stew called to me from the table, but I hadn't said hello to my mother and father yet. I made for Father's study.

Books lined every wall of the small room. The desk lay bare except for an empty ink pot and some old pens—exactly as I'd found it when I'd moved back in years ago, except with a bit of added dust.

"Evening, Father."

I traced my fingers along the spines of his books and wondered again who he'd been. A tutor, maybe, to have so many volumes in his personal library. I didn't suppose there were half as many in the rest of all Pembrone put together. And if he had been a tutor, maybe he'd been stationed with a wealthy family for the bulk of my childhood and taught me stuff when I was a tiny lass. Which would explain why I'd shown up in Pembrone as a six-year-old who could read. Unless it was Nanny who had taught me . . .

I sighed. Most people's lives were stories with mysterious endings. Mine was a story with a beginning I could never make sense of. It was like fifty different unrelated strands I couldn't weave into a solid crystal.

My gaze wandered back to the books. Maybe Father was a scribe?

Farmer and Ma-Bradwir knew who my father was, but they wouldn't talk about him, and they didn't suffer questions about it. Always said it was better not to tread that path.

Once I thought Father might have been a monk or something, since the temples always seemed to have books on hand. Not a priest, as they weren't allowed to marry. But when I skimmed through Father's titles, skipping over the real long words, I didn't see anything about the goddesses in there. I decided he'd have made a poor monk. There was some stuff about the Creator here and there, but I'd shoved those books to the darkest corners of the shelves. That stuff was like as not to get you hanged these days. The priests called it blasphemy. Seemed the Creator and the goddesses were mixed up in a war as old as time, and who had time to sort that mess? Not me.

Maybe Father was a merchant. Pembrone had been a proper port at one time, though now all the ships and boats had moved down the coast past Lewir to Physgot, which had better fishing. Maybe he'd run a business back in the days before Pembrone settled into its pokiness and became a village full of farmers.

I put my hands on the back of Father's chair and pretended he was sitting there. The image of a man formed, even though I couldn't remember what Father truly looked like. My image was tall with dark-gold hair like mine. Seastone-blue eyes like mine appeared at first, but then I remembered what Ma-Bradwir said once—my eyes were my mother's.

I replaced my imaginary father's eyes with brown ones, like Brac's.

"Join me for supper, Father?"

Wished he could.

I sighed and left the study, then traipsed down the hall to my bedroom.

"I'm home, Mother."

It was my room now, but it'd been Mother's when she was a girl. Her curtains—the finest cloth I owned—still hung in the windows. But they were so thin now they hardly kept out the light.

I didn't mind much. All the light streaming in as the sun set lit up my crystallized stories—the first ones I'd ever made. And it helped me see the books that lined my shelves.

Not like Father's dry volumes full of text. Mine were storybooks that had come with me to Pembrone, full of painted pictures in all colors of the rainbow.

Reading those books aloud was what first made me realize I had the storytelling gift. Normal lasses don't make ribbons of light when they read their bedtime stories.

My gaze scanned the crystallized stories. A castle, a star, a white velvet-petal flower.

I picked up my first crystallized story and smiled at it. A tiny pink fluff-hopper, transparent as glass. Fluff-hoppers were cottony-soft, grass-eating critters Farmer Bradwir called pests. But Brac and I liked to catch them for his little siblings to pet and snuggle. They were perfectly tame unless you riled them up. Then they'd bring out their dagger-sharp teeth and hiss at you. More than one Tirian child had lost a finger to an angry fluff-hopper.

A beloved Tirian fairytale told of the pink fluff-hopper who'd grant wishes if you caught him.

I held up my pink crystal fluff-hopper and whispered to it. "I wish for a way out of here."

It hadn't worked the other five hundred times I'd tried it, but you never know when your luck might turn. Maybe mine would tonight.

Tears stung at my eyes.

No. Couldn't give in to that. Never helped.

I forced them away as I slipped out of my peddling clothes—a white muslin dress, brown apron, and brown vest. I pulled my house-dress from the wardrobe.

The rough cloth grated against my skin. Might as well be wearing a watta-root sack. But peddling time was done, and I wasn't about to spoil my nicest clothes by dropping grazer stew on them.

I dismantled my upswept hair, pulled my gold waves into a simple tail, then tied it with a length of twine.

Now I looked just like every other Pembroni peasant girl. Ordinary and poor as dirt.

I shuffled back down the hall and plunked at the table. My stew was cold. I spooned it into my mouth anyway and tried to guess what it'd be like if I could hear Mother's and Father's voices around the table as we ate.

I pretended to feel the warmth of Father's arm around my shoulders, pretended to bask in the glow of some approving words from Mother.

The fantasy was awfully nice. But it was just foolish imagining. The truth was the empty table before me, the dead-silent cottage all around me.

Aye. I wished for a way out.

I popped up in bed with a gasp. Something wasn't right. Had I heard a noise? Felt a touch? An image of the arrogant guardsman from the day before flashed into my head.

The first light of dawn slanted through my threadbare curtains, but the house lay still.

Light of dawn.

Riwor.

I'm late!

I threw back my blanket and flew from bed. I stumbled over my bag, already packed and ready for the journey.

Too bad I wasn't.

Dress, hair—no time for braids or curls—shoes, necklace.

I grabbed the silver trinket I'd taken such care to rescue from the king's guardsman the day before. It wasn't worth much, but the silver charm—worked into a curled, flowery shape—had been my mother's. I never left home without it.

I slipped it over my head and down the front of my dress.

Done?

I patted my dress to make sure everything was in place. To make sure I hadn't accidentally tucked the back of my skirt into the ties of my apron. Wouldn't want to embarrass myself like that.

Again.

I dashed into the hallway, then to the fire. It hadn't completely died through the night, and that was lucky. I added some wood from the pile, then stoked the fire back into flame before I ladled water from a barrel into my cooking pot. No matter how late I was, I wouldn't make it through the day without some manner of breakfast.

I tossed a cupful of grain into the pot, then hurried to Father's study.

Straighten the old pens; make sure all the books are in place.

I paused at a particular leather-bound volume. Father's name was branded on the cover: *Yestin Bo-Arthio.* It looked like a journal. But it was empty, every page blank. I'd flipped through them all a dozen times to make sure.

I frowned. Maybe he hadn't been much of a writer.

A hissing noise reached me from the next room. My porridge was boiling over.

I ran back to the hearth and stirred the gruel with a wooden spoon.

But for some reason, I couldn't shake the picture of Father's journal from my mind.

"Tanwen!"

I started so badly, the spoon dropped into the pot. I fished it back out with a wince, then zipped through the entry toward the angry voice on the other side of the front door.

"Tanwen, I swear I'll leave you behind, you lazy, useless watta root of a girl!"

"I'm coming, Riwor!" I flung the door wide.

Riwor barely waited until the door was completely open to push past me. "We agreed on sunrise. What's been keeping you?"

"I overslept."

Riwor made a noise that sounded like an irritated grazer's huff. Her gaze swept over my cottage. "Well, well. Quite nice for a girl who claims to be so poor."

I turned to scoop out the half-bowl of porridge I allowed myself for breakfast. "It was my mother's family home once."

"Humph," Riwor grunted.

The sooner I got her out of there, the better. Didn't want her to start pocketing my parents' belongings.

I inhaled my porridge, though it burned my mouth. "Ready." Snatched my bag off the floor. "I just have to see someone before I leave."

Riwor's jowls quivered. "Make it quick, or I leave without you."

"Brac?" I peered into the dark barn, but I didn't see him. "You in here?"

There was a poke in my side that made me jump. "Ho, Tannie."

I spun around and punched Brac in the stomach. "You scared me!"

He just laughed at me. "Aye, that was the idea."

I glanced back to the road. I could tell Riwor was glaring at me, even from a distance. "I'm leaving. Be gone a fortnight across the river—Gwern, Afon, and Mynyd."

"I know. You told me."

"Aye, but . . ." I fumbled with my vest hem. "I just wanted to say good-bye."

He tickled me under the chin. "Is that your way of saying you want to marry me after all?"

I swatted his hand away. "Wake up, Bo-Bradwir. You're dreaming again."

His grin slipped.

Blast.

"Sorry, Brac. I didn't mean it. I was teasing."

He let out a long breath. "Easier to tease than talk about it, I suppose."

Double blast.

I bit the inside of my cheek. "There's not much left to talk about, is there? You want a simple farm lass, and goddesses know you'd have a line of them from here to the sea if you weren't so hung up on me."

My gut twisted at the thought of a line of lasses snapping for Brac's attention. But I swallowed the sick feeling. I didn't have any right to it. "One of those lasses will suit you for a wife just fine. She'll want what you want, and you'll both be happy."

Brac stared at me a moment, his mouth a bit open. Finally, he managed words. "Don't you understand, Tannie, after all these years?"

He stepped toward me, and I took an equal step back out of instinct. Closeness to his person never helped me think clearer.

But those blasted lanky arms of his reached across the distance, and he put his hands on my shoulders. "I don't want some lass. I don't want any girl who'll make a fine wife. I want *you*." He pulled me closer. "All of you. The parts that drive me up one side of a wall and down the other, even."

Tears dribbled down my face unbidden. Drat it.

I thought about pulling away. But instead I looked up into his eyes, full of hope over how I might respond. "Brac, I—"

"Tanwen!" Riwor's voice cut into the moment like a scythe. "Get a move on, girl!"

I sighed. "I'm sorry, Brac. I have to go now."

He reached up and stroked my hair. "I get the feeling one of these days when you leave, you ain't coming back."

"I'll always come back." I shouldn't have said it. I shouldn't encourage him, but it just came flying out—and part of me wanted so badly for it to be true.

Brac smiled sadly and traced his thumb down the side of my face to my chin. "Aye, you'll always come back. Until you don't." He sighed and looked away. "Tannie, if only you'd set aside this storytelling business . . ."

Now I pulled away without a problem. I stared hard at him. "Don't. Don't ask me to give up my dreams."

Brac's expression somehow hardened and melted at once. "My fault for trying to put a painted-wing in a cage. Wasn't any way you were going to be satisfied living there."

"Stop it. That's not fair."

"No, it ain't fair. You care more about being the Royal Storyteller and having riches than you do about the people you're supposed to love."

And then I slapped him across the face. Hard. He recoiled, eyes wide.

But I wasn't sorry. If anyone knew how hard I'd worked to take care of myself so I wouldn't be a burden to his parents or anyone else . . .

I took a step closer to him. "Farmhand, milkmaid, barkeep, scrubbing floors, emptying chamber pots. I did all that just to put food in my mouth before Riwor came along and offered to take me on. Story peddling is my only chance to provide three sure meals a day for myself. Every day. And no planting tax or harvest tax or reaping tax. So don't you tell me my dreams are all about having nice things. I just want to have *something*! *Some* life! And just because you're not brave enough to think of a life beyond Pembrone, it doesn't mean the rest of us have to be happy here!"

An ugly red mark blossomed on his face, and I could see a deeper welt blooming in his eyes—one from my sharp words. Regret oozed over me. I shouldn't have hit him, no matter what he'd said.

I tried to say I was sorry, but I wasn't exactly known for letting apologies fly on the regular. "Brac . . ."

"I'm sorry, Tannie. I shouldn't have said that about being the Royal Storyteller."

Blast. I hated that saying sorry was so much easier for him than me.

But he wasn't finished. "You're wrong, though. It ain't that I'm not brave. Being in love . . . Well, that's the biggest kind of brave there is."

Tears came to my eyes again. "Why's that, Brac?"

"Because you have to be strong enough to get your heart broken every day."

A morning breeze blew in from the ocean and ruffled my hair. It didn't do much to calm the heat in my face. "You're going to find a lass. A lass who deserves you and makes you happy. I just know it."

Brac leaned down and rested his forehead on mine. "Tannie, there ain't nobody in all of Tir for me except you."

I met his gaze. "If only I weren't a story peddler?"

He stared back in silence a moment. "Aye, if only you'd set it aside."

"Tanwen!" Riwor's harsh cry carried over the grain fields and beyond the grazer pasture.

I pulled away from Brac. "I have to go. I'll be back in a fortnight. Good-bye, Brac." Then I turned and ran.

"Tannie!" his voice called after me.

But I didn't stop running until I reached the main road and hopped into the cart.

Riwor set to grumbling right away. "Late as it is, fool girl. You want to get into Gwern before sundown or not?"

Brac had nearly caught up with the cart as Riwor slapped the donkey's rump with the reins.

"Tannie."

I wouldn't look at him. Didn't know how to sort through the dozen different feelings swirling inside me like story strands. Heat crawled up my cheeks. "Aye?"

The cart rattled to life.

Brac walked beside us. "Promise you'll take care of yourself while you're gone."

Words wouldn't form on my tongue for a moment. "Sorry I slapped you," was all I could manage.

"Aye, I know. Do you promise to take care, Tannie?"

I think I nodded and maybe mumbled something. Brac stopped walking beside us. The donkey clip-clopped his way out of Pembrone, and I knew Brac grew smaller behind me with each step.

"I love you, Tannie!"

Riwor snorted, but I ignored her. I had to say something to Brac. Anything.

I turned around on the bench and finally made my voice work. "Brac!"

In the distance, I could see his head lift.

"You forgot your hat!"

CHAPTER 4

TANWEN

THE CHILD STARED UP AT ME LIKE SHE'D GLIMPSED A DEAD woman. "Haven't seen a story peddler around these parts since they hanged the last one." Her eyes were so wide I could almost see my reflection in them.

I smiled and tugged one of her thick blonde braids. "That's because that peddler was telling some stories he shouldn't have. There are laws about saying things against the king, you know."

The child gnawed on her thumbnail for a moment. Then she leaned over and whispered to me. "But what if them things are true?"

Riwor saved me from having to think up something to say.

She called the gathering crowd to attention. "Come round, come round," she cried in her deep, rich peddling voice. It sounded nothing like the harsh growl she used when it was just me and her. "This young peddler has a tale to spin for you."

I placed my stool on the cobblestoned ground.

We'd grabbed a prime spot that morning, smack in Gwern's town square. We had gotten to town as the sun set the previous evening and found lodgings in the more respectable of Gwern's two taverns. No giggling girls waiting upstairs for lonely farm boys.

It had set us up nice to get into the square first thing, while the villagers went about their morning business. A decent crowd gathered and waited for me to begin.

I cleared my throat and started with the story Riwor had ordered me to tell. "Once, there was nothing. No ground to walk on nor sky to look up at nor people to do any such thing."

This was my first test. Riwor wanted to hear the crowned story about how the goddesses made the world through their divine beauty. I tried not to yawn.

But no matter how dull or unbelievable I found the story, I aimed to tell it right and fetch a handsome price. If I couldn't . . . well, let's just say I'd better be ready to dodge Riwor's backhand.

"And from the goddess Cethor's flowing azure locks, the wide Menfor Sea and all the oceans of the world were made."

A sparkling blue strand swirled around the crowd. The little girls in front giggled.

"And from the goddess Direth's strong brown arms, the towering mountains, sloping valleys, and sandy shores were made."

A rough swathe of cloth that looked like the bags Farmer Bradwir used to haul his grain soared into the sky, then joined the dance with the blue ocean strand.

"And then from the green eyes of the goddess Lysia, all plant life sprang up and grew toward the radiant sun."

A green strand like a beam of light shot from my hand and bounced around the cobblestones between the people. The children squealed and the townsfolk laughed.

"From the blood-red lips of the goddess Dynole, man was made: like the goddesses but mortal, here to do the goddesses' bidding and please them always."

A slow, satiny ribbon of deepest red poured from my fingers. It slithered around the gathered folks.

Suddenly, something pinched in my stomach.

Uh oh.

It wasn't the first time I'd had to squish down that odd feeling when telling a crowned story. I closed my eyes for a moment and tried to force the squeeze away. As the pinch eased, something like a tiny bubble popped in my head. No pain. Just a tiny release.

I put a hand to my forehead. What in blazes was that all about?

No matter. Back to work.

But as I glanced at the crowd, then at Riwor, I couldn't seem to grab hold of what I'd been saying. In fact . . . I gazed around the unfamiliar town square.

Where in Tir was I?

"Tanwen." Riwor's hiss drew my attention.

Urgency tightened my gut. I remembered I *had* to sell this story. My life or . . . something depended on it. But which blasted story was it?

Riwor mouthed it to me: *Goddesses' creation story.*

I knew the story, of course. It was old as dirt. But where had I left off?

I hoped she'd read my desperate stare. The crowd began to murmur.

"The last bit." Her growl wasn't pleasant, but at least it did the trick.

I forced my smile back into place and made the proper words come out.

"And thus, from the beauty of these four goddesses, all in Tir as you see it today was made. And still we offer our loyalty and praise to the goddesses for this great deed."

The four strands came together and spun so fast that all I could make out were the green and brown strands.

"And we always shall."

At these words, the strands crystallized into a perfect little version of a peninsular evergreen—tiny, transparent green needles and all.

The story dropped into my hand, and a delighted cheer rose from the crowd.

"Prettiest one I ever saw!"

"Look how clear it is. Never saw a story with such fine crystal in my life!"

"Well done, Peddler! A bit dodgy there for a second, but you brought it round."

I stole a glance at Riwor. Her face pulled in a strange direction. Like she wanted to smile—we'd sell this one for sure—despite my flub. But she also looked angry. Because I'd almost made a mess of it again?

Could be. Yet the only thing Riwor really minded about was getting paid.

So why did her brows crease like that? Was it all the praise I was getting from the crowd, maybe? Brac always guessed she was jealous and that's why she smacked me about.

In any case, she erased the grumpiness from her face and called out to the villagers. "Who will pay five coppers for this story? Five coppers, anyone?"

I almost choked on her words. Five coppers as a starting bid! And just after the planting tax. No one would pay it. She'd finally gone mad, good and proper.

"I'll pay five!" a farmer called out. He tipped his floppy hat to me.

"Six! I have six!" An old woman flashed a toothless grin.

The townspeople called out ridiculous bids as I sat there in dumb shock.

Riwor's triumphant crow startled me. "Sold to the priest for one silver piece and six coppers!"

I handed the goddesses' tree to the priest. I hadn't even noticed him in the crowd—a wonder, since priests shaved their heads bald instead of growing their hair long like most Tirian men. They tended to stick out.

But there he was, swishing his plush purple robe to the side to reveal his coin purse. Heavy, by the look of it.

And no wonder. In most peninsular towns, the only coin purses heavier than those of the local barkeep were those of the local priest.

He spared a tiny bow in my direction as he handed me the silver piece and six coppers. "Well done, young peddler. You do justice to the tales of the goddesses."

I pushed a smile onto my face. "Thank you, sir." It wouldn't do to look horrified that my story had sold at such a high price, or that I was exchanging small talk with a priest.

The priest made his way to the back of the crowd, holding out his free hand as he went. Eyes downcast, the townsfolk dropped coppers in his palm.

Temple tax. That one was always due.

I made my voice cheery and spoke to the crowd. "Would you like another story?"

The children seated on the stones clapped and hollered.

"Aye! Tell another, Peddler!"

"Tell a princess one!" The little girl with the blonde braids beamed up at me.

A cool voice with an unusual accent sliced through the clamor of the peninsular farmers. A lad, by the sound of it. "How about the story of Princess Braith? It's a crowned story, so you're unlikely to find your neck stretched on account of it."

What was that odd lilt to his speech? And who dared say such a thing?

I looked up to search for the voice's owner. He lurked at the edge of the crowd, hooded, with his face cast entirely in shadow. His cloak stretched all the way to the ground, but I could see the tips of his boots—definitely not like the ones the farmers wore in the fields. Thicker. And shiny.

I pulled my gaze away from the lurker and smiled at the children. "Shall I tell Braith's story?"

"Aye!"

"Tell it, Peddler! Please tell it."

I glanced at Riwor. She nodded once, so I cleared my throat and took a deep breath. "Not long ago, there lived a king, Caradoc Bo-Dechrau the Blessed. He ruled well and peacefully over all Tir."

A glowing purple ribbon of light began at my fingertips and wound down to the ground as I spoke. It pooled like water at my feet.

"But tragedy struck the good king and his peaceful realm."

The purple light rose into the air before me and formed itself into two dozen flat, round shapes.

"A plague claimed the lives of many, the king and his beloved wife included."

A story strand like molten black metal ran from my palm. It spun in a circle just above the ground, hovering, waiting for my next words.

"The kingdom feared the end of peace and prosperity had come, for who would now rule in place of good King Caradoc? He had died without a blood heir to the throne."

The pinching returned to my gut. I worked to squash it down, like always.

But then something strange happened.

A tiny strand of white light escaped from the littlest finger of my right hand. I blinked, trying to clear it from my vision. The light was so bright it almost hurt to look at it, tiny though it was.

I looked at Riwor. Her face squeezed together in a frown. She didn't seem to recognize the strand either.

But before I could ask her if I should go on, the white strand married with the purple light, lacing itself through the glowing violet shapes. The molten black metal rose into the air, spinning around and around, poised for the next part of the story.

Keep talking, Tanwen En-Yestin, if you want to sell this story too.

I cleared my throat. "But the good king had been wise indeed and thought of his people even as he lay dying. The king named an heir. He bequeathed the crown to his closest friend and advisor, Gareth Bo-Kelwyd the Handsome."

Poison-green satin ribbon cascaded from my fingers. King Gareth's story strand.

A murmur trickled through the crowd. Some people grumbled quietly. But the priest was still about, and who knew when the king's guard might show up? Folks knew to keep their voices to whispers, if they said anything at all.

I watched the satin slip out of my hands. Looking at His Majesty's story strand always made the pinch in my stomach worse.

But I forged on.

"Gareth the Handsome swore fealty to a blood heir, should one ever be found, and an oath to protect the realm." The poison-green fabric twisted until it made a thick cord. It joined with the flat petals, now streaked purple and white.

In a blink, the strands formed themselves into a velvet-petal flower. The black metal strand still waited for me to continue before adding itself to the story.

"But no blood heir could be found. Gareth Bo-Kelwyd, according to King Caradoc's final will and testament, became the new king, bound to the sacred duties of ruling Tir and all the outlying areas of the empire."

The black metal ribbon clamped on to the purple flower like a choking vine. It wrapped around the green stem and wove itself through the delicate petals of purple and white light.

"With his splendid rule, King Gareth gave new life to the realm."

The black metal choked the fragile petals.

"This new life came in the form of Gareth's own wisdom, might, and military prowess, but most especially from his fair daughter, the princess, Braith En-Gareth."

A pale gray mist swirled from my hands. It floated up to the petals, then settled down over them. The mist's fine, dewy shimmer added to the beauty of the flower.

"And that is the story of how our beloved Princess Braith came to be the new blood heir of Tir and the hope of our realm."

The story crystallized, a transparent purple-and-white velvet-petal with a green stem and a metallic vine around it.

The lass with the blonde braids breathed a loud sigh. "So pretty."

A hush settled over the villagers. No lively bidding war this time, but they all seemed captivated by the story in my hand. Even Riwor had fallen silent.

I held up the flower so everyone could see it. "Any bidders?" My voice was barely a murmur.

"I'll buy it." The hooded man stepped forward, just enough to pluck the flower from my hand. Then he tossed two silver bits into my lap.

One coin bounced off my skirt, so I leaned over to pick it up.

When I sat up, he had vanished.

CHAPTER 5

BRAITH

"Shall I wash your feet, Princess?"

Braith glanced up at the sound of Cameria's voice. The Meridioni maid held a burnished bronze basin of water with a cloth draped over the side.

Time to prepare for afternoon council.

"Yes, Cameria. Thank you."

Cameria lowered the basin to the ground, then removed Braith's crystal-encrusted slippers. Braith placed one foot into the water.

Warm, but not hot—just what was wanted, like a quilt on a cool spring evening. How did Cameria manage the perfect temperature every time?

"How long does it take you to ready the water for my footbath?"

Cameria's eyes flickered up to the princess. "I don't know, my lady. I heat it over the fire, then let it cool to the touch." She picked up Braith's other foot and slid it into the water.

The scent of lavendellus wafted up to Braith's nose, and she inhaled deeply. The princess leaned back in her chair and stared out of her bedchamber window. She could just see the tops of the trees in one of the palace gardens below.

"But you do all those things before you ask me if I'd like my feet washed, do you not?"

"Yes, my lady. So as not to keep you waiting should you desire a footbath."

"But what if I say no? Doesn't it seem a waste of your time?"

Cameria did not respond. She wiped Braith's foot, removing any dirt, real or imagined.

A bluebird landed on the windowsill and chirped. The princess smiled. "Do you know what kind of bird it is, Cameria?"

Cameria watched the bird peck around for a moment. Her cheeks lifted as though she were about to smile. "No, my lady. We did not have them in Meridione, and I've scarcely seen them in Tir."

"You miss your homeland, don't you?"

The maid did not answer for a moment, and when she finally spoke, she did not look up. "I miss my family."

A loud *caw* startled the princess, and she looked back at the window to see a coal-black crow swoop down on the little bluebird. With a squeal, the bluebird took off, out of Braith's view.

She frowned at the ugly black bird. "That's a shame."

Cameria dipped her cloth in the water and squeezed it out. Then she began to wash the princess's leg. "We must ready you for council, my lady."

Braith pressed her lips together.

Cameria glanced up. "My lady?"

"Yes. Time to ready for council. If I must."

Cameria smiled wryly. "Yes, you must, I'm afraid." She returned to her washing. "Her Majesty the queen does not plan to attend council this afternoon, as I understand. She was in a temper."

"In that case, it is better that she doesn't attend." Braith sighed. "Mother barely listens during council meetings anyway. I don't know why she ever bothers to attend. Perhaps . . ." She paused. "Perhaps she grows tired of the endless stream of petitioners who suffer under the king's policies. Perhaps she is frustrated at her own powerlessness to help them. Perhaps it is easier not to listen sometimes."

Cameria paused. "It . . . is a thought, my lady."

"You don't think it so?"

"I think my lady speaks for herself and not her royal mother." Cameria met Braith's gaze. "Her Majesty is not concerned enough with her peoples' troubles to be so bothered by them."

"Yes." Braith's smile was sad. "I suppose you are right." She turned her gaze toward the window and lapsed into melancholy silence.

"Your Highness?"

Braith's gaze stayed fixed on the crow, now pecking where the bluebird had been. Had it found insects? Perhaps crumbs left there by Cameria after Braith's luncheon?

"Princess Braith?"

Braith started. "Yes?"

Cameria's eyes trained on her mistress. "Are you unwell, my lady?"

"No, I'm fine." The princess's tone told a different story.

But Cameria did not press. "Very well. Which gown would you like me to prepare?"

"Any is fine. Thank you, Cameria."

Cameria finished drying Braith's feet. She glided off to the adjoining room, where the wardrobe was kept, to select a dress.

Braith stared at the crow unseeingly. "I wonder if the king is in good spirits this afternoon."

Cameria reentered the room, a sky-blue gown embroidered with silver detail and thousands of sparkling beads in hand. "His servants did not say, my lady."

"Princess Braith!" The exclamation preceded the fluttering arrival of Trini, Braith's personal beauty attendant, and her two assistants. "Princess, your hair is in a state!"

Braith allowed Cameria to help her into the blue gown. "And that is precisely why I have you in my employ, Trini."

The laces of Braith's gown were tied, and she was swept onto a padded stool in front of the looking glass. Trini and her assistants fussed and hemmed and hawed. They did not ask the princess's opinion on her hair or cosmetics.

Braith had no opinion on such matters, and they all knew it.

Trini pointed to one of the assistants. "You begin the braiding, and I'll search out those jeweled pins. I'm sure I set them about somewhere." She rifled around in the boxes stacked on the vanity table.

Braith watched them in the looking glass. One assistant began sectioning off Braith's hip-length hair for braiding; the other mixed up the powders that were soon to be smudged onto Braith's lips and cheeks.

The princess eyed her reflection. "Wouldn't it be nice if my hair were a true color?"

Trini frowned at her work. "Your Highness, don't be ridiculous. It is a color. And divinely beautiful at that."

"Yes, as every princess must be," Braith said dryly. "Trini, you know as well as I do every royal or noble woman is said to be beautiful, no matter what she actually looks like."

"Oh, posh. You are the great beauty of the Empire."

Braith frowned at herself in the mirror. Hair so pale as to be white. Large eyes, gray as an overcast day. Skin so fair Braith feared to stroll uncovered in the palace gardens for the sunburn she would receive.

She straightened on the padded stool. "I look quite like a miserable specter."

The princess's beauticians did not venture a response. Instead, they braided, pinned, poked, powdered, lined, shaded, and painted her into a presentable state. When they had finished, Trini stepped back and beamed.

"Almost too pretty for an afternoon council session, wouldn't you say? Better suited to a ball, my lady is."

Trini's assistants nodded and murmured their assent.

Braith bowed her head, now heavy with long braids pinned up on it. "Thank you, Trini."

Cameria ushered the other servants out of the room. She offered a hand to help Braith stand. The princess groaned but proved equal to the task, even in the cumbersome brocade gown and squeezing corset underneath.

"Are you ready, my lady?"

Braith dredged up as convincing a smile as she could muster. "I am."

Braith frowned at Orellwin, governor of the Western Wildlands. He wrung his hat in his hands, crushing the fine leather.

"So you can understand, Your Majesty," Orellwin continued, "why my territory is finding the planting tax a bit difficult this year." The governor shifted his weight from foot to foot.

The king fiddled with a stray lock of hair—once sandy blond but now losing its color with age. He straightened in his throne and let out a sigh. "Orellwin, I've already given your people an extension. The other territories have had the same hardship, and they've managed to pay. I would say I've been more than gracious. What say you to that?"

"Begging your pardon, my lord." Orellwin dropped to his knees. "But they don't call it the Wildlands for nothing. Our soil is already difficult to till, and with the droughts and many infestations, not to mention the fending off of the Wildland beasts at every turn—"

"Enough!" The king's yell boomed through the cavernous hall. "I have shown mercy once, and once is enough. You have until the end of the week to pay the tax in full, or I shall have to find a governor who can better manage his people." He leaned forward, eyes flashing. "Am I understood?"

"Yes, Majesty." Orellwin stumbled over himself in his haste to exit the throne room.

Braith frowned as she watched him go.

"Braith."

The princess jumped at the sound of her name. The king was watching her. "Yes, Your Majesty?"

"Are there many left?" He scratched his graying beard. "We shall not have time enough to meet with the council in private if there are many more petitioners who wish to address me."

Braith scanned the piece of parchment on her lap. "Next we have the steward of the Eastern Peninsula here to bring the last of his territory's tax."

"Ah!" Pleased crinkles formed at the corners of the king's eyes—gray, like Braith's. "That I should be glad to receive."

Braith nodded to Dyrain, the steward. He stepped forward and made a grand bow. "A thousand of the warmest greetings, Your gracious, divine Majesty, Gareth Bo-Kelwyd the Handsome."

Braith swallowed a yawn.

"I bring you the remainder of the tax owed to his most regal and honored person, our king, His Majesty."

The king waved his hand. "Yes, yes, Dyrain, just hand over the money."

Dyrain passed several large sacks to the king's chief political advisor, Dray Bo-Anffir. Dray eyed the contents of the sacks, then turned back to the king. "All seems to be in order, Majesty. We'll count every coin after council, of course."

The king smiled. "Thank you, Dray. You're dismissed, Dyrain."

Dyrain the steward bowed so low his face nearly touched the stone floor. "Thank you, Your Majesty, for the privilege and honor of fulfilling my duty."

The king spared the steward a nod then turned to his daughter. "Is there anything else pressing, Braith darling?"

Braith scanned her list and sighed. Many common folk with petitions, but nothing that would interest the king if his patience had already waned. The peasants would have to wait another day.

"No, Your Majesty."

"In that case, I shall excuse all present who are not members of my council and ask that—"

"Wait!"

All eyes turned toward the back of the throne room.

The king's personal bodyguard drew his sword from its sheath and crouched before the dais, ready to disembowel the intruder who had so disrespected the king.

But Gareth lifted a hand to still the hulking knight. "Peace, Baedden. Who is it that dares to interrupt his king?"

A small man, his clothes covered in bird droppings, and a king's guard knight stepped forward from the entrance to the throne room.

The small man bowed low. "Apologies, Your Majesty." His words were punctuated by gasps for air, as though he'd sprinted up the considerable staircases leading from the palace foyer. "Only just received news, we did."

The king's brows pulled down. He nodded to the knight. "What's happened?"

The guardsman bowed, then gestured to the small man. "Menod here tends the palace carrier birds. We've received a report from the Eastern Peninsula."

Braith fought the grimace that wanted to form on her face. Now that the man covered in bird droppings was closer, she could smell the stench of the aerie all over him.

Menod straightened and sucked in a deep breath. "A message from Gwern arrived, Majesty. Alleged incident with a story peddler, there was."

The king's posture stiffened. "Indeed?"

"Yes, Majesty. One of the townsfolk reported to a local guardsman about a forbidden story strand."

Naith Bo-Offriad, councilmember and high priest of the Tirian Empire, heaved his bulk from his padded chair. The light of the throne room torches bounced off his bald head. "A forbidden strand, you say, but you do not say a forbidden story." His eyes narrowed. "Do you mean to suggest a forbidden strand appeared in a crowned story?"

The bird man nodded. "The peasant said the peddler told the story of our illustrious king's rise to power." His gaze flicked to Braith. "Of how you became heiress of Tir, milady."

Braith's spine straightened. "Oh? Well, whatever is the trouble, I wish to stay out of it."

The king shot a disapproving glance her direction, and she pressed her lips together.

Sir Dray frowned. "How could a forbidden strand have appeared in that story?"

Naith picked imaginary specks of dust from his moss-green velvet robe. "Perhaps—and it's only a suggestion, shrewdest of advisors—if you had listened to my proposal last month, this would not have happened."

Dray's smile dripped icicles. "Yes, I recall your suggestion was to outlaw all stories except the traditional tales of the goddesses. Correct?"

Naith's slightly pointed teeth showed in his feigned smile. "You remember well."

"I didn't understand then, nor do I now, why you wish to outlaw all stories that draw attention to the great deeds of our renowned king."

Naith's face reddened. "Of course that's not what I—I didn't—You—"

The king waved a hand. "Enough, enough. Let us hear the rest of the report, and we can save the squabbles between high priest and chief advisor for private council." He looked at them dryly. "As is our usual custom."

A titter of laughter ran through the courtiers gathered in the throne room.

Braith cleared her throat. "Your Majesty, surely we would not fault a story peddler for some errant bit of story strand." She nodded to Menod. "Sir, is the peddler registered?"

"No, Highness," the bird man said. "The report said she was a young lass, but she travels about with the registered peddler Riwor."

The king shifted in his seat. "Ah, I do think I know the name Riwor. She told us stories at court once. Frightful to look at but had a nice voice when she got down to it."

Another titter of laughter.

Braith ignored his comment. "You see, Father? The peddler is so young she hasn't even been registered yet. Do you think we might overlook this offense, if even there was one to overlook?"

As soon as Braith spoke, the king's face darkened. Apparently he did take offense to this errant strand, and he did not seem to appreciate her dismissal of its significance.

"Princess," the king said, "I'll overlook your speaking out of turn, but a forbidden story strand ought not to be treated lightly."

Braith lowered her head slightly. "Forgive my ignorance, Majesty. But what exactly is the crime here? The peddler was telling an approved story. Surely this strand was an accident."

Dray's dark eyes trained on the princess, Naith's seemed determined to look anywhere but at her, and the king grumbled something under his breath before raising his voice.

"Perhaps," he said, "the princess ought to be taking a full report instead of questioning her father's laws."

His tone hit Braith like a slap. "My apologies, Your Majesty. Of course." She looked at Menod. "Sir, did the witness describe the story strand in question?"

He wouldn't meet the princess's eyes, nor those of his king. "They say it glowed with white light. Just the type of strand His Majesty has warned the guard about."

Braith frowned. "Was anyone hurt by this strand?"

"No, Princess Braith." Menod shifted his weight. "Not according to the report."

"Your Majesty, I'm certain I must be missing something." Braith turned to the king. "Why would a strand of light be forbidden if it is not dangerous?"

"Hold your tongue," the king snapped.

Braith sucked in a tiny gasp. She glanced at the listening courtiers, then clamped her mouth shut and waited for the king to speak.

King Gareth turned back to Menod. "Tell me, aerie-watcher. Did the witness say anything else about the nature of this strand, beyond the fact that it was white light?"

Menod's throat bobbed as he swallowed. "He said it was thin, like thread."

The king grunted. "Anything else?"

Menod glanced up at the knight beside him. The knight nodded and the bird man continued. "The witness did say it was something to look at—stark white and like staring at the sun. Never seen anything so beautiful, he said."

Braith sat up straighter and bit her lip. But she held her peace.

The king stroked his beard. Then he glanced at Braith, stiff as a poker on her throne.

When he finally spoke, the king's tone was deliberately casual—measured. "Perhaps we shall not be overly concerned about this incident. Yet." He inclined his head to Dray, and Dray scribbled something on a piece of parchment.

That never boded well.

The king continued. "Perhaps Dyrain, honored and notable steward of the Eastern Peninsula, shall take this matter to heart, since it occurred in his territory. And perhaps he will keep his king abreast of any new developments as they arise."

In the crowd, Dyrain started at the mention of his name. He had been flirting with a young lady-in-waiting, apparently. "Yes, Your Majesty."

Something churned just beneath the feigned calm of the king's expression. Braith stared at him, trying to read his thoughts.

If this young story peddler on the Eastern Peninsula had indeed done something to offend King Gareth—something so grievous as to be called forbidden—there would be no mercy for her when she was found out.

CHAPTER 6

TANWEN

"The goddess Cethor did not take lightly the offense done to her by her sister Noswitch."

A shimmering blue strand tangled with a velvety plum one, just as the goddess sisters had struggled with each other. The strands danced before me, almost singeing themselves by the large fireplace in the common room of the inn.

"There lived a brave young man named Ean who took up Cethor's cause, for he had fallen deeply in love with the sea goddess."

A flesh-colored ribbon poured out from one of my palms—rough, like Brac's chin when he forgot to shave a couple days in a row. The flesh strand jumped into the fray between the blue and purple strands.

Did Brac forget to shave today? Did he forget his hat, and is his nose burned to a crisp?

After a moment, Riwor grumbled from the chair beside me. "Your strands are dying. Thinking about your own hero, are you?"

I scowled at her. Hated when she could read me so plainly like that. And I hated that she made comments about Brac like he was my lad. But she wasn't wrong—my strands were about to disappear.

Focus.

I did my best to ignore Riwor, slurping at her mug of ale like a thirsty hound.

"Ean sought out the crafty night goddess, Noswitch, and entered into battle with her."

The blue strand hung back now while the flesh and purple strands swirled viciously.

"Ean resisted the night goddess like no mortal man had ever done before. His swordsmanship did not fail him. He fought bravely, all the while thinking of Cethor's love."

The flesh strand swirled around and began to form the shape of a man's head.

"Alas, the goddess of the night's trickery has never been matched. She routed Ean and used his own sword to cut off his head."

Red light floated from my fingers. Where it touched the fabric head, it left bloody stains.

"Cethor was heartbroken and driven to despair by her sister's cruelty. She gave up her immortality and chose to die with her lover."

The shimmery blue strand flooded into the fabric head. After a moment, it popped out of the eye sockets to form Ean's crystal-blue eyes.

"Noswitch regretted her rash decision to kill the hero Ean, and she missed her sister Cethor. So she used her magic to bring Ean's head back to life. Ean's head, and Cethor within it, lived for eighty more years."

The plum strand danced around the fabric head, washing away the bloody marks.

"Then they found their peace in the afterlife, together for always."

The story crystallized—a handsome man's face with striking blue eyes that glittered in the light.

It was a pretty story I'd made, the glass fine and clear, but still I wrinkled my nose. "That story will turn your stomach, no question."

Riwor's grumbling laugh cut through the quiet of the common room. "You just don't like that story because legend has it all blue-eyed people descended from Cethor and Ean."

My frown deepened, and I tried not to think about my seastone-blue eyes. But then I brightened. I turned my story this way and that. "Least it's pretty, isn't it?"

Riwor feigned a wide yawn. "Barely passable."

"Well, the villagers liked my stories today. Sold five. My best day ever." I placed the crystallized head on the low wooden table that stood in front of the fireplace. "What was your best day ever, Riwor?"

Riwor's face turned red. She huffed and sputtered a moment before real words came out. "You wicked girl! How dare you ask me such a question?"

I sighed. "Didn't mean offense. Just wondering is all."

"Well, success isn't always measured by the number of stories a person sells. There's also price to consider. And don't you forget I've been to the palace. Told stories to King Gareth himself."

"Did you ever visit the palace when the other king ruled? King Caradoc?"

Riwor set her mug on the table and stared at me. "Aye."

The sudden stillness in the room chilled my bones. It was just the two of us, plus the barkeep wiping down tables in the back. But the air got calm all at once, and it didn't feel natural.

"Was it different when King Caradoc ruled?"

Riwor pursed her lips. "You trying to get me to speak treason, is that it? Now that you think you can make money without old Riwor, it's time to be rid of her and take the extra cut for yourself, eh?" She tried to run a hand through her wiry gray hair, apparently forgetting it was pulled back into a bun.

"No, that's not it. I was just curious." I picked up the crystal head and studied it. "I was only four when the king died, so I don't remember anything about him."

Riwor settled back in her chair. "Aye, it was different."

I waited for a few long minutes, but she didn't say anything else. I replaced the crystal head on the table.

"Do you ever get bored, Riwor?"

"Bored of what?"

"Only telling crowned stories about the goddesses and the king. Don't you ever want to tell stories about something else?" I thought of the fairy stories secreted away on my bookshelves back at the cottage in Pembrone.

I'd never tell Riwor, but I used to make up my own stories when

I was practicing before she took me on. Never had that pinchy, squished-down feeling back in those days. Felt freer somehow.

Riwor's gaze drilled into me. "Listen well, Tanwen. If you don't want your head to end up like old Ean there, you stick to the crowned stories and never speak another word of this to anyone. Including me." She shifted her weight in her chair, grabbed her ale mug, and took a big gulp. And that was that.

Fine, then.

"I hope I get to tell stories to King Gareth someday like you did."

"Ha!" Riwor's severe tone made the barkeep jump. "He's not an easy man to please, Tanwen. Careful what you wish for, especially if you're thinking of veering from crowned stories."

I studied Riwor's face. Four mugs of ale in. She might talk a little. "Is the king very cruel?"

Riwor shrugged. "He's a fighting man—a warrior. Conquered Meridione, Haribi, and Minasimet all within a few years of his coronation. I suppose a man like that would be used to getting what he wants, when he wants it. And I suppose it'd be natural for him to demand the utmost loyalty from his subjects." She cast a sideways glance at the barkeep.

Aye, I supposed. But I couldn't help wondering what the king really thought of us, his people. Did he love us? I thought a king ought to love his people, but Brac said I was addled. Fanciful.

I turned to Riwor. "I wonder what Meridione is like. Maybe we could take a tour there after this one is done."

Riwor spluttered into her ale. "Meridione is a thousand miles southwest, stupid girl! You think that old bag of donkey bones will pull us so far?" She snickered. "No, I thought we'd do Twen, Bach, and Drefden next."

"Drefden!" Indignation leaped up inside me. "That's where you live! They've heard your stories a thousand times. And Twen and Bach are on our side of the River Abereth. That's hardly even a real tour. I thought at least we might go over the mountains. Past Lake Lyn or something."

"Past the lake, eh? Why, because that's the way to Urian?" Riwor scoffed. "Always about the palace for you, isn't it, Tanwen?"

I didn't answer. I studied the way Ean's dead blue eyes caught the light of the failing fire.

Riwor was wrong. It wasn't just about the palace. I wanted to see those far-off places and meet strange new people. To have adventure. Why did everyone act like that was a crime?

I slumped in my chair. "Someone once told me the Meridionis are lovely to look at. I don't know a thing about Haribi or Minasimet, except the names and some fairy stories. Have you been to those places?"

Riwor snorted again, but this time a belch came out with it. "You'd have to cross the whole of Tir, through the Western Wildlands, to even look upon Haribi—and even then, it'd be a speck on the horizon, across the Cefin Sea. And Minasimet, well, it's a big island way out in the Menfor Sea. Have you ever heard of a Tirian peasant venturing to either of those places?"

I felt my face fall. "No. But we're not ordinary peasants. We're story peddlers. We travel to all kinds of places most people will never see." I bit my lip. "Don't we?"

Riwor laughed. "Perhaps you ought to leave your imaginings to your practice stories. That's the place they rightly belong."

I sucked in my breath. So the old beast knew I used to make up my own stories. I wondered if she'd ever turn me in. Wouldn't put it past her. Best not to push my luck.

I made my voice sound calm. "I was only practicing so I could get better. I don't do it anymore. Not since you taught me the crowned ones."

She cackled. "Ah, yes. I saw many of your practice stories. Always featuring some bachelor prince wanting to marry a poor peasant girl, seemed to me. Too bad there isn't a real bachelor prince in Tir for you to use as the subject of your yarns. Bet you could tell some mighty fine stories about him, eh?"

She took another swig of ale and slapped her knee. "Maybe if you told that story enough, you could crystallize a life-sized bachelor prince for yourself. You could tote him around in a bean cart and introduce him as your husband, heir to the Tirian Empire." She guffawed and a bit of ale dribbled down her chin.

I felt the ugliness of the scowl on my face, but I didn't care. "Aye, very funny."

"I never could tolerate the idea of marriage myself." She rubbed her belly. "But if you're considering it at all, I think you should marry that ridiculous puppy dog who follows you all around Pembrone. He'd make a fine match for you."

My stomach flopped over. The memory of my fight with Brac shot to the front of my mind. He'd wanted to kiss me in that barn, and I knew it. But the idea made my stomach pinch tighter than it did when I told those crowned stories.

A few seconds passed before I could make the words come out. "Brac will make some girl a fine husband one day."

"But not you?" She grinned, revealing the space where one of her top teeth had rotted out.

"I don't know. But if you say one more word about Brac, I'll box *your* ears for a change."

The humor fell from her face. Blood rose in her cheeks. But I wasn't going to back down this time. Not if she was going to bring Brac into it. My mind was scrambled enough about it as it was. Didn't need her ribbing to further confuse matters. We glared at each other in silence.

Then she took a huge swig of ale and burst into laughter. "Sure you will, Tanwen." She took another drink. "Sure you will."

Really, I'd been lucky this was her fourth tankard for the night. Otherwise I would have gotten a stiff slap for my disrespect. But I meant every word, and if she kept talking about Brac, I might even make good on my threat.

What was he doing just then, I wondered. Playing with the little ones at home? Down at Blodwyn's tavern, flirting with the girls upstairs? The idea made my insides twist. But . . . did that mean I loved him? Or did I just want him behaving like a proper gentleman for his own good?

Riwor's growl broke into my thoughts. "Marry the puppy, Tanwen. Live on the farm; have a litter of pups. Best you'll do."

I glowered at her. "Oh yeah? That's not where I've got my sights set."

"Perhaps if you had a father to arrange something better, you could rise out of it. But you don't. You're all alone, and a cozy farmhouse with a loyal lapdog is more than many girls in your position could hope for."

I leaned back in my chair and sighed. Her words tasted like a slap, but for once she wasn't being cruel. She was just speaking truth. The great empty space in my heart threatened to swallow me whole.

The flames of the fire had dwindled to a glow. I watched a hunk of wood char to blackness, then drop away from its log.

Aye. Perhaps if I had a father.

CHAPTER 7

THE ONE IN THE DARK

Second moon of autumn, the 36th year of Caradoc II

The ultimate of blessings has been bestowed upon our household this day.

The Creator has given us a great treasure.

A light cracked the utter darkness. Rats skittered as the young woman entered with a candle in one hand and a basket on her other arm.

She bent down. "I've brought food."

Eyes blinked at her several times, watering at the candlelight. Then looked into the basket. Bread, cheese, two bottles—ale, water. Something else was at the bottom, but hunger gnawed and hands reached for bread first.

"How are you today?" She searched his face with earnest dark eyes. Surely she knew there would be no answer.

She watched as the bread was devoured. "Have you kept busy?" She gently brushed crumbs from the ragged shirt front. "Staying out of mischief, I hope."

A grunt. A tired mind that sensed it owed her a proper answer. But it had been so long.

She took out the item at the bottom of the basket and placed it carefully into a calloused hand.

Better than food. More necessary. Fingers closed around the bottle—the lifeline.

"Use it well. I'll return tomorrow." She smiled. "My lord."

CHAPTER 8

TANWEN

Traveling with hungover Riwor was akin to keeping company with a mountainbeast that'd slept on a prickle-vine. Still, we somehow both survived the day after our chat in the tavern, and we made it to Afon in time for a late supper.

I could smell Afon's smallest inn—aptly named the Greasy Rag—from two buildings away. I didn't want to touch the door or the walls for fear the wood would fall away under my fingers. But the price was a bargain, so Riwor was tickled as a slap-happy hedge-nibbler.

Easy for her to be pleased. She didn't have to sleep on the floor. Although, on balance, the floor was probably better than the flea-infested mattress.

Beyond all reasoning, I awoke in fine spirits the next morning. Another day of peddling. A new town, new people. Excitement bubbled up inside, and even the moldy tavern couldn't dampen it down.

"Hurry up, Tanwen!" Riwor shouted at me from across the town square. She flailed her arms to get my attention. "This is the best spot." She elbowed away a merchant farmer with a cart of withered-looking greens.

I trotted over to her and set down my stool, then nodded a quick apology to the miffed farmer. "Riwor, look at this fountain! You ever seen anything like it?" I peered over the edge of the odd contraption. "It's like a big white bowl!"

Riwor rolled her eyes and yanked me away from the trickling water. "It's called marble. If you ever do make it to Urian, you'll see a lot of it."

"I wonder why we don't have one in Pembrone." I stood on tiptoe and peeked around Riwor's shoulder to get another look at the cascading water.

Riwor shoved me back onto my stool. "Because Pembrone is a burp of a town no one cares about. Afon is the second largest village on the Eastern Peninsula."

I sighed. Much as I agreed with her about Pembrone, it stung to hear the words from someone else. It was the only home I'd known, after all.

But the sun was chasing away the morning fog, and birds came to line the edge of the fountain, twittering a song. And I was far enough from the musty tavern to smell the patches of spring flowers. Riwor's foul mood couldn't dent my spirits.

The children gathered first. They always did. They sat with crossed legs and gazed up at me, waiting for a bit of magic. I played with them until paying customers gathered and Riwor finally decided to announce me.

"Gather round to hear the pride of the Eastern Peninsula—Tanwen, the story-peddling prodigy!"

I almost snorted at her introduction. She certainly didn't mind slapping around the "pride of the Eastern Peninsula" when she had a mind to.

But I just smiled at the crowd. "Any requests?"

"One with soldiers!"

"One with a princess!"

"Tell the story of Trasig and Ramant!"

Trasig and Ramant—a crowned story about two mortal men who fell in love with the same goddess and both ended up dead on her account. Cheery stuff.

Riwor nodded to me. The suggestion had come from an adult, one who might pay, so that's the story I'd tell. A short time later, Riwor added several coins to her purse, and I handed the villager her story—a crystallized heart with a dagger through it.

Riwor always said the young women were suckers for the outlandish tragic romances. Between squelching, ale-scented belches, she reasoned it was because the young women hadn't learned real life was tragedy enough on its own.

Having to smell those belches day after day, I rather agreed.

"What's next?" I asked the crowd. "What would you like me to tell?"

"How about the story of King Gareth's conquest of Meridione?"

A shiver prickled my spine. The requester's voice—too familiar. I looked up to see a hooded man with a long cloak and shiny boots.

The very same boots I'd spied in Gwern.

But how . . . ? Why? Was he following us?

After several moments of silence, I caught Riwor's frenzied gestures out of the corner of my eye. Everyone stared at me, waiting. Either Riwor had forgotten the hooded stranger from Gwern, or else she remembered all too well the heavy coins this mystery man had tossed to us last time. Of course she'd want a repeat performance.

So I tried to ignore the hooded onlooker and began the story. "Once there was a people who lived to the south of the great state of Tir."

Two strands of light—silver, like sparkling fog—curled from my hands. The strands danced around the crowd, and smiles lit up all about.

"Tir lived at peace with her neighbor to the south for many generations, with Tir looking after her lesser neighbor like a father looks after his child."

The silver strands flew up toward the sky together, then dropped to the ground in a swoosh.

The children unleashed excited squeals when the strands whizzed past them.

"But over time, the darkness of pride consumed the people to the south. So much darkness that it swallowed them from the inside out. It blackened their hair, darkened their skin, and they became known as the Meridioni—'Dark People' in their native tongue."

"You're pronouncing it wrong." The hooded stranger's voice nearly sent me jumping from my skin.

My gaze shot back to him. "Huh?" The strands stopped swirling and began to lose their shape.

"You pronounce it like a Tirian peasant. It's not 'Muh-rid-e-own-ee.' It's 'Mer-eed-e-own-ee.'"

"Oh." I pushed out a laugh. "Right."

Riwor faked a wide smile at the stranger and bowed. "Thank you, good sir." Then she turned to me and hissed, "Keep going."

Sure as the taxes, my strands had just about disappeared.

"Oh. Aye." Where was I? Ah, yes. "They became known as Meridioni—'Dark People' in their native tongue." I made the word roll off correctly—like the hooded stranger had said it—even though it felt weird.

The silver strands popped back to life. One rose above the villagers and circled around. The other strand slowly changed. The silvery tip darkened like it'd been dipped in blood. Red spread all the way through the strand until the whole thing was crimson, just like the Meridioni flag.

If I played this right, the red strand would form a scaly fish, and the silver strand would turn the acid-green color of our king. Then the green satin would become a silvery-green sword. The fish ended up with the sword down its throat, showing the dominance of Tir over Meridione. Doesn't sound nice, but somehow ends up being sort of pretty if the story crystallizes well.

"The Dark People to the south became bolder and more prideful by the year, until they had truly forgotten their kind father to the north."

The red strand balled up into a circle, and then wiggled into the shape of a fish with glistening red scales.

I paused. Something seemed to stop up my mouth, like my own words didn't want to continue coming out. Maybe it was the idea of King Gareth being a kind father that seemed strange.

But now was not the time for mulling over such things. I had to keep telling the story. And the way I'd learned it too. It was what the villagers expected, and I aimed to give them what they wanted.

And get paid for it.

"For some time, this father nation had lacked a strong leader to enact discipline upon the disobedient, prideful child. But when its ruler succumbed to the plague . . ." I trailed off as the silver strand turned green, like it was supposed to.

But that feeling. That pinching, painful feeling rose suddenly in my gut again.

I fought hard against it. But the pain struck so hard this time I had to bite down on my lip to keep from crying out. My hand flew to my side, but I forced more story to come out.

"King Gareth Bo-Kelwyd came . . . to power—"

Then the rising feeling gave way, and it was like a coursing river of energy bolted through my body. There was no stopping it. A scream tore from my throat.

Blinding white light set each of my fingertips ablaze. My mouth dropped open. A few of the children shrieked. My head whipped toward Riwor, but her face hung slack and there was no help, no direction, to be found in her eyes.

The only thing I knew to do was keep going. Force the story—and my body—to behave.

"... and with him the strength and resolve of the father nation was renewed. Oh!"

My stomach seared like it was being ripped in two.

The white light shot from my fingertips. The force of it propelled me backward, and I toppled from my stool. Light spilled everywhere—up in the air, around the villagers, weaving in between us and under us.

And then a whisper sliced through the chaos. And I'll be blasted if the whisper wasn't coming right out of my own story strands.

"Lies. All lies from the one who has sold himself to the Liar. It was not a plague that slew Caradoc."

I squinted against the light. The shouts of the villagers carried through the muddled din.

"What did she say?"

"Did she say it wasn't a plague that killed King Caradoc?"

Horror crashed down upon me like a wave from the sea. "No, it wasn't me! I didn't say it!"

But even as I shouted my protest, I realized it *was* my voice coming out of those strands. Like how my voicc sounded the time I took ill for two weeks and could barely swallow. Or when I'd hollered myself hoarse while helping a farmer herd his grazers.

And then more words dripped from my story strands. "By Gareth's own hand did Caradoc sleep."

"She's speaking treason!"

I clapped my hands over my mouth. But my voice wasn't coming from there. The light blasted from my fingers. And within it, the whispers spoke. My voice. My voice accusing King Gareth of treachery.

"Gareth is no king. He dispatched the rightful king. The truth will be known, and the empire of lies will fall."

And suddenly, the accusatory strands shot to the sky and bundled together. They collected into a single beam, then careened down toward the cobblestones. The green satin strand of the king remained swirling in a circle at my feet. The red Meridioni strand was nowhere to be seen.

The light crashed upon King Gareth's strand. They wrestled each other, the light enveloping the green, then the green ribbon rallying back and forcing itself into view. And before I knew what had happened, the light made a clear bottle, like my mother's fine glass ones I had pawned long ago. The green satin funneled into the bottle and stilled. Emerald smoke wafted up from the open top.

One child in front gasped. "It's poison!"

The moment she spoke, the story crystallized. And true enough, it did look to be a vial of grass-colored poison.

Though I tried to clamp my mouth shut, though my tongue lay still and my lips didn't move, that unwanted feeling rose inside me until the hoarse whisper spilled from my throat. "Gareth the Usurper is the poison."

The bottle exploded into a thousand pieces of light.

The villagers gaped. Riwor's mouth still dangled. The hooded figure had vanished.

And I had a desperate feeling my life was lost.

CHAPTER 9
TANWEN

I SHOT UP IN BED WITH A GASP.

Where am I?

Then the last two days settled over my mind like marine fog. A dismal, leaden fog that lingers all day and spoils picnics. After my story blew up, Riwor had abandoned me. I'd barely ducked the king's guard in Afon, then I'd spent that first night in a barn. Next day, I'd begged rides in passing farm carts until I reached the river. I had enough change to pay the ferrying fee across, thank the moon. I'd spent last night in the cheapest room of this tavern in Twen.

I swung my legs out of bed. The icy floor stabbed my feet with pins and needles. Early morning still. I had enough money to pay for my lodgings and some breakfast, but perhaps the innkeeper would let me exchange labor instead. I reckoned it'd be wise to hold on to every bit I could.

A breakfast of watery gruel and a mountain of washed dishes later, I trudged down the king's road.

Only halfway home and no donkey in sight.

Tears bubbled up from deep inside. Where was Riwor? Hiding out too? Or had she officially disowned me and my traitorous story threads?

I already knew the answer. But I couldn't account for how deep it cut me. Right to the bone. It'd been a fool idea to think of Riwor as a grandmother. I'd known that for six moons. And yet I couldn't help wondering. . . . Would I ever find anybody who would take me as his own, stand by me through thick and thin the way family ought?

Brac popped to mind. He stood by me. Always. But then his words rang in my memory: *If only you'd set your storytelling aside.*

Did he really stand by me if he didn't love all of me, if he wanted me to lock up my passions, dreams, and hopes—my gift—and be what *he* wanted me to be instead? My mind swirled worse than a hundred rogue story strands.

If the guard caught up to me, none of it mattered. A girl didn't much need a family when she whiled away her days in the king's dungeon. Or worse, ended her days on his chopping block.

A speck on the horizon snagged my attention. For a moment, my spirits rose. Maybe it was a farmer with a cart who could give me a ride to Pembrone. Then reality deflated me.

He's going in the opposite direction, Tanwen. You blockhead.

Unless I wanted to head right back into Twen, this approaching stranger wouldn't be of any help.

But then my heart pinched like someone squished it in his fist.

The approaching figure was a mounted king's guard knight. I was sure, now that he was closer and I could just make out the seal on his chest. I scurried from the road into a ditch overgrown with tall grass and grasped the silver knot around my neck.

Please, let him pass by me.

I'd seen him, so surely he'd seen me. But maybe if I just pretended to be a simple peasant, gathering wildflowers or berries or some such harmless thing, maybe then he'd pass by me without a thought.

I tiptoed down the ditch, hoping to find something I could reasonably be collecting. A few scrawny flowering weeds were my best and only option.

The clip of hooves sent my breath into my throat. The sound slowed for a moment, then there was silence. My heart hammered in my chest, but I pretend to be busy about my weeds. Checked the scarf I'd tied around my blonde hair. Didn't seem to be any escaped locks trying to shout out my identity.

Was this soldier looking for me? Looking right at me?

I couldn't breathe.

What did it feel like to be hanged?

But then the clopping of hooves picked up again and eventually faded into the distance. All my breath fled from my body, and I collapsed into a heap on my back. Tears of relief dripped down my cheeks.

Goddesses above, please let me get back to Pembrone safely.

"Here is fine." I glanced up at the man beside me.

He tugged the horse's reins. "You sure? Some distance yet to the next town."

I slid off the driver's seat and flashed a smile, praying it was convincingly carefree. "I like to walk."

He shrugged. "Take care, then."

"Thank you, sir."

I let the dust from the cart full of wax beans dwindle before I made a show of following him. The farmer looked back once, so I kept shuffling along behind, pretending to enjoy my walk. Finally, the horse put enough distance between us that the cart showed as a dot on the road ahead.

Then I spun around and took off at a run toward Pembrone.

I had let the farmer pass my town, hoping it would appear as though I were traveling on to Drefden, or even Bach. I didn't want Pembrone to stick in his head as the place where he'd dropped me off. The idea conjured up the image of the poor man being tortured for information about a wayward story peddler skulking about these parts.

I tried to force my mind to sift out those thoughts like chaff. This would all blow over. I was making too big a deal of it.

How many times had I told myself the same thing in the three days since I'd left the tavern in Twen? I'd lost count, and I still didn't truly believe it. The farmer with the wax beans was the first ride I'd had, and I was more tired than a carrier pigeon on mail day.

But not too tired to run full speed back to Pembrone. To Brac's place.

What if the king's guard was there already? What if they'd traced me back to Pembrone, and Farmer Bradwir and his wife and the wee ones were—

No, stop. Settle down, Tanwen. It's going to be fine.

I forced myself to walk. The afternoon sun slanted into my eyes. My hair—greasy after days without a proper wash—simmered under the heat. But I knew this road well. Only a bit farther and I could turn down Pembrone's main thoroughfare. Brac wouldn't be waiting for me this time, pitched against the building and rubbing his sunburned face. He wasn't expecting me for some days yet.

No matter. Today I'd go to him. I started sprinting again.

The first smack of cobblestone under my feet set my bones to clattering. I tightened the strap of my bag, hiked up my skirt, and threw every last ounce of energy I had into my strides.

"Tanwen?" Blodwyn looked up from sweeping the porch of her tavern. "Where's the fire, lass?" She watched me fly past. "Tannie?"

I dodged a group of children playing, then a farmer and a butcher haggling over the price of some grazer meat. I could only think of getting to safety—to the Bradwir stead.

And then there was his voice. "Tannie?"

I ground to a stop right in front of my stone cottage. Brac ambled down the pathway from his place, his eyebrows raised and a basket in one hand.

I sucked in deep breaths of briny sea air to try to calm my ramming heart. Then I jumped up and threw my arms around his neck.

He let out a short laugh. "Well, hello to you too, Tannie. But I thought you weren't back for a few days." He pulled away a little and squinted at me. I could see the wheels of his brain turning, figuring how many days I'd been gone and how many till I was supposed to come back.

"Your family." I gasped out my words. "They're all right?"

Brac frowned. "Were at lunchtime. What's happened?"

"Nothing. Everything's fine."

The lie tasted sour on my tongue. I could trust Brac—in fact, he might be the only person in Tir I could trust. But I couldn't spill it all out just then. Now that I was sure Farmer Bradwir and his kin, most of all Brac, weren't in danger, all I wanted was to be home. Safe inside those familiar walls.

Brac nodded to the basket. "Mam sent me to check on your place, and I thought I might have my supper by the cliffs. I'll share it with you. Ain't really enough for two, but goddesses know you've had your share of scant meals before. Least it's something."

Tears burned my eyes. "Thanks."

"Tannie, what is it?" He put his hand on my arm. "You're about to cry. Don't tell me you ain't."

A tear snaked down my cheek, then another. "I'll tell you everything later, Brac. I promise. I just—I need to go home now."

He nodded. "All right." Then he put the basket into my hands. "You take it. I can get something at home. You eat it and then come see me, all right?" He nudged my shoulder and pulled his face into a lopsided grin. "Good to have you home, whatever the trouble was. I'm sure it'll pass."

I tried to hold in a panicked sob. "Thanks, Brac. Just glad you're safe."

His expression dimmed. "Tannie, what in the name of the taxes happened?" Then his eyes lit up all fiery. "Did she hit you again? Did that mountainbeast of an old hag smack you? I tell you what, if she ever sets foot near me, I'll—"

"No, Brac." I sighed. "Truly, I don't think you'll be seeing Riwor again."

Suddenly, his face lit up. "Won't be seeing Riwor? Does that mean . . . Tannie, does it mean you're leaving it behind, like I said? No more storytelling?"

My chest ached. I tried to imagine what my life would be like with no story peddling, or worse, no storytelling at all. Was I even Tanwen En-Yestin anymore if I didn't tell stories? *Could* I even tell stories after what happened in Afon? Was settling down and setting it aside my only choice now?

I leaned against the wall and dropped my head in my hands. "I don't know anything anymore, Brac."

I could almost hear his smile collapse into a frown. "Well, as soon as you're settled, come up to the stead. We'll sort it."

"Aye." I pried myself off the wall and forced a thin smile. "I will." I slid through the gate, latched it behind me, and then trudged through the front door into the cottage.

I dropped my bag on the floor and went straight to Father's study. Not sure why, but fear knotted my stomach as I paused before the study door. Can't say what I feared I'd find—his chair bolted to the ceiling? The bookshelves overturned and all his books tossed out? His ghost sitting there, waiting for my return?

But of course, nothing like that happened. Everything seemed to be exactly where I'd left it.

The cottage was normal. I just needed to do normal things, and then it would be fine. Everything would be fine.

"Father." My whisper echoed through the empty cottage. "I'm home."

The tears started leaking down my cheeks again, because even I could see how pathetic it was to be talking to the emptiness like it was a real parent. "Something bad happened while I was away."

Silence answered me.

"I was telling a story, and these terrible strands started flying all over the place. White and bright, like the sun."

Outside, a bird chirped.

"The strands made me talk—or else they were talking themselves. I don't even know. I've never heard of anything like it. The strands said treasonous things about King Gareth."

My gaze shifted to the books lining Father's shelves. Bet there was a lot that wouldn't be "crowned" between those covers. Father would have had some answers for me. If he were here.

"Why did it happen? What does it mean?"

The silence, the absence that so marred my life, was the only reply.

And suddenly, I felt like screaming. I needed help—guidance, protection. Something. I needed my parents, now more than ever. The hole in my heart gaped wide.

"Why are you gone?" I cried out into the calm. "Why did you leave me?" My voice shrank. "I'm afraid."

A breeze whispered through the garden outside the study window. And then all lay still and silent again.

Water dripped onto the floor as I squeezed the last of it from my hair. I combed my fingers through the tangled tresses before the fire.

At least I was clean. That was more than I'd been able to say for days, and it felt better than decent to be fresh finally.

I folded back the cloth on the basket Brac's mother had packed for him. Slices of a roasted bird of some sort, a round loaf of crusty bread, a bottle of grazer milk, a piece of delightfully smelly cheese, and a small hathberry pie.

Must be the first hathberries of the year. A bit early, but no one ever complained when the hathberries arrived before summer.

I chuckled. Brac had said it wasn't enough for two, but this could last me a couple days if it had to. Sometimes I wondered how his parents managed to keep that lad fed. I spread the meal on the table.

Stay busy. Do normal things. Think about normal things. Act normal, and it'll be normal.

"Supper's laid out," I said to no one.

I stoked the fire and added another log. A brisk wind seemed to search out every crack in the windows and under the doors. A shudder tiptoed down my back.

Cool spring evenings are normal. Quiet, solitary suppers are normal. Everything's fine.

I took my seat on the bench at the table. The hathberry pie found its way to my mouth first. If I had no parents to guide me, at least I could take advantage of the good parts. Dessert before supper. Sounded good to me.

"Riwor doesn't want anything to do with me now. Don't know if I can keep peddling anyway, with the guard stirred up against me. Brac thinks . . ." I let the thought die on my tongue.

I grabbed a piece of bread and wished I had some butter. "Think

I'd be able to handle peddling on my own?" I imagined Father giving me an encouraging nod. "What if I went across the mountains? Maybe follow along the river and peddle in the river towns. See some new villages."

Surely word of my disastrous white-light story hadn't traveled that far. I could settle down there, or even farther if I had to.

Then that nagging thought pierced my gut.

Brac.

"Maybe he'd come with me." But that forced a startling question into my mind.

If Brac did agree to travel with me, would I be more inclined to marry him? Would it change anything?

I smashed the thought into the ground. No matter. Brac was about as likely to leave Pembrone as Riwor was to win a beauty contest. But peddling downriver on my own. That was an idea. It was just beginning to crystallize in my mind, like a well-told story, when there was a knock at the door.

My stomach catapulted into my throat. The king's guard. They'd found me. My eyes darted everywhere.

Where to hide?

But then my breath came out in a relieved huff. Of course it was only Brac. I'd told him I would come up later and he'd gotten impatient, so he came down himself. If the guard had found me, surely they wouldn't knock first.

"I'm coming, Brac." I wiped the crumbs from my lap. Then I tightened my shawl around my shoulders and made for the door.

The latch complained with a creak as I lifted it.

"Got tired of waiting already? That's not like you, Br—"

Never did finish my sentence.

The moment I had the door open, a hooded figure clamped a hand over my mouth and shoved me into my house. Two more hooded figures pushed inside, and one of them slammed the door and bolted it.

CHAPTER 10

TANWEN

A FAMILIAR VOICE POURED OUT FROM BENEATH THE HOOD OF the one with his hand over my mouth. "Listen carefully."

My eyes widened. I tried to say, "You!" but his hand muffled the sound. I clawed at him to no avail.

"Tanwen, listen."

He remembered my name. I struggled harder.

"The guard is after you. They've been following you since Twen. You need to come with us. Do you understand?"

Another of the hooded figures, so tall his head nearly scraped the low ceiling of the cottage entry, pulled off his hood. Straw-colored hair, sunburnt skin, and calloused palms. Might as well have been Brac standing there, just two hands taller. "Mor, if you want an answer to that question, I reckon you're going to have to take your hand off her mouth."

The hooded man holding me hesitated. "Can I let you go, Tanwen? Do you promise not to scream?"

I struggled in response.

The third hooded figure sighed. "Who could blame her, Mor?" A woman's voice. "I wouldn't trust a hooded hooligan lurking about like a phantom either." She pulled back her hood to reveal light-gold hair, high cheekbones, and mournful green eyes. "We mean you no harm, Tanwen."

Finally, my captor released me. His hood came off, and I got a look at the face belonging to the voice I'd heard twice before. For a moment, my breath was about beaten out of my lungs.

The young man called Mor didn't look like anyone I'd ever seen. He had fair Tirian skin, but his hair was dark as the bitter-bean brew lots of folks drank in the mornings. It was cut short, unlike any farmer lad I knew, and a gold hoop was punched clear through one of his ears.

The lass laughed and turned to Mor. "She doesn't know what to make of you."

Mischief lit up his sky-blue eyes, and he took a bow. "Captain Mor Bo-Lidere, at your service."

"Captain?" Thoughts of the guard slammed to mind.

"Of a ship." He glanced down at his boots—the shiny ones I'd seen before. Sailors' boots, I realized now. Real fisherman didn't often come to our little bay.

I frowned at the shorn hair and gold ring. He had scruff enough on his face for a full-grown lad, but his skin didn't have the leathery, weather-beaten look of one who had spent years and years under the ocean sun like a regular captain.

"You're too young to be a fishing boat captain," I declared. "Are you a pirate?"

The tall, straw-haired farmer folded his arms across his chest and stared at his comrade. "Answer the lass's question, Mor."

Mor grinned. "Aye."

I planted my feet and glared at the trio, even if a handsome pirate was one of their number. "What are you doing in my house? Do you work for the king? I haven't done anything wrong, so you ought to go right back where you came from, thanks kindly."

The lass with the sad eyes shook her head. "Mor, I told you we should have approached her in Gwern. Now we have the guard breathing down our necks and no time to convince her."

Mor straightened his shoulders. "And I told you she wouldn't have come then either. She was still with the old lady and had no more reason to believe us then than she does now."

The lass took a step forward. "Some people listen to reason, even if you don't know how." Her green eyes seemed to glow in her hot stare.

The air in the room felt like when Farmer and Ma-Bradwir had a disagreement about something. Thick and charged with a special sort of lightning between the two.

The other cleared his throat. "Ain't got time for this at the moment. If you want to fight, save it for the Corsyth."

"Zelyth!" The lass's glare shot to the farmer now. "Keep locations out of this until she's agreed to go. I'll not have her betraying us to the guard." She turned back to me. "Tanwen, listen to me carefully. The guard knows about what happened in Afon. The captain of the peninsular guard has issued your arrest warrant. The soldiers are in Pembrone and will be here any minute. They'll have no qualms about hurting the ones you love to get to you. Time is running short. Do you understand?"

I don't know why, but when she spoke in her calm, proper Tirian, I couldn't help but believe her. At least a little.

Just the suggestion of the guard hiking up the road to the Bradwir stead was enough to convince me I should leave with these people, whoever they were.

"Just . . . let me pack my things."

"Hurry." The lass brushed dust from her cloak. "And I am Gryfelle." She curtsied. "Gryfelle En-Blaid."

"Tanwen. But it seems you already know."

A half-smile appeared. "Yes. Tanwen En-Yestin."

My full name—said right aloud like that—hung in the air. I never used it in public. Farmer Bradwir had told me it was better to stick to my first name for safety's sake. Leave Father's name out of my mouth. I'd always been more concerned with wondering what Father had been like, who he really was, so I'd never questioned Farmer Bradwir about why Father's name should be kept silent. Never even wondered why.

Until now.

CHAPTER 11

TANWEN

Mor glanced out the front window before he pulled the shutters closed. "Night's coming on, Elle. You all right?"

Gryfelle's back straightened. "I'm fine. I'll rest when we've reached safety."

I waited for a moment, but no one offered me anything by way of explanation.

Mor tried again. "We've been travelling for days. You sure you're good?"

Gryfelle shot an icy glare at Mor, then nodded to me. "Excuse me." She stepped out the back door and into the garden.

Mor's breath came out in a big, huffing sigh. "Elle, wait." He followed her out to the back garden.

Awkward silence filled the cottage around me and the farmer. I collected some things—clean clothes mostly—while he helped.

"I'm Zelyth Bo-Gwelt, by the by." The accent screamed Eastern Peninsula.

"You're from around here, aren't you?"

"Hauplan. It's—"

"Between Gwern and Afon, and a bit north. I know it." My face relaxed a little—almost smiled. "I'd know a peninsular farmer from a league off."

He smiled. "Aye." But then his smile dimmed. "You're doing the right thing, Tanwen. The guard . . . they're not accustomed to showing mercy."

I knew that to be true enough. But I wondered. Maybe the king would show mercy if I could explain the whole story to him. Those white light strands weren't my fault, after all.

I shoved a clean skirt into my bag. "So who are you three, anyway? Are you all on the run from the guard?"

"More or less." He handed me a clean pewter cup to pack. "I'm doing the same thing you're trying to do. Protect my family."

"Your parents? Brothers and sisters?"

"No. My father would turn me over to the guard if he got the chance." He stopped grabbing things off the shelves but didn't turn around. "It's my wife."

He looked no older than Brac. But Brac was, strictly speaking, of marrying age, so I guess this shouldn't have surprised me. Still, it did a little. A picture popped to my mind—a pretty lass with sun-browned skin and yellow hair, churning cream into butter.

It was nice to think Zelyth had a lass like that back home.

After a second of silence, he started moving again. I glanced out the back window. Mor and Gryfelle seemed to be having a heated conversation in whispers, and Gryfelle looked about ready to claw the sea captain's eyes from his head. "Them too?"

Zelyth rolled his eyes. "Not exactly. We all have our reasons for hiding out, each a little different than the last."

Mor tried to reach for Gryfelle's arm, but she yanked away and glared poison daggers at him. She spun away and took to staring out over the black water of the Menfor Sea. His shoulders sagged, then in the next second, his gaze lifted to me, staring at him through my back window.

A kaleidoscope of painted-wings escaped in my belly. Leastways, it felt like it.

I cleared my throat and turned away, only to find Zelyth eyeballing me.

He nodded to Mor and Gryfelle. "Those two are hopeless. Especially that rakish captain."

I fastened the strap on my leather traveling bag. "Not so keen on Captain Mor, are you, Zelyth?"

"Eh?" He looked up, eyes puzzled. "Mor's my best mate."

I let out a short laugh. "Hard to tell, the way you talk of him."

"Well, him being my best mate doesn't stop him from driving me crazier than a harried hedge-nibbler." He rolled his eyes, but a hint of humor shone through. "And you can call me Zel."

We shared a brief smile. Then the pounding on the front door started.

In a blink, Zel had snuffed out the only candle we had lit. He put a finger to his lips, then grabbed my hand.

Thank the goddesses Mor had closed the front shutters.

Zel moved quieter than a fluff-hopper toward the back. The pounding on the front door got louder.

Then a shout from outside. "Story peddler! We know you're in there. Open up, lass. We won't hurt you."

My breath came in clipped puffs. Zel caught my gaze in the dark and steadied me somehow. He shook his head slowly and eased us both out the back door. The door made but a whisper as it settled back into its frame.

The backyard was empty. Mor and Gryfelle had disappeared. But then I heard a low whistle that sounded so like a bird I'd have missed it if not for Zel's nudging me. Mor's dark hair appeared over the low stone wall on the north side of my yard.

Zel and I ducked through the garden and out the side gate. We crouched beside Mor and Gryfelle. Just in time too. A crash boomed from the cottage, and moments later at least four guardsmen, one with a torch, poured into my home.

My breath stole into my throat. I watched through the window as the guardsmen ripped through the kitchen, overturned the table with my supper still on it, and then split up—two into Father's study, the other two toward my room.

"Tanwen?" Mor's whisper shook me from my horrified trance. "Which is the best way back to the road? We have horses waiting." He touched my arm.

I stared at his hand. He'd asked me a question, hadn't he? Oh, right. The road.

If we crawled around the wall to the east side, we could slip down the cliffs to the beach. But it'd be quite the trek to get back to the road unnoticed, and I didn't know how well these three could climb. The rocks were treacherous, even in the full light of day. If we slipped all the way around to the front of the cottage, we'd end up right out on the road—and probably right into the guard's lap.

"Farmer Cerio's orchard," I said finally, nodding to the fruit trees just behind us. "If we follow them north a bit, we can meet up with the road away from the cottage. Sneak to the other side of town through the grain fields."

Then my breath left me again. Those were Farmer Bradwir's grain fields.

"Brac." I grabbed Zel's arm and whispered as quietly as my panic would let me. "I can't leave Pembrone without telling Brac."

A strange sob escaped my lips, and Mor clapped a hand over my mouth.

I could tell he was trying to fight it on account of the mortal danger and all, but a twisty smile darted onto his face anyhow. "That's your lad's name, eh?"

Fire lit my cheeks. Couldn't quite account for it, but it seemed the last thing in the world I wanted was Mor thinking Brac was my lad.

I pulled his hand from my mouth and made a face at him. "No. He's my best friend. His parents raised me after I turned up in Pembrone."

Gryfelle's delicate hand found my shoulder. Her whisper was quieter than a breath of wind. "Tanwen, there's no time. If the guard sees you, you'll be putting your friend and his family in danger."

"We could leave a note." Mor pulled Father's journal from my travel bag and held it up.

I snatched the journal and my bag back. I hadn't seen the pirate rifling through it. "Can't. I didn't bring any ink. It'd be no good anyway. Brac can't read."

Mor raised an eyebrow. "Can you?"

I was grateful for the dark, lest my fire-hot cheeks be noticed. "Aye."

"Who taught you?"

"Nanny, I guess?" I frowned. "Or maybe my father. I was six when I came here. Mother died and Father went missing when I was four. I'd lived with my nursemaid after that, but she took ill, and since my mother was Pembroni, Nanny brought me back here. Brac's mam and mine are distant cousins of some sort, so Nanny was trying to find my kin. Knew she was dying. I suppose it was her who taught me."

Mor grinned. "Fancy the Pembroni peasant who knows how to read."

"Shh." That was Zel. "Quiet down, you two."

I tried to push Mor's teasing from my mind and stole a glance over the garden wall. Guardsmen were still sifting through my things. I cringed to see them handle what remained of my mother's dishes.

Gryfelle looked at me strangely. Knowingly. "You had a nursemaid and you knew how to read. That's peculiar, don't you think?"

Yes, I guessed it was. I barely remembered the old woman who had brought me here, except that I called her Nanny. Everything before Pembrone was a blur. She always seemed like a character in a fairy story, and it had never occurred to me to ask why I'd been in the care of a stranger.

Not a stranger. A servant.

A crash from the cottage set me to jumping. I nearly hopped to my feet. "My house!" At every bump and bang, I imagined some trinket of Mother's or relic of Father's shattering to pieces.

"It's only things, Tanwen," Zel offered.

I knew he meant it kindly, but my eyes welled. "Those things are all I have left." All the years holding onto Father's books and pens while my stomach rumbled with hunger, only to have the ruddy king's guard wreck it all in one night.

It wasn't fair. None of it.

Mor paused one moment longer, giving me all the time he could allow. Then he said, "Come on." He took my bag back and shouldered it himself. A pirate gentleman? "We need to move while they're still tossing the house."

Zel squeezed my arm. "It'll be all right."

Sure, it would. I was putting all my trust in the hands of three people I didn't know, sneaking out of the only home I could remember to a place no one had even told me about.

Excellent plan.

But I nodded once and hoped my face looked braver than I felt.

And with that, I was leading these strangers—who may or may not be daft—through Farmer Cerio's orchard. I decided not to think about it as I wove through the blossoming trees, focusing instead on keeping my steps and my breathing quiet.

My feet stumbled over a root, but Mor's strong grip on my hand steadied me as I squinted in the dark. The cloud cover blocked all moonlight, and it was harder to see than usual. Good for ducking the guard; bad for trying to find the road.

"There." I pointed just ahead and to the west. "The road winds in close to the trees there. We can slip across to Farmer Bradwir's grain fields. Where are your horses?"

Zelyth tiptoed a few paces ahead to spy the pathway. "They're tethered by the king's road just outside Pembrone. Didn't want to draw attention by bringing them into town."

That sent a shiver through my bones.

But I forced my voice to sound calm. "Then we'll stay to the fields and steads on the west side of town. We'll meet up with the main road that way."

Mor's eyes seemed to glitter, even though there wasn't much light to reflect. "Just remember, they're likely to have guards posted all about. I'll go first."

Before anyone could say anything, he'd darted across the path into Farmer Bradwir's grain.

Zel nudged me. "You next." He checked for the guard one last time. "Go!"

I put my head down and ran. It seemed a league and a half before the stalks of grain swallowed me up. A few breaths passed and Gryfelle appeared, followed by Zel.

Zel nodded to me. "You lead."

So we picked through the grain like we'd picked through the

fruit trees. My chest squeezed around my heart when the Bradwir stead came into sight beyond the fields.

Couldn't I just bolt away, find Brac, collapse into his familiar embrace, and forget any of this had happened?

Just when I started thinking that was a fine plan, Mor yanked me into the dirt. He pressed a finger to my lips. Despite his touch, I was about to hop to my feet and give him a piece of my mind. What kind of gentleman pirate pulls a lass to her face in the dirt? But then I heard it—boot steps in the field.

Way too close.

I tried to slow my breath, but I was pretty sure my heart sounded like a smith's hammer against an anvil. The four of us waited, heard the steps come nearer and stop. Because they were there, I grabbed one of Mor's hands and one of Gryfelle's. I squeezed them both to keep myself still, if nothing else.

Then the steps carried on in another direction.

It was all I could do to keep the air from escaping my lungs in a loud sigh.

Zel nodded, and we took to picking through the grain again, this time practically crawling on all fours.

But one thing was sure—I couldn't run to Brac and pretend this wasn't happening. The guard was here in Pembrone looking for me, whether I liked it or not. Best to leave Farmer and Ma-Bradwir, the little ones, and Brac out of this whole mess. Safer that way. Safer for them to know nothing so they had nothing to give up—nothing to hide.

But safer didn't mean my heart wasn't crumbling to pieces.

"You don't ride." It wasn't a question. Gryfelle frowned as I struggled to mount the sleek mare they'd brought along for me.

I shot her a look. "Don't have lots of blood-mares in Pembrone. If you have a broken-down donkey to spare, I might ride that."

Mor snorted. But when Gryfelle's frown transferred his direction, he covered his snort with a cough.

Zel gave me a boost. "Quickly now. We'll head straight north. Our boat is stowed there."

My nose wrinkled as Zel handed me the reins. "In the marshes? Nobody keeps their boat there. The smell alone would drive a person leagues around it."

"Exactly," Mor said. "Faster and safer."

Hoofbeats cut our conversation short. The lads looked over my head, then glanced at each other.

Gryfelle didn't waste any time. She wheeled her horse onto the path, but I couldn't figure how she did it. Seemed she barely tugged on the reins at all, but the horse knew just what she wanted.

"Come quickly. Fly for the marshes." In a flourish of her dark cloak, Gryfelle vanished into the night.

Zel followed, somewhat clumsier.

Mor and I were left alone. "Say good-bye to Pembrone, Tanwen." Then he took off after the others.

I didn't look back. I slapped the horse with the reins like we did with the donkey, and the creature almost shot from under me with a vengeance—like I'd branded her rear with a hot iron. My lips were silent as I clung on for dear life. But in my mind, I was saying good-bye.

Good-bye, Bradwirs. Good-bye, Brac.

CHAPTER 12

TANWEN

THE SMELL NEARLY KNOCKED ME FROM MY HORSE BEFORE I could even see the marshlands where the river emptied out into the Menfor Sea. And no amount of evening breeze could carry it away.

Zelyth had insisted we not speak most of the way down the main road, but once we'd turned on the eastern offshoot that led to the river, he'd eased up a little.

"Ugh." I pressed my sleeve over my nose. "I never did understand why it stinks so bad here."

"Stagnant water." Mor dismounted and headed for a cluster of reeds. "During the winter rains, the river swells and makes pools, but after the flooding stops, that water gets trapped. It has nowhere to go, nothing to stir it, so it lies still and starts to smell. It isn't so bad in the winter when the floods come through."

"Well, it's not winter now, and I—oh!" Mor cut my remarks short by pulling me from my saddle. He held me until I got my feet beneath me. I dared a glance up at him. He winked.

"Come on, Tanwen," Zel said. "Best we get on the water sooner than later."

I stepped away from Mor and straightened my skirts. "I think you can stop worrying, Zel. We lost them back at the fork."

Gryfelle glided down from her horse. "I wouldn't be too sure of that. Some of these guardsmen are from the mountains. They're expert trackers accustomed to trapping mountainbeasts for their winter furs. If they have an idea we might head for the river, we're not safe. Not by a long shot."

"From the mountains?" I tried not to let a look of provincial awe settle onto my face. "Truly?"

Gryfelle pulled packs from the saddles. "The peninsular mountains are less than a week's ride from Pembrone. You've never been?" She paused and looked at me. "That you remember, at least?"

I shook my head. "Hoped Riwor would take me on a tour through there—past there, even. But I guess that's not happening now."

Gryfelle heaped the packs onto her graceful shoulders, and it didn't look quite right. "No, Tanwen. That won't be happening now."

With some effort, Mor pulled a small boat from the protection of the reeds. "Ah. Here we are. Zel, help me get her to the water."

I patted my mare's neck. "But what about the horses? I think she likes me."

The mare snorted, and a spray of horse snot flew from her nostrils. I stumbled backward.

Zel motioned to the other side of the marshlands. "We'll set them loose there. Our contact in Drefden will round them up after the guard is out of the area."

I forgave the horse and moved closer to her again. "Sure, if the guard doesn't get them first." The thought of a metal-clad, lunkheaded guardsman on the gentle beast didn't sit right.

"These horses are fast and agile, Tanwen, not like the bulky destriers the guardsmen ride. All that metal slows a horse down. Ours won't be caught." Zel helped Mor shove the boat the last little bit into the mossy water. "We should be more worried about the guard catching us."

That was all the prodding I needed. I took Mor's hand as he helped me into the boat. "Is this your ship, Captain?"

"Hardy-har." He grinned, but it fell almost immediately. "No, I lost my ship six moons back."

I didn't know if I should be feeling sorry for a pirate. Especially since I didn't know if he'd come by that ship through honest means in the first place. But still.

"I'm sorry, Mor."

He shrugged. "We've all lost things. Some more than others."

Everyone paused then, and it was like we were counting all our losses. I numbered mine. My cottage, for one. Could I ever go home now? If I could, had those guardsmen left anything to go home to?

But worst of all was Brac. What if I never saw him again?

"Come on now," Zel said. "This ain't over yet."

"True enough," Mor said as he helped Gryfelle over the side, and we were all four in the little boat. "One, two, three!" He and Zel shoved with poles until the boat obeyed and we started to move.

Zel stayed standing in the back of the boat, pushing with his pole, and Mor moved to the side so he could guide us off the banks of the river when it narrowed.

"We'll be going upstream till we get to Lake Lyn and pass through the mountains," Zel said. "Then it's easier going, but more dangerous. Rocks and strong currents and such."

Past the mountains. I was finally going to leave the Eastern Peninsula. This wasn't exactly how I'd imagined it, but I'd take it.

Gryfelle huddled on one bench in the middle of the boat, I on the other. She looked as out of place in the tiny riverboat as I would have at a palace ball.

"So tell me," I said.

Gryfelle looked up. "Beg your pardon?"

"Tell me where we're going. You said no locations until I agreed to come, and I think it's clear I've agreed to come."

The three shared a look.

After a moment, Gryfelle said, "The Corsyth."

"Great. What in Tir is the Corsyth? Never heard of it."

Mor laughed. "As well you shouldn't. Gareth would be none too happy if word about the Corsyth got out. We'd be welcoming newcomers from all corners of the empire, I reckon."

Gareth. I'd never heard anyone speak about the king so familiarly. Without his title and honorifics and whatnot.

"Do you know the king, Mor?"

Mor's face clouded. "He knows me."

"Got in trouble with your pirating?"

"No," he said lightly, smirk returning. "Forced into piracy after

Gareth made legitimate fishing impossible for me. I had to run once too, just like you. But I took to the seas." All humor fell from his face. "My family was all gone by then anyway."

"Sorry." I studied the stubble on his jaw again. "Fisherman, pirating sea captain, outlaw all before your—what—twentieth birthday?"

His catlike smile stretched across his face again. "I was twenty last moon."

"Ah, well. I was close." I turned to Zel. "And you. You're easy enough. Farmer, wife at home. I picture her with sun-browned skin and yellow hair, churning butter. She's my age, maybe."

Zel nodded. "Aye, she's about your age. But her hair's orange as a sweet-root."

"Close again, but not just right. Seems to be my lot in life." My gaze settled on Gryfelle. "Not even sure I should try with you. Don't know what to make of a lass who keeps company with the likes of these two but sounds like she was turned out of a Urian school for ladies."

Her lips curled in the corners. "That about covers it. In broad strokes, at least. I suppose if things had gone differently, I'd be presenting my first infant to the court at some point this year. Eighteen is about the age for that."

"Truly?" Now I knew my eyes had gone provincially wide. "Urian? The capital? Your own babies presented at court!"

"It isn't as wonderful as you imagine." She looked straight at me. "Babies don't remember being presented, do they?"

I frowned. She was driving at something again, but it was like a wisp of story strand I couldn't quite get to crystalize.

Mor huffed. "Court life isn't as wonderful as we lowly peasants imagine, she says. Then why are you so wistful for your old life, Elle?"

Gryfelle's eyes flared. "Because whatever it was, it was mine, and it oughtn't have been taken from me." She sat back on the bench and stared at the reedy banks. "Nor should my second life have been."

Mor shut right up then and kept his eyes fixed on the banks. Whatever fire existed between the two of them, it burned so hard I could almost singe my fingers on the heat. I made a mental note not to sit directly between Mor and Gryfelle again.

"None of you has told me *why*, you know."

Three pairs of eyes snapped to me, but only Zel spoke. "Why what?"

"Why . . . any of it. Why you've come for me. Why you're on the run. The guard's after me for some treasonous stories, which, I feel I should add, were not my fault. What did you do that's got you on the wrong side of the king?"

Mor's gaze hardened. "He's not the king."

Zel sighed. "Mor, would you get off that? It only makes it worse."

"Worse? It can't get any worse, Zel!" Mor dug his pole into the bank and righted the boat's course.

Silence wrapped around us like fog. Two solid minutes ticked by.

I cleared my throat. "No one answered my question."

"Same as you, Tanwen," Mor said. "Weavers on the run."

"Weavers? You mean you're all story peddlers?"

"Not peddlers. Story*tellers*." Mor shrugged. "Some of us anyway. But best you wait until we get to the Corsyth for a full explanation. For now, get some sleep while it's still dark."

"Here." Gryfelle scooted gingerly beside me on my bench. "Lean on me and rest."

"You sure? Don't you need sleep, too?"

"I'll be all right. Rest now."

"Elle . . ." Mor frowned at her.

"Rest, Tanwen," she growled. Though I didn't get the impression the ire was directed at me.

Mor shook his head and looked away.

I leaned against Gryfelle's shoulder, and she wrapped her arms around me to hold me up. With the strain of the past week—and especially tonight—I slipped into sleep quicker than I imagined possible.

As I dozed, I could have sworn I heard the sweetest birdsong ever sung lulling me into my dreams.

✦

"Tanwen?" Gryfelle's soft voice poked into my mind—reached me somehow through my sleep. I heard her sigh. "She's not ready to wake. Let the poor thing sleep as she will."

"But the mountains." Zel's voice. "She'll want to see them. Besides, it's more suspicious to have a sleeping lass in the boat in the middle of the day. We'll need to get through the ferrymen of Waybyr, and don't be surprised if the guard has a checkpoint there too."

Mountains. The word forced me to open my eyes.

"Did someone say mountains?"

Mor chuckled. "You were right, Zel. Though it was kind of you to think of her sleep, Elle."

Gryfelle barely cracked a smile. Couldn't tell if she was still cross at Mor or if she was just exhausted.

I blinked in the full sun. The river had widened and flowed clear now, no longer marshy like it was near the coast. "What time is it?"

"Past midday." Mor held out a chunk of bread. "You slept through breakfast and lunch."

I took the bread and set to devouring it. "You all haven't slept?"

Zel stretched his arms. "We've taken shifts. But I won't lie. I'll be glad enough to reach Lake Lyn and cross the mountains. The lake feeds the Endrol River, and bless the stars, the Enrdol flows inland. It'll be easier going from there, least as far as paddling is concerned."

I felt rather than heard Gryfelle suck in her breath. "That's a king's guard checkpoint."

Our boat glided toward the crowded Waybyr waterway, where rafts and small riverboats ferried people from one side to the other. Sure as the taxes, a smattering of soldiers dotted the banks, scanning the boats as they passed through.

"Tanwen, I'm a lady from court," Gryfelle said suddenly.

"Huh?"

Gryfelle caught my eyes. "I'm a lady from court and you're my servant. We were here visiting my uncle in Waybyr, and we hired these two lads to take us on a day trip up the river. Understand?"

"Oh, right. Got it."

A guard hailed us. "Ho, there!"

Zel stopped poling and Mor lifted his chin toward the guardsman, then they stayed silent, like good hired men would do.

Gryfelle inclined her head slightly. "Good afternoon, gentlemen."

The guardsmen stood a little straighter in an obvious attempt to look sharp for the lady. A bearded guardsman, who appeared to be the lead man at the checkpoint, bowed at the waist. "Afternoon, milady. What finds you so far from Urian today?"

Gryfelle let out a glittery giggle unlike anything I'd heard from her before. "Oh, my uncle lives in Waybyr. He's taken ill of late, and I came for a visit. But if I had to spend one more moment shut up in that tiny hovel he calls a cottage, I thought I might burst!" She laughed again. "My maidservant and I hired these river lads to take us on an adventure."

"Nothing too taxing, I hope, milady."

I'd never heard a guardsman speak so respectfully before—especially not to a lass as pretty as Gryfelle. But I'd never seen the guard around real lords and ladies either. A younger soldier with no whiskers seemed to have his gaze fixed on me, the "servant." The leering look on his face was something I was a bit more familiar with.

But Gryfelle just smiled. "You're kind to worry over us. But it's just a short trip to the mountains and back. I'll be locked in my uncle's hovel again before long."

The glittery laugh sounded again but then cut off abruptly. The smile dropped from Gryfelle's face and her eyes went blank. Mor and Zel stiffened.

Mor took hold of Gryfelle's arm. "El—milady? Milady?" He shot a desperate glance at Zel.

Should I say something? My heart pounded out a rhythm of utter terror at the thought of speaking up. But I imagined myself telling a story to any regular crowd of peasants—and our lives depended on selling it. "Forgive my lady, good sirs. She's been such an attentive niece these past days, caring for her uncle. She's fairly worn out."

A wisp of story puffed from my fingers, like a tendril of pale purple smoke. I shooed it away and flashed a smile I prayed was charming. "Poor lass."

The lead guardsman frowned at me, then Gryfelle, then at the "river lads." But he nodded to his fellows. "Let them pass."

Thank the moon and all the stars.

Zel dug his pole back into the riverbed, and we set to fighting upriver again. I wouldn't release my breath until the guard was out of sight. Just a few more moments and we'd be through. I glanced at Gryfelle. Her eyes were like the empty windows of a deserted cottage. What in blazes . . . ?

"Ho!" a deep voice from one bank cried out. "You there! Stop!"

The lads pretended not to hear.

"Lady!"

Gryfelle suddenly seemed to come back to herself. But she stared around, confused, like she didn't know where she was or why.

The shouting guardsman crouched down, then stumbled along the bank to try to keep up and get a good look at us as we pushed up the river. Then he suddenly came up short. "It's them! Stop them!"

Mor's river-lad façade dropped and the sea captain was aboard once again. "Go!"

Both lads poled now. Downriver behind us, a handful of guardsmen clanked into a boat.

"The third pole." Sweat beaded on Mor's forehead. "Tanwen, can you grab it?"

"No, I will." Gryfelle was with us again—clear and present. She grabbed a third pole that was hidden along the edge of the boat. It didn't look as long as the other two, but if the river was shallow enough here, it could reach the bottom.

Gryfelle dug in a few times and we propelled forward a little faster. But then something like a huge bug zipped past my ear and plunked in the water.

An arrow.

"Tanwen, get down!" Mor grabbed Gryfelle's pole. "Elle, get in the bottom of the boat!"

She snatched the pole back from him. "Let me help. It's hardly the first time I've been shot at!"

Another arrow whizzed by, and this one nearly skinned a line down my back, even though I was crouched.

"Elle, please!"

She cast a pained look at Mor, then dropped the pole and ducked down beside me. "Lie flat as you can, Tanwen," she said.

Mor and Zel settled into a rhythm. Zel never said a word, but both lads dripped sweat, and I wondered how long they'd hold out like this.

The mountains loomed all around us, and the guard nipped at our heels.

Mor grunted. His arms looked ready to fall off from the work. "Can we lose them, Zel?"

Zel didn't answer.

"Zelyth?"

I looked up to see Zel grimace and nod to his arm. His shirt was stained through with blood. It looked to be spreading to his torso. I couldn't help the gasp that escaped me.

Zel glanced at me for half a second, then took to poling again. "Don't worry, lass. Just grazed me is all." He winced. "Aye, Mor. If we make it to the lake, maybe we can lose them up ahead."

Mor frowned. "Hold on, mate."

With his best friend injured and bleeding, Mor seemed to double his strength out of nowhere. An arrow thunked into the back of the boat. I closed my eyes and squeezed Gryfelle tight.

Made me feel a bit better that she squeezed back just as hard.

I thought of praying but abandoned that notion. Didn't really believe in the goddesses, so what was the point?

An awful minute passed, and I heard shouting—closer than it ought to have been.

"Stay down, Tanwen!" Mor looked ready to thwack me with his pole.

I hadn't realized I'd lifted my head to see what was going on.

"Are they close?" My voice rattled.

"Aye, they're close."

For the next moments, Mor and Zel called a series of commands to each other—working their way around obstacles, I supposed, or else figuring how to push upriver as hard as their arms could manage. The boat scraped up against something, and I thought Mor would shout himself hoarse.

"Easy now! To the left. Left, I said!"

Zel bellowed back, "I'm trying! Ain't got a ship's wheel, you know."

But suddenly the water didn't seem to be pushing so hard, and the boat evened out some. Gryfelle and I stopped sliding back toward Zel. I looked up again and saw Mor's face light up.

His lips moved, but his words were lost in the roiling of the river. Even so, there was no mistaking what happened next. A cloud-gray story strand swirled before him. He spoke a final word, and the strands became rocks—a dozen and a half of them. They splashed into the river just behind us as we crested a rise in the water.

My head popped up in time to see the guardsmen's boat make a go for the uphill slope—and get batted back down by the grouping of sharp stones. The ones Mor had just made from his story strands. Their boat reeled backward, then nearly tipped over before they righted it again. But by then they were too late. They'd never get up speed enough to top that rise and still maintain enough control to navigate the gauntlet Mor had thrown down.

The bowman pulled out one last arrow and took aim.

I hollered at the top of my voice. "Look out!"

Gryfelle and I hit the bottom of the boat, and Mor dodged as the arrow sailed past his ear. He spared a wink in my direction—which I guessed was a pirate's way of saying thanks. The lads gave one final push, and the boat evened out completely as we reached the edge of the lake. The guardsmen's boat remained stalled some distance back. We were out of shooting range within moments.

Our boat stilled and the lads just about collapsed to the deck.

Gryfelle took one of the poles to help keep the boat from drifting to shore, and I pulled a skin of water from my bag.

"Here." I opened it and handed it to Zel. "Drink some."

He took a swig, then passed it to Mor.

Mor drank, then gave it back to me with a dry smile. "Welcome to our world, Tanwen. To *your* world."

CHAPTER 13

TANWEN

Crossing Lake Lyn was downright tranquil after the fight up the River Abereth. We sailed across in what felt like no time flat, then Gryfelle and the lads guided our boat toward the mouth of the Endrol River.

Since I was fairly useless at boat work, and since I no longer feared my immediate demise, I gazed around at the mountains. They were beautiful but somehow not what I'd expected. They soared taller than anything I'd ever even thought about. Being under them, winding along down the Endrol, was surely something to experience. Craggy ledges towered into the sky, capped in glistening snow lingering from winter.

But truly, I thought those mountains would be more exciting. I'd been hearing—and telling—tales of mountainbeasts since I was a wee lass. Why couldn't I see one for real?

When I voiced my question aloud, Mor laughed. "Those creatures are taller than Zel by half and wickeder than that peddler who used to slap you around."

"Mor!" Gryfelle frowned up at him.

"Sorry, Tanwen." His smile just about melted my knees. "Didn't mean any offense. Just wouldn't fancy watching you get your pretty face ripped off by one of those things."

Gryfelle's frown deepened. She turned away from Mor and settled on Zel instead. "How is your dressing holding up, Zelyth?"

He flexed his arm and wiggled his fingers. "Seems sound. I'll be needing some of Karlith's care when we get back, I'd wager."

"Yes, of course." Gryfelle dug around in one of the bags she'd pulled from the saddles. "Would you like some creamleaf for the pain? Crushed goddessflower would help fight infection, but I didn't bring any with me."

Zel smiled. "I'm all right. You rest now, lass. You've had a day too."

Gryfelle brought her hand to her forehead. "Yes, I suppose I should." She winced like her head throbbed.

"Gryfelle?" I tried to think of how to ask without prying. But there wasn't any way around it. "What happened back there? It was like you disappeared for a spell."

She smiled thinly. "Later. I'll explain later. For now, I must rest." She settled into the bottom of the boat.

And that was that, I reckoned. For now.

Gryfelle had barely shut her eyes for two minutes when her breathing evened and the creases on her forehead smoothed out.

I stared at her sleeping form and lowered my voice. "What's wrong with Gryfelle?"

Both lads looked at me, but neither said a thing. I raised my eyebrows, hoping to wiggle a response from someone. But nothing.

Fine then.

"Will you never answer any of my questions, the lot of you?"

Mor looked out as the water slipped past in silence, but Zel smiled a little. "It's a question for Gryfelle to answer."

I glanced down at her. She managed to look regal even lying in the bottom of a tiny, smelly riverboat. An image of those rocks—the ones Mor conjured out of thin air, like he was a wizard—popped into my head. "There's something wrong with all of us, isn't there? That's why the king wants to get rid of us."

Mor's angled jaw tightened. "The only thing wrong with us is that we have the ability to create things—things the king might not be able to control." He spat into the water. "Gareth doesn't like things he can't control."

Weariness creased Zel's face. Suddenly he looked old. Old and tired, like the farmers on tax day. "Sometimes the answers to questions ain't easy, Tanwen. I don't know if our gifts are wrong. But sure as fire is hot, they're dangerous."

Mor looked at Zel like Zel had punched him in the gut. "You don't know if our gifts are wrong? You still wonder? Just because your father doesn't understand them or the king outlaws them does not make our gifts wrong. When will you realize that?"

Gryfelle stirred under Mor's raised tones. Mor stared hard at his friend, then shook his head and looked out along the dark water again. Zel's expression teetered between defiance and shame.

I started watching the water too. Like rolling black glass. It looked just how I imagined the great empty space inside me would. "Sometimes, when I was telling one of the king's crowned stories, this feeling would rise up inside. Like something was working to get out of me, and I'd have to squish it back down so I didn't spew it all over my audience." I sighed ruefully. "But in the end it poured out anyway, and there wasn't a blooming thing I could do about it."

Both lads stared at me a moment. Then Mor spoke. "Tanwen, promise me you'll never stifle it again. If Gryfelle were awake, she'd beg you."

I tried to read his eyes, but they offered nothing more than a glimpse into two endless blue pools. "But wasn't it those crazy strands that landed me in this whole mess? If only I could have squished them down like usual, I wouldn't have the guard on my tail."

"Tanwen, trust me on this. Please."

The fire of his gaze moved me to agree. I couldn't refuse, though I barely knew him. "Aye, Mor. I won't squish it down again."

He smirked. "Don't you mean 'Aye, Captain'?"

"Tanwen."

I stirred sleepily but didn't open my eyes. "Hmm?"

The voice again. Mor's. "Tanwen, wake up."

I cracked one eye open. "Ten more minutes."

Zel, manning the pole to steer us, nodded to the north bank. "Bowyd up ahead. Best to keep low for now, but it's almost time to go ashore."

I sat up and peered ahead. True as a tumbleweed, the endless stretch of riverbank was finally interrupted by a few rickety docks jutting out into the current. But otherwise, Bowyd's shore looked quiet and deserted.

"Past Bowyd is where we stop," Mor said. "We'll hide the boat, then travel into the Codewig."

"The Codewig Forest?" Another place I'd dreamed of seeing.

Mor smiled. "Aye. That's the one."

"Is it true the trees are so thick that people have gotten lost in them and never returned? Because I've heard that."

"Aye." Mor's grin stretched wide as a sail. "Which is why it's the perfect hiding place for the Corsyth."

Trying to get a riverboat out of a river current, onto a riverbank, and hidden in a thick cluster of river bushes isn't as easy as a person might think.

Least it wasn't as easy as I thought it'd be.

But we finally managed it, even with Gryfelle being half asleep, as anybody would be when she's slept hard for half a day after not sleeping for goddesses know how long.

My legs complained and fairly creaked like Riwor's climbing down from the donkey cart. "Oy. How long have we been sitting in that boat anyway?"

Zel glanced up at the sky. "A full day and a half now."

"My legs aren't happy about it."

"Don't worry." Mor patted me on the back as he passed. "You'll have plenty chance to loosen them up again on our hike to the Corsyth." He disappeared into the trees.

"Hike?" Now my legs complained in a different way. "Is it far?"

Gryfelle shook her head as we followed after the lads. "No. There is a place where a spring bubbles up just a short distance into the forest. That's where our camp is."

"More marshes?" My nose wrinkled at the thought.

Gryfelle smiled. "They don't smell half as bad."

"Of course there's marshes," Mor said over his shoulder. "That's where the name comes from."

Gryfelle must have seen the question on my face. "In the old language, it's Mae Corsyth yer Gweyth: the Marshes of the Weavers."

I scooped up a little pebble and chucked it at Mor's back. "Hey, just because I can read, it doesn't mean I speak Old Tirian."

Mor glanced back and smiled. "I'm not even sure you speak modern Tirian."

Gryfelle rolled her eyes. "Mor, not everyone gets a chance at a formal education. You'll remember most of your fellow fisherman didn't. Your father was . . . unique."

Ahead, Mor paused. "Aye. He was different. That's what started the trouble, wasn't it?" Then he continued walking without looking back.

After that, heavy silence settled around us again. These people and all their secrets sure could weigh one down. I wondered how they managed to wade through their ghost-filled pasts at all.

We zigzagged through trees that grew so close together there couldn't have been a path through had someone wished to make one. Which I'm sure the outlaws didn't. Still, I noticed Gryfelle covering whatever tracks we left behind us—stirring up the underbrush, shuffling broken twigs about, bending branches on shrubbery in directions we weren't going. As if a body could track us in a forest so thick anyway.

I kept expecting the stench to smack me in the face like it had at the Menfor Marshes. But it never did, and I had a fair shock when Mor's serious face finally eased into a relaxed smile.

"Just through here."

He pulled back a curtain of hanging moss, and I thought I'd stepped into one of my beloved fairy stories.

Like Gryfelle said, water bubbled up from the ground somehow and made a wide pool in the middle of the forest. Soft moss dripped from every tree, climbed up every trunk, webbed between every branch. I guessed the water mustn't have been stagnant, because it sparkled clear, even in the dim green light filtering through the tops of the trees.

Spring flowers bloomed along the drier banks, and wide, waxy water flowers dotted the surface of the pool. Reeds shot up everywhere, which seemed strange to me in the middle of a forest.

The colors of the place would've been strange anywhere, but lovelier than even a story peddler could tell you about.

Splashes of every color I could imagine, dashed all over the trees, the rocks, the forest floor. Like story strands had turned to paint and streaked onto everything. Then there were balls of crystal hanging from the trees. Crystallized stories, I was sure.

But then I remembered Mor making rocks from story strands without actually telling a proper story. So maybe not crystallized stories, exactly. But what? Crystallized thoughts? Ideas?

In any case, they dangled from the trees like lanterns. How enchanted it would all look at night with lights glowing inside!

"It's pretty as can be." I turned to Gryfelle. "But where's your house?"

She paused and looked at me.

"I mean, where do you settle down at night?" I tried again. "Where do you stay?"

Gryfelle's gentle lips curved into a smile. "There's one. And just over there, on that rock. And here's one." She nodded to a bunch of moss-covered rocks all around the pool.

She might've finally cracked.

But then, as if she'd appeared out of nowhere, a woman crawled from one of the nearby rocks. I blinked, because surely I was seeing things. Or else *I'd* finally cracked.

But if I ducked my head just right, I could see that the moss wasn't covering a rock—it covered a raised crate of some sort, like the ones I'd seen full of salted fish that had been shipped to Pembrone from Physgot.

Except much larger. Large enough for even Zel to sleep in without trouble. And if you weren't crouching just right to look for them, the moss draped in such a way as to make them invisible. Or at least make them look like moss-covered rocks and nothing more.

The woman hoisted herself over a boulder, then scrambled up beside us. Her long, gray-streaked blonde hair fell over one shoulder in a curly plait. Her blue-gray eyes were half-lidded, but she wore a wide smile.

"Yer back safe. Praises to the Creator."

Instinctively, I looked around for guardsmen or priests. Wouldn't get away with saying the Creator's name so loud anywhere but a marshland hideout, I guessed.

"Aye, we're back." Mor kissed the woman on the cheek.

Zel followed suit. "Good to see you, Karlith. Didn't know that we'd make it back this time, to be telling the truth."

Gryfelle and Karlith embraced, then the woman held her at arm's length. "Oh, dearest. Was it so bad? Did you suffer?"

A wan smile stretched onto Gryfelle's lips. "I'm just worn. I'll rest awhile and be quite well."

Karlith didn't seem satisfied. "I'll brew some tea."

"No, I'll take bitter-bean brew."

"Tea would do ya good."

Gryfelle smiled again. "Just the bitter-bean, please."

Karlith shook her head. "I blame Mor. He's the one who's always talking about the Spice Islands and their bitter beans. Got all you young ones worked up about exotic things that wasn't even on the map when I was your age." She shrugged her defeat and then turned her gaze on me. Her smile bloomed in full again. "And this must be our peddler."

So . . . I'd been expected?

"Aye. I'm Tanwen." I stuck out my hand for her to clasp in greeting, the way I might to any farmer's wife. Then I paused. Was that proper? Was that the way ladies were supposed to greet each other?

I tried to remember what Gryfelle had done when we'd first met.

But Karlith took my hand and gave it a strong squeeze. "Karlith Ma-Lundir." Love and kindness seemed to travel from her fingertips into mine, then journey up my arm, straight into my heart.

The feeling of it hitting my empty insides nearly dropped me like I'd taken a punch. Tears sprang and a knot bunched in my throat.

I fought to clear it. "I'm Tanwen. Did I already say that?"

Karlith smiled, but Gryfelle glanced up from where she was sitting on a hidden crate, pulling out pewter cups from somewhere I couldn't see. "Tanwen En-Yestin."

This meant something to Karlith—something more than it meant to me. "Aye. Tanwen En-Yestin." Tears filled her sleepy eyes. "Welcome home, dear one."

Irresistible warmth seeped through me, filling up the hollow spaces. And something inside me wondered if this was what it felt like to have a mother.

CHAPTER 14

BRAITH

"Would you like more wine, Princess Braith?"

Braith held up a hand to excuse the royal wine steward. "No, thank you, Gwin."

Gwin bowed, then retreated to his place among the other servants lining the hall, his flagon of wine clutched in his hands.

"Darling," the queen said, "I simply insist Braith meet with the Haribian prince tomorrow afternoon." She smoothed her long pale braid and took a sip of wine. "How much longer can I be expected to put him off?" She glared at Braith. "He is a prince, after all."

The king set down his goblet with a clang. "A prince, but a Haribian prince. You really want your daughter marrying one of them, Frenhin? Imagine the grandchildren."

The princess winced and cast an apologetic look toward the handful of dark-skinned Haribian servants who stood alongside the pale Tirians and the caramel-skinned Meridioni.

She pursed her lips in silence a moment, then cleared her throat. "I would be pleased to meet our Haribian guest, Mother. I understand Prince Huku has been quite gracious during his stay in Urian."

The queen's pointed chin lifted. "I don't want you to just meet him, Braith darling. I want you to marry him."

Father's goblet slammed to the table again.

But Braith put a soothing hand on the king's arm. "Perhaps Prince Huku and I might meet to discuss the issues currently vexing our Haribian subjects." She turned to the queen. "I fear our policy of imperialism has made us unpopular, and Prince Huku would not take me as his wife, even if I did agree to your attempts to marry me off to our guests."

Queen Frenhin's face colored. Her head looked ready to pop off her neck.

But Braith continued calmly. "In any case, perhaps a meeting with the prince would help ease Haribian relations. I can listen to the problems of his people. Help him where I'm able."

"*My* people, Braith." The king's eyes filled with warning. "Prince Huku's people are my people now."

Braith smiled weakly. "Yes, of course. I'll have to brush up on my Haribian, of course. The prince doesn't speak much Tirian, does he?"

The king snorted. "Hardly a word."

"Good. That will give me a chance to practice my Haribian. It has been too long since I've had reason to exercise it." Braith's eyes lifted a moment, only to find Dray Bo-Anffir smirking at her from across the table.

Braith's gaze dropped. That smirk—somehow boyish, despite the gray showing at Dray's temples—had seduced more ladies of King Gareth's court than Braith cared to count.

Naith Bo-Offriad sniffed. "The Haribians still refuse to worship the Tirian goddesses. Have a pantheon of their own, apparently. That alone would deter me from marrying any daughter of mine into that heathen country." He smiled. "Were I allowed to marry and father children myself, that is."

Still, the queen wasn't ready to let the subject drop. "I don't care about the grandchildren or who they worship; Braith would be the uncontested queen of the Haribian province. We could leverage her position for the Bellithwyn conquest we've always talked about."

Braith took a long sip of wine. Would talk of expanding the empire never die?

The queen's voice was firm as she turned to the king and pressed the issue further. "With Haribi standing between us and Bellithwyn, there is no way to mount an offensive against the countries there without first establishing strategic positioning in Haribi."

Braith set down her wineglass. "Mother, whether I'm married to

Prince Huku or not, launching a Bellithwyn offensive from Haribi would be suicide. Prince Huku and his line will always have the loyalty of the people, whatever banner flies above the Haribian plains. Do you honestly think dispatching our soldiers through their vast continent would result in anything less than utter annihilation? And that before we could even sight the shores of Bellithwyn on the other side."

The king huffed. "We beat the Haribians once, you know. Conquered them fair on their own soil."

"Indeed." Braith smiled thinly. "Battles fought within sight of the Tirian shores. Battles that conquered their important coastal cities. So, yes, a fair conquering by the technical definition.

"But it was not a war waged in the Haribian wildlands," she went on. "The tribes there may be primitive to our minds, but they are warriors with mettle to match any of our knights. And they will fight for their prince if we presume to march through their territory on our way to expanding ours. It would be the end of the guardsmen's glory and the destruction of the king's empire."

After a moment of silence, Dray chimed in. "The princess speaks wisdom, Your Majesty." His unsettling gaze turned back toward Braith. "I don't suppose she learned military tactics at her dancing lessons."

Braith laughed shortly. "No, indeed, Sir Dray. Despite what critics would suggest, I was not appointed to our king's council to add feminine charm to the proceedings."

A ripple of polite laughter ran through the courtiers at the table.

Dray leaned toward her. "And yet you provide that too."

Braith lowered her gaze to the blood-colored liquid in her goblet.

"Very good." The king drained his wine, then signaled for Gwin to bring him more. "Braith will meet with Prince Huku for the reasons she's agreed to, and only those reasons. Is that clear, Queen Frenhin?"

The queen visibly bristled under the public command. But she fixed her features into a mask of calm. "Of course, Majesty."

"Good. Now, we will enjoy our supper. If that were possible."

The king poked at a lump of purple mash on his plate. "What is this muck? Ginia, are you trying to poison me?"

Ginia, the palace cook, stepped from the line of servants, her hands trembling. "No, Majesty. You know our Tirian crops have not been good this year. We've had to be . . . creative in the kitchens. Those are pureed plum wattas from Haribi. And I . . ." She glanced at Braith and swallowed hard. "I thought our guest, Prince Huku, might like them."

"I'll thank you to serve me good Tirian food from now on, Ginia, or perhaps you'll find yourself on your own butcher block."

Ginia's voice shriveled to a squeak. "Yes, Your Majesty." She scuttled back into line with the others.

"Poison," the king muttered, squishing his fork into the purple puree. "Poison, poison, poison." A storm shadowed his face, and he looked like he might begin shouting at the staff any second.

Braith put a hand on his arm. "Majesty, Ginia wishes to please you. All your servants do. But everyone in Tir is feeling the effects of the blight on the land this year. I don't see that we should be any different. If the people suffer, so should we. And they have not the opportunity to sample fine foods imported from Haribi and the other corners of your vast empire."

It wasn't clear if the king had even heard her.

"Majesty?"

Just then the doors to the dining hall flew open. Baedden the bodyguard stiffened at the king's shoulder, but his tension eased when he registered the intruders. Guardsmen knights—five of them, led by General Cydinol, commander of all king's guard soldiers stationed in the eastern half of Tir.

Cydinol bowed. "Permission to speak, Your Majesty."

The king frowned. "Eh?"

The general glanced at one of the knights, who shrugged. Apparently taking the king's response as authorization, Cydinol continued. "It seems there was a severe offense in Afon nearly a week ago." He lowered his voice. "Forbidden story strands, Your Majesty."

The fog around the king evaporated and he snapped back to

himself. "Story strands on the Eastern Peninsula? Again?" He scowled. "Is it the same peddler—the unregistered girl?"

"We believe so, Your Majesty."

The king crashed his fist onto the table. Goblets and plates rattled, and several diners jumped. "Nearly a week! Why have I not heard of it until now?"

Cydinol held his head high, but he visibly steeled himself. "Captain Wyren—he's commander of the guard in the trans-river cities, my king—it seems he wanted to capture the offending party before notifying you of the offense. His men tracked her from Afon to Pembrone. Indeed, they found her residence. But she was gone when they arrived. Wyren has dispatched several units to checkpoints around the Peninsula. He says he'll be sending word frequently by his fastest birds. He realizes his error now, Your Majesty. As soon as we received the message, I came here directly. I apologize for interrupting your meal."

The king gripped his goblet until his knuckles whitened. "Explain the nature of these forbidden stories, Cydinol."

The whole of the king's guard company before the royal table paled and stood in silence.

Queen Frenhin scoffed, her dark eyes glowing with indignation. "Your king has asked you a question, General. Answer at once!"

The general cleared his throat. "They were most accusatory, sire. The offenses the peddler laid out against you were so treasonous, I daren't repeat them. And that's not all. There's something else I think you should know, Majesty."

"Then tell me quickly."

"The Pembroni house the guard tracked the peddler to—it appears to be the family home of Glain Ma-Yestin."

"Yestin?" The king scratched his beard over and over. "Yestin." His eyes grew wide. "Will some ghosts never leave us?"

A sliver of red appeared along one of the king's cheeks.

"Father!" Braith grabbed her napkin and blotted the blood. "You're unwell. Let me accompany you to your room at once. Please."

Braith rose and the entire company, excepting the king and queen, rose after her.

The king finally followed suit, but trouble stirred his features. "Yes. I shall retire now."

Braith took the king by the elbow and they moved past the knights.

Just as they quitted the room, the king turned back to his general. "Cydinol?"

"Yes, Majesty?"

"Tell your men to find this girl. Tell them to search for her as if their lives depended upon it. Because, indeed, they do."

"Yes, Majesty."

"And put the word out to the peasants. Anyone who captures or leads to the capture of this story peddler will be rewarded. Say, one hundred gold pieces. That ought to inspire some loyalty from the starving provincials."

"Indeed, Majesty."

Braith's eyes widened. One hundred gold crowns? A large sum for a peasant. Huge, actually.

But the princess stayed silent and led the king to the stairway outside the dining hall doors.

The king paused at the bottom of the stairs and called back over his shoulder. "And Cyd? Bring me Captain Wyren's head in a basket."

CHAPTER 15

BRAITH

BRAITH LEANED AGAINST THE CLOSED DOOR TO HER FATHER'S private chambers. She'd seen him in, gotten him comfortable, then escaped to the hallway where the air didn't threaten to smother her.

She tried to put the captain's fate out of her mind.

A hundred gold pieces.

Truly, a king's ransom. And for a peasant girl.

It defied reason. The peninsular peasants would be clawing each other's eyes out trying to find the story peddler. An entire family could live for years on one hundred gold pieces.

Braith pushed herself off the door and began a distracted trek to her own chambers.

Clearly, the king would see the girl silenced at any cost.

But why? He was proud, true. But he valued gold even above his pride. A hundred gold crowns because of some story strands. Unbelievable . . .

"Princess."

"Oh!" The princess clutched her chest. "Sir Dray. You startled me."

Dray slipped from the shadows of the hallway. His chiseled features caught the flickering torchlight. "Apologies, Your Highness. I didn't mean to frighten you." He took her hand and bowed, then lifted his eyes to meet her gaze. "I have a confession."

The stays of Braith's corset suddenly felt too tight. "Oh?"

"I was waiting for you. Hoping to catch you on your way back to your chambers."

Braith glanced at her father's chief advisor, then resumed her stroll down the hallway. “It disturbs me somewhat that you know where my private chambers are, Your Grace.”

“I’m chief advisor to the king. I know many private things about many important people. It’s my duty to know such things, do you not agree?”

“Even about the king’s daughter?” Braith stopped walking and turned to look the politician squarely in the eyes.

It didn’t seem to unnerve him. “Especially the king’s daughter.” He smiled. “Might we dispense with formality at last? I’ve known you since you were a child, but you’re no longer a little girl, are you? Call me Dray.”

“What would the king and queen think of such familiarity, I wonder?”

He took a step closer. “I should think they’d be pleased to see their daughter become more familiar with the king’s closest advisor. May I call you Braith?”

Braith clasped her trembling hands behind her back. “As you wish.” She walked again—slowly, with measured paces.

“Don’t you think we ought to become better acquainted?” Dray pressed.

“I’ve known you all my twenty-three years and we see each other daily. Call me Braith, if you must, but are we not well enough acquainted already?” Her voice rattled a little.

She did not want to be alone with this man.

Dray stopped walking and stepped in front of Braith. “I thought I knew you quite well. And then, as we sit around the king’s table enjoying supper, Your Highness delivers the best-reasoned speech I’ve heard in an age, effectively deterring her father from what could be a regime-ending military campaign. And I find I don’t know Braith at all.” He moved in closer. “Perhaps I’ve too long thought of my lady as a child.”

Braith retreated a step.

“Perhaps I’ve missed the extraordinary woman Braith has become, right before my eyes.” Dray advanced.

Braith scooted away so quickly her back thumped into the stone wall behind her. "Dray, you wanted to speak plainly, so we shall. I understand my father trusts you with his life. But I fear you overstep your bounds. You're making me very uneasy. You do not wish to agitate the princess, do you?"

Dray placed his hands on the stone wall behind Braith, trapping her between his arms. The scent of brisk-leaf hovered on his breath, and the musky smell of whatever he used when he groomed his cropped beard filled Braith's consciousness as he leaned in. "Maybe I do wish to agitate the princess." His mouth inched closer. "Just a little."

Before Braith had time to move, he brought his lips to hers. Softly, as though he and she might be lovers. A split-second passed. Then Braith caught her breath and pushed him back.

"Your . . . Your Grace." Her voice stumbled. "This is a transgression my father would not overlook." It came out weakly. Because, truly, would the king object? Perhaps having his daughter marry Sir Dray Bo-Anffir would suit him just fine.

And Dray knew it.

He pushed himself away from the wall and gave Braith some room to breathe. "Forgive me, Braith. I couldn't help it."

She lifted her chin. Her voice regained some muster. "Try next time. I'll disregard this offense but no others. Is that clear?"

The lines of amusement around Dray's mouth deepened. "I'd expect nothing less of Your virtuous Highness."

Braith glared at him. "Does Lady Feistrys not wait for you in your chambers right now, Your Grace?" The words came out dry as the Haribian desert.

"Kind of you to call her a lady, Braith."

"She is a lady, is she not?" Braith straightened her skirts and resumed her dignified passage down the hall.

"Yes, she is called a lady," Dray answered. "But only because she's been my mistress for so many years, and your father thought he ought to give her a legitimate reason to be at court." He smiled. "I know you don't approve."

"Must you be so crass?" Braith turned her gaze straight ahead and stared at the gray stone wall at the end of the hallway. "I'll recognize any lord or lady my father so declares. That is my duty as princess."

"Ah, yes. Your duty. Is that why I unsettle you? Because you are ever duty-, rule-, and honor-bound. And I am not."

In spite of herself, Braith stopped and rounded on him. "Some people see value in tradition and honor—and yes, rules, if you want to put it that way. Clearly, you don't see value in those things."

Dray laughed. "I suppose you could say that. Do you know what interests me most at present?" He reached up and touched Braith's cheek, then unleashed the disarming smile that had undone so many ladies.

"I do, Sir Dray." She pulled away from his touch and leveled her gaze at him. "The throne."

Dray's face showed genuine surprise for a moment. Then his smile spread wider. "Clever lady."

"Princess Braith!" Cameria's voice carried down the hall like a ray of sunshine after a storm.

Dray backed away from the princess with a jerk as Cameria rushed toward them.

"Cameria," Braith said, and the relief was clear in her voice.

"There you are, Your Highness." Cameria's dark gaze bounced between Dray and the princess. "I came to escort you back to your room after supper, but they said you'd taken your father to his room. Is the king ill?"

"Yes, I believe he is ill. Sir Dray was just going back to inquire after him." She turned to the king's chief advisor. "Isn't that right, Sir Dray?"

He cleared his throat. "Yes, of course."

"Thank you for escorting me to my chambers, Your Grace. Good night."

Without another word, Braith turned, took Cameria's arm, and strode to her door. Once inside, Braith nearly collapsed to the floor.

"Highness!" Cameria ducked under Braith's arm to support her.

Braith steadied herself against her rescuer. "I'm fine, Cameria. Shaken, but fine. If only my wobbly knees would believe it."

"Did he hurt you, my lady?" Cameria's eyes blazed. "Tell me if he did. I saw his hands on you."

Braith steadied her breath as Cameria helped her onto one of the lounges. "No, he did not hurt me."

"What did he want with you, my lady?"

"To advance his political designs, of course." Braith leaned back against the embroidered cushions and swallowed. "Cameria, I do believe I was just speaking with my most formidable adversary yet."

CHAPTER 16
TANWEN

My mouth flew open as I watched another person crawl out from a hidden crate—a woman, older than me but younger than Karlith. Her hair was shorn off at her chin and black as night. Her milk-white jaw was set in a hard line.

And I'll be blazed if she wasn't wearing trousers like a lad. What's more, she was strapping a sword belt around her hips as she hopped over the rocks toward me and Karlith.

She nodded at me and smiled a little. "Welcome, Peddler. They've finally got you here, have they."

Wasn't a question, the way she said it. "Aye. Guess they have. With the guard's help."

"The guard has a way of flushing us out, don't they? I'm Aeron En-Howell." She stuck out her hand for me to grasp.

I clasped it. "Tanwen."

"En-Yestin," Gryfelle added from beside a fire she was starting.

I looked at her. "Why do you keep on doing that, Gryfelle? You know something I don't?"

Mor patted my back. "Gryfelle probably knows a lot of things you don't." He punched Aeron in the arm as he passed her. "Good to see you, En-Howell."

She raised an eyebrow but didn't really look cross. "Likewise, Bo-Lidere. I see you managed to squeeze by the guard again. One of these days you'll end up with an arrow in your gut, you know."

"Long as it doesn't come from your bow, soldier." Then he crouched beside Gryfelle to help her with the bitter-bean.

"Soldier?" I stared. "Are you a guardsman? Or a . . ." Had to think about the right word. "A guards*woman*?"

Aeron glanced over. "Was."

I turned to Karlith. "Never heard of such a thing. I guess they must all be in Urian. King's guardswomen." The word sounded backward on my tongue.

Karlith laughed. "No, I think Aeron was the only one—or one of a handful, leastways."

I heard rather than saw the next arrivals to the Corsyth. A few muffled shouts and crashing sounded through the forest underbrush.

Karlith glanced at Mor. "Warmil and Dylun are back from watch."

Mor rolled his eyes. "I hear."

"No, no, no!" One male voice carried into camp. "When will you understand this is bigger than your personal agenda? There's a principle here, and you're so apt to lose sight of it I wonder if you aren't going blind in your old age."

Another voice growled. "Watch it, boy. You may use words as your weapons, but you forget I carry an actual sword."

Two men suddenly appeared on the edge of the Corsyth pool and stopped short at the sight of me. The taller of the two, silver-haired and thin to the point of gauntness, pulled his sword from its scabbard. "State your name!"

The other one—shorter, stockier—snorted. "Warmil, she's obviously the peddler they've been tracking. Might you remove the guard training from your brain long enough to be reasonable? Just occasionally. It'd be a nice breath of air."

Silver-haired Warmil didn't pull his gaze from me. "Just protecting your high-principled cause, Dylun. She could be a spy. She could have forced the others to lead her here under threat of death. They could be under duress right now."

I glared at him. "If there's been any duress, I've been the one under it."

Zel glanced up from his seat on a rock, where he'd been quietly changing his dressing. "It's all right, War. We fairly dragged her here with the guard at our heels. She ain't a spy."

Warmil seemed satisfied by Zel's words and sheathed his sword. "I see they got a bite out of you."

Zelyth kept wrapping his arm. "Not the first; doubt it'll be the last."

Karlith hiked up her dress and shuffled over to Zel's side. "Don't wrap it so tight. Let me get some herbs for that."

Dylun stepped forward and took my hand. Then he bowed at the waist. "Dylun Bo-Ino, according to Tirian custom."

Couldn't quite guess what he meant by that, but I eyed his black hair and burnt-sugar skin. "I'm Tanwen. Are you . . . are you Meridioni?"

Dylun turned to Mor. "She is from the country, isn't she?"

Flame leaped into my cheeks. "Well, excuse me, but some lasses haven't had the opportunity to travel. A simple 'yes' would've been answer enough."

Dylun seemed to consider this, looking me up and down. Then he nodded to Mor. "Yes. She'll do."

Mor laughed. Then his gaze flicked to me. "Aye, she will."

The flame on my face blazed hotter.

"Glad you approve, Dylun," Mor said. "Always makes things easier when you manage to."

Whatever he meant by that.

"So . . ." My attention bounced around the Corsyth trying to swallow it all—seven people, plus me, all surrounded by streaks of color and dripping moss. "So you're all weavers?"

Karlith smiled. "Of one sort or another, all run to ground by the guard for our art."

"Not me." Aeron turned and busied herself about something. "I'm not a weaver."

"That ain't strictly true, lass," Karlith said. "And you know it."

Aeron shoved a pair of boots onto a rock and began to polish one a little too hard. "It is if I want it to be."

Gryfelle frowned at Aeron. "Is that how it works—we get to decide now? If only I'd known." Bitterness laced every word.

Aeron didn't look up from her boot.

After an awkward moment of utter stillness, I broke the silence. "If you're not a weaver, why're you here, Aeron?"

She stayed fixed on her polishing. "Warmil is my captain." Finally she glanced up. "I mean, he was my captain when I was in the guard. I came with him."

That mute fog of secrets settled around us, and I'd about had it with these people and their locked-up pasts.

"That seems a big leap to make if you weren't an outlaw yourself," I said. "Leaving your living, going on the run. Warmil must be some captain."

Warmil glanced our way from across the Corsyth. Mor seemed to be fighting a laugh, whether because I'd said something funny or on account of his discomfort, I couldn't tell.

But Aeron looked up and held my gaze. "Yes. He is."

Fair enough. Least it was a straight answer for once.

I nodded and then stumbled my way over tree roots and rocks to Mor and Gryfelle, who finally had some water boiling over the fire. I set about helping with the bitter-bean. Although I didn't care for it myself, I'd learned to make it when I worked a couple mornings a week in Blodwyn's tavern as a little lass. She gave me a few coins for my trouble, and it helped me buy food before I could make a living peddling.

I spoke to no one in particular while I worked. "Mor says you're not all story peddlers. Or storytellers, anyway. I guess you're not peddlers if you don't sell them. So, if you don't tell stories, what do you do?"

"Master colors." Warmil went back to cleaning his blade with no further explanation.

"Spin songs." Gryfelle smiled and took the cup of steaming bitter-bean I held out to her.

"Storytellers, colormasters, and songspinners." Karlith smiled, then glanced at Aeron. "*All* of us."

"I heard of a songspinner once," I said thoughtfully. "I would have sworn the old man telling me had lost his mind. Or was drunk. Actually, I'm sure he was drunk, because he always was."

Dylun snorted. "Yes, I'm sure he was. He'd have to be to speak openly about songspinners, since they're completely outlawed now."

I frowned. "Totally outlawed? But aren't there—I don't know—song peddlers, or something? I mean, there's only two songs, anyhow. How could a songspinner get into much trouble with just two songs to sing?"

Seven sets of eyes bored into me, and I knew I'd said something wrong. But fried if I could tell you what.

So I kept talking. "I mean, right? 'The Ballad of the Goddesses' and 'The Song of the King.'" They were the only two songs I'd ever heard in my life.

Dylun looked like he might pour steam from his ears. He jabbed a finger in my direction and turned to Warmil. "That! That is what our fight is about. Two songs! There are only two songs, she says!"

He stepped toward Warmil, and it looked like a threat. "Gareth's work is almost complete. He's already enslaved my people, the Haribians, the Minasimetese. And now he works to enslave his own people by stamping out every shred of human creativity that's left. 'Crowned' stories, two approved songs, and no colormastery allowed at all, except to paint portraits of his royal backside!"

All of a sudden, his hands lit up with fire—true and actual fire. Flames licked his fingers and palms, and he threw one arm forward like he was chucking a snowball. A stream of flame tore through the Corsyth.

I screamed, stumbled over, and fell to the ground. The trail of fire slammed into a tree and burst into an image against the bark—a golden crown, half-melted in a wreath of flame.

Karlith held up her hand. "Peace, Dylun." A stream of glowing water poured from her palms toward the tree. When the water splashed onto the tree, the melting crown disappeared, and the image in its place was a stack of wood with flames all around it, quite as normal as a campfire.

Karlith glanced at Dylun. "You'll frighten the poor lass to her death."

Dylun looked down at me like he'd forgotten I was there. "Apologies." His voice still cut hard as edged steel. "Some things disallow proper manners."

I swallowed hard and took a new look at the color-splashed trees around the Corsyth. Sure enough, the splashes weren't random splatters of color. They were picture upon picture upon picture, all layered over each other and each telling a different story.

Flowers, horses, knights, trees, birds, castles, cottages, people, ships. Everything you could dream had been strewn about the place.

I'd never seen or imagined anything like it in my life.

After a moment of thick silence, I cleared my throat. "So what you're saying is there's more than two songs."

For one dreadful minute, I thought Dylun might throw a stream of colormaster's fire at me. Instead he burst into laughter. "Yes, Tanwen En-Yestin." He grinned wryly. "There are more than two songs."

"You mustn't mind Dylun." Gryfelle sipped her bitter-bean and spoke quietly to me. "He doesn't mean harm. It's harder on him than on some."

I glanced at the young Meridioni man. "It's not hard to see why he's on the run from the guard. I can't imagine he'd be able to stay out of trouble."

"No, indeed. But it's more than being a colormaster. He's Meridioni, and that fact alone makes him worthy of slavery in the view of Gareth Bo-Kelwyd."

I peeked at Dylun quickly, hoping he wouldn't catch me. I'd never seen hair like his, so black it was almost blue, or skin such a rich brown. "How come he speaks Tirian so well? Better than me, like he had a fancy tutor or something."

"Dylun was raised in the palace, like I was." She paused thoughtfully, weighing her words. "He's Meridioni but he was born in Tir.

His family was a respected part of Caradoc II's court." Her face tightened. "All that changed when Gareth took over. No matter how noble-blooded or well-educated, every Meridioni in the palace was either executed for some crime or forced into servitude."

My stomach twisted. "That's . . ." For all my supposed storytelling talent, words failed me just then. "How did I not know that?"

Gryfelle shrugged. "How could you? You're just young enough not to remember how it used to be. Imagine the next generation of Tirians Gareth is raising up. They'll only know those who used to be our neighbors as our king's subjects, and they'll only know the crowned stories." She smiled a little. "And two songs."

My head drooped. I was making a pretty good run at being part of that generation. "You said you're a songspinner, right?"

"Yes," Gryfelle answered.

"Will you sing something for me—something besides those two songs?"

"Very well." She paused, and something flickered over her face. "If I can remember."

But in the next moment, the sweetest sound I'd ever heard drifted through the Corsyth. I couldn't understand the words—Old Tirian, I guessed. But as Gryfelle sang, wispy strands of color and light danced around us—like story strands, but less solid. Airier. Thinner.

A blue wave of light, rolling like the sea. Then a tiny ship made of smoke.

The song seeped into my ears, filled my whole body all the way into my soul. I closed my eyes to listen fully.

Some minutes later, when Gryfelle's melody wound to a close, my eyes fluttered back open. Her song still shimmered in the dim forest light, but to my surprise, a near-exact copy of it hovered right before me.

"Oh!" The thing crystallized and fell in my lap—a perfect, tiny glass ship. I looked up at Gryfelle. "Did you do that?"

She laughed. "No, you did."

My mind felt like it could burst. Too many new things all at once. Story strands that appeared from mere ideas, not stories that had been taught, memorized, and practiced. Stories that crystallized into real, actual things, as Mor had conjured those rocks. Not crystal figurines, but actual stones. Stories that poured out accidentally while listening to a song, even when I couldn't understand the words.

I didn't comprehend how any of it worked. And how I hadn't known any of it existed.

I felt a hand on my arm and turned to find Karlith smiling gently at me. "Do you understand now why we're so dangerous to Gareth the Usurper?"

I shook my head dumbly.

"Art—real art, the way you see it here—has a queer way of revealing truth. And truth, in all its forms, would be the undoing of Gareth Bo-Kelwyd."

CHAPTER 17

TANWEN

"ABOUT TIME TANWEN'S MILITARY TRAINING BEGAN, DON'T YOU think?" Warmil tore at a hunk of roasted meat at supper. "The guard will be tracking you lot. No idea which of you has been seen, or where. Best to train her up sooner rather than later."

"He's right," Dylun said, like it settled the matter.

I stopped chewing my roasted light-foot. "And what, exactly, is involved in military training?"

"You have to spar with Aeron." Mor grinned. "You can borrow War's sword."

I made a face at him, then returned his smile.

Warmil didn't smile. Ever. Seemed to be a habit of his. "You'll take first watch tonight with Aeron and Karlith. Should be easy enough. Just a few scans of the perimeter."

"If it'll be easy, why's it needed?" I asked. "If we're being tracked, seems like we could get ambushed just doing a perimeter scan, or whatever you called it. Which is why you want me getting the practice in the first place, isn't it?"

Dylun's laugh crackled through the heavy forest air. "Ah, yes. This one will do nicely."

Warmil almost broke a smile. "True enough, lass. Starting you out as easy as we can, then. That's how we'll say it."

"Fine with me." I squared my shoulders. If I was to stay around the Corsyth, seemed I'd have to at least pretend I was brave, even if I didn't feel it.

"I'll go too." Zel's voice fairly startled me, as he'd been so quiet and spent since we got to the Corsyth.

Gryfelle frowned. "Zel, you're injured. You should stay at camp tonight and rest."

"I've rested enough. I don't want the ladies out alone with only Aeron's sword for help." He smiled. "Not that you're not a lady, Aeron, or that your sword isn't more than enough. But, you know. Doesn't seem right to send the womenfolk out alone."

Warmil made a noise that I think was supposed to be a laugh. "Zel, no offense meant, but I'd trust Aeron's sword more if she didn't have you to look after too. But go if you must."

Aeron, tough a lass as she seemed to be, turned pink in the cheeks. Suddenly her fingers didn't work, and she dropped a piece of bread on the ground.

A thought struck me like a bolt.

I wagered I understood why she'd followed her captain into hiding. He wasn't just some captain. He was *some captain*.

Tough Aeron was sweet on old Warmil. Wondering if the captain had any idea, I eyed his grim face from across the fire.

No. Definitely not. Warmil looked like he hadn't even realized women were a thing, and even if he had, he hadn't noticed they might be nice company to have once in a while.

If he ever did realize that, maybe he would smile more.

Karlith, Aeron, Zel, and I traipsed through the underbrush. Aeron tried to show me how to step so I wouldn't make much noise. But I still felt like a marsh-grazer barreling through those crunchy leaves.

"This is as far north as we go during our perimeter sweep." Aeron pointed another direction. "Then we head east, then circle back around to the river in the south. It's not a wide sweep, but the Corsyth is well hidden. The guard would have to get pretty close to be able to find us."

"Have they ever gotten close?"

"Once or twice. But those guardsmen didn't live to tell their commanders about it, I can promise you that."

I shuddered. Didn't want to think about that, really.

"Zel," I said, by way of changing the subject, "what's your sweet-root–haired wife's name?"

His face softened. "Ifmere."

"What's she do while you're away?"

"She takes care of the house. Last I heard, my father and brother had taken over tending our bit of land for her. She's . . ." He swallowed hard. "She's expecting our first child soon."

My walking slowed. "You're going to be a father?"

He faltered. "Aye. If I ever get to see the little one." He squared his shoulders and started walking again. "But now you know why it's doubly important to keep her safe."

"Aye." I trudged in silence a moment. Zel's child would have its mother, at least. But with Zel in hiding, seemed Tir was gaining another fatherless baby.

Welcome to the party, wee one.

I shook the gloomy thought from my mind. "Nice that your family helps while you're gone."

Zel snorted. "My mam's behind that. I think my father would leave Ifmere to starve if it were up to him." He shook his head. "I shouldn't say that. It ain't fair. He's just scared, you know? He's scared of the king and the guard and the goddesses."

"He's scared of the goddesses?"

"Aye. Scared they'll punish my family because my stories are . . . wild."

"Wild?"

"Aye. That's what I said."

He didn't offer up anything else.

Karlith's voice startled me from behind. "Your father needn't fear the goddesses, Zel. Seeing as they aren't real."

I turned to stare at her. Lots of people didn't believe in the goddesses these days. I mean, only the most superstitious of the peasants truly thought the goddesses were real and might rain hellfire down on the world at any moment. But the priests—*they* were real, and they could have your head cut off for speaking words against the goddesses or failing to offer the money and food we were supposed to.

Still, I'd never heard anybody say aloud and so plainly that the goddesses weren't real. It was a shock to the ears.

Zel laughed shortly. "Well, if ever you meet ol' Farmer Gwelt, you can let him know."

"I will." Karlith smiled. "And I'll tell him all about the Creator too."

Another thing that could see you on the chopping block or swinging from the end of a rope—mentioning the Creator. Aye, so now I knew why gentle Karlith needed to hide out with the likes of fire-throwing Dylun. She wasn't a revolutionary rebel, strictly, but she did have a mind about things, and the king wouldn't be pleased with her conclusions.

I stepped around a big tree root. "You don't think you'll ever see your father again to tell him yourself, Zel?"

"Even if I did, he wouldn't listen to me. He doesn't understand people with our gifts. Thinks we're cursed or something."

I wasn't sure Farmer Gwelt was wrong about that.

We continued on our perimeter scan, making a fair amount of racket. Then Aeron held up a hand to slow us. "Quiet now. That's the river. More likely to be guard about."

Karlith pulled me back, and we let Zel and Aeron go on in front. I was about to ask Karlith about her family—she'd said her name was Ma-Lundir, and the *Ma* meant she was married—but Aeron's shout cut me off.

"Down!"

Karlith yanked me to the earth just as an arrow streaked overhead.

I peeked up ahead to see a blur of steel with shorn black locks whirring in the middle of it. Aeron looked like a story strand come to life. Except it wasn't an actual strand. It was just how she moved. Though to tell the truth, I could swear I saw an odd purple light playing around Aeron's hands as they gripped her sword—purple light like Karlith's blue colormastery strands.

Even if she didn't want to be a weaver, it was plain to see why having Aeron around the Corsyth would be handy. Under her blade, two guardsmen clanked to the forest floor.

But she wasn't finished. "Zel," she roared. "The third one's getting away!"

She took off in a flurry with Zel just behind.

Karlith and I panted on the ground next to each other. She took my shaking hand. "Just stay low. Aeron and Zel will return soon, and we'll go straight back to the Corsyth. We'll be safe."

I nodded but didn't say anything. Of course she didn't know we'd be safe. She was just saying the stuff mothers say when their wee ones are scared. My chest pinched at the thought. I squeezed Karlith's hand a mite tighter.

I wondered. Could it be possible that, even after meeting me only today, Karlith could think of looking out for me like a mother might?

She caught my stare and patted my hand. "They'll be back, love. Don't you worry."

Maybe so.

A few moments later, Aeron and Zel did show up—in one piece, thank the stars.

But Aeron's scowl could be seen a league off. "Didn't get him." She sheathed her sword abruptly.

Karlith climbed to her feet and helped me up after her. "Well, maybe that isn't a bad thing. No need to be celebrating loss of life, is there?"

Aeron frowned. "Yes, but I heard him shouting back to the rest of his unit, in case we stuck him with an arrow before he could get out of range, I guess."

Karlith's half-lidded blue eyes suddenly looked concerned. "He saw Tannie?"

Hearing my nickname in her voice warmed my achy insides.

But Aeron shook her head and stared stone-hard at Karlith. "No, I don't think they saw Tanwen. But I did hear him shout *a* name to his wretched fellows." Aeron's gaze turned from stone to steel. "Karlith Ma-Lundir."

CHAPTER 18

BRAITH

THE PRISONER'S CHAINS RATTLED. BRAITH'S GAZE KEPT WANDERing to his eyes—hollow, dead, yet still desperate. She forced her attention back to his voice.

"Majesty, please. My family will starve without me. My wife has a baby on the way, and four others besides. Mercy, my king!"

"Ah, so that's where my taxes have gone." The king scratched his beard. "Into your brats' mouths."

The man collapsed to his knees. A piece of his shirt fairly disintegrated with the motion.

Dray's nose wrinkled. "Goddesses' tears. How long has he been in the dungeon? He looks a sight."

The prisoner clasped his hands together. "Majesty, surely you would not execute a poor peasant for putting food in the mouths of his children. Mercy, I beg you."

Braith winced. She could hope the king would have mercy—for once. But history suggested this hope would be vain.

The king leaned back in his chair. "I would not fault a man for feeding his own children." He reached over to Braith and patted her arm. "Do not forget I am a father myself."

He must not have noticed Braith's rod-straight back and clenched fists.

"But I will fault a man for taking food off my table. Which is exactly what each peasant does when he refuses to pay the tax." The king sighed. "I do not understand why this is so difficult to grasp.

It's such a simple idea, and yet the rustics fill my hall day in and day out, complaining of my punishments. Is the law not clear?"

The council members nodded concurrence. Except Braith.

"See this?" The king looked like he might smile. "My council says the law is clear. Are you simple, man? Do you not understand the law?"

"No, Your Majesty. I understand it."

The king sighed. "You do not claim ignorance. And so, by your own admission, you chose disobedience. There is no mercy to be had here. You will be punished to the fullest extent of the law."

Braith gasped. "Death, Your Majesty? This man is a father of five. Surely there can be mercy for him, if for anyone."

"Never saw such a tenderhearted creature in my life, Majesty." Dray's voice dripped flattery. "Your daughter's kindness does you credit as a father."

Braith cast a reproachful glance at Dray. That man had the ears of a night-flier.

"Yes," the king said, tone clipped, "but her tenderness borders dangerously on weakness, and one ought never to show weakness. Ever."

Dray's gaze stayed fixed on Braith as if welded there. "Indeed, Majesty."

"Majesty . . ." Braith cast a desperate glance at the prisoner bowing face down on the throne room floor. "Father, please."

"Braith, you would show mercy to every piece of rubbish that kneels before this throne."

"But Father, this man has only done what is right."

The king wrenched his arm away from Braith. The familiar storm brewed in his eyes. "Breaking the law is right? Did you just suggest that?"

Braith bit her lip. "Your Majesty, a man fed his children. Fed them food he grew himself, with his own two hands. If he must break a law to do so, perhaps it is the law which is not right. It seems to me he has acted in accordance with his conscience and with what natural law would demand. Surely natural law is higher than kingdom law."

The king eyed Braith for a full minute. It was impossible to tell what he was thinking, except that he was displeased.

Finally, he spoke. "Braith, you overstep your bounds."

Braith took a deep breath—weighed her options. Then she placed her hands on either side of her throne. It took every fiber of muscle in her arms and legs, but she pushed herself up, heavy velvet dress and cinched corset notwithstanding. She lifted her voice so every council member and courtier in the hall might hear.

"I demand mercy for this man and his family!"

A murmur rippled through the crowd. Tirian tradition required that a royal lady's call for mercy be obeyed. Braith did not dare to exercise the right often. The king would remove her from council faster than she could swoon. And what good could she ever do if she didn't sit on council?

But she must take the risk sometimes.

King Gareth shifted in his seat, then glared at Braith with disapproving eyes. Finally, he rose. "Very well. Princess Braith calls for mercy, and mercy the prisoner shall have." He lowered his voice so that only those advisors at the council table in front of the dais could hear—Dray, High Priest Naith, and a handful of others.

"The princess must know how displeased I am."

Braith bowed her head. "Forgive me, Majesty. My heart is too soft. But I could not sleep tonight knowing we had made a widow and a cottage full of orphans today. Not when our table is full and this man's taxes mean little to us. I ask your mercy for myself too."

Braith did not look up for a long time but kept her head bowed before the king and prayed. Not to the goddesses, for she knew them to be fables. But to whatever force of good and justice might exist in the world.

If there were one.

The moments stretched excruciatingly.

But then the king reached out and roughly patted Braith's hand. "There, there. You know, a fair few people thought I'd gone mad when I put my daughter on the council. They prophesied womanly weaknesses such as these. I had hoped you'd try harder to prove the naysayers false. You must not realize you have detractors, daughter."

As if Braith could forget her enemies when she sat at the council table with them every day.

A swell of loneliness surged through her. "Yes, Father. Thank you, Your Majesty."

The king took his seat again, then waved at the guardsman next to the prisoner. "See to it that this man is released."

The guardsman bowed and hoisted the prisoner off the floor.

The peasant locked onto Braith's gaze. "Thank you, Highness. Bless you!"

Braith nodded to him. Poor soul.

The king cleared his throat. "One last prisoner for the day. Dray, do tell them to bring in the next."

But the king's chief advisor wasn't there.

The king swiveled around as far as his ever-growing stomach would allow. "Where is that man? Supposed to be my advisor, isn't he? A bit hard to advise me when he's so far from my person, I daresay."

But then Dray appeared at the back of the hall. He must have slipped out when Braith and the king had been speaking. Now a guardsman was with him, but Braith didn't recognize the soldier. He must not be high ranking.

Dray lowered himself to one knee with a flourish of his hand. "Forgive me, Majesty. But this soldier called me out of council on urgent business."

The king nodded to him, and Dray rose and reclaimed his position at the table below the royal dais. The guardsman stood at attention and waited to be addressed.

"Well," the king said, "what was so important as to divert the attention of my chief advisor in the middle of council?"

The soldier spoke. "Majesty, we just received a message. We set a watch in the aerie to bring you word as soon as we heard anything about the"—he cleared his throat—"ah, troubling matter of the Pembroni story peddler."

The boredom drained from the king's face. "And?"

The guardsman unrolled a piece of parchment. "She managed to escape all the guard's checkpoints, Majesty."

The king's jaw tensed. "And?"

"It is believed she had help."

"From?"

The guard shifted his weight. "The rebel band of weavers, Majesty."

Braith turned to the king. His face showed no surprise. Only anger and something else. Dread, perhaps. But clearly these rebel weavers existed within her father's knowledge, even if Braith had never heard of them.

"Majesty," Dray cut in. "Might I speak?" An expression of sincerest obedience was plastered over his fine-featured face.

The king nodded curtly.

"My advice would be to pursue this matter with the full force of your power. Rebellion must be stamped out." Dray glanced at Braith. "There is no mercy to be had in such matters. These weavers, or so they call themselves, have plagued you with their insurgence long enough."

A loud yawn from the other side of the council table startled Braith. Naith, who had been relatively quiet this afternoon, daintily touched his lips. "Oh, do forgive me. Let me guess what the great chief advisor's counsel will be." He steepled his fingers in front of his chin. "Kill or capture?"

Dray glared. "Yes. Kill or capture. Perhaps a man of your deep religious convictions doesn't understand such matters, but it is the proper way to handle an uprising. And that is exactly what this will become if we don't act decisively. These weavers claim their gifts come from the goddesses themselves. There is no end to their audacity."

The king leaned back on his throne. "Kill or capture. Dray, I fear your harshness will scandalize the princess, delicate as she seems to be today."

Braith forced a smile. "No, Majesty. I'm only surprised. This is the first I've heard of a band of rebel weavers."

Heavy silence filled the room.

Finally, the king nodded to the guardsman. "Bring me that note."

The soldier stepped forward and handed the note to his king.

As the king read, Naith muttered to the council table. "I suppose Sir Dray will send the king's men on another expensive vanity campaign. Dray Bo-Anffir's notion of domination has been insulted, and now blood and coin must be spent at will."

A retort seemed to be welling up inside Dray, but the king interrupted. "It says here Karlith Ma-Lundir was spotted with the rebels moments before the writing of this note." His gaze lifted to Naith, and a whisper of amusement danced in the king's eyes. "That name means something to you, doesn't it, Naith?"

Naith's round face colored, then paled. His hands squeezed into fists. "Karlith Ma-Lundir? Were the witnesses sure it was she?"

The king glanced back at the parchment. "Seems so."

Naith straightened in his chair and looked past Dray to the king. "My lord, I must agree with your advisor's suggestion. Kill or capture. It is the only way."

Dray laughed scornfully. "Indeed! Whose vanity campaign is it now?" He leaned forward. "I think I remember this Karlith Ma-Lundir. She's that colormaster—the one who is a Creator fanatic. Isn't that right?"

Naith's fists tightened until his knuckles stood out white, even against the paleness of his flesh.

Dray sat back into his chair. "She had a husband, didn't she? A songspinner. You speak of the blood on my hands while managing to forget that which stains yours. Lundir's blood is there, among many others. And didn't Karlith and Lundir have children? What became of them, I wonder?"

"Enough." The king waved his hand as though he were shooing flies.

Braith leaned toward him. “Father . . .”

“Hush now, Braith. Surely you’ve spoken the word *mercy* enough for one day.”

The king snapped his fingers, and a scribe appeared at his hand opposite where Braith sat. She stretched in her seat but couldn’t see what the king had scrawled onto the back of the report about the outlaw band of weavers.

The king scribbled his signature, took the wax from his scribe, and placed the royal seal on his words.

Without making a verbal declaration, the king reached across the table and showed the parchment to Dray. Dray scanned it, then met the king’s eyes. A flicker of satisfaction skittered across his face.

The king retrieved the parchment and tucked it into an inside fold of his tunic.

Braith frowned. What had he written? And why did he not wish her or the other council members to see it?

“Well, now,” the king said. “Let us move on to pleasanter matters. Sir Dray, tell me. How went the executions yesterday?”

CHAPTER 19

TANWEN

COLOR-SMATTERED TREES POPPED INTO MY VISION, AND I COULD have collapsed with relief. "There! It's the Corsyth, isn't it?"

Aeron nodded once, then strode ahead as though she hadn't just been slaying king's guardsmen and running through the forest like a light-foot. Surely she was more tired than I was, and I felt like I was going to keel over any second.

"Captain Bo-Awirth," Aeron said.

Warmil looked up, and he seemed to know immediately we'd had trouble. I guess the big streak of blood down Aeron's white shirt and brown trousers was a clue.

"What is it?"

Whatever summary of happenings Aeron gave the captain, I couldn't hear it. But I did see her nod over to Karlith once or twice.

Zel's bandage was soaked through with blood again.

"Zel, your arm."

He looked down at it. "Guess I overdid it."

"Want me to rewrap it?"

"Nah." He shook his head. "I can ask Gryfelle. You need to get some decent sleep."

Truly, my body was right worn out. I scanned the mossy rocks, knowing there were those crate beds underneath, even if I couldn't see them. "Where do I . . . ?"

"That one there. Between Warmil's rock and Aeron's. You'll be well protected."

Gryfelle's sigh sounded behind me. "Oh, Zel. Come on. Let's get that arm patched up again. I told you to take it easy."

He shrugged. "The guard mustn't have heard you."

She smiled a moment, but then her face fell. She put a hand to her temple and frowned. "What was that, Mother? I can't seem to find the gold ones."

I felt the confusion settle onto my face, and I must have looked lost as a fluff-hopper in a mountainbeast stampede.

"Gryfelle?" I reached for her.

But Mor swooped in just then. "Come on, Elle. Let's go sit." He didn't even seem to notice me, but he gave Zel a quick nod. "Karlith will patch you up, mate."

I didn't have energy left to wonder at this. Not just then. I scrambled over to the rock Zel had pointed to, slipped under the cover of moss, and climbed into the makeshift bed. Truly, it was like a large fishing crate half sunk into the marsh. But all the open spaces between the slats had been plugged and patched so it was drier than wheat ready for storage.

A collection of straw-stuffed pillows lined the bottom. I flopped onto them and felt the crate shift in the sloppy marsh mud.

Whoops.

Guessed I should move with more care, lest I invite a flood of muck and water into my new bed. I pulled up a blanket thicker than the ancient ones I had back home. It welcomed me into its cozy folds, and in a few moments, there was only the blessed blackness of exhausted sleep.

The sound of the world being ripped in two jolted me awake.

Least, that's what I thought it was at first.

The noise came again—a scream or a howl, I couldn't really tell. Maybe both.

I crawled out from under my moss covering and met a flurry of movement around the Corsyth.

Mor's voice cut through the night. "Elle, stay calm. Everyone get back!"

The howl came again—animalistic, soul-chilling. It couldn't . . . I mean, that growling, guttural sound couldn't be coming from Gryfelle.

Could it?

"Tanwen!" Karlith's heavy-lidded eyes found me in the blackness. "Back to your bed, my girl. Hurry now."

My heart galloped. "Karlith, is it the guard? Have they come for us?"

"No, lass. Back to your crate with you."

I bit my lip, grasping for control over my panic. "Karlith, what's happening?"

Karlith opened her mouth, but Zel's holler cut her off. "Karlith, we need you!"

She met my gaze for a moment. "Stay here." Then she took off full-speed toward the commotion.

And of course I followed her. Though looking back, I wish I hadn't.

Gryfelle lay splayed in the middle of a small clear spot of ground. The other six weavers huddled around her. Warmil and Zelyth each pinned a leg to the earth. Aeron and Dylun gripped her arms. Mor held her head in his lap. Karlith seemed to be crushing some kind of herb and shoving it under Gryfelle's nose.

Gryfelle screamed like they were pulling off her limbs.

Horror doused me like a bucketful of ocean water. "Stop it!" I stumbled toward them. "What are you doing? You're hurting her!"

"Tannie, don't—"

I silenced Mor with a stiff shove.

Dylun felt the sting of my indignation next as I toppled him and freed Gryfelle's arm. "Let her go!"

"Tannie, look out!"

Mor's warning came too late—especially for my unthinking, grazer-brained self.

Gryfelle let out another howl, then swung her free fist smack across my jaw. I fell back in shock.

Mor didn't let another heartbeat pass before he was back by Gryfelle's head. "Easy, Elle. It's us. You know us."

Gryfelle screamed out, but she hardly sounded herself. "No!" She yanked against her restrainers and shrieked that awful, animal cry.

Dylun recaptured her free arm, but his cheek took a swipe from her fingernails in the process. Even in the dark, I could see the gashes oozing blood.

How hard did she have to gouge to make such a wound with naught but her nails?

"Karlith, the herbs." Mor struggled to hold his grip on Gryfelle's head as she wrestled about. "Please. It's going to be a bad one."

Going to be? Gryfelle growled and yanked against Zel and Warmil at her legs. If this wasn't the worst of what was to come, I wasn't sure I wanted to see the rest.

Karlith crushed the herbs in her palm. "Nothing in it, Mor. They don't help her anymore, and you know it."

Desperation swallowed Mor's face. Like a man caught in a war he knows he must fight but can't possibly win. "We have to try. I can't . . ." His voice caught. "I can't lose another."

Gryfelle's howls dwindled to moans.

Warmil glanced up. "She's crossing into it." He seemed to be waiting for some sort of approval from Mor.

Mor nodded to them all. "Now!"

Everyone except Mor released Gryfelle.

I scooted away from her as fast as I could scramble. My jaw still smarted where she had hit me. "Wait, what about—"

Never finished my thought. Because in the next moment, I knew why they'd let her go.

Gryfelle's eyes blanked into empty windows, like they had on the river. Vacant. Hollow. And then it seemed every muscle in her body got shot through with lightning. Tensed. Contorted.

She twisted onto her side. Mor followed her movements, her head protected gently in his hands.

"Hold on, lass," he murmured. The sound carried through the still nighttime forest. "Hold on, Elle."

Gryfelle's only response was a gurgle deep in her throat. Then the thrashing began.

It wasn't like the other thrashing, where she'd strained and fought as if some spirit of violence had taken hold of the real Gryfelle for a spell. These were the thrashings of someone entirely cleaved from her own will—from her own mind. She flailed like she hadn't a thought in her head or a speck of control over herself. Like lightning zapped her, except there wasn't any coming from the sky.

The lightning was inside her.

It struck again and again. Then again. A full minute rolled by. I felt Zel's arm loop around my shoulders as we, all of us, watched Gryfelle's body beat itself against the ground.

"What is it, Zel?" I whispered through my fingers, only then realizing I'd been covering my mouth in horror. Even so, my whispered words seemed loud against the silent spectacle before us.

He shook his head and barely seemed able to make his voice work for a moment. Finally, he managed words. "The curse."

Gryfelle whipped to her other side so that her usually elegant face turned toward us. Dead eyes, twisted features, frothed spit around her lips. I hardly knew her.

At the next strike of invisible lightning, Gryfelle's mouth opened. A moan escaped—and so did a flurry of song strands. The melody of them spun softly toward us. A quiet song that felt like warmth and care and service.

"What is it?" I choked from a throat that felt two sizes too small.

As I spoke, the strands collected together. Vials, bandages, herbs, bowls of powders.

I looked up. "Zel?"

But it was Karlith who answered. "It's the healing arts. All I've taught her." She clasped her hands to her chest like it hurt to speak it—like her heart would crack in her ribs.

Gryfelle jolted again, and her head slipped from Mor's hands. He cried out but couldn't move his hands fast enough. Gryfelle's head slammed to the ground and more song strands escaped. Then again as she jolted. And again.

"No!" Mor's frustration could have felled a tree as he fought to recapture his moving target.

And Gryfelle's head hit the dirt again. All the while, her song strands grew more solid, glowing in the dark forest. Every blow to her head sent new strands out into the night air.

Karlith rushed to Mor's side. His hands slipped off Gryfelle on one side, but hers found purchase. Karlith's lips moved silently as she cradled Gryfelle's head.

"Five minutes." Aeron glanced at Zel, then Warmil. "Longest yet."

A lump rose in my throat. Tears spilled down my face. "Will it ever stop?"

No one seemed to have an answer for me. In the light of Gryfelle's song strands, I could see that Mor was crying too. The anguish etched in his features showed that every thrash of her body was felt in his soul.

Our eyes locked across the clearing, and I don't know as I ever saw a more helpless, hopeless lad in my life.

My heart pinched in my chest.

A wail from Karlith broke the connection between me and Mor. She looked up to the dark, tree-covered sky. "Mercy! Please, mercy!"

Gryfelle thrashed.

"Six minutes." Aeron frowned at Warmil. "Captain, should we—?"

But a loud sigh from Gryfelle cut short Aeron's grim question, whatever it was. With every breath out, Gryfelle uttered long, loud sighs. Her body stilled but for her heaving chest. The song strands that Karlith said were the healing arts slowly disappeared into the night.

"Gryfelle?" Karlith put Gryfelle's head in her lap and stroked the sweaty golden hair. "Can you hear me, lass?"

Gryfelle sighed.

Mor placed a hand on her forehead. "Gryfelle En-Blaid, do you know me?" He chuckled, but it sounded more a weary sob. "Do you know Mor Bo-Lidere?"

Gryfelle sighed again.

Karlith's colormastery strands poured from her fingers. "Do you remember being a wee lass in Urian with the great marble fountains and the palace as tall as the heavens?"

Strands like paint splashed together in midair to form the bubbling fountains.

A moan hummed from Gryfelle, and her eyes fluttered.

Mor touched her face. "Remember the vast parties in fancy ballrooms?" As he spoke, strands of story formed pictures—fine gowns swirling through the air of the Corsyth. "Remember the dancing lessons?"

Karlith pushed back Gryfelle's sweat-soaked locks. "Remember your sisters and your wee brother?"

Gryfelle's eyes fluttered again, and this time they stayed open. Her voice was the saddest song. "No, Karlith. I do not."

Blue waves of light rolled from Karlith's palms as tears coursed her cheeks. "Do you remember when Mor found you on the Isles of Gael?"

Mor winced. "Karlith, if ever there was a memory to be stolen forever, it's that one."

Karlith didn't pause. Her soothing murmur kept up its rolling hum. "Do you remember your friends in the Corsyth? You don't have to hide your gift here, lass. The Creator gave it to you. It were an act of love, dear one. You don't have to be afraid anymore."

Dylun touched my arm, and I nearly parted from my skin. His dark eyes burned in the low light of the story and color strands. "Gryfelle need not fear anymore. But we must."

"What do you mean?" I whispered.

"More is at stake than just the freedom to create, Tanwen. Don't you see? Gryfelle's curse—it's because of what Gareth has done. What Gryfelle had to endure as a child with the songspinning gift, living inches from the pretender king who would silence her as soon as look at her. The suppression, the denial, the secrecy. It's what brought this sentence upon our friend. Suppress the art inside a weaver long enough, and the gift turns curse."

I stared at the huddled mass of bodies before me—Gryfelle, Karlith, and Mor. "And so she's . . . ill?"

"Not just ill, Tanwen." Dylun's face pinched and the others went silent as a winter midnight. "Gryfelle is losing herself, bit by bit, memory by memory. She's being erased. The curse won't relent until she's gone. An empty canvas."

I could barely speak for lack of breath. "And then?"

"Her body will die." He gently turned my face back toward his. "It's too late for Gryfelle. But you see our fight is a matter of life and death. For us, and for you, too."

I turned back to the bruised, crumpled, lovely, broken creature who lay shattered on the forest floor.

And I saw my future.

CHAPTER 20

THE ONE IN THE DARK

She was there again with the basket. Hands reached out to take the offered cheese. The candlelight revealed blackened fingertips. Not a warm, living black, but black like the darkness that surrounded them. As if the darkness had seeped into the fingers.

The young woman seemed to sense these thoughts. "I've brought more for you." She slowly brought a bottle out of the basket.

Of course. Ink.

"Here." The word is encouraging and kind.

Hands take it. The acknowledging grunt of thanks.

She closed the blackened fingers around the bottle. "For your journals, my lord."

Second moon of winter, the 1st year of Gareth the Usurper (40th year of Caradoc II)

I escaped just in time. Gareth has been aware of my presence—and the fact that I escaped his "plague"—for several days, but today was the first attempt on my life. My dear wife heard them coming and practically shoved me into the passageway. She told them I'd been gone from the palace for several days and she feared I'd contracted the plague after all, since I'd not yet returned. I'm almost certain Gareth did not believe her, but it was enough to keep him away.

For today.

But how long before he comes again? How long before he comes for her? How long will he wait to create another accident, and will he come for the child, too?

Not my dear, sweet girl.

I know the palace better than anyone alive and could hide in these secret passages for ages if I had supplies enough. But I cannot leave my family, nor could I bear having them trapped in this dark, desolate place. The young one could never manage to stay hidden, in any case. How to free them from the palace before Gareth's noose tightens?

And what of the others? We've managed to spread the true story. But slowly, for we know not who can be trusted, and not much can be done while I am locked away in hiding.

Glain says it is imperative I stay alive. She says the truth must be preserved in me, the only witness. But all I can think of is keeping those dearest to me safe.

Fingers dug into familiar divots in the stone wall. Muscles strained and pulled up. Then again and again. One hundred times per day to keep the muscles strong. Limber. An old soldier's habit.

Ninety-nine. One hundred.

The fingers released and feet dropped to the floor.

A sound in the darkness.

The young woman. She held out a basin of water. "My lord?"

Wash day. He came slowly from the corner and sat in the light of the candle.

The woman placed a pile of clean clothes by the basin. She dipped her cloth into the steaming water. "I warmed it." She smiled. "Not so hot as last time." She wrung the cloth and pressed it to the face, beard, and neck.

"I'll have more food for you tonight. Did you finish what I left?"

No answer. She must not expect one.

But she doesn't ask questions to find answers. She wants his ears to remember voices. Words. Questions. People.

She was taking care of a weary and wasted mind.

"Let me see those hands, my lord."

They reached out to her. Fingertips black, stained.

But she took them and rubbed them until the blackness faded—now transferred onto the cloth instead.

She dipped a cup into the water and poured it over the head. A bar of soap came out and she made suds in the hair.

"Hold still." She met his eyes, and there was a smile in hers. "My lord."

She poured the water again, then wiped the face. A final rinse and squeeze of the rag, then she dropped it into waiting hands. "I'm going to wait by the passageway door. You finish washing, then I'll come back for the basin. Do you understand, my lord?"

She turned to step out. It was not proper for a lady to help a gentleman bathe.

With the young woman in the darkness of the passage, the bath continued, then finished.

Legs slid into clean trousers, and a tunic slipped overhead. The dirty clothes went on the floor.

A grunt. The woman reappeared in the candlelight.

"All done?"

A nod. She collected her things. And then . . .

"Meridioni," his throat croaked.

She froze. "Yes. I am Meridioni."

"Ben . . . na . . . ti."

She gasped. "Yes. My father was Bennati."

A slow nod.

"It . . ." She approached and knelt beside him. "It has been so long since you've spoken," she said, her own voice breaking. "Since you've remembered."

Another nod.

She was quiet for a moment, looking at him with tear-filled eyes. She rose. "I must get back now." She reached down and picked up the dirty clothes and water basin again.

He began to retreat back toward the dark corner.

But as the candlelight disappeared down the passageway, there was a rasp. “Wait.”

The woman stopped and turned. “Yes, my lord?”

“Name?”

A smile shone in the flickering candlelight. “Cameria.”

CHAPTER 21

TANWEN

If there's a way you're supposed to act the morning after you see the dark, desolate possibility of your future, I never learned it. If there's something that's to be said to one suffering as Gryfelle was suffering, I don't know it.

Everyone moved about the Corsyth like a veil of shadow covered the place—somber and serious, like we were at a burial ceremony. And in a way, the whole of life in the Corsyth was like a burial ceremony. Because with each passing day, Gryfelle En-Blaid died a little more.

The veil of shadow lingered all through the morning meal. I tried to kick up some conversation while we sipped our tea and bitter-bean, but nobody was listening. We sipped in silence, keen not to mention the goings-on of the night before.

So when Gryfelle eased beside me with a tied-up rag in one hand and an open look about her face, I was fairly shocked.

"May I sit?"

I nodded to the ground beside me. The story I'd been building hovered in front of me—an old legend about a beast called a starwolf that looked human through the day then flipped to a dread beast in starlight. I hadn't told it in years because it wasn't crowned. The wolfish beast made of gray-brown fabric story strands twirled slowly. When Gryfelle lowered herself beside me, the story wolf opened its mouth in a silent roar, and a beam of red light shot out.

I waved my hand to make the blazing thing disappear and felt my face go hot. "Sorry. Not exactly the prettiest story, is it?"

She didn't look at me but smiled a little. "No one would fault you for having that tale on your mind—the beast revealed by starlight. I suppose that's what you witnessed last night." She held up the bundle in her hands. "Karlith tells me these cold river stones might soothe your sore jaw."

"Oh. That." I'd barely thought of it, but it was achy.

"I don't remember using cold river stones or packed snow to ease pain and swelling, but Karlith says we've had need to do so dozens of times."

"Oh." Part of Gryfelle's healing arts that had disappeared into the night air.

I hadn't a notion what to say next. And being lost for words isn't exactly what I'm known for.

"May I?" Gryfelle held up the bundle of stones.

I frowned. "May you what?"

She smiled. "Your face."

"Oh, yes. All right."

She gently pressed the cool bundle to my sore jawbone.

I studied her—the high cheekbones and the delicate lips, the smooth skin and the thick lashes shielding those green eyes. "Can you get it back, Gryfelle?"

"Pardon me?" The lashes curled back and the green eyes lifted to me, a giant question mark swimming in them.

"If Karlith taught you the arts again. If Mor retold your life story over and over, would it make a new memory for you?"

Her eyes lowered back to her work. "It doesn't quite work that way. I know for this moment that cool things help reduce pain and swelling. But the knowledge will not lodge fast in my mind. Furthermore . . ." She trailed off a moment, and great tears began to roll down her cheeks.

But then she gathered her voice. "Furthermore, the desire to learn the healing arts has fled with the knowledge. It was a part of who I was, now lost. It's worse than if the knowledge had never been there in the first place."

"Like a rockslide." The picture popped into my head—along

with a hollow dread in my heart. "When a big squall sweeps through Pembrone, sometimes the water lashes at the cliffs above the Menfor Sea. Rocks that've been sound enough to scramble across for years might suddenly break free and tumble down, taking hundreds of others with them. After that, the cliff face there is so smooth that no Pembroni would dare to test it for some years to come.

"It's a bit like that, isn't it? Things that were once stuck fast in your mind come tumbling down, and the face of it is so smooth nothing else will stick there."

Gryfelle paused a moment, testing the temperature of the not-so-cool stones. "Yes. It is a bit like that." She sighed and sat back. "Tanwen, I'm very sorry."

I stared at her. "You're sorry? For what?"

"I never meant to strike you last night."

I recoiled. "Of course you didn't! Nobody means to lose herself." I winced. Hadn't come out like I'd wanted. "I mean, it isn't your fault, Gryfelle."

She nodded and stared down.

I sat on the fallen log beside her and spoke hesitatingly. "Dylun said the curse was from suppressing your songspinning gift. Suppressing—that's the squashing down?"

"Yes. That's correct."

"And that's why Mor made me promise to stop squashing it down?"

"Yes." Gryfelle paused. Then she looked me in the eyes. "I'm dying, Tanwen."

A thought suddenly struck me in the chest, though I couldn't account for the way it knocked the breath from my body. "That's why you won't be with Mor."

A little smile broke through the cloud on her face. "Mor feels a great responsibility for me. But I think it'd be quite a shame to allow him to waste his heart on someone like me—a candle burned down to a stub. The flame will only hold out so much longer, I fear."

"But—" A lump in my throat cut off my words. I swallowed it

down. "But if you love him, Gryfelle . . . I mean, you do love him, don't you?"

Her smile wilted to a pained grimace. "I'm sure I did. Once."

I'd never imagined what it would feel like if hope and despair waged a war inside my mind. But I supposed it was something like the battle raging inside me in that moment.

I cleared my throat. "Do you remember what your life was like in Urian?" The name of the city I once dreamed about tasted like ash in my mouth.

"I remember some things I'd rather forget. Imagine what it was like for the weavers at court when Gareth stormed to power. Suddenly, something that had been considered a gift from the goddesses was looked down upon like a curse. My parents—"

She closed her eyes for several heartbeats before she could continue.

"My parents did their best. I was only five years old when King Caradoc died, and they supposed I could be trained to ignore my songspinning ability." She glanced up at me and raised an eyebrow. "That didn't go so well."

"Did you run away, then?"

A sad sort of smile turned up one corner of her mouth. "No. When it became clear the experiment hadn't worked—that the suppression of my songspinning hadn't made me 'normal' but had instead pushed me past a threshold into something truly cursed—my parents turned me over to Gareth and the king's guard."

My mind got stuck on that one. Her own flesh-and-blood kin turned her in? Maybe I didn't have much nice to say about life in a small farming town. And maybe I talked a lot about how poky and ordinary Pembrone was. But such a thing as turning in your own blood kin when you were the one who'd made them what they'd become. . . . Well, I could only think Gryfelle's mam and dad wouldn't be able to show their faces in Blodwyn's tavern after what they had done. Not if they'd been Pembroni.

I wanted to reach out and take Gryfelle's hand. But it was pale as milk, and she was shaking. I didn't know if she'd want me to.

"Gryfelle?"

She looked up again. "Yes?"

"How did you escape after you were arrested?"

"I didn't. I mean, not at first. I was exiled to the Isles of Gael."

"The Isles of Gael!"

Of course, then I remembered that Karlith had said it the night before. But I'd been so addled by the commotion I hadn't comprehended what she'd said in the moment.

I'd heard about people being banished to the islands of the prisoners. But for serious crimes. Like thieving from a temple or something. Something that wasn't bad enough to earn a date on the chopping block but was so bad the king didn't think you were worth feeding for ten years in his dungeon.

But exiled for being a songspinner? And a young lass too!

"Yes, the Isles of Gael." Gryfelle sighed. "I hadn't been on the island two minutes before I realized I'd have to get off somehow. The other prisoners—" She shook her head as if to clear it. "Well, that's another memory I'd not mind losing. They'd all but turned into beasts. Savages. All the society and humanity chased from them by starvation, violence, and cruelty."

Suddenly, something clicked in my mind. My heart wrenched. "Is that where you met Mor? Because he was sailing around and pirating and all?"

She smiled ruefully. "I suppose that's the short version of what happened." But she didn't give me a chance to ask what the long version was. "Are you cold, Tanwen?"

"Eh?"

"You're shivering."

I guessed I was a bit chilly. The sun was all but blotted out by the trees, and the Corsyth felt damp and misty this afternoon. "I suppose I am."

"Shall I warm you?"

"Warm me? But how—"

My question died when she opened her mouth again. Because this time song poured out. Strands like hazy fire flowed from her lips. I couldn't figure the words—Old Tirian again. But it felt like she sang of the kind of summer afternoon when all the work stops for a minute and everybody lies in the shade and sips something cold.

Whether she truly sang about that or not, I don't know; but as I thought about those summer afternoons on the farm, strands for those ideas ribboned from my fingers. Pale blue satin for the sky and sparkling yellow mist for the sunlight. Then a ribbon of amber-colored light that looked as though it bubbled. It could only be Brac's mug of ale. Then another strand so clear I could scarcely see it but for a shimmer here and there. That was my mug of cold well water, never so appreciated as on those hot, sunny days.

Gryfelle's song drew to a slow close. Her strands disappeared, but mine crystallized into a tiny glass haymow, just like the ones on Farmer Bradwir's farm that Brac and I would lean against when we rested.

Gryfelle smiled. "You miss him."

It wasn't a question, and I realized Gryfelle was in the habit of doing that. Observing things and saying them aloud.

"Aye, I miss him." A lump of guilt bigger and colder than a river stone settled in my stomach. I bit my lip. "Think I'll ever see him again?"

"If Mor and Dylun and Warmil have anything to say about it, you all won't be in hiding forever."

"And you?"

She smiled weakly. "My purpose is to serve as a warning to others. Beyond that, I have no future."

I swallowed and watched the leaves flutter above us. "That's the saddest thing I've ever heard, Gryfelle."

"Is it? Well . . ." I could hear her take a long breath. "Then I have warned you well."

CHAPTER 22

TANWEN

It's a strange thing to feel empty and full at the very same time. Empty on account of the fact that, in so many ways, my life had taken a turn for the worse. Curses, doom, death, and the ever-lurking loneliness billowed around me like a dark cloud.

A few days had passed, and with it, the fear of discovery seemed to ease a little. Aeron and Warmil had dumped the guardsmen's bodies in the river, and I guessed that was supposed to make us safer for the time being. Harder to trace us back to the Corsyth if the guard didn't have a couple of dead bodies to use as a starting point.

The thought made my stomach lurch.

But as I stared around the Corsyth from my favorite perch on the fallen log—at the beauty shaped by creation and by the hands that lived here—it tickled something inside me. Something that had been so long asleep I didn't even know it existed.

I felt like in this place, with these people, I could discover the real me. The storyteller. The weaver.

And here I didn't feel afraid of who she might be. I didn't feel so much like an orphan.

I pinched the stem of a fallen leaf and twirled it between my fingers and smiled. Brac would scoff at such fanciful notions. If it didn't have an everyday application on the farm, Brac wasn't much interested in thinking on it very long.

Suddenly, I felt like my backbone had been switched out for an iron rod.

Brac.

Was it wicked of me to say the Corsyth weavers felt the closest to family I'd ever had? Brac had been by my side most of my life. I'd known the Corsyth weavers for a few days, and I was ready to say they somehow filled the great emptiness in my heart? Ridiculous.

And yet it didn't stop the feeling. Or the truth of it.

Mor's mischievous ice-blue eyes popped to mind.

Aye. There was that too.

If I were being honest with myself, the great pit inside me wasn't just on account of the awful possibility shown to me in Gryfelle's curse. No, part of it was on account of the fact that Mor was the first lad to ever set those painted-wings loose in my stomach. But if ever there was a lad's whose heart wasn't free, it was Mor.

You're a wretched creature, Tanwen En-Yestin.

I crumbled the dry leaf between my fingers and let the crushed bits flutter to the ground like snowflakes.

"Now, that's a shame."

I nearly crumbled to pieces myself at the shock of a voice. Especially since it was *that* voice. "Ho, Mor," I said. "Scared me half to death. What's a shame?"

"It's a shame when something beautiful looks so desolate and forgotten."

I stared at the spot where I'd sprinkled the dead leaf bits. "It was just a leaf."

Mor laughed and his eyes twinkled. "I was talking about you, farm girl."

Heat swallowed me like I'd fallen into a fire. Except the fire was inside my face. "I am not a farm girl."

He grinned. Then he plunked down on the log beside me.

We sat in silence a minute. Then I ventured, "Sometimes it seems . . ."

He waited.

"Nah." I shook my head. "It's a fool idea."

"Tell me anyway."

That's right, Tannie. Open your heart to the lad you'll never have.

I ignored that pesky voice again. "Sometimes it seems I'm forever meant to be without a family. My parents are gone. It didn't take too many years before I became such a burden to the Bradwirs that I needed to strike out on my own. Then there was Riwor. Can you believe I tried to fancy her my granny for a bit?"

Mor gave me a look that made me wonder if his noontime meal might resurface.

"And just the other day, on my first rounds with Aeron, Zel, and Karlith, I had this fool idea that Karlith felt like . . . a mother."

Mor smiled. "She does feel like a mother. She is a mother, and she'll love you like one if you let her."

"Well, not a moment after I'd thought it, in crashes the guard, shouting her name and looking to arrest the poor lady." I sighed. "So maybe it's just the way it's meant to be. Maybe I'm not supposed to have a family."

He laughed humorlessly. "If it makes it any easier to swallow, I know how you feel."

It didn't make it easier to swallow. It just made me feel bad for the both of us. "Mor?"

"Aye?"

"I'm sorry about Gryfelle."

He smiled in a tight, sad way. "Aye."

"I've only known her a short while, and the other night was . . ." I had to hold back a shudder. "Well, I can only imagine what it was like for the rest of you." I looked down. "Especially you."

He didn't speak for a moment. Just sat there, staring.

"Tannie?" He was looking down at the ground like life's toughest questions were written there in the dead leaves. "How do you know if you're . . . I mean, sometimes the right thing is hard. But you should do it anyway, no matter how hard it is. Right?"

I nodded.

"And do you think doing the right thing when it's difficult can somehow erase . . . ?" He trailed off and kept looking at the leaves on the ground. Though I don't think he was seeing them at all.

I nudged him. "Can somehow erase what?"

"Times when you didn't do what was right."

"Oh." The question struck like a slap. "What'd you do?" Instantly, I wished I could suck the words back in. "Oh, sorry! Forget I asked that."

He smiled. Warm and thunderous like a summer rainstorm. He brushed a strand of hair off my face. "Don't ever change."

Then he rose and strode away.

I was left alone on the fallen log with a stomach full of painted-wings and the sharp knowledge that I was in for a world of trouble with this pirate.

CHAPTER 23

TANWEN

"YES, PLEASE TELL ME AGAIN ALL ABOUT YOUR HIGH IDEALS. Really, I can't get enough." Warmil launched a withering glare across the fire at Dylun.

We all sat there, eating our evening meal, but they were the only two talking. As usual.

Dylun snarled back, "So your cause is the only one worthy of attention, is it?"

"Not what I said. Don't twist my words."

"Then don't make such twistable declarations."

They both harrumphed and folded their arms across their chests. They may as well have been two of Farmer and Ma-Bradwir's youngsters arguing over whose turn it was to grub the watta root slips.

"Seems to me," I cut in, aware but not caring that I probably didn't have a right to speak up, "that you both want the same things."

Seven sets of eyes shot to me.

But I figured I best explain myself, now that I'd started. "You're both aiming at freedom, aye?"

After a moment of silence, Warmil nodded. "Aye, I suppose."

"Never going to happen like this."

Dylun's eyebrows rose. "Pardon me, but like what?"

"With the two of you bickering like a couple of wee ones. Not meaning any disrespect, but if you both want the same things, I don't think arguing over stuff like this is going to help anyone reach that end. You know?"

A soft snuffle of laughter seemed to come from Mor's direction, but I ignored it.

"Seems to me if you're after the same thing, no matter what your reasons are, you should be talking about how to get there rather than what makes the journey worth taking."

Warmil's blue eyes narrowed, but then he nodded once and settled back into his moody silence. Dylun's face relaxed a little, though his mouth twitched, and fried if I knew whether that meant he was angry or thought it was funny.

Mor smile wryly. "What Warmil and Dylun mean to say is your point's well taken, Tannie."

I shrugged and fought the glow that wanted to surface at his attention.

Lots of silent chewing followed. *Lots* of silent chewing.

How did these folks manage to talk to each other so little? I had more mealtime conversation back in Pembrone—when I ate by myself.

Out of sheer need to be doing something other than count the number of times I chewed each bite of my roasted light-foot, I took to staring at Warmil. Seemed a better choice than Mor, given the way of things. Warmil was sitting right next to me, so he was the lucky one who got to be studied.

The former captain was probably the least forthcoming of all the secret-keepers around this Corsyth, except when he and Dylun got to arguing with each other. He was handsome, I supposed, but those cold blue eyes of his—there was something behind them. Something lost, maybe?

No, not lost. Wounded.

Farmer Bradwir had taught me wounded animals were dangerous. They were like as not to lash out and hurt those trying to help them.

So naturally, I decided to poke this wounded animal with a stick to try to figure out what was wrong with him.

"Warmil?" I made my voice sound as sweet and safe as I possibly could.

He didn't answer me. Just tore another piece of bread off the half-loaf he was eating.

I raised my voice a bit. "Captain?"

"Hmm?" He turned to me, eyes wide like I'd startled him. "Yes?"

"How old are you?"

He paused like he had to think about it. "Thirty-seven last moon."

I fairly choked on my dinner. Thirty-seven! Nearly as old as Farmer Bradwir. And I'd just thought the captain was handsome.

"Well, I guess the silver hair should've given you away, but I didn't realize you were so old."

He frowned at me.

My cheeks heated. "No disrespect or anything. But I've seen young lads in the guard with silvery hair before. Not since I was a lass, though. Ma-Bradwir said it was the hard life of fighting wars that turned their hair gray. But now there aren't wars to fight. Just peasants to bully, and I guess that doesn't turn a lad's hair silver before its time."

Warmil's lips pressed together a moment. "No, I don't guess so."

"Bet you didn't bully anybody back when you were in the guard."

"No, I certainly did not."

I paused to look at him another second. "You're not from the peninsula."

"The Western Wildlands, actually."

"Oh!" I leaned forward. "I've never met a Wildlander! What's it like there?"

He swallowed his bread. "Would you be satisfied if I said 'wild'?"

"Not a chance."

He sighed but humored me. "The land isn't any good for farming, but it's rich in minerals Gareth wants. So that's how he bleeds us dry."

"Do you come from a mining family?"

"Aye. Like most Wildlanders."

"But you didn't become a miner."

"No, I joined the guard." He picked up a stick from the ground and tossed it into the fire. "Back when it meant something different."

"Caradoc was still on the throne?"

"Yes. I joined up when I was fourteen. Caradoc had a good many years left at that point. Joining gave me the chance to study in Urian, which I'd always wanted to do. I couldn't get enough of it once I started. Learning and fighting." He stared hard into the fire. "But now I'd just as soon forget everything I know. Useless."

"Useless?" I thought of what it would be like to read all the books in Urian. I'd grown up surrounded by a fair handful in Father's study, but I couldn't even fathom the libraries of Urian.

Dylun's voice surprised me. "Warmil Bo-Awirth is a dangerous sort of fellow."

I looked across the fire at the Meridioni, but his eyes weren't filled with anger this time. Only thoughtfulness.

Dylun leaned back against a tree trunk. "He's the type who knows everything and believes in nothing."

Warmil spared Dylun a glance, flat as a hotcake. "Indeed."

"Well," I said, "that doesn't seem true to me. If you believe in nothing, why do you care about getting rid of Gareth or getting freedom for weavers? Seems a man with nothing to believe in would be fine with everything staying the way it is."

For the first time since I started poking around in Warmil's mind, Aeron glanced up. But she wasn't looking at me. Her gaze fixed hard on Warmil like she wanted to say something. Or maybe like she wanted to run across the circle and hold him in her arms.

Probably both.

"Redemption," Warmil said. "I need redemption, and that's why I care about those things."

"Redemption." I didn't know the word.

"I need to redeem myself. That is, I need to make amends for something I've done."

"Redemption." I liked the way that word felt in my mouth.

"Yes. And I desire the kind of redemption a person needs when he's failed so miserably his life will be forfeit without it."

"So you failed at something?" If I was a betting lass, I'd wager this was the wounded part. "You failed and now you think you need to make up for it."

That reminded me of a certain pirate. I glanced at Mor. He was looking straight my way.

Warmil went on. "I don't *think* I need it. I must have it." His words spiked edgier than a prickle-back on a poker.

I thought about the idea of someone redeeming himself. What if he had to make some sort of payment every time he didn't succeed in the mission his commander gave him, or he was bested in sword training, or he didn't polish his armor shiny enough?

Or she didn't sell enough stories?

Or she snapped at Brac?

Or her big mouth ran away with her again?

The thought was unsettling enough to make me shift on the log where I sat.

"Seems to me—" I began.

"Uh oh," Mor said. "Something *seems* to Tanwen again. Everyone beware."

I made a face at him but kept on. "If your whole life is about measuring up, you're in for a load of trouble, aren't you? I mean, there wouldn't be a person in Tir with any friends left if we all expected perfection of plain ol' people all the time."

Karlith laughed. "The lass speaks truth, Warmil. Whether she means to or not."

Warmil turned to face Karlith. "I respect your faith, Karlith, because I respect you. And out of that respect, I'll say nothing further."

Karlith's eyes turned sad, though she smiled still. "For all your book learning, you'd think you would understand about the Creator. Funny thing, that."

"Just because I don't believe it doesn't mean I fail to understand."

Karlith's smile brought Ma-Bradwir's motherly ways to mind. "I'll always pray that the Creator's love will find you, Warmil. Or that you'll find it. I don't see how you'll ever be free from your fetters otherwise."

Warmil's mouth pulled into an even grimmer line until his lips fairly disappeared. "Noted."

"What did you do that was so bad, Warmil?" It bounced out of my mouth before I could stop it.

The grim line of Warmil's mouth collapsed into a grimace.

I shook my head. "You don't have to tell me. My big mouth just runs on without my brain sometimes. Pay it no mind."

"No." He brushed crumbs from his trousers like he was calm inside, but he wouldn't meet my eyes. "It's just as well that you know so you're aware what sort of man you share a camp with."

He seemed to be swallowing—gathering his courage. "It was after Gareth's rise. Everything had changed already. Caradoc's guard was a distant memory, and the new sort of guard had been mobilized to fight Gareth's wars for several years. My unit was . . . different than the others. The men didn't like Gareth's policies. We weren't the only ones, of course. There were many soldiers across Tir who'd sworn to protect the realm, not die on a distant battlefield to satisfy the new king's lust for land.

"But my men were too vocal about it. My fault, of course, because I was too vocal about it. They followed me."

My throat tightened. "So what happened?"

"We were dispatched to the Haribian front." The captain flinched. "But we never made it. And I abandoned my lads to die at the hands of their own countrymen."

"That's not how it happened!" Aeron cried. Fire might have started shooting from her eyes for how they blazed. "That isn't the whole story, Captain."

Warmil shrugged, and suddenly it seemed he'd found something really interesting on the forest floor.

Aeron's face hardened. Her features were severe in any case, and even more so when she got riled up—but somehow she was full of a fierce sort of beauty.

And she turned that fiery gaze on me, like I'd accused the captain of cowardice or something. "We were ambushed. Urian wanted us silenced, and they accomplished it. Simple as that."

"But I . . ." The words died on Warmil's tongue. His fists clenched by his side.

The knuckles on all ten of his fingers whitened. Then—no mistaking it—they began to glow. Warmil's face pulled and his jaw clenched.

On the other side of the circle, Mor rose. "War—"

Then Aeron practically shouted, "It wasn't your fault!"

Warmil's clenched fists slammed into the rock where he sat. Explosions of color burst down the boulder and scattered across the Corsyth floor so far that I couldn't see the end of the color trail.

The captain spit out the words. "I abandoned my men. All dead, except Aeron."

I craned my neck to look at what the colormaster had made.

Across the fallen leaves and jutting roots of the trees, dozens of bodies lay. Not a perfect reflection, like Dylun's pictures had been. These pictures writhed—stretched and twisted, as if the world had been spinning when the images were made.

Gaping mouths frozen in silent screams.

Bodies torn open; blood splashed everywhere.

The banner of Tir draped across the corpses.

Warmil's mouth worked. His fists clenched and unclenched. "All those lads . . ."

The way he said "lads" finally made something click in my mind. They'd been his family. He'd cared for them like an older brother might. And how would Brac feel if all the wee ones in Farmer Bradwir's brood were murdered and Brac felt he'd led to its happening?

In that moment, Warmil began to make sense to me. And I pitied him.

I forced my eyes away from the battle scene on the ground and closed them tight. I dug into my memory and pulled up a day that hid there, tucked away safe. Early autumn last year, just as the winds were cooling and the Menfor Sea wasn't fit for swimming anymore.

Brac and I stood on the pebbly beach below the cliffs of Pembrone. He'd said something to me. I couldn't remember what. In my mind's eye, his mouth moved, but I couldn't hear the sound. Must have been jesting, though, because I threw back my head and laughed. Brac beamed. And the breeze whipped through his straw-colored hair, loosed from his tail while we rested after a long day of harvest.

I set my mind harder on that breeze until I could feel it about my face and working through my hair.

My eyes fluttered open back at the Corsyth. Story strands so clear I couldn't see them but for the way they made the light shimmer curled through the air. My laughter and Brac's carried on the strands, and the breeze of them ruffled the leaves on the ground.

I squinted and directed them down. The wind quivered through the leaves, turning them over and around. In a moment, Warmil's painting of anguished death had fairly vanished, and clean leaves settled back into place on the forest floor.

Karlith reached out and touched Warmil's arm. "See that, Captain Bo-Awirth?" she said softly. "All things made new. Redeemed."

CHAPTER 24

BRAITH

BRAITH STOOD BEFORE THE KING'S DOOR. HER HAND WAS POISED to knock, but she hesitated.

Had enough time passed since council? She had taken her evening meal in her chambers the previous night, then avoided the king's table for breakfast this morning. But would she find him angry still about her call for mercy the previous day?

Braith almost turned to leave. But no. She must find it if she could. The king's behavior had become too troublesome to ignore.

She rapped on the door.

The wooden barrier creaked on its hinges. The face of Baedden, the king's bodyguard, appeared in the opening. He grunted.

The towering man never spoke more than a rumble or two.

Braith fixed her features into a pleasant mask. "Good morning, Baedden. Is my father available?"

Baedden paused, glanced over his shoulder. Then he turned back to Braith and nodded once. He opened the door fully and allowed her access to the king's front chamber.

Oil lamps dotted the walls of King Gareth's room. The firelight shimmered along the scar that stretched the length of Baedden's face on the left side.

Braith shuddered.

Baedden escorted her to the door of the king's study. His face bunched into a scowl and he nodded to the door.

Braith inclined her head. "Thank you, sir."

She used "sir" in the loosest sense of the word. Baedden was nothing more than a gruff mercenary.

Braith knocked on the study door. "Father?"

Silence.

She tried again. "Majesty?"

Movement stirred within the study. Then his brusque voice. "Yes?"

Braith steeled herself and entered the room. The king stood behind his huge desk, fingers drumming the polished writing surface. He stared at the floor and mumbled to himself. He had not changed from his dressing robe.

Braith frowned. "Father?"

The king started like he'd forgotten anyone had been at the door. "Oh, hello, darling."

Darling. Did that mean she'd been forgiven?

She smiled. "How are you this morning, Father?"

"Unwell, Braith." His face twisted into a troubled grimace. "Quite unwell."

Braith hesitated. It seemed the events of afternoon council the previous day had been forgotten. Perhaps it was best not to bring it up. But if he was still offended, better to apologize now than feel his wrath later.

"I hope you are not unwell on account of me, Your Majesty," Braith said.

"What?" The king's stormy gray eyes lifted from the floor and he turned to her. "You, darling?"

"Our disagreement at council yesterday."

"Oh, that." The king waved his hand. "No, no."

"Oh." Braith paused a moment, frowning. Then she crossed the room toward the king and placed her hand on his shoulder. "Then something else troubles you."

"Hmm," he murmured. "Nothing to be done about that."

He seemed to speak more to the late-morning air beyond the glass panes than to Braith. After a moment, he gave a fierce shake of his head and resumed pacing. Braith's hand slipped from his shoulder.

Then his voice boomed so suddenly, Braith jumped. "It is the disloyalty of my people that troubles me."

"Disloyalty, Your Majesty?"

"Do my armies not protect the people of Tir? Do my temples not keep the people pious and holy before their goddesses? Did I not expand the boundaries of their empire, fill their homes with slaves and servants? Do I not allow them to farm the land that belongs to me?" His fist slammed to the desk. "Why do they not love me?"

Braith swallowed hard. "They fear you, Majesty. Is it possible to have both the love and the fear of your people? I think it must, perhaps, be one or the other."

The king scratched his beard. "Yes." He nodded. "They fear me. And fear is better."

"Is it? They cower when they could be kissing your hand. If you had their love, you would also have their loyalty. Is that not better than their terror?"

"It is much too late for love and loyalty. That time has passed," the king said sharply. Before Braith could respond, he turned to her. "Braith, your virtues do you credit. But you must temper them if you are to rule one day, which you surely will after I'm gone. We must find you a strong husband. You will rule well together, he as the enforcer king and you the diplomatic queen. Just as you and I rule well together."

Braith stiffened. "A strong, ruthless husband—like Sir Dray Bo-Anffir?"

The king seemed to pay no attention to the name. "Yes, a strong husband is in order. You'll carry my mantle well after I'm gone. With him by your side."

"Naturally."

The king turned back toward the window. "It is important, Braith."

Braith glanced at the king's desk. There. Right on top, easily accessible. "Yes, Father." She reached for the parchment—what she had come for.

"Yes . . ." He moved as if to turn back around.

She froze, fingers outstretched toward his desk.

But he paused another moment, and Braith took her chance. She snatched the parchment and slipped it into the wide sleeve of her gown just in time as the king turned away from the window.

"Was there anything else?"

Braith inclined her head slightly. "No, Your Majesty. I'll retire to my chambers now. Cameria will see to luncheon before council. I just . . . couldn't bear it if things were uneasy between us for long."

The king patted her on the cheek. "Farewell, my dear. I'll see you at council."

Braith curtsied and then slipped from the room. She brushed past Baedden, who barely spared her a parting glance, then skittered into the hallway.

The parchment in her hand seemed to burn a hole through her palm—it was the first thing she had ever stolen.

She rounded the corner toward the east wing of the palace. And slammed bodily into a mass of purple velvet robes. Naith Bo-Offriad.

The parchment fluttered from her hand to the stone floor.

"Forgive me, Highness." Naith straightened his robe and smoothed hair that didn't exist on top of his head. "I did not see you."

Braith steadied herself. "Your Holiness." The calm of her voice belied the rattling breath in her lungs.

The stolen item lay on the ground in full view several feet away. The king's writing and wax seal were recognizable on the back, even from Braith's distance.

"There is no apology necessary, Your Holiness," she continued. "I was not minding my steps as I ought to have been."

The doughy man's face dimpled in all the wrong places with his humorless smile. "Well, I suppose that makes two of us. Now, shall I escort you wherever you might have been going?"

"That's not necessary, Your Eminence. I was just off to my chambers to take luncheon before council."

"Ah, perhaps we might dine together. I have something I wish to discuss with you."

Braith took a step. "Is that so?"

"Did you drop something, Highness?" Naith seemed to have just noticed the parchment. "Is that the king's writing?"

Before he could get a closer look, Braith leaned down and snatched it up. She nearly tumbled over in the process. "Indeed. I've just come from the king's chambers." She didn't offer anything else, and she prayed he daren't ask.

She cleared her throat and began a measured stroll. "Why should we not speak as we go?"

"Surely." Naith kept pace with Braith in silence for a moment. "Highness, I pray to the great goddesses that you'll forgive me any impertinence."

Braith smiled thinly but did not look at the high priest. "Avoid impertinence and I shall not have to."

Naith's chuckle held no warmth. "Sometimes duty demands that which one may find uncomfortable."

"What troubles you, High Priest Bo-Offriad? Is there something I can do for you?" The parchment moistened beneath her sweaty fingers.

"I've noticed, Highness, that your visits to the temple have been sporadic of late."

Once per moon. It was all her father required of her, though this clearly disappointed him. Even so, it was no secret between Braith and the king that she only attended temple services for the sake of the peasants. So they might see their rulers carrying on Tirian traditions. And that had been the agreement for some years.

"I attend as often as the king deems necessary," she said at last.

Naith's tone cooled. "As spiritual advisor to the royal family, I find this troublesome. Highness, I fear you've lost your faith."

"Have I? Well, if you are concerned about my weekly offerings, never fear. They will continue as always. Nothing has changed."

"But Princess Braith, if perhaps you were more intimately connected with the happenings at the temple in Urian . . ."

"It would strengthen your position at court?" Braith said dryly. Her patience had been spent. "Naith, my family keeps your temples well furnished. We keep your coffers—and your own pockets—quite full. Is that not enough? Surely this must be a raft you do not wish to upset, for fear of drowning."

Naith reddened. "I was only worried about your spiritual well-being, Highness."

"Of course. Thank you. Now if you'll excuse me . . ." She stepped toward the hallway leading to her chambers.

"What about our luncheon? There are still several things I'd like to discuss with you."

The parchment in Braith's hand grew slick. If she held it much longer, the ink might be washed away by her perspiration.

"I'm sorry, but I have other plans this afternoon. Another time, perhaps."

Naith's face hadn't calmed. "But Highness, it's really rather important that I—"

"You're too late," an intruding voice cut in. "The princess has plans already." Dray Bo-Anffir stepped from an adjoining hallway. "With me."

Braith's gaze hopped between the two men.

Naith's eyes narrowed. "You? The princess is to dine with you? I can hardly understand that. What could you have to discuss with her?"

Dray slipped an arm around Braith's waist. "Personal matters."

Braith swallowed down bile.

Naith's eyes widened, then narrowed to slits. He glared at Dray, then turned his fiery gaze on Braith. "I see."

Braith pushed Dray's hand from her waist. "Sir Dray forgets himself. There is no such personal business between us."

"But we do have plans for luncheon." Dray smirked at his adversary. "Sorry to disappoint, Your Holiness. You must save your wheedling and flattery for another day."

The two men stared each other down, and Braith decided whatever hatred sizzled in those gazes had little or nothing to do with her.

She cleared her throat. "Excuse me, gentlemen."

She managed several paces down the hallway before Dray caught up and matched her stride. "You're welcome."

She glanced at him but didn't dare stop walking. "Am I?"

"Got you out of having lunch with that insufferable toad, didn't I?"

"I suppose. But what is your price, I wonder? Must I now dine with an insufferable serpent?"

Dray threw his arm out in front of her, and Braith jerked to a sudden stop. "Now, now. That's not very nice, is it?"

"Forgive me." She shrank away from his blockade. "I grow weary of being used as a game piece."

Dray pressed his other hand against the wall so that Braith was trapped between his arms.

She glanced down the hallway, but Naith had already disappeared. She was alone with this man. Again.

"Sir Dray—"

He inched toward her. "I thought I told you to call me Dray." His breath found her bare neck.

Braith gasped. "Sir, my chambers are near and my servants are inside. I will scream."

Dray pulled back, what appeared to be genuine astonishment on his face. "Scream?"

"You guess rightly my father would probably welcome some manner of union between the two of us. But if you simply take what you're after, I assure you, you will find a permanent home in the dungeon." She lifted her chin, though it quivered. "Please do not dishonor me by forcing me to be more specific."

Something Braith had never seen there before settled onto the face of Dray Bo-Anffir—a wounded look swimming in his eyes, like a child who had been unfairly reprimanded. "Braith, did you think I would—"

"Please. I beg you not to continue. You have quite the reputation, as we both know. You have been cultivating it for years. But I'm not a lady-in-waiting or a kitchen maid or the lass whose father manages the stables that you might similarly take advantage of me with no repercussions."

Dray stepped back. "I—I'd not force you, Braith. That's not what I—"

"Please, Sir Dray!" Braith's face flamed. "I do not wish to discuss the particulars with you."

The wounded look hardened. "Oh, now I understand. I have a reputation at court, therefore I must surely have forced those women. I'm a godless man, therefore I have no scruples at all. I make no attempt at piety and am honest about my designs and so am rewarded by you thinking of me in the most heinous of terms. It is quite a bit easier to think in black and white, isn't it, Princess?"

The fire spread from Braith's cheeks all throughout her body. Not embarrassment now, but utter indignation.

"If a lady has been seduced and deceived, do you call that willingness? If you assert your political power, promise her wealth or even just your affection, perhaps you have not used force. But you have used manipulation, and it is the same in my eyes."

"Yes, it would be." He snorted. "Black-and-white Braith. Braith the ice princess."

She bristled. "Call me what you will, sir, but any man who freely admits to seeking himself above all things disqualifies himself from my esteem—whether he can understand why or not. Whether you seek to force, seduce, manipulate, or try to coerce me into agreeing to your plans, your aim is the same. You wish to set yourself upon the throne of Tir when you've no right to it."

Angry tears burned her eyes. "And that makes you a wicked man."

Dray's voice turned to stone. "So be it."

The next moment, Braith's back slammed into the wall and Dray's lips pressed against hers. She only just managed to keep the stolen parchment between her fingers under the force of the blow.

Braith struggled. She jerked away and screamed. The shriek, high and panicked, echoed down the hall.

Dray backed away of his own accord. "You'll want to make sure that parchment is well hidden before the guardsmen arrive, Princess."

He knew. The blood drained from Braith's face.

Clanking armor announced the guardsmen before Braith could see them. Moments later, two soldiers came into view. Both skidded to a halt at the sight of Braith and Dray alone in the hallway.

One soldier spoke. "Highness?"

The threat slipped away from Dray's face. "Ah, well done, good knights. Your quick response does you credit. But there's nothing to fear. Her Highness merely saw a rope-tail skitter down the hall, as they will do. I happened to be nearby, and all is well now."

Braith's knees wobbled beneath her gown. He knew. Her position was tenuous at best.

So she turned to Dray and flashed a wan smile. "Thank you, Sir Dray. Hopefully the rope-tail has skittered away for good." She nodded to the guardsmen. "Shall we?"

The soldiers shuffled behind her as she hurried to her chambers.

Cameria stood in the hallway before the princess's chamber doors. "My lady?"

The clanking of the guardsmen's armor stopped as they resumed their positions beside Braith's chamber doors. Braith grabbed Cameria's outstretched hand but couldn't seem to find words yet.

"My lady, I heard you scream." Cameria's dark eyes were wide enough for Braith to see her own reflection in them. "What's happened?"

Braith glanced at the guardsmen, then nodded toward her door. "Let us take luncheon, Cameria. I've had a fright."

The two women slipped into Braith's chambers, and Braith instantly sank into a chair in her front room. She slapped the parchment to the table beside her lunch, then dropped her head into her hands.

"Princess." Cameria fell to her knees beside Braith. "Tell me what happened."

"Officially, I saw a rope-tail," Braith said shakily. "So let us hold to that if anyone asks."

"And the truth?"

The truth stuck in Braith's throat. She forced it out. "I had another encounter with Sir Dray. His intentions have been made quite clear. Also . . ." She hesitated, but then continued. "I stole this from my father's desk." She slid the parchment across the table toward Cameria.

Cameria gasped. "Stole, my lady?"

"I suppose there truly is a first time for everything."

"But what is it?"

Braith eyed the wretched thing. "I don't know yet. Something the king scribbled during council yesterday afternoon. I couldn't see it from where I sat, and I had to know." She frowned at her friend. "Something is amiss, Cameria."

Cameria's lips pressed together. She kept her gaze focused on Braith. "I'll leave you, my lady." She slid the parchment back toward the princess without looking at it. "So that you might read it alone." She hesitated. "If you think it's safe for you to be alone."

"I have the soldiers outside my door. If they can't protect me, we'd be lost anyway." She sighed. "Thank you, Cameria."

Cameria nodded. She picked up a basket with a cloth over its contents. "May I take this extra food, my lady?"

Braith nodded. "Of course."

Cameria curtsied, then slipped from the room. Braith rose and bolted the door behind her.

Then she returned to the table and stared at the parchment. She almost didn't wish to read it now, so great was her dread. But the king's stormy expression and the distracted way he muttered to himself—and his adherence to secret laws Braith had never heard of—forced her hand. It was too much to ignore.

She picked up the parchment—the one the king had shown to Dray at council.

She flipped it over and scanned the words. A warrant for the story peddler, Tanwen En-Yestin. Braith gasped at the next words. "Arrest or execution. Reward: two hundred gold pieces."

The king never issued such a warrant with any other design than to kill. If the girl could be captured alive, it would only be so she might be tortured for information or some other purpose before her eventual demise.

And the king was willing to part with two hundred gold over it.

Braith let the makeshift warrant flutter back to the table and covered her face with her hands.

If there was any god to listen, Braith prayed Tanwen En-Yestin would meet with a quick, merciful end.

CHAPTER 25

TANWEN

"KARLITH?"

Karlith looked up at me from the fire where she was getting an iron pot situated for the evening stew. "Aye, lass? Something bothering you?"

"No. Not exactly." I scooted beside her and absently added dry twigs to the blaze. "I just wondered . . ."

Truly, I felt a fool for even thinking of asking.

"Aye, Tannie?"

"I want to be able to do more with my storytelling," I blurted. "If you all are on the side of right—and I believe you are—then I should be doing all I can to help. But I feel like my stories are nothing more than practiced loads of fluff that the king wants me to know, and a couple bits of fairy stories left over from my childhood. Can you teach me how to be a real storyteller?"

Karlith smiled, but I could tell it was a smile that meant no. "Tannie, we agreed before we brought you here that our aim was to protect you. We're not asking you to join a revolution or stick your neck out. We've been watching you all this time to keep you safe."

"I've been here a week." I knew it sounded feeble as a new hatchling. "It isn't long, but it's long enough for me to know."

"Know what, child?"

"That everything you've told me is real. The pieces fit together—the king and who he is. Why we're all stuck hiding out in a swamp. All I need to do is look at Gryfelle to know that all this business with crowned stories and squashing things down isn't right. I want to learn to be a different sort of teller."

Karlith sighed. "Believe me, Tannie, I'd like to help you. But—"

"Karlith, aren't you the one always going on about truth? You say art has a way of revealing it, but you don't want to let me learn how. Why?"

She chuckled. "I was going to say I can't teach you because I'm not a storyteller. I'm a colormaster, lass."

"Oh. Sorry." I bit my lip. "Maybe Zel could—"

Karlith shook her head before I could finish. "Zel is still shackled to the ghosts of his past. He isn't sure we ought to be using our gifts. Leastways, not in the way War and Dylun would like. He's frightened of his weaving gift, and I don't think he'd help you grow yours."

And that left . . .

"I'll teach you, Tannie."

I glanced up. Of course. There he was, leaning against a tree, arms folded and smiling at me.

Sure as stars in the sky, it wasn't that I didn't want Mor to teach me. But I'd scarcely been in the Corsyth a week and already it was becoming unbearable to be around Mor without speaking my mind to him.

Or in this case, my heart.

Not free, Tanwen. Not free, not free, not free.

Didn't help much, but the constant reminders would sink in eventually—wouldn't they?

But I smiled and tried to be casual about it. "Aye, Mor. That'd be nice. . ."

"Catch." Before I could even blink, Mor shot a strand of story toward me—sparkling, silvery mist.

In a flash I answered with a strand of fire that swallowed the mist before it could reach me. "Hey, now! What was that all about?"

Mor grinned. "Test number one. You passed. Good reflexes."

I glared at him. "Rude."

"Aye." He laughed. "But I'm a pirate. What did you expect? And you answered, didn't you?"

"I suppose. Hey, how'd that happen? I didn't even think about it. I didn't have an idea and make it come out as a strand. I just reacted."

"Exactly." Mor moved to an open space between the trees and beckoned me to follow. "It's a good sign. You're beginning to fuse back together."

"Was I broken apart?"

"Yes, actually." He touched a finger to his temple. "The story peddler lived here, building stories as she'd been taught with the aim of selling them. The weaver lives here." He placed a hand over his heart. "When you've rejoined the head and heart, the art will happen without you needing to think about it."

Fear tweaked my stomach. "But I can control it, right? I mean, all my heart isn't going to pour out into the air without me wanting it to, is it?"

"Eventually. We've all had a couple slips we wish hadn't happened." He took a step away from me. "Now I want you to close your eyes. I want you to think about what Karlith always says. Art has a way of revealing truth. Don't think too hard—you already know how to think a story. I want you to *feel* this one."

I obeyed. I tried to wipe away all the practiced words of the crowned stories, at least for the moment. My fingers tingled. Strands poured from them, I knew. But I didn't dare open my eyes to see what they were.

Another moment ticked by. I exhaled. It had crystalized. I could feel it the way you sense the presence of someone nearby before you turn around and see him.

I opened my eyes. A clear glass heart hovered in the air between me and Mor. Painted-wings fluttered inside the hollow heart.

I stared at it. "They're moving. My crystallized story is moving."

"Aye." He nodded. "Another good sign—you're making stories that can do things."

"But . . . what is it?"

"You tell me."

I studied the heart. A symbol was etched in the glass—a round, twisted knot, just like the charm I wore on a cord around my neck.

"It's mine," I realized aloud. "It's my heart. Look." I pointed. "There's a painted-wing made of leather that's like Father's journal. And that sunset-pink one? Mother's curtains in my room are that exact color."

A sparkling-blue painted-wing with gold circles on its wings caught my eye. Gold circles that looked a lot like gold hoop earrings. Best not to explain that one.

"See there? The one that looks like it's made of straw? That's Brac."

"All the people you love." Mor glanced at me for a heartbeat, then looked away.

"Something like that." I bit my lip. "Mor—"

But before I could say anything else, the heart split apart with a loud crack. The glass shattered to pieces before the shards disappeared into the air. The painted-wings hovered for a moment, then an unseen force sucked them down to the ground. A sound like squealing animals filled my ears, then the painted wings vanished as if pulled into the earth by invisible hands.

The Corsyth lay deathly still as I stared into the void where my heart had been.

I swallowed the lump in my throat. "What happened?"

Mor frowned. "A warning, I think. Your heart knows what's at stake, Tannie. It knows what you stand to lose."

"I've already lost my parents."

"But you have memories—ideas of them, at least. Those trinkets and relics of your family. You've preserved all you've been able to."

Tears stung my eyes. "And if I don't stop squishing down the art—the truth—that wants to be told, I'll lose those too."

"Aye. You'll lose everything."

With a last, lingering glance at me, he turned and strode toward the log where Gryfelle sat, a hand to her temple. Like her head ached again. Or else like she was trying to grasp at rocks that wouldn't stop sliding.

CHAPTER 26

TANWEN

MOR FOLDED HIS ARMS ACROSS HIS CHEST. "I DON'T LIKE IT, Warmil. I think Tanwen should stay here."

His worried glance simultaneously made my cheeks flush and my heart fill with dread.

Warmil chewed his lip a moment. "I understand your objection. But you see my point, don't you? It's been a full two weeks. Tanwen is one of us now, and we all have to be trained. What if Aeron, Dylun, and I are ambushed on our watch tonight? What happens when Gryfelle has another spell? You know she could take one of us down with her."

Gryfelle's intake of breath could be seen from where I stood. She lifted her chin like she felt the point of a sword at her back. Mor's eyes blazed blue fire.

Warmil stiffened. "Forgive me. I don't mean to be unfeeling. But we have to consider the possibility. Tanwen needs to be fully aware of how we function here—where we get our supplies, who our contacts are, which areas to avoid. Bowyd is our main supply center, and if our allies there don't know Tanwen's face, they'll never help her." He shook his head. "We can't bring her into our fold if she's sheltering in the Corsyth."

"I'll be all right, Mor." I flashed a smile at him—hoped it hid the shakiness I felt. "I don't mind. If I'm going to stay, I need to learn."

Mor didn't smile. He glanced at Zelyth. "What do you think, mate?"

Zelyth looked up at me from where he sharpened a dagger. "I

don't like it any more than you do." He pushed himself to his feet and winced. "But I think War's right. We can't guess who'll make it to the next sunrise around here, so Tannie needs to learn."

The drawl of his accent on my nickname served me a sharp reminder of the life I'd left behind. It'd been two weeks since I'd heard Brac's voice, his drawl, ripple through my name like that. It seemed a lifetime ago.

I missed my best friend.

"Lass." Karlith put her hand on my arm. "What troubles you, love? Are you afraid to go to Bowyd?"

I pressed my lips together. "It's not that. It's nothing, really."

Karlith didn't push, but she squeezed my shoulder like maybe she understood.

Mor nodded once. "All right. Seems I'm overruled. I'll let this happen on one condition. I scout up ahead. If there's any danger—any at all—Tanwen must be brought back to the Corsyth immediately. Top priority, War. We brought her to the Corsyth to protect her, and I'll be flayed if harm will come to her on my watch."

Warmil's sky-blue eyes glittered. "I'd not see harm come to the daughter of Yestin Bo-Arthio either. You know that."

Father's full name. "Warmil, did you know my father?"

Dylun looked at me. "There's not a subject of the *true* king alive today who doesn't know your father's name."

My father, with his sleepy study in the dusty, poky village of Pembrone was known around Tir?

"But—" I could barely splutter the words past my disbelief. "But why?"

"No time." Warmil nodded toward the treetops. "If we want to be back before nightfall, we need to start now."

"Then tell me on the way." I wasn't backing away from this one so easy. "I deserve to hear."

Karlith squeezed my shoulder again. "Course you do, lass. But Yestin's name is best not spoken within a league of civilization."

Cethor's tears. What had he done? This man I'd always imagined as a merchant or a shopkeeper. What if he'd been a villain instead?

I frowned at the others, all staring at me like I had any idea what to say. "Was he bad?"

Warmil shook his head then dropped his gaze to the ground. "No, Tanwen. He was very good."

And that seemed to be all I was getting until our mission was over. And if that was the case . . .

I squared my shoulders. "Right, then. Let's go to Bowyd."

I studied each face in turn while the riverboat slipped through the water toward Bowyd. Who'd be most likely to divulge some secrets?

"Karlith?"

Her sleepy eyes lifted to mine. "Yes, love?"

"Did you know him? I mean, did you ever see my father with your own two eyes?"

Karlith smiled a little. "Sorry, lass. I never saw him. But I sure knew of him. You've seen him more than anyone else in this boat."

I slumped onto the bench. "But I don't remember."

"I know, lass. And I don't pretend it's not been hard on you. Life, that is."

"So . . ." I didn't want to say it aloud. "So, then, he's really dead?"

"Yes, lass. Not seen or heard from in over a decade."

"Karlith, please. Tell me who he was."

She paused a moment.

Warmil's hiss silenced anything she might have said. "Bowyd's dock ahead. Time to cut the chatter."

Karlith whispered kindly, "In good time."

Mor, Zel, and Aeron eased the boat toward the dock. A chilly breeze stirred through the trees lining the shore.

All faces tensed. Every eye watched.

"War, you take Tanwen there." Mor nodded to a rocky part of the bank a bit off the main dock area. "Guard her while I scout up ahead." He looked at the others. "You'll secure the boat, then keep to the trees. Aye?"

Nods and ayes all around.

"Good." He turned to set off. "See you soon."

Warmil didn't do a very fine job acting like a normal person. At the rocks he looked exactly like a soldier guarding a peasant lass for no apparent reason—back stiff, eyes scanning the area, hand ready on the hilt of a short sword hidden beneath his cloak. I didn't suppose he was great at secret missions.

"Warmil, what's our story to be?"

He grunted. "Story? I'm a colormaster, not a storyteller."

"Not like that. I mean what if someone stops to question us?"

"A cover story?"

"Aye. One of those." I stifled a laugh. "You're not blending into anything at the moment, if you want to know the ugly truth."

He frowned. Seemed like he tried to relax his posture somewhat, but he only ended up looking like he was crouching down to spring.

"How about you be my father. And you've taken me to Bowyd to shop for some material for a new dress. But we traveled a long way in our boat, since our farm is far, so we stopped here to rest. You're spent, as a person would be, rowing a boat all the way from our farm, which is why we're resting here. But I really want to get to the shops so I can find the perfect fabric—for my wedding dress! And—"

"Tanwen!"

I jumped at his harsh growl. "What?"

But then I saw the wispy strands of story dancing before us—pale yellow, just like Evan Ma-Griod wore to her wedding last year. Blushing, I waved my hands to clear the strands before anyone saw them. "Oops."

Guessed I wasn't good at secret missions either.

Warmil cleared his throat. "You were saying something about blending in?"

I smiled wryly.

A moment of silence passed, then he glanced at me. "You really think I look old enough to be your father?"

I snorted. "You *are* old enough to be my father."

Warmil grunted and turned to look out across the rippling water. "Odd how one's life slips by unnoticed sometimes."

I wound a lock of hair around my finger, then shifted it back and forth to watch it shimmer gold in the sunlight. "I don't think my life's too keen on slipping by unnoticed." I nodded to the river. "I seem to ping off one bank of the river, then bounce off the other. Then slam into a rock or two. Or twelve."

Warmil smiled—really and truly smiled, right there in that rocky outcropping by the river.

I laughed. "You have a nice smile!"

"What?" He started like he'd taken a bolt of lightning.

"Your smile is nice. You should use it more often." I tucked my knees up under my chin and tugged on my skirt hem so my toes were covered. "Why didn't you ever marry, Warmil?"

He shrugged. "It didn't occur to me."

"Didn't occur to you? Like, you managed not to notice every person around you was married?"

"I was busy with my command."

I quieted a touch then, because I knew he was thinking about those lads he'd lost. "You could get married now, couldn't you?"

All traces of smile dropped off his face. "No."

"No?"

"No. Of course not. Who in the name of the tax collector would I marry?"

I had to bite down on my lip to keep from shouting out her name. "There are some lasses about, Captain. And you're still handsome enough to convince one of them to get married, don't you think?"

"No. I thought you said I looked old enough to be your father."

"You do. But old people can be handsome too."

He tossed a half-hearted glare in my direction, and I giggled.

He cleared his throat. "Yes, I suppose you think I should marry Gryfelle, or some other such nonsense. That poor lass has enough to contend with."

Maybe if I banged his head against the rock it would knock some sense into him. "No. Even if she were well, Gryfelle's not for you. It'll have to be someone else."

"Not Karlith." Warmil rolled his eyes. "You know little of her heart if you think she'd ever give it to another. Lundir is the only man she could love. She's a decade older than I, in any case."

"No, not Karlith." I fixed my gaze on him and aimed to keep it there until he understood my meaning. Should only take him about a moon. He suddenly looked at me with a touch of horror.

I stared back, puzzled, but then it dawned on me. "No! I didn't mean *me*!"

He just gave another glare and muttered it was all nonsense.

"Try again," I pleaded.

Suddenly those blue eyes went wide, and I knew he'd finally stumbled upon it. "Aeron?"

"She's in love with you. Never noticed?"

"Impossible." He waved his hand, spluttered something that didn't even sound like Tirian, then plopped down beside me on the rock. "She couldn't possibly."

"Why not?"

"She was just a lass when she joined up. A child. I'm sure she looks at me like a father."

"A child!" I threw back my head and laughed. "Old enough to die in the king's service, though. How old was she when she joined? Think hard now."

He shook his head a little. "Fifteen. Maybe sixteen."

"Fifteen." I looked at him. "I'm only a lass of seventeen and I know more about love than you do. Hardly a child."

"Excuse me, but—"

"Oh, Captain, really. Poor Aeron's probably been in love with you since she joined up at fifteen. How long ago was that?"

"Ten years."

"So that makes Aeron twenty-five. Still lots of years for having wee ones."

Warmil froze so still he might've been a statue.

I mused, "Wonder if they'll be born with your gray hair."

"This is . . . ridiculous."

"Warmil." I made sure to catch his gaze. "Ask her."

He jerked to his feet. "What? Where?"

I pulled him back down by his cloak. "Not now. Maybe when it's just the two of you. Like when you're out on watch together. You could make sure you're well away from the Corsyth so you'll not be heard. Take her to a place where the trees aren't so thick and the starlight is sparkling overhead. Then you take her hand in yours and tell her you've been thinking a lot lately, and you wonder if she might be willing to let you be *her* knight for all the rest of her days!"

"Tanwen!"

A black-and-white story strand snaked through the air while a silver-gray one followed behind. The strands swirled into a heart when I paused.

"Oops." I waved the strands away. "Sorry."

Warmil opened his mouth, but before he could say anything, a sharp whistle brought his hand to his sword hilt again. "That's Mor. Follow me."

He slipped back into the trees, me just behind. Another whistle sounded, and a moment later I saw Gryfelle's green dress appear from one clump of trees, Zel's straw-colored hair from another, and all the others from different directions. Finally Mor appeared, chest heaving and something clutched in one hand. Paper, it looked like.

"We need to get out of here. Now." Mor smoothed out the crumpled paper. "Look. These are all over Bowyd."

My hands dropped to my sides and I took a step back. "That—that's me."

An image so perfect—so exact—that I might've been looking into a still pond on a clear day stared back at me. My nose, my seastone-blue eyes, my dark golden hair, pinned up in fancy braids and curls the way I liked it when I was peddling. And the words screaming across the top of the slip weren't lost on me: TANWEN EN-YESTIN, CAPTURE OR KILL. REWARD: TWO HUNDRED GOLD PIECES.

"How?" I shook my head to make the fog of horror clear away from my mind. "How did they do this?"

Dylun snatched the paper from Mor. "Gareth must have a

colormaster. Probably locked in the dungeons, doing the tyrant's business under threat of noose or chopping block."

Warmil snorted. "Or working for the usurper quite willingly—for a hefty salary. High ideals be fried, Dylun. Not all weavers are on our side."

Dylun didn't raise a fuss. This once. "Whatever the case, it's a colormaster." He glanced up at me, then back at the paper. "No other way a portrait could be this exact without you sitting for it. They must have spoken to many witnesses." He turned his dark eyes on me. "Friends. Family."

"There's no family to talk to." But as soon as it flew from my mouth, I realized it wasn't true. "Except Farmer and Ma-Bradwir." I almost couldn't get the word past my heart. "And Brac. And the little ones."

Zel peered over Dylun's shoulder. "What's it say?"

Dylun's face stormed. "Kill or capture. Says here capture is preferable—which means Gareth plans to torture you."

I supposed they were used to this business, but I couldn't quite grasp how he threw that out there so callously.

"Ah, here it says it's suspected Tanwen is 'in league with the outlaws who live in Codewig Forest.' That puts a nice fine point on it for the bounty hunters."

"Bounty hunters?" The squeak didn't sound like it could have come from my mouth. "People will be hunting me?"

Dylun held up the paper. "Two hundred gold pieces, Tanwen."

"Two hundred!" Zelyth practically shouted. "I could feed Ifmere, the baby, myself, and my father's whole family for years on two hundred gold." He glanced at me, and I must have had terror written all over my face. "Not that I would, Tannie. I only mean to say Gareth's turned every peasant from here to Haribi against us by offering such a bounty. Nowhere is safe now."

Gryfelle sighed. "Well, it's not as if anywhere was truly safe before. We shall simply stay to the Corsyth as much as possible. It's well protected, and if we can manage to hide out long enough, the bounty hunters will move on to their next mark and the peasants will be less alert."

"We need our supplies before we leave," Mor said. He crossed his arms. "I'll not take Tanwen into town now. Not for any reason."

Warmil nodded. "No, of course. We'll stay and ready the boat. But don't you go either, Mor. You're too known around here. If the peasants are looking, someone's bound to notice you."

"Aye, then it has to be me," Zel said. "I can blend in to the marketplace like any of the other dozens of farmers there to sell crops."

Gryfelle put a hand on Zelyth's injured arm. "But not alone."

"I'll go." Aeron fastened her cloak around her shoulders. "Of the rest of us, I'm least visible."

"Least visible?" I eyed the tall woman in trousers with hair shorn at her chin like a lad's.

She spared me a tart glance. "I didn't say invisible. I said least visible. Mor, War, and Karlith have appeared on far too many kill-or-capture orders themselves. Any noble or official might recognize Gryfelle." Aeron rolled her eyes. "And one can hear Dylun's loud mouth a league off."

Dylun shrugged some manner of agreement.

"Aeron . . ." Warmil's gruff voice might've made me smile under any other circumstances. "You'll be careful?"

Aeron frowned. "Of course, Captain." She eyed him like he'd grown an extra head.

"Right," Zel said as he checked his hidden dagger. "It'll be me and Aeron getting the supplies. The rest of you ready the boat." He turned to me. "And Tannie—stay hidden, lass."

I nodded. I leaned in closer to Dylun to read over his shoulder. "Dylun, what's that say on the bottom there?" I pointed to the smaller words printed along the bottom of the page, which I couldn't quite make out from my distance.

Dylun scanned the lines. "Says anyone who withholds information about you or your whereabouts will be tried for treason."

My insides twisted. "Meaning what?"

Dylun shrugged. "If the guard wants information about you,

they'll question the people in your town. If they can't get what they want easily, they might arrest or torture the holdouts."

Without another word, I took off at a run toward Bowyd. The others called after me, and I could hear crunching in the brush behind me. But I didn't care. I could only think of one thing.

The Bradwirs.

CHAPTER 27

TANWEN

"Tannie!" Mor's cry tugged at one heartstring while all the rest pulled me back to Pembrone.

I could just see the town of Bowyd ahead—the low stone buildings of the shops and the makeshift tents and barrels of the marketplace. I could hire a riverboat once I got there. Promise some riverman a heap of coins to get me where I wanted without asking any questions. Then I'd—

Before the rest of the plan could crystallize, a whole mess of hands grabbed me from behind.

"Put me down! I have to get to Pembrone!"

"Slow down, Tanwen." Warmil set me back on my feet, but he, Zelyth, and Mor didn't let me go. "Tell us what's wrong."

A fire-orange story strand shot from my hand, quite by accident, and a frustrated growl rolled out with it. Warmil dodged the strand, but his eyes said it all. *Get it under control, Tanwen, or we'll all be caught.*

I took a deep breath and willed my hammering heart to slow. "Farmer and Ma-Bradwir. The wee ones. Brac." I swallowed the rising bile. "If the guard questions them, they'll never cooperate. And the guard will arrest Brac and take him to Urian to be tortured, or worse. I can't let that happen. Not because of me. I—"

But I couldn't get the last bit out. What I felt for Brac had been turned upside down and inside out since I left Pembrone. If it'd ever been right-side up to begin with.

I stole a glance at Mor and his dagger-sharp gaze. "Farmer Bradwir and the family is the closest thing I've known to kin."

Mor's eyes flickered—like I'd stoked something he was hoping to smother. More secret pain and unspoken mysteries. But all he said was, "Believe me, Tannie. We understand."

Tears pricked my eyes. "Brac asked me to marry him," I blurted. "I always said no . . . for a lot of reasons. Not the smallest being I couldn't imagine getting stuck on a farm in Pembrone the rest of my life. I wanted to go to Urian and be Royal Storyteller."

The words tasted sour in my mouth, and I realized I'd been keeping them stuffed inside for fear my new friends would despise me if they knew. Oh well. It was out now.

I wiped tears from my cheeks. "I knew the king wasn't kind, or anything like it." I sniffled. "But I hadn't guessed—I mean, the things you've told me. I didn't know about all that. I thought I could finally stop struggling to keep my belly full if I were Royal Storyteller in the palace." I looked at Warmil. "Stop pinging off the banks of the river, you know?"

Warmil looked like he understood.

"And now everything's a mess. Brac's going to be killed because of me." I smacked a hand to my forehead. "I gave him hope, you know. Just before my disaster of a tour. Told him I'd consider settling on him. He'll die, thinking it's for his future wife. I'm a traitor to all who have ever shown me kindness." I hiccupped like a sniffling toddler. But I couldn't help it and I didn't care.

Zel squeezed my shoulder. "They mightn't have got to him, Tannie. Think he would've known enough to hide out for a while?"

I snorted. "No. He's like to be out looking for me. Left him no note, no warning. Just disappeared on him."

I knew it had made sense at the time to leave Brac and Farmer Bradwir's family out of this whole mess. But now it seemed utterly foolish. What were they to think when I just disappeared one night, and the next day the guard is crawling all over Pembrone looking for me?

"I have to get back. I have to see what's happened. If he's been taken already and there's not a blazing thing I can do about it, at least I'll know." I fired off my gaze into each of their eyes. "I have to know."

They looked at each other—Mor, Zel, and Warmil, with the others behind us just a bit. They seemed to be talking through their eyes, but I couldn't guess what was being said in this silent sort of conversation. Tanwen En-Yestin never went in much for silent.

Finally, Warmil nodded. "All right, Tanwen. We'll travel back to Pembrone so you can see your lad."

I cringed at the word. Hadn't he been listening?

He went on, "But you can't just go charging into Bowyd. We need a plan."

Mor smiled. "Don't know if you've noticed, but you seem to be losing control of your strands a bit."

"Good." Dylun's voice from nearby. "She's finally getting in touch with her gift, not just spitting back those blasted crowned stories."

Warmil rolled his eyes. "Artistic freedom aside, it's dangerous."

"I'll try to get it under control," I promised. "Whatever you want, if you'll only take me back to Pembrone."

The jest in Mor's eyes ramped up, but it looked a little forced. "Sure you're not settled on Brac for your lad after all?"

I shot him a glare that could peel the skin off a watta root. "Quite."

"Fine, fine." Warmil nodded. "First we'll need to—"

"There!" An intruding voice cut in from the edge of the trees. "I see her!"

No.

Next thing I knew, an arrow whizzed past me. But it had come from our party. I whipped around to see Aeron pull another from the quiver at her hip. Mor grabbed my hand and began to tug me back toward the boat. But a half dozen guardsmen leaped from the cover of the trees beside us. Then more from behind.

Surrounded.

A split-second passed—just enough time for a loaded glance from Mor. Then he shoved me unceremoniously to the ground and ducked beneath the sword of a guardsman.

Metal clanged—swords crossing. Arrows flew by. Bursts of color, light, and fire exploded all around.

Mor yanked me back to my feet. Sweat glistened on his forehead already. "Run."

I tried to obey, but I didn't know which way to turn. My feet felt plastered to the earth. Then, without warning, white light shot from my palms. One beam smashed into the chest of a guardsman, and he stumbled backward.

I stared down at my glowing palms. What in the name of the goddesses was happening to me?

"Tanwen, run!" Gryfelle's voice, but I couldn't see her.

I picked up my skirt to go, but then an arm circled my waist from behind and yanked me back.

"No!" I struggled against the death grip. "Let me go!"

I looked ahead and saw Warmil take a cutting stroke from a guardsman's sword. Karlith barely held a soldier back with a stream of water pouring from her hand. Fireballs blossomed all around Dylun.

"Tannie!" Mor's voice. But where was he?

Then my heart sank. A stone's throw away. Surrounded on all sides by guardsmen playing for keeps.

Zel, Gryfelle, Aeron. . . . All surrounded, all battling for survival. I had to help them.

I strained against my captor. What strands could I make that'd sting real nice and make him let go? But before I could sprout a real plan, a dull thump sounded by my ear. Then another. Pain in my head, then only blackness.

CHAPTER 28

TANWEN

A HAZE OF VOICES FLOATED TOWARD ME, BUT I COULDN'T SEEM to open my eyes. I shifted, groaned, then collapsed back to the hard surface beneath me.

"How hard did you hit the lass, Bo-Milwir?"

"By 'lass,' I suppose you mean the prisoner accused of treason?" A harsher, older voice. "Don't go soft on me, Bo-Ifun."

A sigh. "She's barely older than my sister."

"Well, she ain't your sister, I'll remind you. And I'd wager your sister's never been accused of high treason."

"Will both of you shut up?" A reedy voice behind me. "These docks are difficult enough to traverse without you two rambling on like a couple of women."

A spark of annoyance flickered in me.

Then the harsh, growling voice again. "I'll speak when I feel like it, Bo-Forir. And I'll thank you to keep your sentiments in your head, else I'll knock it from your shoulders."

A grumble from the reedy voice.

The kinder voice: "Didn't have to hit her so hard is all I'm saying. Been out for ages. Could have done some real damage."

Great. That was all I needed. A little brain injury.

"And she didn't have to land herself on the king's kill-or-capture list, but there we have the way of it." A gravelly laugh. "Calm your conscience, lad. We'll dock before long, then it's a short stretch into the city. We'll deliver the girl like Captain ordered, and that'll be the end of it."

The kind voice lowered. "For us, I suppose. Not for her."

"Not your concern. Besides, I don't think it was my knocks to the head that put her out. Didn't you see her get hit by one of them strands? That's what kept her down so long, if you ask me."

"And it wouldn't have happened if you hadn't been using her as a shield."

A snort. "It's a wonder you ever joined up, Bo-Ifun. You haven't the stomach to be a guardsman."

"Oh, no?" Now the kind voice colored with anger. "I can best you with a sword."

Another gravelly laugh. "Takes more than a swift sword to make the kind of guardsman that serves the king the way he likes. Most young soldiers I know wouldn't be thinking much of the lass's safety just now, if you catch my drift."

I caught his drift fair enough, and I fought the fog in my head to get it to clear. A lass needed her wits about her if she had any hope of keeping herself safe around a man such as this Bo-Milwir gem.

"Besides, you saw what them outlaws was doing back in Codewig. The lass herself knocked Bo-Forir here on his backside with one of them strands of light. Safer for all of us if she's out for the trip."

"I guess."

I forced my way through the haze. "D'others?" My mouth felt full of pebbles, but I managed to pry open my eyes.

"Look who's up." A pockmarked face came into view. "It's your lass, Bo-Ifun."

Bo-Ifun and I both ignored him. "The others?" I asked again, clearer this time. Then I pushed a hand against my throbbing temple. "Where are they?"

A long moment of silence answered me.

Then pockmarked Bo-Milwir grinned. "Don't worry, lass. I'm sure their bodies have sunk to the bottom of the river by now."

Dread rose inside me until I thought I'd be sick all over the floor of the boat.

"Oh, enough, Bo-Milwir." A hand appeared in front of me, then a new face—young and kind, if a bit grim. He had very fair hair pulled back in a tail, just the same color as Celyn En-Rhys's back home. "We don't know what's happened to them. Our orders were for you, so we got you out as quickly as we could."

I took the young man's hand and let him help me to a sitting position, only then realizing my hands were bound with rope in front of me. Even so, relief trickled from my head all the way to my toes. There was still a chance my Corsyth friends were alive. Still a chance Mor was—

But I squashed that thought before it could fully blossom.

Bo-Milwir shook his head. "No sport to be had when Bo-Ifun's around. Might as well be serving in a unit with my mother. Or worse, my wife."

I blinked, trying to focus the jumble of shapes and colors swirling before me. We were still on the same river, I supposed, for it looked much like the river by Bowyd. Except it had widened to triple the size. Might've been a lake, if I didn't know better.

Docks poked out from the shoreline, just like the ones I'd seen before in the small river towns on the peninsula, but there were dozens of them here. Every few yards, it seemed, another dock jutted into the water. And people swarmed all over each of them. Soldiers, peasants, ladies in fine dresses like Gryfelle's, only not so worn. Stands and tables and barrels seemed to grow right out of the very ground, and each had a young lad shouting his wares—fish hooks, new rope, hot flatcakes, fresh berries, salted fillets. Seemed a girl could find anything she might want or need for a day of fishing or lounging by the river.

I didn't suppose I'd be fishing or lounging today.

Every dock gave way to a paved stone pathway. It seemed they met up to make a proper street in the distance—three times the size of Pembrone's main thoroughfare, which was the only paved street we had.

"Ashton?" I couldn't seem to form my complete question aloud. But I knew the city of Ashton lay some distance beyond the Codewig forest, and I'd heard the main street was larger than anything we had on the peninsula.

Bo-Milwir threw back his head and roared. "You are fresh off the farm, aren't you?"

I glared at him and tried to swallow the feeling of rocks in my mouth so I could speak properly. "I've heard Ashton's main street looks like that one there." I pointed with my chin since my hands were bound.

Now even Bo-Ifun was smiling at me. "That's not the main street of this city, lass."

I felt my eyes go large. "Truly? It's so wide."

Bo-Ifun nodded. "It's one of dozens like it, all leading to the center of the city. Wait until you see King's Way."

"King's Way?" I sat up straighter. "That means . . ."

Bo-Milwir's smile wasn't friendly. "Welcome to Urian, Tanwen En-Yestin."

CHAPTER 29

TANWEN

Apparently, Guardsman Bo-Milwir hadn't been trained in the art of keeping a lass's arms attached to her body while he yanked her through the crowded streets of the capital. He tugged at will, and it was all I could do to keep from stumbling.

And those uppity capital folks pointed, stared, and whispered the whole time. Even the peasants.

Is this what it'll be like when they lead me to the noose? Probably. Only then they'll be throwing rotten vegetables and booing at me.

I tried to squish the thought out of my mind.

"Bo Milwir, easy up the steps!" Bo-Ifun shouted. "She's not running anywhere." He sheathed his sword. "Let me lead her. You guard."

I appreciated his concern, but I hated that he was right. I wasn't running, and I wasn't fighting. Maybe I should've been. The others from the Corsyth would've fought like mountainbeasts to get away from their captors. But I hadn't trained enough. I didn't feel sure what my strands would do if I let them loose. What about all the innocents standing about?

Bo-Milwir shrugged. "Suit yourself." He drew his sword and waved away the people crowding around some steps leading to a courtyard. "Make way, make way. Have ourselves a prisoner." He shoved a dark-haired lass so hard she nearly tumbled down the steps. "On our way to see the king."

Bo-Ifun pressed his lips together, but he didn't say anything. He led me up steps that looked like they were made from the same white stuff as the fountain I'd marveled over in Afon. Marble—I could hear Riwor's voice growling it out at me. No wonder she'd scoffed at my interest in the fountain. Seemed the whole inner city of Urian was carved from this smooth white stuff.

"Ho." I nudged Bo-Ifun beside me. "Thanks."

He looked away and guided me up a few more stairs. "For what?"

"For being kind, even though you didn't have to. Bo-Milwir's right, though."

He stopped. "You mean you are a traitor?"

"I mean you don't belong in the guard." I nodded up to Bo-Milwir, who was pushing his way through a cluster of townsfolk. "He belongs in the guard."

We continued on in silence for another moment or two, then Bo-Ifun spoke again. "My mam told me once that if you want to see something change, the best way to do it is from the inside. You know, instead of sitting on your backside, talking about the way things should be." He frowned. "Think that's a fool idea?"

"I think that's a brave idea."

But anything else I might've told this young soldier stayed locked inside my mind. Because we'd cleared the last of the stairs, and now the biggest building I'd ever seen towered over my head.

My mouth dropped, and I'm sure I looked daft. But I didn't care. Thousands and thousands of gray stones were set upon each other so perfectly, it didn't seem possible human hands could have done it. I wondered if perhaps they hadn't. Perhaps it had been some kind of magic.

Gardens spilled flowers all around the outside of the huge structure. Courtyards with benches, pathways overhung by trees—more beautiful than any gardens I could have imagined. People zipped in and out, and everyone looked to be on important business.

Horses, carts, guardsmen, ladies with servants.

It was the palace.

The closer we got to it, the finer the clothes became. Even the men had lace about their collars and brocade for their waistcoats. I thought of what Brac would say if he could see these primped men in their finery. *Lads and grown men prancing about like ladies at a ball! I'd like to see that fine white lace after half a day in the fields. Lovely to know our taxes are spent on such fluffery.*

But then the thought sent dread shooting into my throat again.

Brac.

The Corsyth weavers may have escaped the guardsmen back at Bowyd. But I still had no clue if they'd gotten to Brac, and if they had, what type of fate might await him. Or had already come to pass. And now I might never be able to find out.

I caught Bo-Ifun's gaze. "Please, sir. Do you know anything about the guard's search for me in Pembrone?"

"Not much. Why?"

My true designs almost came tumbling out, but then I stopped myself. If Brac had managed to slip away or convince the guard he didn't know anything, it'd be foolish of me to out him like this.

"Nothing. Just wondering if my friends are all right. You know how it goes with the guard sometimes."

"I don't think there were any arrests, if that helps. I know there was some lashing, but nothing beyond that."

Lashing. I'd only seen it once before, and never in Pembrone. It was half a year past, when I first started peddling with Riwor. We were in her town, Drefden, and some drunk farmer had gotten into a brawl with a guardsman. He was sentenced to twenty lashes, and I thought I'd never seen anything so awful in my life. The farmer's back looked like raw grazer meat by the time the guardsmen were done with it, and he could hardly stand. Even if he had been sober.

"Do you know who was lashed?" I didn't even want to imagine if it'd been one of the wee ones.

"No. Sorry, lass." He nodded up ahead where a huge pair of doors loomed before us. "Don't take this wrong, but if I were you, I'd be worrying about my own skin. King Gareth's thrown every available soldier into finding you and your mates. I don't know what he has planned for you, but it can't be a summer holiday by the sea. Understand me?"

My gaze scanned the length of the giant doors. I swallowed. "Aye. I understand."

Bo-Ifun took my elbow. "I'm not a betting man, but I'd wager the king will want to see you directly."

And he would have won that bet. Soon as we made our way through the doors and into the cavern of an entryway inside the palace, commotion erupted everywhere. Guardsmen shouted to each other and darted here and there. Everyone in the king's service seemed to be anxious to be first to get word to him that the treasonous story-peddling wench had arrived.

Bo-Ifun tried to shield me from the crush of people, but it really was no use. Bo-Milwir grabbed me and thundered up the stairs at the far end of the entryway. We pushed through a series of hallways until I couldn't have found my way back out if the king had paid me in gold to do it.

"Halt." A calm-faced knight in fine black clothes held up a hand to stop the overeager Bo-Milwir.

My pockmarked captor wasn't keen on this, judging by his scowl. "I have the prisoner. Sir," he added, with a touch of annoyance in his voice. "The one the king's been looking for."

"I know. Do you think a few lumbering guardsmen can pole their way downriver faster than our birds can fly? We received the message of your coming hours ago."

Bo-Milwir shifted his weight. "Two hundred gold pieces. That was the bounty on her head."

"I'm aware. Surely the king will reward you. But that's not my concern." He turned his searching eyes on me. "We must go through the proper channels. I'll not have you crashing into His Majesty's throne room and interrupting council because you're anxious for a ransom."

"Yes, sir." His grip on my arm tightened.

A figure appeared down the hall. I could just barely make out that it was a man when he crossed beneath the torches. We must have been in the belly of the palace—no windows at all.

The man came closer, and I couldn't take my eyes from him.

Handsome as anything, though he was probably older than Warmil. His jaw cut a sharp line through his close-cropped beard—dark, but sprinkled with gray. His eyes brimmed with cleverness and reminded me of Dylun's, except where Dylun's eyes were always on fire, this man's eyes looked like they were carved from ice and stone.

His clothes were cut from the finest leather I'd ever seen. I could tell, even without touching it, that it'd be soft as new-sprouted grass. But he didn't wear any of the fancy frills that looked so funny to me. I immediately felt the need to smooth my frazzled hair and rumpled dress. But I couldn't move with my hands bound.

The man's cold eyes scanned me, then turned to the soldier in black. "What have we here?"

"The story peddler, Sir Dray. She's here for His Majesty, whenever the king is available."

Sir Dray. I'd heard his name once or twice, spoken of as someone who was important at court. A councilmember. He smiled at me. And though I knew he'd likely send me to the chopping block as soon as speak to me, the charming smile sent a flutter through my stomach. I would have been thoroughly shamed to have Brac know that. Or Mor.

"Yes, I think His Majesty will make himself available for this one."

And that did nothing to calm my stuttering heartbeat.

What does it feel like to die?

"En-Yestin." Sir Dray looked me over again. "Yes, I see it, though there's much more of your mother there. This way, my dear."

My dear? I wondered if the king would be angry to know one of his councilmen was being friendly with me. Except maybe it wasn't really friendly. Maybe it was a threat.

The knight in black turned to Bo-Milwir. "You're dismissed, soldier."

Bo-Milwir didn't look at all like he wanted to be dismissed. But he let go of my arm and slunk away toward the wall. The knight in black took my arm now and followed after Sir Dray.

"Sir Dray," he called. "I believe that guardsman is anxious for the bounty on the peddler."

Sir Dray's tone was light. "Indeed. If anyone ever sees that two hundred gold, it'll be his unit commander." He glanced back over his shoulder. "But I have a feeling the king will make a very convincing argument that the ransom offer did not apply to guardsmen, as they're already in his paid service."

"I'm sure that'll be a very convincing argument, sir," the knight replied.

We entered a large, open area, then Sir Dray stopped before another set of doors. I felt like I'd been hauled through a maze.

Sir Dray smiled unnervingly at me again. "Here we are. Do try to look your best. You're about to stand before your king." He signaled two guards, and they threw the double doors wide.

CHAPTER 30

TANWEN

WITH A ROUGH TUG ON MY ARM FROM THE KNIGHT, I FOUND myself stumbling into a room lined on one side with tall windows and packed with richly dressed people. Whispers broke out behind the fluttering fans of the ladies. The lords looked me up and down and nudged each other.

At the end of the green carpet stretching the length of the room sat a long table surrounded by seated men, and up above on a dais, three big chairs. Took me a heartbeat to realize they weren't just chairs but thrones.

One for the queen, one for the princess, and one for King Gareth.

The queen's was empty, and Gareth's was full to bursting. I'd never seen a man with a bulging stomach such as his. Not enough food in all Pembrone to make it so. But as I glanced around the court, I realized several of the lords' bellies strained their brocade waistcoats. I guessed they had enough to eat here in the capital.

On the last throne sat the lady who could only be Princess Braith En-Gareth. I'd told her story many times, and now I realized why that lovely pale, silvery mist shimmered down onto the flower petals when Braith became part of the story. Because that's exactly what she looked like—a pale silver mist. Her skin looked as if it had never seen the sun. I glanced at my own browned hands and tried to pretend they weren't covered in callouses on the undersides.

Everyone knows when you speak of a royal or noble lady, you're supposed to say she's beautiful. So everyone talked of Braith like she was prettier than a rainstorm during a drought. But truly, she wasn't half as beautiful in her features as Gryfelle. If she could scrub all that makeup off her face, unpin her hair, and change out of that heavy-looking gown, she'd probably look fresh and bright—just as pretty as all the farm girls back home when they'd had a bath and a good night's rest.

But now she looked like a miserable, powdered-up doll, and the sadness in her eyes ran deep.

Sir Dray stepped in front of me and bowed at the waist. "Your Majesty, Tanwen En-Yestin, the story peddler." Then he took an empty seat at the table.

The knight beside me elbowed me in the ribs, and I tripped forward a step. I glanced at the princess. She shifted in her seat, then inclined at the waist. It was just a hair of a bend forward, but it was enough for me to catch her meaning.

I curtsied, but I couldn't quite bring myself to choke out the words *Your Majesty*, or some other such grovelly sounding thing. Felt like I'd be spitting on the weavers of the Corsyth to honor this man, and if Gareth aimed to kill me anyway, there wasn't much point in pretending.

"Tanwen En-Yestin." Gareth spoke each word of my name like a punch to the gut. "At last we meet."

I glanced at the princess again. Was I supposed to say something? But she sat still as a statue, and I realized several of the men at the table were looking at her. She couldn't really give me any cues without being seen.

So I cleared my throat and took a chance. "Yes. I reckon you knew my father."

Around court the fans fluttered harder, the whispers grew louder, and the mumbling deepened to low thunder.

Gareth's eyes narrowed. "I did indeed. What do you remember of your father, child?"

"Nothing. Sir," I added, just so the knight didn't run me through right there.

A smile touched the corner of Gareth's mouth. "I see. I suppose your parents wouldn't have had much hand in raising you, would they?"

"No, sir. They've been dead long as I can remember. I only just learned my father was someone you might've known." I left out the fact that I still had no clue *why* the king might have known him.

Gareth eyeballed me for a minute. "What do you remember of your mother?"

The question felt like an arrow made of ice shot through my heart. "Nothing at all. Sir."

"Would you like to know what happened to your mother?"

A little sob I couldn't quite smother hopped up into my throat. Princess Braith stared at her father now, something stewing in her eyes.

I swallowed down my feelings. "Yes, sir."

"Your mother was just a simple peasant girl, like you. But she caught the eye of an important man—your father. Do you know who he was?"

"No."

"Yestin Bo-Arthio was First General to King Caradoc, may the goddesses preserve his royal soul."

The king looked genuinely pious as he said this, while Sir Dray practically smirked. But I was stuck on what the king had just said.

"My father was First General?" I needed to sit down.

"Yes, he was." The king settled back onto his throne. "Your parents were fine servants of King Caradoc. Friends of his. They took it rather hard when the king passed. We all did, but it seemed some couldn't accept it. Your parents were two such people."

The accusations I'd heard about Gareth swam through my head—those that had come from my friends at the Corsyth, but also the ones that poured out of my own story strands without my meaning to do it. Art has a way of revealing truth, Karlith said. My parents somehow had known the truth. And that made them dangerous to Gareth.

If he understood I was catching on to the truth, I'd be dangerous too.

The king studied me. "Your parents betrayed me because they couldn't accept what had happened to King Caradoc. They tried to convince people I'd stolen the throne from the late king, but Caradoc was my friend as well as my king. You can imagine how deeply offensive your parents were to me."

I pressed my lips together and nodded.

"They staged an uprising. Or tried to. You understand why I couldn't let them live."

I tried to force the picture of my mother with her head on Gareth's chopping block or a noose around her neck out of my mind. I swallowed it all down and lowered my head. "Yes."

"Did you know your mother was a storyteller too?"

My gaze snapped back up to the king. "No!" Something stuck in my throat. "I didn't know."

"Indeed. She told beautiful stories that amused King Caradoc and Queen Wynne greatly. But Glain's stories turned sour when she did. She was the reason we passed the laws about crowned stories. Couldn't have treasonous falsehood flying around Tir in wild strands, could we now? Best to keep a tight rein on such things, don't you think?"

I tried to understand his words. But all I could think about was what it would've been like to tell stories with my mother instead of Riwor.

"I asked you a question, lass."

"Yes, sir." I bit my lip.

"And your father . . ." The king trailed off. Shifted in his seat. His patronizing smile slipped. "Well. Perhaps we won't discuss that unpleasantness."

And it seemed the subject was closed.

King Gareth leaned forward then. "Are you afraid, Tanwen?"

I met his gaze and pushed down my tears. "Yes."

"Because you think I mean to kill you too?"

"Yes, sir."

He laughed. "You know, I did mean to kill you, lass. Especially when we'd heard who you are and what the witnesses had seen. You can understand why I'd assume you sought to continue your parents' legacy of treason."

"Aye."

"But I've had a change of heart."

Princess Braith's eyes widened, and she looked at her father like he'd just fallen through the ceiling.

"New information has come to light, and it's changed my mind on the matter." He sat up and smiled. It was supposed to be friendly, I'm sure, but it made my skin feel like it was covered in scuttlebugs. "I think what happened in Afon and Gwern was a result of bad blood, not malicious intent. Am I right, child?"

Malicious was a word I hadn't heard before, but I could guess its meaning. "Aye, I suppose that's it."

"You're young yet, and we'll simply have to train those treasonous rumblings out of you. Understand?"

"Aye."

"So, why don't you tell me a story, Tanwen?"

"A story? For you? Now?"

"It's what you've always wanted, isn't it?"

How does he know that?

Unease blossomed in my stomach. I wondered what "new information" had changed his mind—and how he'd gotten it.

But now it was time to tell the king a story. Apparently. I held my bound hands up to the knight, and he loosed the knot and set me free in a blink.

Then I faced the king again. "Shall I tell the story of Cethor and Ean?"

The king laughed. "I have enough bloody heads in my collection, thank you. How about the creation story?"

One of the men at the table seemed pleased with this. Clean-shaven head and rich velvet robes—obviously a priest. It seemed beyond my comprehension when I realized he was probably the high priest. How had I ended up in this place with all these important people when just last moon I'd been trudging through the fields of Pembrone with Brac, carefully avoiding grazer dung?

But the king wanted the creation story. Time to focus.

I cleared my throat and began. "Once, there was nothing.

"No ground to walk on, nor sky to look up at, nor people to do any such thing. And then from the goddess Cethor's flowing azure locks, the wide Menfor Sea and all the oceans of the world were made."

The sparkling blue strand of Cethor's hair rippled from my palm. It swirled around the courtiers, and many of the ladies giggled. I was reminded of the little girls in the peasant villages who oohed and aahed over each new bit of story.

"And from the goddess Direth's strong brown arms, the towering mountains, sloping valleys, and sandy shores were made."

The rough swathe of brown cloth soared up to the ceiling, then danced with the ocean strand.

So far, so good.

"And then from the green eyes of the goddess Lysia, all plant life sprang up and grew toward the radiant sun."

The green strand like a beam of light shot from my hand and whizzed toward the king. It pinged off the back of his throne, just beside his head, then zoomed around the room between the nobles. Everyone laughed, like always.

"From the blood-red lips of the goddess Dynole, man was made: like the goddesses, but mortal, here to do the goddesses' bidding and please them always."

The ribbon of man—slow, satiny, deepest-red—poured from my fingers. It slithered around the lords' leather boots and ladies' jeweled slippers.

And then my stomach pinched. Same spot, just as it had the last time I told this story.

Before I could stymie it, the image of Gryfelle that night in the Corsyth came to mind. Writhing. Jolting. Her mind and her very self disappearing like a puddle on a sweltering day.

I had promised them—Gryfelle and Mor. I had promised I wouldn't squish down that pinching feeling anymore, lest Gryfelle's nightmare become mine. But *now*? In front of the king? Was it really the time to stop squishing?

I forced the next words out while holding the pinch in my stomach at bay, just for a moment. "And thus, from the beauty of these four goddesses, all in Tir was made as you see it today."

The four strands came together and spun into a green-and-brown blur. I eased up on the pinching in my stomach, just the tiniest bit.

But as I did so, two threads of white light uncoiled from my smallest fingers on each hand. They swam around the spinning green-and-brown blur, and from the strands themselves, my own voice spoke.

"And He saw that it was good."

At these words, the strands crystallized into a perfect peninsular evergreen, like they were supposed to. But this time, a layer of wintry snow settled onto the tiny transparent needles. The tree dropped into my hand. I stared at it, and I wasn't the only one. The whole room stared. After a full minute of silence, I dared a glance up at the king.

His gaze fixed hard on the story. Princess Braith sat rigid, eyes wide. The high priest didn't look pleased anymore. Sir Dray broke the silence by bringing his hands together in applause.

"Well done, Miss En-Yestin. Well done, indeed."

Applause rose from every corner of the room now, and I wasn't sure if I should curtsy or make a run for it. So I just stood there.

The king finally lifted a hand, and all the noise died. "Some bits to work out still, but well done." He sat back in his throne again. "I have a proposition for you."

I swallowed. "Aye?"

"As I said, I believe you to be a victim of your blood, and breeding can overcome blood. I think there's hope for you yet, and I'm willing to provide help so you can live a life on the good and proper side of my law. Does that make sense?"

Not in the least. "Yes, Majesty."

"Good. But in return for my benevolence, I'll expect certain things from you, Tanwen. I'll expect you to set your mind to using your gift properly. I'll expect you to entertain my court, as the storytellers in Tir have always done. And most importantly, I'll expect you to aid me in whatever way you can with the capture of those who would seek to defile my name. Do you understand what I mean?"

You want me to give up the weavers from the Corsyth.

"I believe so, Your Majesty."

"Then you accept?"

My gaze flitted to the knight beside me. His hand rested on the hilt of his sword. He met my eyes, and nodded ever so slightly. But I knew he'd read my thoughts—I'd been wondering if I truly was being offered a choice, or if my "choice" was accepting the king's offer or taking the point of that soldier's blade in my back.

Then I thought of the young guardsman who'd been so kind to me. Bo-Ifun. I remembered what his mam had told him about changing something you didn't like from the inside out.

I looked back at the king. "I accept."

Gareth clapped his hands together. "Excellent. You realize what's just happened, don't you? Tanwen En-Yestin, you've just become my Royal Storyteller."

I managed a smile. A moon ago, I would have burst with happiness if this had happened. Now it felt like a death sentence.

But something about Bo-Ifun's words gave me strength. Change from the inside.

Only I wasn't looking to change Gareth's regime from the inside, exactly. I was looking to pull it apart at the seams.

CHAPTER 31

TANWEN

"SHOW STORYTELLER EN-YESTIN TO HER FAMILY'S APARTMENTS." Gareth nodded to Sir Dray, who then nodded to the knight beside me. "They're still vacant, aren't they?"

"Yes, Your Majesty," Sir Dray answered. "They've remained so all these years."

"Good." The king looked at me. "Be ready, Tanwen. I'll call on you to entertain me whenever the mood strikes, so you must always be available with a story."

"Yes, Your Majesty."

"And someone please see to getting the lass some proper clothes. Can't have her appearing before me like this again."

Laughter rolled through the room, and I hoped my face wouldn't burst into flame.

The knight led me back down the green carpet. I glanced over my shoulder once, and my gaze landed on Princess Braith. She seemed carved of marble, like the rest of Urian.

"Sir?" I shuffled to keep up with the knight striding ahead of me. "How will I ever find my way around? Is there a map or something?"

He took another turn down another hall. "Lass, you'll not be picking up and leaving without an escort. His Majesty isn't a fool. Two of my men will be stationed nearby at all times. Should you require anything, you'll have to ask."

We took a set of narrow stairs that spiraled up, and I could only guess we were in a tower. Then we crossed a long hallway—into another tower, maybe. Then the hallway opened up into a larger area with several doors. Finally, the knight stopped before one of those doors.

"Here."

"Here?" The halls looked totally empty, with none of the hustle and bustle of the downstairs areas of the palace.

"Yes, here." He pulled out an iron ring with about a thousand keys on it. He slipped one of them into the lock and turned until it clicked.

"Do I take the key?"

He snorted. "No. Like I said, His Majesty isn't a fool. He'd not give you the only key to your apartments, understand?"

I understood. The guardsmen, or anyone else the king saw fit, would have access to my room at all times.

"Sir? Why is the king keeping me alive?"

"New information made him less inclined to believe you'd meant to cause harm. And you're useful. Got his sights set on the whole lot of you, if you know what I mean."

I knew what he meant.

Bait.

I thought of all the lads by the riverbank selling fishhooks and buckets of worms. That was me. One of those squirmy things about to get impaled on a hook to draw in the fish.

"The king knows what he's about." The knight gestured into the room. "Well, go on."

I couldn't rightly say why, but I didn't want to cross through that doorway. Something felt too final about it. "What's your name, sir?"

"I'm head of the palace guard, and that's all you'll ever need to know. Won't be seeing me again, except when you come to court to amuse the king." He shrugged. "Or if the king wants you for interrogation."

I swallowed. "Interrogation?"

"Never mind about that now. Get yourself cleaned up."

I nodded and stepped through the doorway into my family's old chambers.

Then the door banged shut. A click. And I was alone.

I stood frozen just inside the doorway.

How many times did Mother and Father stand in this very spot?

I shook my head. Best not to allow those ghostly thoughts. If I were going to live in this place without going mad, I would have to learn to snuff out those musings.

The front room was bigger than any I'd ever lived in.

Two carpets covered the floor before me, so big a full-grown grazer might've settled onto each of them for a nap. I hadn't ever seen a thing like those rugs before—all swirling patterns, as if they were half-formed stories woven in thread. I wondered if they might be something foreign—maybe brought over the wide Menfor Sea from Minasimet or some other place I'd never even heard of.

Or maybe it was a story trapped in fabric. I'd seen stranger things this past moon.

Left of the rugs, two stuffed couches covered in velvet ran along the wall. I'd never worn a dress of so fine a material in my memory. Imagine covering a whole sofa with it, just so your backside felt properly attended to!

The farthest couch sat just beneath a window, and I instantly wished I had Father's whole library and mine. I could curl up on that couch and read in the sunlight. But I didn't have my books. In fact, even the travel bag I'd packed from home was back at the Corsyth. I had nothing except the clothes on my back.

Suddenly I grasped at my chest as I remembered the one thing I owned that a guardsman might have had a mind to take while I was passed out. But it was still there—a curled knot of silver beneath my dress, hanging by its leather cord, like always.

My breath escaped in a long, slow stream.

To the right of the rug furthest into the room sat a desk—just like Father's desk back home, except finer wood and not so worn. I supposed palace servants polished the thing to keep it looking so nice. Made me feel sorry for the one back at the cottage, since I had no servants nor desk polish nor any such thing to keep it looking healthy.

A table twice the size of the one back home was just to my right, in front of the desk. It had proper chairs around it—six of them—instead of the benches we had around our tables in Pembrone.

Along every wall but the one with the window, shelves ran from top to bottom. Bookshelves that could have housed hundreds, maybe even thousands, of books. But not a single book sat upon them. I wondered what had been there when my father lived. If he kept such a fine library at the country cottage in Pembrone, what must these shelves have looked like?

First General. I still couldn't believe it.

It had all been stripped away now. Shelves empty, desk bare. Nothing remained that spoke of Yestin Bo-Arthio and Glain Ma-Yestin. And why should there be anything left? It'd been thirteen years. The king had no reason to keep the rooms of his enemies as a shrine to them. Still, it felt hard, somehow, to walk into this place and know my family had once lived and breathed here, and now it was just an empty shell.

I let out a shaky breath. Two doors beckoned me from the opposite side of the window wall. I wondered if they joined up with others' rooms and maybe I ought to knock. I hesitated a moment, but then I tried the handle on the door furthest back, just beside the desk. The knob turned easily, and I opened the door to what could only have been my parents' bedroom.

A bed three times the size of any I'd ever slept in sat against the far wall of the room. And by the look of it, that mattress had genuine feathers in it, not the straw I was used to. A beautiful carved wardrobe lay to my right—empty of all clothes now, surely. Opposite that was a real looking glass with a stool in front of it.

I moved closer, a little hesitant. The glass was so clear I was afraid to look.

With good reason. No wonder the courtiers had mocked me.

A trickle of dried blood streaked the side of my face where my old friend Bo-Milwir had popped me. I looked like I had rolled around in a farmyard or some other such dusty place. Leaves and twigs stuck in my hair, bursting out like I'd put them there for decoration. My sun-browned arm showed through a long gash in my sleeve.

I was a sight—no mistaking that.

But a pitcher and basin had been laid out for me, along with clean cloths and a bar of tallow soap. At least I could clean up when I had a mind to.

In the back corner, an area was curtained off by fine brocade drapes. I pulled back on one side of the curtain. Only in Urian would you find fine material used to conceal the chamber pot. Brac would have had a laugh over that.

I left the bedroom and paused before the other door. I had a fair idea what I'd find inside, and it took me a minute to decide to look. I breathed deep and twisted the knob. Sure enough, a small bed in one corner, a child-sized version of the carved-wood wardrobe, and a pretty little rug spread on the floor—a rug that showed what had always been my favorite fairy story. The mythical pink fluff-hopper who granted wishes if caught and bared its wicked fangs to try to keep people away.

My room.

It was stripped to its bare bones, except the rug, so I couldn't really imagine what it'd looked like when I was a tiny lass and I'd actually slept in that bed. I supposed my mother would've had some nice wall-hangings and maybe a rag doll for me to cuddle. A warm quilt for the drafty nights in the stone castle, maybe?

The achy hole in my heart twinged.

I closed the door without entering the room. No need.

I made my way back to the basin. The tallow soap burned in the cut on my head, and scrubbing dried blood out of a wound not yet healed isn't a holiday, in case anyone was wondering. But I managed to chip away at all the dirt and grime, and though I still looked every bit the peasant when I was done, at least I was a clean peasant. Except my dress, but there wasn't a thing I could do about that.

Boredom pushed me back into the front room. I didn't think I'd been in my new place an hour yet, and I was already itching to escape outside. A walk in the gardens. A late picnic lunch on one of those benches. Dip my toes into the cool river. *Something.*

But, no, this was to be my life now. Gareth's "Royal Storyteller," but really his prisoner.

I walked along the bookshelves behind Father's desk, tracing my fingers over the wood like I used to do at home. I'd passed three shelves and was onto the fourth when I halted before it. I cocked my head to the side, looked at the other shelves, then back to the fourth one.

"It's just a frame," I said aloud out of habit. I had always talked to my parents like they were around the cottage, just to keep myself from getting too lonely, and I was every bit as alone here.

This set of shelves was just a frame, not a finished bookcase like the others. The others had solid wood at their backs; this one showed through to the stone wall behind it. Odd. Why would it not be finished also?

I supposed when all those shelves were full of books, as surely they once were, it wouldn't look different than the others. Especially if you picked taller books to sit on this one and cover the stones. But why was one different than the others? Didn't make sense.

I put a hand through the frame and felt the cool stones behind.

A knock on the door sent my heart pounding. I took a huge breath to try to get some kind of normal beating back into it.

Who would be at my door? Could Gareth be summoning me already? The thought of appearing before all those courtiers still dressed in my torn-up peasant rags wasn't a happy one.

I heard a click on the other side of the door. Supposed my guard had unlocked it. My hand on the front door knob, I took another deep breath, then I pulled the door open to face whatever waited on the other side.

It was Her Royal Highness, Princess Braith.

CHAPTER 32

TANWEN

Princess Braith offered a smile. "Hello, Tanwen."

I stared at her and the woman beside her.

After a short pause, the princess tried again. "You needn't worry. All is well. We have some things for you. May we come in?"

I nodded dumbly and stepped back to allow Princess Braith and the dark-haired maidservant entry.

Braith nodded to her maid. "This is Cameria, my most trusted servant and friend. The gowns she has are for you. I hope you don't mind, but they're my old ones. The queen had a whole wardrobe made for me when I was about your age. Only I grew an inch a moon after they were finished." She smiled ruefully. "The queen was not pleased, but it did give her an excuse to design a wardrobe full of new dresses. In any case, you are a bit shorter than I, so I thought they might fit you."

I gaped. What . . . what was happening right now?

Braith waited for me to say something, but when I couldn't manage, she kept on. "We . . . brought food as well. I didn't suppose you'd had a proper luncheon, and it's closer to supper at this point. But . . ." She held out the basket in her arms. "Would you care for something?"

I jolted back to life. "Aye, thanks. Do . . . you want to sit?" I gestured to the small table in the front room.

Braith nodded. "Thank you. That's most gracious." She pulled out her own chair, and I wondered if I was supposed to do that for her.

Needless to say, I hadn't entertained a princess before.

Cameria bowed. "I'll just hang these gowns if you don't mind, miss."

A moment of silence passed, then I realized she was talking to me. "Oh! Aye, that's fine. Thank you. Wardrobe is in there. Just hang them . . . anywhere."

I sat opposite Braith as she cleared her throat. "I did not know what might suit your appetite, so I brought a few of my favorites. Herb-stuffed fowl, sandwiches with soft cheese and fresh cucumber, miniature hathberry pies with sweet crystals, garden salad, and"—she pulled out the last, steamy bundle from the basket—"Cameria's favorite from Meridione. Hot, sweet maize cakes."

I gazed at the spread without a word.

Braith's expression fell. "Does it not suit? I can have whatever you like made in the kitchens, of course. If this is unappetizing—"

"Unappetizing!" I found my voice again. "No, it isn't that. I've just never seen food like this before. It's so . . . dainty."

"I suppose it is." Braith smiled. "Please, eat."

I picked up one of the pies. "Stars, this is pretty. The sugar looks like crystallized story."

The princess laughed. "I hope it tastes better than that."

"Only one way to find out." I popped the whole thing in my mouth at once, tiny as it was. "Mmm. Delicious."

Braith smiled, then folded her hands in her lap. "Tanwen, I came here to bring you lunch and the gowns, but I also wanted to speak to you." She looked down at her pale fingers covered in rings of gold and precious stones. "Whatever has happened in the past or will happen in the future, you have at least one friend here in Urian."

I blinked.

Braith looked up and smiled kindly. "I mean me. I would like to be a friend to you."

Did I hear her right?

"I could use a friend," I said slowly. "But . . . meaning no disrespect to you, Your Highness, I think your father would be pickled if he knew you had been trying to make friends with me. I know he says I'm Royal Storyteller, but I think I'm a bit more like a royal prisoner, if you understand." I looked at the crumbs and empty napkins on the table. "A fancy prisoner, but still a prisoner."

Braith nodded. "You are wise to understand your situation, Tanwen. You are a captive here. But let me trouble about the king. You work on keeping out of mischief. My father doesn't suffer mischief well, and I would hate to see anything happen to a friend."

I swallowed. Hard.

"That is a warning, Tanwen," Braith said with another smile. "Not a threat."

I nodded. "I think I understand."

"Good. You are right to be wary of speaking freely in the palace, but you needn't feel that way around me. Or Cameria," she added, as the maid made her way back into the front room.

Cameria's cheeks were flushed, and the black pigment lining her eyes was smudged. She had been crying.

Braith looked at her quizzically, but then turned back to me. "Tanwen, you have an open invitation to dine at the king's table any meal you wish. Just summon your guards and someone will escort you. You will hear meals called throughout the palace."

"Thank you, Your Highness." My heart warmed at her offer. "That's kind of you. Though it's hard to imagine me eating at the table of the king."

Braith smiled. "You'll learn. Did you know my family was lowborn? In fact, you have more high-born blood than I do, since neither of my parents were nobles and one of yours was."

My breath caught. I hadn't realized that. "Seems a bit hard to figure, but I guess it's true." Maybe Braith could answer some of my questions. "Highness . . . was my mother . . . I mean, was she a scruffy farm girl from Pembrone, like me?"

"I had tea with Glain Ma-Yestin many times when I was a girl. She was very gracious and refined, as I recall." Braith paused. "I know she was from Pembrone and her father was a farmer, but I believe your grandfather was quite the successful businessman. The peninsular farms thrived in those days. Do I remember correctly that he had orchards of some kind?"

"Aye! We do have an orchard along the cottage land, but it belongs to Farmer Cerio now. I guess it must have been sold at some point."

Braith nodded. "Yes, I remember now. Queen Wynne had a taste for fruit preserves, and I think Glain's father was the queen's chief supplier of such things. That must be how Yestin came to meet Glain."

I tried to smile, but tears began to trickle down my cheeks. "What did she look like?"

Braith looked at me, and the pity was heavy in her eyes. "Like you."

"Truly?"

"Yes. Truly." The princess rose and Cameria followed. "I regret we must leave now, Tanwen. But thank you for graciously hosting us this afternoon."

I jumped up from my chair. "Thank you for the food. And the company."

Braith glanced at the empty bookcases lining the walls. "Shall I have some books sent for you? I'm sure we can spare some from the palace library."

I hardly knew what to say. "I'd like that very much."

"Very well. I'll see it done." Braith gathered her basket and headed toward the door.

I hurried to open it for her.

"Do take care, Tanwen," Braith said.

"I'll try."

"Come, Cameria." They slipped into the hallway and I slowly closed the door.

Whatever I'd stumbled into here, at least I had one friend in the palace. But how far could that friendship stretch under the strain of Gareth's wrath?

CHAPTER 33
BRAITH

BRAITH EYED HER REFLECTION IN THE MIRROR. "CAMERIA, DO you think my hair would look prettier if I wore it down?"

Cameria smiled. "You mean like Tanwen, my lady?"

"Yes, I suppose." Braith smiled wryly. "Am I that transparent? The girl is so . . ." The princess searched for words. "She is full of spirit. And sometimes I feel hollow."

The reflection of her gray eyes looked empty. Tired.

"I think Your Highness would look as well if you had fewer cares and could enjoy life in a small farm town."

"Indeed." Braith sighed and abandoned her vanity table. "Shall we head to supper?"

"Yes, my lady."

Braith stopped and studied Cameria's face. "Cameria, may I ask you something personal?"

"Yes, my lady?"

"You were crying before—in Tanwen's room."

Cameria had been readying Braith's midnight-blue cloak. Now she paused but did not look up. "Forgive me, my lady."

"Cameria! I was not scolding you for having sentiments." Braith crossed the room. "Will you not tell me what troubles you?"

"I wish I could tell you the whole of it. But . . ." She shook her head. "It distresses me to see Yestin's daughter. I remember him very well."

"I didn't know. I'm sorry."

"He and my father were great friends. I spent many hours with my mother in Glain Ma-Yestin's sitting room. And the girl looks so like her mother, doesn't she?"

"Yes, she does." Braith searched her friend's dark eyes. "Cameria, I don't begrudge you your privacy. But you know you can trust me with whatever troubles you—especially if telling someone would help ease your burden."

Cameria's gaze flashed up to Braith's face. "I trust you with my very life, Braith," she said quietly. "But I would not put you at risk by sharing all my secrets. Some things are better left in darkness."

"Very well. But you will tell me if there is anything I can do to help?"

"Of course, my lady."

"Good. Then why don't you go on ahead and prepare my place at the king's table? I'll be along shortly."

Cameria frowned. "Are you sure, my lady? Should we not walk together? What if you happen upon that wretched man again? It seems Sir Dray stalks you in the halls these days."

"Yes, it does seem that way. But he's exactly who I would like to run into this evening."

"My lady?"

Braith bit her lip. "I don't wish to burden you with my secrets either."

"Oh, Braith." Cameria's distress swam in her eyes. "Please do not put yourself in danger."

Braith reached out and hugged her friend. "Thank you for seeing to me, Cameria." She pulled back. "I hope you understand that I must continue to look into the matter of Tanwen En-Yestin. If I need to dance around Dray Bo-Anffir to get more information, so be it. But I promise to be very careful."

Cameria did not speak. But she nodded her acceptance, then took Braith's cloak and slipped from the room.

Braith drew a deep breath and followed Cameria into the hallway.

Braith had taken the long way through the halls. Then she lapped the perimeter again in search of the weasely Sir Dray. Nothing. But when Braith was distracted, hoping to get back to her room quickly or carrying stolen bits of parchment up the sleeve of her gown, she couldn't seem to help running into the man.

The callers sounded the final alert for supper. Braith knew she must head to the dining hall if she were to make a prompt arrival and not provoke a flurry of questions.

She circled back down a pathway she had already covered and made her way toward the dining hall. Just as she was about to round a corner, familiar voices brought her to a halt.

It was Naith and Dray. Unmistakably.

The high priest was mid-growl. "—an offense that shouldn't be overlooked. You saw it yourself."

Dray's boredom punctuated his words. "So what? So a thread of white light appeared during her story. The king didn't seem bothered."

"Don't be coy, Bo-Anffir. You know it's a problem and so does the king. That strand did not belong in that story."

"Look, I'm terribly sorry Your Holiness has been offended by the suggestion that something in the universe exists beyond the lauded goddesses of your temples. But I haven't the slightest idea why you think this matter concerns me."

Naith scoffed. "Ha! As if you believed in either the goddesses or whatever that blasphemous peddler was suggesting with her white light strands."

A brief pause from Dray, and then, "I'm not the only one who doesn't really believe in the goddesses, am I, Naith?"

Braith couldn't have speculated how the high priest would take that suggestion—if he'd begin shouting or if his head would simply explode in indignation. But to her surprise, he responded calmly.

"We're to speak plainly, are we?" Naith asked, his voice low and smooth.

"Oh, please, let's. For once. It'll be refreshing not to dance around your insinuation and posturing."

"Very well. No, I don't put faith in the goddesses as real entities like the peasants do. Or even as the king does. But if you believe there is no power behind the institution I serve, you are sorely mistaken."

Braith's breath caught. Whatever did Naith mean by that?

But the high priest breezed past it without further explanation. "Whatever you choose to accept as truth about the goddesses or the power behind them, I think we can both agree that the church holds an important place in Tirian society. I do believe in that tradition."

"And you believe in money."

"Ha! Says the son of a lowly merchant who clawed his way into position in Urian."

A pause. Braith would have given much to see the look on Dray's face. She knew well he did not appreciate mention of his humble beginnings.

Finally, Dray spoke. "Ambition is not a sin, is it, Your Holiness?"

"You said we would speak plainly, so I shall. We each have interests beyond what others might consider appropriate for our positions. Perhaps it is—unusual—for a man of the faith to enjoy luxury as I do. I don't deny it. But how much less appropriate is it for a king's advisor to seek his master's throne?"

Dray didn't skip a beat. "The throne? And why would I have designs on such a thing? My influence is unparalleled in Tir. No man beneath the king has the pull I have. What more could I possibly want?"

Naith breathed an oily chuckle. "You stumbled upon it yourself, didn't you? No man *beneath the king*. Since when is Dray Bo-Anffir content to be second-best to anyone?" His tone sharpened. "And it runs deeper than that, doesn't it? Deeper and more personal. I think you truly do want the princess for yourself."

Braith's heart ceased its hurried rhythm. For a moment, it stopped entirely.

"Me?" Dray said, casual indifference lacing the word. "With ladies surrounding me and a mistress who lives in my chambers? Please, Your Eminence. You try my patience."

"Ah, but Braith is different. She may not be the beauty of the court, like that insufferable cream puff who dangles from your arm.

But Braith is the brains. And the grace and the goodness. Something about her draws you, though you yourself probably couldn't guess why."

Braith put a hand to her chest.

"She's unconquered," Naith continued. "You're not a soldier, but you are a military man. All who know about such things acknowledge you were the strategist behind His Majesty's military campaigns. With you as the strategist and he as the soldier, Tir's enemies hadn't a prayer. And now that the lands are conquered, you've set your sights on a new outpost—only this time, it's the princess."

Braith's knees felt ready to collapse beneath her.

An interminable silence stretched on. Dray's always-ready words didn't come, and with sinking realization, Braith understood that Naith must have struck close. Too close for Dray to play it off.

"All right." Dray's voice had quieted, but danger edged his words. "What do you want, Naith?"

"It behooves us both to make sure this peddler girl and weavers like her do not make a disadvantageous rise to power. Remember what it was like in the old days? There were the stories, yes. Harmless enough. But also prophecies. Interrogations done with the use of storytellers. Crime scenes recreated with the use of colormasters. What was the old saying, hmm?"

"Art has a way of revealing truth."

"Indeed. And the last thing you or I need are specific truths to be revealed. Was it not part of your own plan to make sure the weavers could be controlled before our good king's—er—rise to power?"

"It was hatched jointly with the king. I'll not take all the credit for that. The weavers needed to be controlled or silenced."

"Precisely. Controlled or silenced. Do not fail to remember that as we use this peddler to our advantage."

"*Our* advantage?" Braith could imagine Dray folding his arms across his chest. "How does she benefit you?"

"She benefits the king, though I don't pretend to know why. Anything that benefits the king who keeps me secure in my position benefits me."

"Wise answer. And true, no less. Do you care to know why Tanwen En-Yestin benefits the king? You know that if anyone is able to shed light on the matter for you, it's me. And if we're to be allies—albeit temporary ones—it serves us both for you to know."

"Go on, then."

"The king indeed received new information about the peddler from a source close to her—information that showed her to be less of a threat than originally feared. She's not part of the Corsyth band of weavers, though how they managed to end up together, I'm not exactly sure. But I am certain that Tanwen's original transgressions were accidental, like what we saw in the throne room today."

"And since when does our king show mercy because a transgression was unintentional?"

"Since I pointed out to him that the daughter of Yestin is the likeliest thing in Tir to flush the old general out of hiding, if he hides still."

"Hiding?" Naith spluttered. "Yestin is dead!"

"Shh! Do moderate your tone, Your Holiness. Do you want to draw a crowd?" Dray's voice lowered too, so that Braith had to lean forward to catch his words. "That's the official story, of course. But he was never found. If he made his way out of the city, it'd be a miracle. I had the king set up a tight perimeter, more heavily guarded than the princess's bedroom. And Yestin was never caught, no body was ever found.

"For years, King Gareth was sure the general had somehow managed to hide in the palace. That may be possible, but it's likelier he had help to somehow move past our perimeter, though it would have taken an entire unit of guardsmen loyal enough to him to risk their heads. Not such a stretch to imagine. He was well loved under Caradoc and became a folk hero after the attempted uprising.

"And if he escaped Urian, he could be anywhere. He had friends everywhere, thanks to his diplomatic policy. But the king knew him better than I, and he swears Yestin would not have left his family here, not even the little girl, if he knew there was a chance she was still alive. So Gareth believes if Tanwen has been in Tir this whole time, then Yestin has too."

"If he still lives, of course."

"Correct."

Naith breathed a slow whistle. "Astounding."

"Indeed."

There was a pause of several seconds. Braith's head spun, but she couldn't miss her chance. They might go on for an hour, divulging secrets with no opportunity for her to break in without suspicion she'd overheard something dangerous.

She rounded the corner, then gave a start of feigned surprise. "Oh!"

Both men startled.

Braith curtsied to each of the men in turn. "Your Grace. Your Eminence. I thought surely I'd be last to the supper table tonight."

Dray recovered his wits quicker than the priest. "I'd be late to supper every night if I thought it might afford me the honor of escorting the princess to her father's table."

Braith faked a pleasant nod. "How thoughtful." She took Dray's offered arm, then turned to Naith. "Your Eminence, I don't suppose you'd be willing to act as a second escort for me. Perhaps my tardiness would be less offensive to the king and queen if I had the two most honored servants of my father at my arms."

Naith blushed nearly up to his bald pate.

But he bowed politely. "The honor would be mine, Your Royal Highness."

So, with a snake on either side of her, Braith strode to the dining hall. Her mind buzzed with all she'd heard, but one thing sounded above the rest.

Yestin Bo-Arthio couldn't truly be alive. Could he?

CHAPTER 34

TANWEN

YOU'D THINK A GIRL USED TO SLEEPING ON A STRAW TICK—OR IN a crate in the Corsyth—would find a feather bed to be pure bliss. But I tossed and turned all night like I lay on a mattress of thorns instead of soft down.

I finally had everything I'd been after for so many years. I was in the palace, living in the luxury apartments of Tir's former First General, no less. The princess's own gowns hung in my fancy wardrobe. Not only that but she'd called me her friend, and if I judged her right, she truly meant it. The king had hired me as part of his staff, and I was going to do the thing I loved most in the world all day, with none of the tiresome bits of hard work in between.

And yet everything was one big upside-down mess. I had no clue what had happened to my Corsyth friends or the Bradwirs in Pembrone. Seemed fairly certain someone had received lashes on my account—and that alone made me feel I'd lose my fancy breakfast all over my elegant couch. But what if Bo-Ifun had been wrong? What if arrests had been made? Would they be released now that the king and I had struck a deal?

The folks from the Corsyth sure wouldn't. They were wanted for their own crimes, not mine. If they'd been caught . . . Well, I couldn't escape the feeling that their lives were forfeit, and nothing would save their skins. Not even the kindness of the princess, if she had a notion they ought to be saved.

Which I wasn't sure she did.

Something gnawed at my stomach. Every time I thought of my

Corsyth friends, their faces cycled through my mind. And each time, the image of Mor's mischievous stubbled face with its twinkly blue eyes stuck twice as long as the others. And the pit in my stomach grew.

I rested my chin on the back of the couch and stared out the window. The view was downright pretty, no lie, overlooking a garden with huge, lush velvet-petals down below. I'd never seen velvet-petals as red as blood before, as folks mostly grew white and purple ones in Pembrone. I'd always thought my cottage was pretty unique, having the only butter-yellow velvet-petals in town. But these red ones would have made all the Pembroni ladies' heads spin.

Still, as I looked at the lovely flowers far below me, and even as I watched the people about the palace scurry around in the gardens and on the pathways below, I knew I might as well be in the dungeon.

Only difference was my room had a better view.

With every beat of my heart, the lonely muscle pumped the truth.

Prisoner. Prisoner. Prisoner.

I sighed. Wished Karlith was here to sip some tea with me. Or Gryfelle to teach me how I ought to act around these fancy people. Or Zelyth to remind me of the lads back home. Or most especially Mor.

Karlith's words skipped through my mind—all her ideas about the Creator. I wondered if they were true. And I wondered if that was what the mysterious "He" was all about in my botched creation story.

Karlith said He was listening always, no matter what. I guessed that meant He could hear me in this place, prisoner or not.

I figured it couldn't hurt.

So I closed my eyes and thought some words toward Him. They always said prayers to the goddesses really loud in the temples, so as to be heard above the din of everyone else shouting their praises and requests. But I figured if the Creator truly existed, He ought to be able to hear my thoughts. Otherwise, he didn't seem any different than the make-believe goddesses of the temples, and He didn't deserve to hear my words anyhow.

Creator, if you're real and if you're like Karlith says you are, then you can see all the folks I'm missing right now. Please, help them. Keep them safe.

When I opened my eyes, a blazing white tree hovered before me. It was one of those weepy, lazy ones that grew by the riverbanks and swayed in the gentlest of breezes. They'd always been my favorites.

"Amen?"

The tree crystallized and dropped into my lap—so clear it was almost like it was air made solid. If such a thing were possible.

I settled in to say another prayer. One for the folks in Pembrone. But I couldn't even let my mind settle on it anymore. Not knowing their fates was eating away at me too heartily.

I set my river tree on the windowsill and hopped off the couch. I took to pacing like a caged animal.

Which I basically was.

A caged animal in a luxury prison, praying to some god who may not exist. I sighed. But, fairy story or not, it was worth trying.

"Creator, if Brac is alive—"

Before I got any further, someone knocked on my door. The lock clicked from the outside.

I froze on the fancy rug. Could it be the princess again? Maybe a summons from Gareth? Maybe the guard, come to throw me in the dungeon after all. Just in case, I grabbed the river tree off my window and tucked it behind one the throw pillows on the sofa. Then I squared my shoulders and marched to the door, pretending I'd bravely meet whatever waited on the other side of it. I twisted the knob and pulled it open.

If a mountainbeast had been doing a jig in the hallway, I couldn't have been more shocked.

Straw-colored hair, sun-pinked nose, lopsided grin.

"Brac!"

And it was. Really and truly.

But he was decked out head to toe in the black uniform of the palace guard.

CHAPTER 35

TANWEN

"BRAC!" I JUMPED UP AND LOOPED MY ARMS AROUND HIS NECK. I breathed in his scent—sunshine and sweat and mischief.

"Tannie." He exhaled the word into my ear like he had thought he'd never see me again, which I guessed was basically true. "You're alive."

Suddenly, I pushed him away with both hands and took a good look at him.

I hadn't been addled. He truly was dressed in the uniform of a palace guardsman. Ever since Brac had been able to grow whiskers, he had always been clean shaven or sporting a couple days' lazy stubble. But now his face showed the beginnings of a close-cropped beard.

Just like all guardsmen wore.

"Brac . . ." I took a step away from him.

War broke out in my mind. He was here. Safe. Alive. In one solid piece I could touch and see. But he looked like one of *them*—those he'd once despised. Those who had become my enemy.

"Brac, how . . . ?" My warring mind couldn't seem to quiet long enough to piece together a sentence.

His lopsided smile shone at me like the afternoon sun. "It's all right, Tannie. Everything's going to be all right now."

"But you're . . . a guardsman?"

"It's all right."

"Stop saying that!" I took another shaky step backward.

Brac's smile melted like a pat of grazer-cream butter left out in the summer heat. "Tannie."

"A *guardsman*, Brac? How could . . . I mean, what in the wide world is going on?"

Brac's lips pressed together. Then he turned to face someone I couldn't see outside in the hallway. "Sir, permission to speak to the storyteller in her own chambers?" The formal speech grated against his Pembroni accent and made me want to throw my hands over my ears to block out the unnatural sound.

A rumbling laugh sounded just outside my door. "Permission to 'speak' in her chambers, eh, Bo-Bradwir?"

Brac's cheeks reddened, even under his sunburn. "It ain't like that, sir. Well, it is a bit, but I just want to talk to her. The lass has had a shock and is a bit scrambled at the moment."

Well, at least he could still speak like a proper farm lad when he was embarrassed.

"Right, right, Bo-Bradwir. Didn't mean to question your courtly honor." Another rumbling laugh. "Be quick about it, and report down to the stables when you're done. I hear Captain's got a surprise for you—at the stables, so two guesses what it is."

The laugh faded with the sound of a couple pairs of heavy boots.

Brac barely seemed to notice me anymore. His eyes glowed like a couple of Harvest Moons shoved in his face. "Did you hear, Tannie? Captain's got a horse—for me!"

I stuck both my fists on my hips and glared something terrible at him. "And just what could you have done that would earn a horse out of Gareth's stables!"

Brac sighed. "I know we've been a bit hard about the king in the past. But, honestly, I thought you might've changed your stripes after all that's happened."

Something caught in my chest. The swirl of emotional chaos—like a bunch of rogue story strands or Dylun's fiery colormaster magic—stilled to a deathly stop inside me.

Wait, the strands seemed to say to me. *Listen to what he has to say.*

My rational mind filled in the last blank.

Because Brac doesn't know the whole story.

I fought my shaking body into quietness. "Tell me what happened."

A gentle smile—the summer sun again—broke over Brac's lips. "There you are, lass." He strolled into my chambers and stopped in the middle of the embroidered rug. "Whoa. This is quite the place they've fixed you up with, ain't it?"

"Yes." I ground out the word out through clenched teeth. "It was—" But something made me stop short of telling him my family used to live here. Not until I'd heard his story. "It was empty for a long time," I finished instead.

I could say that much truthfully.

Brac flopped onto the couch by the window, then winced. "I'll tell you what. These guardsman uniforms may look right nice, but they ain't so comfortable as a body might hope."

I gawked at the breastplate over his chest. Couldn't get over how odd it looked on him. "No, I wouldn't guess so."

I'd never seen him dressed in anything so fine—never seen him in anything at all except homespun wool and linen. I'd think him as handsome as anyone I'd ever seen if not for the fact that he now looked exactly like all those men who'd threatened me. Or let their hands wander while I scrubbed tables in Blodwyn's tavern just before I started peddling. Or treated me like I wasn't worth the spit to shine their boots.

Something pinched inside me. Had I once been willing to suffer all that from the guardsmen if only they'd get me closer to Urian? And barely a moon ago at that.

The realization roiled around in my stomach.

"Tannie?" Brac bolted up on the couch. "What is it, lass? You look sick."

"I'm fine." I lowered down onto one of the chairs at the dining table. "But I need you to start talking."

The grin reblossomed. "Been a wild couple of weeks, eh?"

"Brac, *please*. They said there had been lashings," I remembered aloud.

"Aye." His smile dipped and he leaned forward with his elbows on his knees. "That was a right shame. She should've cooperated."

My throat squeezed. "Who?"

"Blodwyn."

I closed my eyes and forced myself not to vomit. "What happened?"

"The questioned her about you—your whereabouts, who you might know in other towns. She didn't know nothin', even, but she was right feisty about it. Earned those lashes, I'm afraid."

I couldn't form a reply. My gaze drifted back to the black uniform. "And that?"

His smile reappeared. "That all started when you were kidnapped."

And there it was. Kidnapped.

"When those folks came and ripped you from your own cottage—kidnapped you in the dark of night. Well, I couldn't sit by, could I? Even if it meant working with the guard and getting all friendly with the king. Right?"

I nodded. Of course that's what it'd looked like to Brac. I'd left no note. How could he have known I was going with Mor, Zel, and Gryfelle of my own free will?

Well, free-ish will. Hadn't felt like much of a choice back on that night a few weeks ago. But thank the heavens it had been the right one.

Because I'd met Mor.

Why did those rogue thoughts pop into my head, unbidden, at the worst possible moments? My fluttery stomach and nonexistent romance with Mor should have been the least of my concerns, yet I couldn't seem to stop thinking of that pirate.

Brac cut into my thoughts. "Mam and Da and I—we all worked with the guardsmen to find where the kidnappers had taken you. I told them no one knew the town, or you, well as I did. I told them I'd help them if they'd give me a spot in the guard."

Brac crossed the room and knelt on the floor before me. He grabbed my hands in his. "I didn't care what it took. I was going to help find you. Imagine me, son of Farmer Bradwir, getting to travel around the peninsula any other way."

I swallowed down my resurfacing breakfast. "That's true. I understand why you did it, Brac."

"Plus, I had to explain to them that you wasn't guilty of all them things they were accusing you of. I mean, I know you've had some things to say about the king, but it was always you that calmed *me* down. I knew you wouldn't commit nothing like treason. Especially not when you was working so hard to get to be the king's storyteller. It was me that convinced them you were innocent."

Another war erupted in my head.

Should I tell him I wasn't really kidnapped? Did I tell him about the Corsyth and the weavers there and why they were hiding? Should I tell him the guard was just using him? Did I tell him that Gareth was worse than we had ever imagined?

I looked at his eyes, shining with hope.

No. It was safer for him if he didn't know. Knowledge—truth—was the greatest danger around Gareth. The more I shielded Brac from it, the better off he'd be.

I tried to squish out a smile. "So, what'd you do to earn one of the king's horses? And get promoted to the palace guard, for that matter?" I eyed the sleek black uniform again.

Brac chuckled. "Turns out a peninsular farm lad is just what's needed in some 'royal investigations,' as the captain would say."

I frowned at that. What did he mean?

"Don't bother about it, Tannie," he said as he squeezed my hands. "Soldierly business. Let's talk about happier things."

I gently freed one of my hands from his and smoothed his hair back into its tail. "Like what?"

"Haven't you noticed?" He laughed. "We're here!"

"Where?"

"Urian! Just like you wanted. You're the Royal Storyteller, and I'm a guardsman, real and true. Don't you realize you finally have all the things you've been wishing for?"

Of course, he was absolutely right. If we'd been talking about the

Tanwen who existed a moon ago. She seemed more like the vapor of one of Gryfelle's song strands. At least to me.

"Honestly, Tannie." Brac reached up to touch my cheek. "I thought you'd be happier after you got over the shock. You sure you're all right?"

I forced my head to nod. "Sure. It's just been . . . a lot to take in. You know, for a farm lass."

Brac's grin stretched a league in each direction. "Not a farm lass anymore. Royal Storyteller. I'm so proud of you, Tannie." He kissed my hand.

"Thanks, Brac." A flood of tears welled behind my eyes. Couldn't even figure what they were for this time. Just the utter mess of it all, I supposed.

"Tannie, I'm a guardsman now."

"I know it, Brac."

"Maybe I'll be a knight someday."

A wave of dizziness swept over me. "That'd be . . . real nice."

"If I do . . . I mean, it's much more respectable than a farmer."

Suddenly, Brac sat up so that his mouth was level with mine. Then he kissed me. I inhaled sharply. Felt wronger than snow in summer to have Brac Bo-Bradwir on my lips.

And that's when I knew everything was changed between me and Brac. Forever.

How in the wide world would I ever explain that to him?

He finally pulled away. "Do you think we could have it all, Tannie? Your dreams and mine? Could we really be together and raise a family in Urian?"

A shower of tears leaked from my eyes before I could stop them. "I . . . I don't know, Brac."

I didn't have the strength to tell him I was trying to tear Urian to the ground. Or that my heart belonged to another.

CHAPTER 36

TANWEN

I shot up in bed. Felt like I'd barely slept a wink again, with all the tossing and turning I'd been doing over Brac.

But that wasn't what had startled me. A racket sounded somewhere—distant, like I was listening to it under water.

No. Not under water. Through two heavy oak doors.

I slid my feet into silken slippers the princess had handed down to me and shuffled out of my sleeping chambers and into the front room of my apartments. Early morning sunlight streamed in through the window. Day two of my nightmare had begun.

"Tanwen En-Yestin," an unfamiliar voice barked on the other side of the door. A man—guardsman, no doubt.

Had the king finally changed his mind? Decided the daughter of his old enemy Yestin shouldn't be allowed to keep breathing?

Either way, it wasn't like I could hide out in my chambers. *They* had the only key. Might as well open the door.

I pulled the door open.

Sure as a shipwreck, there was a black-clad guardsman I'd never seen before.

I squinted in the glare of his torch. "Morning?"

"King Gareth requests your presence."

I felt the creases on my forehead deepen. "Now? What time is it?"

"Not now. At afternoon council, of course." He stared at me like it was perfectly normal to wake a lass at sunrise to tell her she was wanted in the afternoon.

"He thought it'd take me this long to get ready?" I covered a yawn with one hand.

The guardsman snorted. "The king summons when he pleases. Best get used to it, lass." His eyes roamed up and down the length of me, like he was seeing me for the first time. "Must say, I don't mind seeing the sun rise if it means I get to call on lasses in their chambers—especially not ones as pretty as you."

I didn't even try to fake a smile. "Thanks for the message." I closed the door with a snap.

And so it begins.

The stiff corset jabbed into my ribs and squeezed the breath from my lungs. The princess's hand-me-down gown added several inches and what felt like several dozen pounds to my frame. Braith's borrowed beauticians had twisted my hair into curls, yanked it into braids, and pinned it all onto my head until I felt like the dressmaker's poke cushion.

Still, if I were being honest, I felt pretty. Couldn't help wishing that when I walked through the heavy doors to the throne room, Mor might be standing in the crowd.

Of course, if he were, that'd probably mean he'd been arrested. Then neither he nor I would give a flying flatcake how pretty I looked.

Just the idea of him being arrested set my rabble of stomach-dwelling painted-wings fluttering at an impossible pace.

"King's calling for you, lass." A guardsman keeping watch by the door nodded to me. "Ready?"

"Does it matter?" My sharp reply tumbled out before I could stop it. I tried to suck it back in with a smile. "Sorry. Nervous."

The guardsman only managed a weak smile in return. "Don't blame you, lassie."

With that extra splash of terror doused over my head, I stepped into the throne room.

Gareth's council was seated around its table—His Majesty of

Deceit and Princess Braith in their thrones on the dais. Another lady sat up there, and she could only be the queen. She looked much like Princess Braith—tall and pale. But without Braith's gentleness and grace, the queen's features seemed ugly somehow.

"Tanwen En-Yestin." Gareth smiled beneath his beard. "Welcome to court."

For some reason, this made the sea of overdressed courtiers titter.

Out of the corner of my eye, I saw the princess incline her head toward me, ever-so-slightly.

I scrambled to curtsy. "Thank you, Your Majesty."

Another titter through the crowd, and I guessed I looked pretty awkward trying to curtsy in this heavy sea-blue dress.

Braith cleared her throat. "Tanwen, you look lovely. You wear that dress far better than I ever might have."

Queen Frenhin laughed. "I knew I recognized it." Then she turned to her daughter. "Has it become your custom to give your gowns to the servants, Braith darling?"

I never thought I'd be in a fix where I'd rather be standing before all Gareth's court in my skivvies than in a fine gown. But I might've preferred my skivvies to this moment of humiliation.

Braith only smiled at her mother's rudeness. "Tanwen fits beautifully into these gowns, Mother. Remember? They're the ones I outgrew before I even wore them. And besides"—she cast a tight-lipped smile at me that seemed an apology—"I'd hardly call the Royal Storyteller a servant. Would you?"

"I suppose not," the queen said stiffly. She glanced at her husband. "Is she here to perform for us?"

"Indeed," the king answered. "I was in the mood for a little entertainment."

At sunrise, I added to myself. How strange to be a king and not worry about inconveniencing anyone else.

I curtsied again. "What story may I tell to you, Majesty?"

"Oh, Your Majesty," the high priest said. "Do have her tell one of the goddesses'." He turned toward me. "I would love to see her make another attempt at orthodoxy."

I couldn't stop staring at his head, smooth and bare as a river stone.

Wasn't quite sure what his words meant, but I didn't need to be a palace-educated courtier to know he wasn't happy with me. Guessed he was angry about the white light strand that escaped during the traditional creation story.

Sir Dray scoffed. "The goddesses again? Let's hear something of our beloved king's military conquests. I do so tire of the goddesses."

The high priest lifted one barely there eyebrow. "Careful, Your Grace. You wouldn't want to incur the wrath of those goddesses you find so tiresome."

"Oh yes. That would be a travesty."

Princess Braith's pale skin colored green, and I wondered if Dray and the priest's banter always made her ill.

The two councilmen traded barbs like sword strokes. On and on they went, and I pondered how anything was ever accomplished at court. How could it be, with these two looking to insult and undercut at every turn?

"Your Majesty?" I said, realizing a heartbeat too late that I'd interrupted the high priest of the Tirian Empire and some important Sir Whatsit of the council.

Oh well.

"Majesty, what would *you* like to hear?"

Even under his heavy, graying beard, I could see the king smile. "Well thought, Tanwen. Sometimes my nobles forget they're meant to be looking out for my interests and not their own."

Because I didn't know what in the wide world of fluff-hoppers to say to that, I curtsied a third time. Sir Dray and the priest glared daggers at me.

A familiar snicker in the crowd snagged my attention. I found Brac, guarding the edge of the clustered courtiers, just in time to watch him get his face in order and stop laughing. As he was on duty today, several additional pieces of plated armor covered different parts of him.

Seeing him fully dressed like one of Gareth's henchmen made

me want to curl up in the middle of the throne room floor and give up entirely.

Gareth scratched his beard. "Let's see. How about the one that speaks of my benevolence to my people?"

Sir Dray looked in triumph at the priest. A political story, not a religious one, had won out.

Made no difference whatsoever to me.

I cleared my throat while I dragged up the words of that tale from my memory. It was a short, easy one I'd learned in my early days with Riwor. "Once, Tir was without a shepherd."

A cream-colored strand of rope slipped from one of my hands. It swirled lazily, then looped itself into what looked like a hangman's noose.

"The people were lost without a strong hand to guide them."

The purple satin that always signified King Caradoc slithered from my other hand. Though his name wasn't spoken, the idea sure got across. He was king, but he wasn't a strong shepherd to guide Tir.

Which was all right as rain, except I was fairly sure the exact opposite was true.

The cream-colored rope and the purple satin danced through the air in slow circles.

"Then the goddesses sent us a true leader, one who would expand our boundaries, extend our influence, and, in the furnace of the world, forge the great Tirian Empire."

Gareth's poison-green satin wrapped around the purple strand until all the purple had been swallowed, like a great garden snake had swallowed its prey whole.

And then my stomach pinched.

No. Not again!

The feeling rose. I could barely scrub from my mind the images of wild strands of story, song, and color careening around the Corsyth. The energy of something creative and real and true bubbled around inside me until I thought I'd burst.

"The . . . shepherd . . ." I could barely force the words out for fear of what else might fly from my mouth if I opened it too long.

The green strand paled to yellow, like it was supposed to, but the tone was off. Looked a sickly sort of color rather than the golden wheat it was supposed to be turning into. My body swayed, and I wondered if I might faint.

The clank of armor drew my gaze. Brac had taken a step toward me. Concern was stamped all over his face, but he seemed stretched between two duties—one to me and one to the guardsman who kept signaling him to stay right where he was.

Hoping to keep Brac out of trouble, I choked out the next words of the story. "The shepherd led his people well."

There, that'd helped. The story looked a little less nauseous now. But the rising feeling inside me didn't go away.

Everything around me started to blur. I couldn't see Brac anymore. My legs fought to keep me upright. I darted a wild glance at the courtiers surrounding me on both sides.

And Gryfelle came to mind.

She could have been any one of these pretty ladies—rouged up and flirting with the knights and lords. How many times had she stood in this throne room as a child, smashing down the bubbling feeling inside? And look what it'd done to her.

Suddenly, I knew what story was trying to spill out of me: the story of a graceful young noble whose life had been stolen from her—who lived a waking nightmare. A fairy story, but backward and inside-out, where the ending was horror forevermore instead of happily ever after.

I prayed for forgiveness, because I was about to break my promise to Mor again. I hushed the story that wanted to come out. I hushed it with every ounce of will I had.

"The shepherd tended his people like a kindly father."

The sheaf of wheat glowed golden, and the cream-colored rope wrapped around it and tied itself into a knot.

"And they loved him for it."

The story crystallized. The perfect, transparent bundle of wheat dropped into my hand as though it hadn't nearly killed me to get it out.

Silence echoed through the throne room. Then a sudden eruption of applause.

Braith rose from her throne as she clapped. "Well done, Tanwen! It's the finest I've ever seen. The glass is clear as our best glass-blowers could make."

The other courtiers clapped and nodded, and council seemed pleased. Even the king and queen smiled.

I smiled back—hoped I looked gracious and mannered enough.

But inside, I wondered. How long could I smash down those churning stories of truth before I slipped into a nightmare myself?

CHAPTER 37

BRAITH

The storytelling had ended, and Tanwen had been escorted from the throne room so that council might begin.

Braith sighed.

"Something the matter, darling?" The king leaned toward her.

"No, Your Majesty." Braith didn't even bother forcing a smile. "Just thinking."

"Well," the king said as he leaned back, "perhaps glad tidings would cheer you."

"Glad tidings, Your Majesty?"

"Watch and see," the king instructed. "It all begins to fall into place." He nodded to Sir Dray, who nodded to a guardsman at the back of the hall.

Some commotion erupted in the hallway, then there was a muffled cry, and a cluster of people appeared in the doorway.

Braith might have known only something truly dreadful would have the king in such a fine mood.

Four guardsmen marched down the green carpet. Two of them clutched a girl between them. She was doubled nearly in half—either beaten into submission or exhausted beyond her ability—and the guards dragged her more than she walked.

The poor lass had the most vibrant sweet-root–colored hair Braith had ever seen. But it tumbled in front of her face in a knotted tangle. Braith could only guess what she had been through.

One of the guards shoved the girl. "Stand before your king."

The girl swayed and nearly fell to the floor, but the guards beside her hoisted her back to her feet. She seemed to take a deep breath before straightening as best she could.

Braith leaped from her chair. "Your Majesty!"

A murmur shot through the crowd, but Braith's gaze stayed fixed on the girl before her.

"Majesty, this girl is clearly with child!"

A full, rounded belly showed, even under the girl's loose peasant clothing. A couple short weeks from delivery, at most. Perhaps days. She swelled to the point of bursting.

The king didn't show any hint of alarm. In fact, a smile bloomed on his face. "Indeed she is." He turned to Braith. "One of the Corsyth weavers—the farmer. This is his wife. Don't you see, darling? She's the perfect lure. If anything will draw the farmer and the others from their cowardly hiding, it's her."

Braith stared at her father for a long moment. Live bait to draw his enemies from hiding. Just as he was using Tanwen.

Braith strode down the dais steps toward the girl. "What is your name, child?"

The lass's lip trembled. "Ifmere."

"Ifmere, you will not be harmed. Do you understand me? I'll see to it that you will not be harmed." Braith raised her voice to the rest of the room. "No one will harm this girl or I will pay you back for your wickedness tenfold! I swear it by my own blood. Stars preserve you if you test my words."

Thunder might have sounded from the king's throne and Braith wouldn't have been surprised. But only silence answered her oath. Finally, Braith turned to look at the king.

He eyed her with no passion at all. Only cold amusement brewed in his expression.

Braith supposed she should be pleased, but somehow it stoked the fire swimming in her veins.

Sir Dray rose from his seat and came to stand beside Braith. He spoke quietly to her. "Of course, Your Highness. The lass will not be harmed. Only used to our advantage—to your king's advantage."

Braith's lip trembled, but not because she might cry. She could barely keep her voice steady through her anger. "Look at the girl. Curses of Noswitch, Dray! Look at her face!"

Purple bruises blossomed on Ifmere's pale skin. Red lacerations striped what bits of flesh Braith could see—her arms, her legs, her face.

"Don't tell me she's not to be harmed," Braith hissed to Dray. "She already has been."

The king inspected something under his fingernail. "A necessary inconvenience for the greater cause. Come, come, Braith. You must think of the larger good being served here. One girl in exchange for a band of outlaws who have evaded capture for a very long time. I count the cost and find it suits."

Sir Dray placed a hand on Braith's arm. "Majesty, it is difficult for one so tender as Her Highness to properly weigh the cost in such matters. Do forgive her. Isn't it why we love her so?"

Dray reached up and stroked Braith's cheek—right there in front of the council, the nobles of the court, and the guardsmen keeping watch. Such of gesture of familiarity in public—Dray might as well have sent the town criers about Tir with an engagement announcement.

Before Braith could collect her wits, excited whispers and giggles raced throughout the room. The court was clearly pleased at the suggestion of romance between His Grace and Her Royal Highness.

Braith felt sick.

She shot a desperate look in her parents' direction. The queen looked puzzled, but not displeased. She would probably prefer a prince of some stripe to a lowborn merchant's son. But, despite his humble roots, Dray certainly had made something of himself. He was a powerful nobleman and technically a knight. He held sway over much of the kingdom's business. The queen would easily be persuaded to accept the match.

The king tented his fingers before his mouth as he eyed the prospective couple. And Braith could see a look of pleasure in his eyes.

She stared at her father and wondered how he had become a stranger—someone she didn't recognize.

Or perhaps she had never known him at all.

CHAPTER 38

TANWEN

If I didn't watch myself, I was going to pace a blazing hole through my fine rug. Seemed all I did anymore was walk back and forth on that blasted thing.

Trapped. The guard watching my every move.

A black strand of frustration slithered from my finger. I blew it away, then walked into the space where it'd been.

Maybe I could plot an escape while Brac was on duty. Maybe he could be assigned to guard my door.

A strand of brown leather spun itself into a floppy farmer's hat before I could even think it into existence.

But, no, that wouldn't work. I'd have to tell him everything and put his life in danger. Even if I did tell him and he did want to help me, there were never fewer than two guards nearby.

I waved my hand and made the hat disappear.

Maybe I could escape out of the window somehow.

A strand burst from my palm and coiled into a rope in three seconds flat. But then what? I could only crystallize it and make it into glass. I didn't yet know Mor's trick of making other things, like rocks. If I didn't crystallize it, I'd be working with an idea strand that could disappear from my fingers at any minute if my concentration wobbled.

That was likely to end with my dead body in the courtyard below.

I flicked the idea rope away with a sigh.

I reached down for the familiar bump that always rested over my chest—the silver knot on my necklace. But I couldn't feel it anymore.

Not beneath my corset and the many layers of satin and brocade. All these fine clothes sure could stifle a girl.

I pulled on the leather cord to retrieve the knot from the front of my dress. The silver trinket stared up at me from my palm.

"What would you have done, Mother?"

The silver didn't venture a response. But it caught a ray of sunlight from the window and winked at me. I flopped onto the couch.

"Not helpful." I turned the charm over between my fingers.

Even if Brac didn't agree with me or understand why I needed to escape, he'd never sell me out. Was there some way to take advantage of his position in the guard without risking his neck?

No. Just didn't seem possible, no matter which direction I tried to look at it.

I dropped my head into my hands.

Useless. I'd been a blazing fool to think I might be able to bring down Gareth from the inside. How could I possibly, when he was my captor and I was powerless as a hamstrung hedge-nibbler?

After a good solid minute of feeling sorry for myself, I peeked between my fingers. The hollow bookcase along the back wall caught my eye. The one where the stones showed through the back instead of being all finished with wood like the others.

I climbed to my feet and crossed to the bookcase. A person wasn't likely to just leave one bookcase different for no reason.

I looked down at my right hand. I had begun fiddling with the charm again without realizing it.

With my left hand, I felt the stones at the back of one shelf in the mystery bookcase. Nothing unusual. Just regular old stones, like you might expect.

I ran my hand along the stones on the shelf just below. Nothing.

Then I stretched to my tiptoes and reached for the shelf above. Normal, smooth stones. What had I possibly been expecting to—

My breath froze in my chest, and my hand stilled on the wall. One of my fingers had caught a small rough spot. Wouldn't have thought a thing of it, except the pattern was familiar to my touch.

In fact . . . I stared down at the silver charm in my right hand. I was feeling the exact same shape in my left hand as my right.

A moment of deathly stillness passed. Then it was like the room exploded into motion.

I darted to the desk and grabbed the chair behind it. Took some doing, but I dragged that blasted heavy thing over to the shelf like a grazer hitched for plowing. Scrambling onto a chair in a corset and gown is not the easiest of tasks, but somehow I hoisted myself up so I could see what I was doing.

And there it was—a small, round chink out of the stone, with grooves in all the right places. No one would notice such a thing, except the shape was the most comfortable in the world to me.

I ducked out of my necklace and held it in my hand. One deep breath and a silent prayer later, I pressed the silver charm into the dent in the stone.

Click.

Something gave. I could barely wrangle a breath.

The stone with the hole in it loosened. I wrapped my fingers around the edges of the stone as best I could, then wiggled. A fresh shock ran through me when I pulled the stone out and found it wasn't a stone at all. Not truly anyway. More like the face of a stone locked into place so it'd look like part of a wall. But a big, hollow space stood behind it.

And in the space was a lever.

I grabbed it and pushed forward, hard as I could. Then a pang of fear darted through me. Maybe I ought to have thought about that for half a second before I did it. What if it opened some kind of trap door that made me fall into Gareth's garderobe or something?

Too late now.

But I didn't drop through the floor, and no one fell from the ceiling onto me. Instead, the whole piece of the wall behind the hollow bookcase clicked like the false stone had done.

And I felt the whole panel budge away from the wall.

Puffs of dust billowed around the bookcase. Seemed safe to guess the door hadn't been used in some time.

I shoved the chair out of the way, then pulled on the panel with everything in me. Though these stones were just faces too, a whole panel full of them was heavier than a side of grazer. And the rusted hinges didn't help me much.

But finally the hidden door squealed its last protest and gave way.

An empty hallway, black as pitch, gaped at me.

I dashed forward, then stopped just short of the entrance. Could be dangerous, after all. Who could even guess where it would lead?

But now that I was closer, I could see the hallway wasn't empty. There were more bookcases all along the sides.

And these weren't bare like the ones in my room. Leather-bound books filled every shelf from top to bottom. The light from my room only shone into the passageway so far, but the books went far as I could see.

I dared a few steps into the darkness, then reached out and pulled one dusty volume from the nearest shelf. I angled the cover toward the light so I might catch the words branded on the front.

The book bobbled in my hands. It landed with a flat plunk on the floor.

Because those words branded across the cover shot strange fire through my heart: Yestin Bo-Arthio.

CHAPTER 39

TANWEN

My gaze flew over the pages and pages of script. An entry for every day—decades worth, it seemed.

The goings-on at court. Observations about King Caradoc. Reports of military campaigns. Notes about "dear Glain"—my own mother. Detailed lists of what plants had been set up in Father's personal garden, and which of them had yielded the best harvest.

The entries bounced from mundane details about life to items of "national importance," as Father said. I stumbled over a few words. Father seemed to have swallowed a glossary of fancy speech at some point, for all the words he knew that I'd never even heard of. And his handwriting was so fine—he must have had very good schooling.

I couldn't even imagine that he was my father. Not truly. Didn't seem possible.

I replaced one book and pulled out another from the next shelf over.

I opened the book to a page in the middle . . .

Second moon of winter, the 40th year of Caradoc II

Tragedy has struck our kingdom this night. All of Tir will mourn when they hear the news. Caradoc and Wynne, the good king and queen, perished in the same night. I fear there will be a struggle for the throne. Every lord with a speck of noble blood within him and every councilman with a trace of ambition will make a play for Tir if we do not act quickly to secure whichever heir Caradoc has specified in his will. Surely it will be his nephew Rhydian, but the lad is only a child. Or perhaps it is Kharn Bo-Candryd—more distant a claim, but at least that lad is old enough to grow whiskers.

The sorrow is oppressive. I feel I must escape the palace. Alas, I cannot. Reports have trickled in all through the night via the servants. The plague, whatever it is, has struck at least half the council by my count. It is my duty to stay here. There will be work to do once the quarantine is over, and as King Caradoc's First General, plenty of it will fall to me. And yet something inside me tells me to run. It's unconscionable, but I cannot seem to quiet it.

Perhaps Glain and I will take the child to Pembrone when the snow melts. The ocean cliffs are the place to be if one feels pressed down by grief. A place to heal. To stare at the great, wide Menfor Sea could only act as a salve on these horrible wounds.

They are sleeping now. One last night of peaceful sleep, then they will awaken into this nightmare with the rising of the sun.

I stopped reading and pressed the journal to my heart—just where my necklace usually hung.

These were my own father's thoughts about the terrible night that changed the course of all our lives—the night that changed the course of all Tir.

I reopened the journal and skimmed through page after page. And then stopped.

Second moon of winter, the 40th year of Caradoc II

I may be the only man loyal to the king who knows this. My life is already forfeit. If I can preserve any shred of the truth by recording my overhearings, then may it be so.

Creator help us all.

I became restless this afternoon. I can't count the number of times I've gone through all my books. I ignored the quarantine and ventured out. The halls echoed with every step I took, so empty were they. As I walked, I listed the remaining council members in my mind.

Arian, the steward of trade. Goncro, my second-in-command. Both had been at odds with the king of late, but I was glad to hear they and their wives survived the plague.

And then there was the other. Fire and sulfur could rain down from the heavens and it seemed he would persist. Like a great scuttlebug. But even as his name crawled through my mind, churning up unpleasantness, I heard his voice—not in my head, but echoing through the halls. His voice, and that of his lapdog.

They made no effort to moderate their volume, as I'm sure they believed the castle halls deserted. The two of them were recounting the very same ruminations which had just been rolling through my mind.

"Goncro attended the supper feast, but didn't drink the wine. He lives and will move into his new role as Protector of the Realm immediately. Arian begged off the feast altogether, and he is already drafting proposals to increase royal revenue via trade tax."

There was a pause. "I haven't seen the bodies of Yestin and Glain turn up yet."

The other laughed. "Rotting in their beds, most likely. Must have keeled over too late to be brought down before the quarantine. No matter. We'll get them in the next day or two when I lift the confinement order from the palace."

Conspiracy.

Murder.

Poison in the wine at the king's table. And he—the betrayer—the king's closest advisor, Gareth Bo-Kelwyd.

I flipped through a few more pages, then this: *Glain says it is imperative I stay alive. The truth must be preserved in me, the only eyewitness.*

Suddenly weak, I leaned against the shelves for support. Thoughts and emotions began to clash inside me as the pieces clicked into place. If Father died, the truth died with him. His story would dwindle and fade like a dying fire until it was nothing more than whispered gossip. So my mother decided to sacrifice her own safety that he might live on, and the true story with him. Then he would stage an uprising and all Tir would know the truth. The throne would be reclaimed for the line of Caradoc II.

And that's how my father had become a folk hero to all the rebels.

I thought of what my friends at the Corsyth had said. Everyone in Tir knew who Yestin Bo-Arthio was. The Corsyth weavers had said he was very good.

But the uprising had failed. It had all been for nothing.

A bolt of anger raced through me. I slammed the book shut and shoved it back on the shelf.

Not anger at Father. It wasn't his fault. He hadn't asked for any of it—who would?

But just at the whole of it. So many lost years. Everyone in Tir knew my parents, but I'd never had a chance to.

I stared at the spine of the journal I'd just been reading—one of what seemed a hundred, at least. How many years had he journaled every day? Were they mostly blank? How old was he when he disappeared? I tried to make a guess at it, but the figuring was too full of question marks.

I grabbed another journal off the shelves and began reading.

CHAPTER 40

THE ONE IN THE DARK

Third Moon. Winter. Usurper's Year.

Glain is dead.

The child is gone. Did Glain smuggle her from the palace? How will I ever know?

The uprising has failed. All are dead.

Unless Bennati remains somehow. He knew of these passages that are now my prison. But does he know I'm here, or shall I rot in these walls?

Where is Tannie?

CHAPTER 41

TANWEN

I SQUEEZED THE JOURNAL SO TIGHT I WONDERED IF IT MIGHT crumble in my fingers. It was like I was meeting my father for the first time through his writings.

He'd once hidden in the palace walls. Secret passages no one knew about except his friend Bennati, who seemed to be a Meridioni noble or something. Bennati was dead. Father's grief had poured out through one of the other entries.

Without his friend, had Father starved in the walls? Had he remained undiscovered, or had Gareth's goons sniffed him out?

I picked up the next book.

With a bracing breath, I forced myself to look at each word—to chew on it, remember what it meant, and move to the next one.

Father's sentences began to ramble in places. Some things didn't make any kind of reasonable sense. Sometimes Father even sounded like Fethow, Pembrone's most loyal tavern customer. I didn't think Fethow had been sober two days together the whole time I'd been alive.

But Father hadn't been drunk when he'd written these entries.

Reading his words reminded me of the time Ma-Bradwir had knitted a new pair of socks for Farmer Bradwir. She hadn't quite finished them when one of the wee ones darted by and got his trousers hooked on the yarn strand. Before anyone could stop him, the little lad had run clear to the other side of the house—and taken that whole strand of yarn with him. Ma-Bradwir's work disappeared in five seconds flat, and she was madder than a tea kettle.

Father's mind was like that pair of socks. Unraveled.

He had started referring to himself in a strange, removed way—like he was witnessing his own life from somewhere outside his body. Odd.

I turned through several pages of rambling, then something new caught my eye.

Someone had discovered him in the passages. She was dark and beautiful, it seemed. And she helped him. In some of his words, it seemed he knew her, perhaps from before his time in the wall. But in other places, he spoke of her as a mysterious stranger. One he wanted to trust but wasn't sure he ought to.

I took half a moment to find my candle on the desk. The sun had failed for the day, but I had to keep reading. I lit the candle and returned to my spot, just inside the very passageways that had become my father's private dungeon.

A loud thump muscled me from sleep.

"Tanwen En-Yestin?" a muffled voice I vaguely recognized was coming from the other side of my door. "Open the door, in the name of the king!"

I rubbed the sleep off my face. The burned-down stub of my candle sat in its holder next to me. Two journals were stacked just beside me, and a third lay open under my face—the page smudged by my drool.

"Ah, just a minute!" My gaze bounced all around the room, from the journals to the open secret passageway. "I'm still dressing. Be there in a moment!" I prayed my visitor wouldn't just barge in, as he easily might.

I shoved the journals and my candle safely into the passageway then scrambled to get the door closed. With a mighty shove, everything clicked back into place. I thrust the false stone into its hole, then yanked my silver necklace away and pulled it back over my head.

The muffled voice sounded again. "What was that noise?"

"Oh, you know . . ." I dropped the leather cord and silver charm down the front of my dress. "Just . . . girl stuff." I smoothed my hair, though it can't have helped much, plastered on a smile, then pulled the door open.

The high priest with his bald head and rich robes stood before me, a guardsman on either side of him. He frowned so deep he would've given Riwor a run for her money in a race for sourest face.

"Oh," I began. "Your . . ." But I couldn't remember what I was supposed to call him. Not Your Majesty. Your Baldness? Your Sourness? Your Honored Fussiness?

His frown deepened. "Your Eminence. Or Holiness. Whichever you prefer."

Rather preferred my own titles for him, if His Pompousness wanted to know the truth.

But I curtsied. "Your Eminence."

He gestured to the guards. "Thank you. I will speak with Tanwen alone now."

The guards bowed and returned to their places beside my door. It was the only time I could remember wishing the guardsmen would stay closer. The thought of the high priest in my chambers with me, alone, made my stomach wrench.

But His Holiness glided into my room and closed the door behind himself like he had more right to be there than I did.

"So. Tanwen En-Yestin."

I stared at him. "Yes, Your Eminence?"

"The king requests your presence in the throne room in one hour. Are you aware that you missed morning meal?"

I prayed my laugh sounded natural. "Did I? Oh dear. I stayed up late last night. Practicing," I added on sudden inspiration. "My stories. For the king. Obviously."

He eyed me for a long, awful moment. "Of course."

A heartbeat of thick silence passed between us. I didn't really like to lie. Felt like it left a film on my tongue.

I cleared my throat. "Will that be all, Your Eminence?"

An oily smile slid across his mouth. "I must tell you something, and you have great need to hear it, Tanwen."

I stared. "All right."

"Remember who you are."

My blank stare must have gotten blanker.

Remember who I was—what did he mean? My father's daughter? My mother's daughter? A weaver of the Corsyth? I'd never forget any of those things. But I didn't suppose that was what he was driving at.

"Your Holiness?"

He took a long, slow breath, then began to pace my room. "You are a peasant, Tanwen."

In spite of myself, a little pang of hurt shot through me. Still couldn't quite break away from that lass who wanted to *be* someone. But I hid it behind a smile. "Aye, Your Eminence. I am. Can't hide that, even though I'd like to."

His smile got oilier, slicker, and more arrogant. "Indeed. You are also a story peddler, Tanwen. Do you know the purpose of a story peddler?"

"To sell stories, sir?"

He paused. "No. Such is merely the means to support the livelihood of a story peddler. But the *purpose* of the peddler is to glorify the goddesses."

For some reason, the shrewd face of Sir Dray came to mind. "And to glorify the king, Your Holiness?"

"Of course." He narrowed his eyes. "But to glory the goddesses is to glory the king, for it was they who appointed His Majesty. Isn't that true?"

I chewed on my answer for a moment. "That's what the stories tell us." That wasn't a lie, at least.

He looked at me. "You shall fit in well here at court."

Wasn't sure that was much of a compliment.

Naith inclined his head slightly. "I'll leave you now." He turned for the door, then stopped. "Oh, and Tanwen?"

"Yes, Your Eminence?"

"You ought to change out of that gown. Is it not the one you wore yesterday?"

He didn't wait for an answer. In another breath, he was gone. I looked down at my heavy dress and secondhand jeweled slippers. Guessed he knew I had been lying about taking so long to answer the door because I was changing.

But he was right. I ought to dress and report to my devil of a master before he decided to free my neck of the burden of my head.

I heaved a sigh. Dream job, my jewel-encrusted foot.

CHAPTER 42
TANWEN

I STOOD BEFORE THE COURT IN ANOTHER OF BRAITH'S HAND-ME-down dresses, a deep purple gown with shimmering gold embroidery. I'm sure I'd imagined gowns as fine, but I don't think I'd ever thought I would truly own one.

It didn't sit well on me.

The king gestured with a flourish. "Well, well. Here's my little storyteller. We have need of entertainment today, I think."

"Good afternoon, Your Majesty," I said.

"We missed you at morning meal."

"My apologies. I stayed up too late last night."

"Yes." The king chuckled. "Lasses will sometimes, I suppose."

Sir Dray rose from his seat and stood before the dais. Braith leaned away from him noticeably.

"Majesty," Dray said, standing near the princess but addressing the king. "Might I request a story?" He reached up and took Braith's hand.

The fine leather of his gloves was the only barrier between their hands, and even from my distance, I could see Braith trying to pull her hand back.

She shot a worried glance at her father, but Gareth looked downright jovial. "Yes, Sir Dray. What story would you like to request?"

"I don't know. What's your fancy, Braith dear?"

Braith's face ignited. "Sir Dray, I—"

Gareth cut her off with a laugh. "Come now, Braith. Surely you can think of a story you would like to hear."

His gaze roved to the front of the crowd. There Cameria stood, dignified and stately. Gareth's jolly demeanor slipped. "I see you brought your pet with you today."

"Father." Braith's tone was bordering on severe—at least for her. She stared hard at Gareth while attempting to pull her hand away from Dray. "Please do not dishonor my friend. She so rarely comes to court with me as it is, and I'd not see her treated poorly."

"Friend?" Gareth glared poison back at his daughter. After a long moment, he nodded to me. "Very well, storyteller. Tell the story that would honor our Meridioni guest. I think you know the one."

Dray gave Braith's hand an obvious squeeze, then winked at her so openly I'm sure the whole court saw it. The crowd's whispers rustled like wind through the throne room. Braith's face couldn't have been any redder if she'd stuck it into the fireplace.

Dray finally released her hand and returned to his chair, thank the moon for Braith's sake. As he sat, he gestured to Cameria. "Don't be shy, woman. Go stand with your mistress."

Cameria's gaze lingered on Gareth for a long moment, fire dancing in her eyes.

She finally turned and moved gracefully toward the dais, chin high and eyes straight ahead. Braith shot her friend a glance—one that seemed to beg forgiveness for the indignity she was about to suffer. Then the princess turned toward me and frowned. My face felt clammy and must have been pale as mist. Last time I told this story, it turned my life upside down.

But I cleared my throat and began the practiced piece. "Once, there was a people who lived to the south of the great state of Tir."

Two strands of silvery light cascaded from my hands. The strands swirled through the air. The crowd gasped, and some of the ladies clapped.

"Tir lived at peace with her neighbor to the south for many generations, with Tir looking after her lesser neighbor like a father looks after his child."

The two strands soared together, then dove toward the ground. More gasps, more grins, more applause.

"But over time, the darkness of pride consumed the people to the south. So much darkness that it swallowed them from the inside out. It blackened their hair, darkened their skin, and they became known as the Meridioni—'Dark People' in their native tongue."

One of the silvery strands shot above the crowd and circled the air near the ceiling of the throne room. The other slowly transformed. The silvery tip deepened. Blood-red color, spreading like ink, seeped through the strand until the whole thing was consumed. Red, just like the Meridioni flag.

"The Dark People to the south became bolder and more prideful by the year, until they had truly forgotten their kind father to the north."

The red strand tightened into a circle then waved into a shape—a fish with glistening red scales.

I saw Braith look over at Cameria's frozen face.

For the love of fluff-hoppers, I didn't want to continue. But Gareth was staring at me. What else could I do?

I swallowed hard. "For some time, this father nation had lacked a strong leader to enact discipline upon the disobedient, prideful child. But when its ruler succumbed to the plague, King Gareth Bo-Kelwyd came to power, and with him the strength and resolve of the father nation was renewed. The father to the north knew it was time to discipline his unruly child in the south."

The silver strand transformed to green satin, then it whizzed up into the air. With a sound that brought to mind the clash of two swords, the green strand formed itself into a blade, now silvery green. A beautiful greatsword, like those belonging to the knights of the high guard.

"With King Gareth on the throne, Father Tir brought his child back under his wing to retrain and correct her as only a kindly father can." Bile rose in my throat.

The sword floated upward. Then in a swift thrust, it speared the fish through the mouth. The story shrank down and crystallized into a smaller version of itself. It dropped into my hand.

I held it up toward the royal family on the dais, devoid of all feeling except the sickness washing over me. "For King Gareth, protector of the Meridioni people and benevolent ruler of the Tirian Empire."

"Ah. Thank you, storyteller." Gareth took the story and handed it over to Braith. "For your servant, darling. Lest she or her fellows ever forget." He raised an eyebrow at the princess. "Lest you forget, too."

The story—beautiful in form, wretched in symbol—looked heavy in Braith's hand. She hesitated. Didn't seem keen to hand it over to Cameria, and who could blame her?

But Cameria stepped close. "It is all right, Princess," she said. "Hand it to me."

Braith paused another moment. Then she passed the impaled fish to her trusted companion.

Cameria gripped the story. For a moment, it seemed the crystallized words might shatter in her palm. But then she dropped the story into her apron pocket. "Thank you, Your Majesty," she said to the king. Just the slightest hint of a Meridioni accent rolled through her Tirian speech. And tears rolled down her face—silent, strong.

Tears shed on account of Gareth Bo-Kelwyd seemed enough to fill the Menfor Sea.

CHAPTER 43
TANWEN

I STARED AT THE LUMP IN CAMERIA'S APRON POCKET. IT HAD never been my favorite story. I had always wished the fish would've crystallized without the sword. It was such a pretty creature, all glistening red scales and glittering black eyes.

But now the symbol of the Meridioni fish run through with a sword was a hundred times worse than before. Now I knew Meridioni people like Dylun and Cameria. And now I knew the real truth of Gareth—what he'd done to Meridione, what he'd done to Tir.

He took whatever he wanted and murdered anyone who resisted.

Like Father's friend, Bennati. He'd been the Meridioni ambassador, according to one of the journals. Obviously, he'd had to go. Probably even before a war was declared right and proper.

I looked harder at Braith's beautiful Meridioni maid. Father's journals spoke of his helper as a dark beauty—someone he had known. Someone who had been connected to Bennati and who stayed in the palace after the Meridioni were enslaved. I studied Cameria's face again.

Could it be?

I drew a sharp breath.

Why hadn't I made the connection last night? Braith's maid had to be the woman who had kept my father alive in the walls—the daughter of Bennati. Who else could it have been?

I wanted to run up to her and beg her to tell me exactly what had happened to Father. Maybe I could finally know the true story of Yestin Bo-Arthio. I had been after it my whole life.

I felt frozen in time. But only for the space of a breath. Because suddenly, a huge commotion exploded at the back of the hall. Armor clanking, shouts, screams.

Gareth and half the council rose from their chairs. King's guard all around the room drew their swords.

Gareth's voice boomed above the racket. "What is the meaning of this?"

A guardsman stumbled down the green carpet toward us. "We found them, Majesty! But they're not coming easy."

A smattering of guardsmen burst into the room, my Brac among them. It took four of them to drag their captive before the king. It couldn't have been worse if the ceiling had crashed in on us at that moment.

Smirky-faced, dark-haired, gold-ringed Mor was clutched between four of the soldiers. My heart plummeted to my toes.

On seeing me, his eyes went wide. "Tannie. You're alive."

Brac stood rigid. "Tannie?"

Too familiar for Mor to have been my captor, as Brac still believed him to have been. Maybe too familiar, period.

I shut my eyes against the wave of dread swelling inside. Everything was fixing to crumble to pieces. And there wasn't a thing I could do to stop it.

CHAPTER 44

TANWEN

"Mor," I whispered through tears. "They found you."

Mor stopped struggling for a moment. "We didn't know if they'd spared you. And if they had, we couldn't leave you and Ifmere here alone in the dungeon, could we now?" He scanned my fancy getup. "Although . . ."

Brac had drawn closer. "Alone? Now listen here, pirate. Tannie ain't been—"

But a shout from the back of the hall cut him off. "Let me go, you dirty, ruddy hunk of metal!" Zelyth writhed in the hands of a half dozen of Gareth's men.

Just behind him, Gryfelle, Karlith, and Dylun stumbled into the room at the shoves of their captors. And then my heart fell, for Aeron and Warmil also appeared—hands bound and weaponless.

Hopelessness oozed from my very skin. All captured, totally defenseless. The Corsyth weavers were doomed.

But if it was their time to die, I'd rather it be my time, too. If I didn't have my allies on the outside, any thought of tearing down Gareth's regime from the inside would be for naught. How could one lowly peasant hope to unseat a tyrant? I glanced at the princess. She'd gone white.

I stepped away from the royals and toward the ragged band of prisoners—toward Brac in his palace guard getup. "Guess you better bind me, too."

"Huh?" Brac shook his head, like it was full of chaff that wanted clearing. "Tannie, what're you—"

"Silence, all of you!" Gareth's voice fairly ripped the air in two. "I demand an explanation immediately."

The first guardsman spoke up. "They were sneaking into the palace, Your Majesty. Bo-Bradwir was making his rounds and saw one of them. He alerted his unit, and it wasn't long before we'd nabbed them all."

"Where is my wife?" Zel shouted. He yanked an arm free and took a wild swing at the nearest guardsman. The soldier, who wasn't wearing a helmet, took the blow to the jaw and stumbled backward.

Zel twisted around to find another guardsman to clobber. "Where is Ifmere?"

At the council table, Sir Dray lounged back in his chair, as though he were reclining in a palace garden. "Your wife's chances would have been better had she not been in such a useless state."

If they could have, Zel's eyes would have shot streams of flame. "What're you driving at?"

"You're young yet, lad." Sir Dray shrugged. "But soon you'll learn that the uses for a country lass are few, and your wife's advanced state of pregnancy made her profitable for none of them."

By the puzzled expression on Brac's face, the meaning of Dray's words had sailed over his head. But Zel got the point. His face reddened by the split-second. Nothing seemed lost on Princess Braith, and by the looks of her, she was absorbing the full implication of Dray's words. Her face was ashen and she was shaking.

"Your Majesty," she said to the king, "have you killed this man's wife—the one who was nearly ready to deliver a baby? The one I swore to protect by my blood?"

Thundering silence followed, and my insides twisted. Would they have? Would they have taken the life of an innocent lass and her unborn baby?

But I knew the answer.

I looked at Brac. He stared back at me, eyes swimming with all the dozen things he must be feeling. If only we'd had a true moment alone where I could have poured out my heart to him. If only things hadn't worked out just as they had, I might have found the right time to explain. Might have been able to make him understand what had really happened, danger be blazed.

Couldn't help feeling like I'd made an even bigger mess of things by not telling him.

Brac turned to the king, and in what could only have been a moment of daftness brought on by his confusion, he spoke without being addressed first. "It ain't true, is it, Majesty? Whatever these outlaws done, you wouldn't murder someone's wife and baby, would you?"

Gareth rose, terrible and slow, like a great dragon taking a breath before spewing fire onto its enemies. "Boy, you might reconsider addressing your king thusly."

Brac's throat bobbed up and down. "Apologies, Your Majesty. But . . ." He frowned.

Poor lad couldn't seem to clamp his mouth shut.

So before he could say anything else, I opened mine. "Don't you see now?" I forced Brac to meet my eyes, then nodded to the captive weavers. "They're not the enemy."

Brac's mouth opened a little, and he took a step back.

Zel's anguished cry cut through the tension in the room. "Where is Ifmere? What have you done to her?"

I glanced at the princess. She'd risen beside her father. Her milk-white cheeks had colored pink. Seemed she wanted the answer to that question near as much as Zel.

Sir Dray was laughing again, and I could only shake my head. Did he think he could ever make Princess Braith love him after such a display of callousness? Seemed he didn't understand her at all, or else he was scheming greater designs at the moment.

"Come now, everyone," he said. "Unless something terribly unfortunate has happened, she should be locked safely in her cell." He turned to a huge guardsman knight that always seemed to be about the king. "Isn't that right, Baedden?"

The knight grunted. "Aye. In 'er cell."

"Cell?" Braith's voice pitched high and angry. "I arranged a guarded room for the girl, comfortable and well furnished with a midwife to attend to her. I saw to it she was placed there myself. Why were my orders disobeyed?"

Gareth glanced at his daughter. "Last I checked, my orders superseded even those of the princess." He snatched her arm in his heavy hand. "No matter how presumptuous that princess has become."

Braith winced at his grip. The courtiers looked to have turned to stone. Every fan stilled. Every whisper quieted.

"Come, come," Dray said, and even he looked uncomfortable. "The girl is well enough. Although . . ."

Braith stared daggers at him. "Although what, Dray?"

"Last I heard, her time had just about come."

Braith put her free hand to her chest. "That girl has been laboring in a dungeon cell? How long?"

"As of this morning," Dray said.

Braith wrenched her arm from her father's grip and gave him a look like she'd just seen him for the first time. "How could you?" She took a step away from him. "You're a monster."

"Tanwen." Mor's low whisper barely caught my notice.

I turned my eyes away from Braith and Gareth on the dais. Mor's gaze burned into me, like he was trying to tell me something important without using words. He nodded to Zel.

But Zel seemed defeated—bent double, body shaking—with big breaths or sobs, I couldn't tell. What was Mor trying to tell me?

But then I saw what he saw.

Strands, curling through the air. Clear, almost invisible. But there, for certain.

What was it Zel had told me about his stories—something about them being wild? I swallowed hard.

It was like time slowed and every movement dragged as if through water.

Zel sucked in a long breath. The other weavers fought against their restrainers and Mor's eyes widened.

Then his shout—odd, muffled, and slow—floated to my ears. "Tannie, duck!"

I didn't waste a second to consider Mor's command. I dropped to my hands and knees on the green carpet. And just in time. Zel's clear strands exploded into ribbons and ribbons of orange fire.

No, not fire. Hair—sweet-root–colored hair, like Ifmere's.

It blasted into the air all around and knocked the nearby guardsmen onto their backsides and knees, some flat on their backs. Courtiers screamed, ladies fainted. Strands raced everywhere. Orange bedlam.

"Tannie!" Brac's voice reached me through the confusion, but I couldn't see him. Couldn't see anything through the swirling orange strands.

I glanced behind me, and as a strand lifted, I saw Warmil wrestling with his captor. Trying to get the guardsman's sword.

"Brac!" I called. "Brac, where are you?"

Then a strand waved away in front of me and I saw him. He had Mor around the throat from behind, and his sword was drawn.

CHAPTER 45

TANWEN

"BRAC!" DOUBTFUL HE COULD HEAR ME THROUGH THE DIN. "Brac, don't!" I scrambled closer, but I didn't think I'd reach him in time. Couldn't possibly.

Not Mor. Please, not Mor.

Whether Brac heard me or not, something seemed to be staying his sword. He could have made the kill stroke many times over. But he hesitated with his blade at Mor's throat.

Just as I neared them, Brac released Mor with a bit of a shove. Then he turned his sword round and handed it to Mor, hilt first. "Better use it right, pirate."

Mor took it, mouth slightly open.

A moment later, I stumbled to Brac's side.

"Tannie!" Brac embraced me, then held me at arm's length. "Are you hurt?"

I shook my head. "I should've told you. I'm sorry!"

"So what in the blazes actually—"

But he never finished his sentence. Instead, he hurled me to the ground and ducked under a guardsman's sword seconds before it would've struck him. The clash of metal sounded. Mor crossed blades with the guardsman over our heads.

Brac's breath came in quick, frantic gasps as he worked to get his balance under him again.

Our eyes met for a heartbeat. "Tannie, run."

"But, Brac—"

"Go!"

My heart lurched. I'd never made a habit of listening to Brac's orders, and it didn't seem like I ought to start now.

Mor spared me half a glance before parrying another strike. "Tannie, please go!"

Couldn't ignore them both. At least I could try not to get sliced in two.

I crawled under an orange strand toward what I thought was the front of the throne room. Weapons flashed in the sunlight streaming through the windows. I saw a strand of orange smash a soldier square in the chest. He crumpled to the floor, and my breath stopped in my throat. The soldier's eyes gazed unseeingly. Open. Blank.

Was he dead—from story strands?

Wild stories, Zel had said. Boy, he wasn't kidding.

I scrambled away from the fallen soldier as quickly as I could. I heard a cry, the voice familiar: Aeron. But before I had time to find her, the body of her opponent crashed to the floor beside me. I accidentally stuck my hand right in a pool of his blood.

I gasped and fell back. Without thinking about it, I wiped the blood on the plum-colored skirt of my gown. I stared down at the dark smear on the fine material.

A scream nearby tore through the sounds of battle.

Braith's. Unmistakable.

"Let me go!" she cried.

I spun around. Where was she?

I finally managed to get my bearings—windows on my right, large entrance doors behind. The thrones, and hopefully the princess, should be straight ahead, and close. Probably just beyond the knot of fluttering ladies before me. I shoved through their screams and gasps.

I finally saw Braith, and my heart stopped.

Dray had her by the throat. His fingers dug into her flesh and he growled in her face. "I said, you're coming with me. Don't make me use force, because I will. I *always* get what I'm after."

Braith spoke around his grip with some difficulty. "Seems a bit late for threats, Dray." The words came in spurts. "Is this not force?"

"Even now you'd defy me, when I'm trying to keep you safe," Dray growled. "Can't you ever do as you're told?"

Braith clawed his hand from her throat and jerked away. "I'll not be manipulated by you," she fumed. "I'm not my father."

Then Sir Dray reached back and slapped the princess across her face.

"No!" Cameria's shout startled me. I hadn't seen her on the dais. Blood trickled from one corner of her mouth, but whatever battle she'd been fighting couldn't trump Braith being struck. She drew a dagger from a hidden scabbard beneath the folds of her apron and charged toward His Grace.

CHAPTER 46

THE ONE IN THE DARK

Racket sounded, and his fingers slipped around the bow. Arrows. Blades.

Always a soldier.

Keen ears were drawn to the noise. Body scaled the wall, fingers and toes in holds they had climbed hundreds of times before. Toward the noise. Toward the usurper's throne room.

The last place this face should be shown.

Pause. Investigate? Take the risk? Perhaps not. Perhaps turn back.

But the clamor. Men shouted. Women screamed. Metal clanged on metal, and a wild whirring sound. Like giant painted wings had taken to air, whistling and whipping.

Scurried closer. Slowed to a crawl. Brightness of daytime streamed from the room, assaulting the eyes. Stopped and waited to adjust to the burn.

Then hurried along the ceiling beams. Close to the walls, in the shadows.

And then the view into the room was clear. Battle, come to Gareth's seat of comfort at last.

So many years . . . his heart lurched. So many years since these eyes had seen this room where King Caradoc once held court.

Story strands flew everywhere—the unidentifiable whirring noise. Strands of pain and vengeance.

He unslung the bow to nock an arrow, just in case. Settled in to observe. Who had brought the sword to Gareth after all this time?

Easy to pick out the rebels from the armored guardsmen. A

dark-haired lad, handy with a sword. Short hair, no tail. A sailor. A tiny glint from a piece of gold in his ear.

A pirate.

There was a woman fighting. Holding her own with the men. Shorn hair and trousers on a lass.

Puzzling.

There was a Meridioni lad. Art raged from his fingertips.

Colormastery strands. Ablaze.

A wispy cage surrounded a pretty lass who might have been one of the courtiers if not for the shabby state of her gown. The cage of wisps—defensive songspinning.

Another colormaster at the back of the room. Water rolled around her, and a half dozen courtiers huddled in the safety of the fluid wall. Protective colormastery.

A farmer lad was warding off three soldiers at once. Yes, it was he who created the orange story filling the room.

What had Gareth done to stir such violence, such angst?

Ah, there was the old pretender himself. Surrounded by protectors, his massive bodyguard in a heap on the floor.

Had the usurper forgotten how to fight? It was the only thing he did well.

Seeing him, thoughts poured out in waves. Memories.

Another rebel pushed toward Gareth. An old soldier, gray hair and vicious swing. His profile looked familiar.

There was the fox-faced Sir Dray, his fingers wrapped around the throat of the princess. Scoundrel.

He could make the shot from here. His fingers tightened around the nock of the arrow, the string of the bow. But wary of the princess's movement. Could hit her if she didn't remain still.

And then a blur of familiar black hair. The young woman from the darkness. Cameria rushed toward the princess and Dray, her dagger drawn.

His heart skipped.

Another young woman. A lass with golden hair. A lass who looked like . . . Glain.

Something shifted. Mind jolted. And . . . the waves of fuzzy memory burst into clarity. Realization locked into place.

He looked down at his hands, wrapped around the bow. He was Yestin Bo-Arthio, First General of Tir, and there was the miraculous possibility that this golden-haired lass before him was his daughter, Tanwen. He was almost sure.

He drew the bowstring taut, sighted Dray, then released. Dray moved, last second, and the arrow nicked the back of his neck. Dray flinched and stumbled. Cameria missed her mark and tumbled to the floor.

Go. Move. Now.

He swung down the wall—plunging over unfamiliar curves in stones his fingers had never touched.

His sword was drawn before his feet hit the ground.

CHAPTER 47

TANWEN

I couldn't see where the arrow had come from. Seemed like someone was protecting the princess—or maybe all of us. But it must have been a stray from some guardsman.

Unless one of my Corsyth friends had managed to snag a bow somehow.

In any case, Sir Dray stumbled under the sting of his grazing wound. Braith flung herself toward Cameria. I was swallowed up in the mass of frantic courtiers again before I could see where they had gotten to.

I prayed they would find safety.

I shoved a swooning lady off me and turned back toward the fray of battle.

Where was Brac? I needed to find him. Make sure he'd managed to get out of the thick of it.

But where? How?

I forced my feet to slow and listen to my brain, not my wild, thumping heart. Didn't have a weapon on me, of course, so it wasn't like I could take off with a shout and start splitting folks in two the way Aeron might. And even if I did have a weapon, blazed if I'd know how to use it. But . . .

My gaze floated upward to Zel's wild strands.

I guess I did have *one* weapon.

I slipped to the side of the room, half-hidden behind some court ladies. At least my fancy dress helped me blend in while I worked to fish something from the dark recesses of my worn-out mind.

But none of those crowned stories would do. I needed to make something new. Something real and true and powerful. I needed to create, as Mor had shown me.

My eyes drifted shut, and I worked to build a picture in my mind.

A dry land. Parched. No green things, nothing living. Just cracked, dead earth, screaming for water through the gashes in its surface. And then the water came—not as drops of rain, but as a great flood of color.

Waves of orange and watery blue—for Zel and Karlith—and a ribbon of fierce black and white, which could only be Aeron. Flame wreathed the edges of the waves—that was for Dylun. A river of red flowed through the middle of the flood—deepest red for Warmil and the death he was so bent on atoning for. The airiest green vapor for Gryfelle. Glittering gold for Mor.

And a wide swathe of sparkling, seastone blue. It took me a moment to realize that was me. Looked like my eyes in sunlight.

Truly, it wasn't until that moment that I realized I really was a part of this just as much as the other weavers. I was one of them, and we were all in this together—live or die.

Live, I hoped.

The tide of color rolled over the parched land like water—healed it. Restored it. Truth and beauty returning to a land starved of it for so long.

My eyelids fluttered open. Guardsmen roundabout stared down at their armor. The silver was now splattered with all the colors of my imagining.

I almost laughed aloud.

Guessed my creations didn't have quite the bite of Zelyth's deadly strands. But I squeezed my eyes shut again and forced my mind back to the idea.

Grass poked through the earth. Plants sprang up—trees, flowers, vines. Through the greenery trod a beast, partially of my own making and partially what I imagined the golden Haribian animals we called halo-heads would look like. Never could get Riwor to tell me whether those things were real or just something from Haribi's fairy stories. But I always pictured their proud gold manes ruffling in the breeze all about their catlike faces.

The animal pawed through the fresh grass, lifted its head, shook the dew from its fur.

When I opened my eyes, the creature stood before me, in real and actual flesh and twice as large as I'd pictured him. The bottom of his belly came up to my shoulder. And he seemed to be waiting for my command.

I sucked in my breath and stepped back. Had I . . . had I made this creature? He yawned wide, then rumbled a low noise almost like a purr.

Guessed I had.

Ignoring a fresh wave of swooning and screaming around me, I thought one word: *Go.*

In a single, powerful bound, the beast cleared half the room. He made for one of Naith's priests.

And shredded the man to bits in two seconds flat.

I stumbled backward like I'd been struck. With a scream, the man—all fine robes and bejeweled fingers—disappeared into wisps like story strands. Then the gold-furred beast lunged for another priest. And another.

Then he turned on the one who had threatened me—High Priest Naith himself. His Eminence took a couple halting steps away. Then his gaze found me, and if glares could slice, I would have been flayed right there.

Next moment, I saw his lips move. A strand of shimmering blackness, like the star-speckled night, burst from nowhere and wrapped around my beast. Something invisible pulsed out from that story and hit me in a heartbeat. Set my stomach roiling and skin prickling.

What was it? Death? Evil? I wasn't sure. And I wasn't sure I wanted to know.

For one long breath, my beast was shrouded in the night. Naith spared me a final glower, then used the cover of his darkness to slip away from his attacker.

Before I had a moment to wrangle my wits, Naith had escaped from the throne room.

Was His Holiness a . . . storyteller? A storyteller with dark, wicked stories? I had to tell someone—Mor, Karlith, any of the others. They would know what it meant.

Then a tiny bubble popped in my mind. The sense of urgency, of burning information, weighed in my chest.

But I couldn't remember why.

A giant halo-head-looking creature pawed the ground before me, and I vaguely remembered I'd made him. That must be the sense of urgency weighing on my chest. Surely. I felt the burden of my own power—power I'd never asked for and didn't know quite how to use.

Guessed my stories did have some of that deadly bite, when they had a mind to.

I stopped counting how many guardsmen my beast shredded. Part of me relished the revenge I was finally getting on all those soldiers who'd bullied me and Brac, pushed us around, taken coppers from Farmer Bradwir's hands.

But the other part of me couldn't shake a nagging question. How many of these men were like Bo-Ifun, who'd been kind to me? Guardsman Bo-Ifun, who hoped to change the guard from the inside out. Had my beast ended any men like him? Even when you were fighting on the side of right, it wasn't all black and white.

But with the blades of the guard at our throats, I supposed it was us or them. Why did so many things in life come down to us or them?

The throng of people in the room thinned. It was starting to look like a field that's been harvested out. My eyes searched for my friends and found Warmil near a band of guards surrounding the king. He looked tired, like his swings weren't as swift as they ought to be.

Gryfelle crouched across the room. Our eyes met, and it was plain to see the relief ooze all over her face at finding me in one piece. But my stomach jolted when I realized she was crouched over Dylun.

Wispy feathers of song hovered over the colormaster—I supposed that meant he was simply injured and not dead if she was protecting him still.

But I couldn't help wondering how bad it was and if some protective song strands would be enough.

Zel struggled in another corner of the room. Blood flowed from a wound in his side, and it didn't seem reasonable that he'd be able to keep his attackers at bay for long. I sent a silent message to my story beast: *Help him.*

And there was Aeron with Sir Dray at the end of her sword. Lucky for him he was *at* the end of her sword and not *on* it. The councilman had his hands in the air, but he didn't look too pleased about it. Aeron appeared whole, if spent. Karlith sheltered a group of courtiers with a bubble of her colormaster's water—looking out for the unarmed, as one might expect of her. And then my heart gave a great sigh of relief, because there was Mor with a group of guardsmen whose weapons lay at their feet—guardsman who had surrendered, by the looks of it.

But who in the name of mountainbeast milk was that man with the bow?

He looked to have crawled out from under some rock where he'd spent the last twenty years—bedraggled and wild, like a wide streak of savage ran straight through his core. In those twenty years spent under a rock, or whatever uncivilized place he'd been camping out in, it seemed he'd survived on heavy lifting and half a piece of bread a day. I'd never seen muscles so lean, like they were ready to rip through the skin.

And he might've been an immortal from one of the goddesses' tales the way he loosed those arrows with such an eye. While I watched, he didn't miss a single shot. Every arrow found a mark. And by those marks, it wasn't hard to figure he was on our side.

But . . . why? Had he been the one to shoot the rogue arrow that allowed the princess to escape from Dray?

The bowman's head turned toward me, as if he could hear my thoughts. To my surprise, his eyes looked kind—and startled. He stood utterly still while we stared at each other. Then, quick as a flash of regret, he darted away and fairly disappeared.

I blinked and scanned the room for him. But he was gone. Seemed like he'd vanished, or else flown away, up to the ceiling.

But before I could complete a ceiling inspection, a shout from Warmil sent my heart to my throat. A guttural, animal cry of war like my ears had never heard and didn't care to hear again.

The old captain stood before Gareth. The king stared down at the blade by his throat. His many defenders lay in a heap at his feet.

Warmil edged his blade closer. "It's finished! The usurper, murderer of Caradoc II, has surrendered!"

Relief swept through me. It was over. Done. No more fighting; no more killing. Perhaps there could be peace at last.

Everything stilled, and only the heavy breathing of tired warriors, injured rebels, and scandalized ladies could be heard. I found my golden beast circling around Zel, and sent him a silent message: *It's done now.*

Like his very fabric had been caught up in a breeze, the creature swirled a moment, then wisped into nothingness. I couldn't decide if I ever wanted to see him again.

"Tannie?"

The voice, so faint it almost didn't register, seemed to come from the floor. But it didn't matter how soft the words were spoken or from how far away. I'd know that voice anywhere.

"Brac?" I spun in a circle—scanned the piles of bodies on the floor. But I couldn't find him. "Brac!"

"Here." Barely above a whisper, but close.

Something stirred under a nearby pile of guardsmen. I dropped to my knees and shoved with everything I had left.

And there he was—broken, collapsed on the floor. His lips, his mouth, glistened red—like they had many times when we'd eaten our fill of hathberries off the vines around Pembrone. Or like the times we'd sneak a couple fresh hathberry pies off his mam's kitchen windowsill as they cooled. He would suck out the sweet red filling from the holes on top of his, then place it back on the sill—an empty crust sitting there like a broken promise. Ma-Bradwir had caught him once and whipped him good. Then she had whipped him again after he insisted he'd taken the second one too. The one I'd eaten.

I supposed this was something like that. Just one more fall Brac had taken to protect me.

The last fall he'd ever take for me, for it wasn't hathberry juice on his mouth. It was his own blood, bubbling up from inside his broken body.

CHAPTER 48

TANWEN

I SWALLOWED THE CRY THAT WANTED TO ESCAPE FROM ME. "Brac." I touched his armor gingerly, so as not to disturb him any more than I had to. I could see that it had been knocked sideways somehow—probably wasn't fitted or attached properly in the first place. The spear, sword, dagger, or whatever else might've done the deed had slipped right past Brac's breastplate.

And into his gut.

Blood blossomed on his guardsman uniform around the wound—blacker spots on the crisp black of the palace guard.

Tears rolled down my face. I took Brac's hand. "Does it hurt?"

He tried to turn his head. "Don't reckon I can tell anymore."

"Oh, Brac. I'm so sorry." I tried to force my gaze away from his wound, from his lifeblood spilling all over the stones of Gareth's throne room.

"My fault much as yours, lass," he said. "Reckon we both been fools." He seemed to swallow with an effort. "Hey, Tannie?"

I squeezed his hand. "Aye?"

"I wish I had my hat, you know." He nodded his head slightly, and his helmet clinked against the ground. "This blooming thing don't fit me right."

"I know it doesn't." I resisted the urge to curl up on the ground beside him.

He cracked half a smile. "Never did, I suppose."

He'd never spoken truer words. I did my level best to lift his head and get the blasted helmet off without moving him too much.

My fingers fumbled as I loosened the ties on his breastplate. "That better?"

His eyes slipped closed, and my heart stopped for a moment. But then his eyes opened again and he smiled weakly. "Still wish I had my hat."

I laughed, watery through my tears. "Well, then I reckon I'd better get it for you."

His lips had faded to gray, like a winter morn by the sea. But his eyes stayed focused on mine.

I made the words come out. "Once, there was a farmer lad from Pembrone."

A ribbon of earth-toned leather unwound from my fingers.

"He could drive his best friend half mad when he wanted to."

The leather swirled in a slow circle above Brac's laboring chest.

"But even so, I loved him best of all."

The leather solidified into exactly what I'd been picturing in my mind's eye—Brac's floppy hat, complete with every blemish and sweat stain he'd collected over the years. Real leather. Not crystallized story.

I fingered the soft, worn grazer hide, then placed it on his chest. "How's that?"

"That's fine." His breath jagged. "Didn't know you could do that."

"Didn't know either, till the others showed me."

"You forgive me, Tannie? Can you?"

I brushed a lock of hair from his sweaty forehead. "What's gotten into that sunbaked brain of yours? What's there I've got to forgive you for?"

"For—" His own cough cut him off, followed by a sputter of blood. "For betraying your friends. Didn't know better at the time."

"Of course you didn't. And of course I forgive you."

Can I ever forgive myself?

Couldn't wrestle with that now. Not while Brac was slipping away from me.

"Tannie?"

"Shh. You rest now." I moved more sweaty hair off his face. His skin grew colder and more ashen by the moment.

"Can't. I got to ask you. Once more."

"Ask me what?" But I already knew, and I also knew what I'd say. Just this once before he was lost to this world.

"Will you marry me, Tanwen?"

I smiled, even though I was sobbing and my nose was running. I picked up Brac's hat and pulled it onto my own head, over my collapsed, deflated curls. Must have looked a sight with my fine dress, covered in blood and sweat. "Yes, I will."

He smiled—tried to reach up but couldn't find the strength and let his hand fall back. "If anything could make me stick around, it'd be that yes."

A dart of guilt shot through me. For that yes would never have come in any situation except this one—his final moments of life.

But I leaned forward and kissed his pale forehead. "Quiet now."

"What's this?" Warmil's booming voice nearly sent me leaping from my own skin.

I hadn't paid a bit of mind to whatever else had been going on around us in the throne room. But now I saw all the guardsmen, councilmen, and Gareth had been rounded up in one place. They stood under the careful guard of Aeron, Mor, and Zel. Dylun sat, propped up between Karlith and Gryfelle. It seemed his wounds had been attended to, at least for the moment.

Warmil dropped to his knees beside me. "Where's the trouble?" But before I could say anything, he answered his own question. Then he shot me a quick glare that I tried not to take personally. "'Sakes, Tanwen! Why are you sitting around here yapping while his life's on the line? Bandages, Karlith! We need to bind this properly."

"But . . ." I barely had time to jump out of the way before Warmil and Karlith descended on Brac. "But he's got a wound to the stomach," I said. "He was half dead by the time I got here. I thought . . ." I couldn't recall now where I'd heard that stomach wounds meant death, but I knew I'd heard it.

"It ain't in his stomach, Tannie." Karlith spared me a quick smile. "His stomach is up here." She touched a spot above Brac's wound.

"Yes, whoever took a bite out of him managed to miss everything important," Warmil said. "Luck was on his side today." He ripped a strip of cloth from the petticoat Karlith had handed to him. "But if you sit here shooting the breeze, he will bleed out. That I promise. What could possibly be so important?"

My face heated up at the reminder of my dishonest acceptance of Brac's proposal, but Brac only smiled. "Asked her to marry me."

Karlith kept her head down as she worked, but I didn't miss her heartbeat-quick glances—one at me, one at Mor across the room.

So. She'd noticed.

But Warmil just rolled his eyes at Brac. "Well, if you'd like to be around to make good on that offer, I suggest we bind you properly. We'll need to stitch this when we have the tools, but this will stave off the bleeding." He looked Brac directly in the eyes for the first time, and there was a fierce sort of kindness radiating from his gaze. "Hold on, son."

"Not sure"—Brac coughed again—"I can."

"Well, then don't. And my afternoon clears right up." Warmil rolled his eyes again. "Just hold on, will you? I can't make you stay alive, lad. Need to meet me halfway." He didn't look up, but raised his voice to a shout. "Karlith! We need gethweed. Now."

Karlith hustled toward us. "Already got it, Warmil." I hadn't realized it, but she'd disappeared for a moment. She handed him a wad of curly leaves—a plant I'd seen Ma-Bradwir yank from her garden hundreds of times.

Karlith noticed my stare. "Tirians have forgotten the old uses of the gifts the Creator gave us. Gethweed—means bloodweed in Old Tirian. Stops bleeding, prods along the blood in clotting like it's supposed to. A useful plant that everyone rips up and throws into the fire. We're lucky to have found some in the palace gardens at all."

Warmil stripped the leaves from the delicate stems of the gethweed. Then he packed Brac's wound with as many leaves as he could stuff in there. Brac winced but the result came swiftly. Blood stopped dripping to the stones beneath us. After Warmil wrapped the strips of bandage around Brac's middle, color returned to Brac's lips, then his cheeks. His breath deepened and became less labored.

"Rest here now, lad," Warmil said. "Sip some water if you can." He stood and wiped the blood from Brac's wound onto a rag—must have had some of Dylun's blood on it already, for it was a proper mess. Then he nodded to Mor. "What of the prisoners?"

My gaze followed Mor's to the group of prisoners huddled near the wall. Gareth looked like a riled snake, ready to strike. If not for the blade at his throat, I think he'd have made a go at escape—or maybe combat. But Aeron held her sword so close the king could scarcely swallow without catching a nick.

Mor nodded back at Warmil. "You tell me, Captain." His eyes flitted to me for a moment, then back to Warmil.

And me, with Brac's floppy hat on my head.

Warmil lifted his chin toward the door. "Dungeon. Until we can decide what to do with them."

Sir Dray growled in his throat. "You'll never get away with this."

In a heartbeat, a dagger Zel must have swiped from a guardsman was at Dray's neck. "I reckon your king will tell you to do whatever we say, or else he'll get a sword through the belly, and so will you. And I reckon, seeing as we'll be down in the dungeon anyway, that you'll show me where my wife is."

And I guessed Zel reckoned right.

A sorry procession of battered guardsmen, disgraced councilmembers, and one dethroned king trailed Mor from the throne room. Zel and Aeron kept the line orderly, even though Zel was still bleeding from the wound in his side. I wondered if I should spin my golden beast into existence again. Just in case they ran into any more guardsmen on the way to the dungeon. But the threat on Gareth's and Dray's lives seemed enough to keep my friends safe for now.

Gryfelle set to getting Dylun on his feet. Karlith put a hand on Warmil's shoulder. "This is your redemption, Warmil."

Warmil paused. But after a moment, he nodded once. "The

capture of the pretender king. Yes, I suppose it's the best I could ever hope for."

Karlith smiled. "No. That's not what I meant. You saved two lives today—Dylun and Tanwen's lad. Perhaps . . ." She nodded to his sheathed sword. "Perhaps it's time to stop taking life and start giving it back. Put your book learning to good use."

I turned to the captain. "You mean you have *useful* book learning in that brain of yours, not just stuff about politics and military tactics?"

A wry smile barely tugged at one corner of his mouth. "Aye, guess you could say that."

"He studied medicine," Karlith put in. "The old folk ways and the newer bits, too. You'll see all that when he stitches up your lad later." Karlith moved toward Dylun and Gryfelle. "Think about it, War. Giving life instead of taking it."

Warmil seemed to mull this over, even as he set about directing courtiers and picking up useful items from the throne room that had been turned into a battlefield.

"Tannie?" Brac's voice pulled me away from the captain and Karlith.

I crouched beside him. "Aye? What can I get you?"

"Nothing. It's just—oh!" He had tried to pull himself up on his elbows and didn't make it halfway before he collapsed back again.

"Here, you big dope." I propped him up and scooted around him so his head could rest in my lap. "That better? You're going to have to start using that sack of watta roots you call a brain if you don't want to undo all the good Warmil's done for you."

"Aye, that's better. I just needed to tell you something."

"Aye?"

Even upside down, I couldn't escape the wideness of his grin. "I love you."

A battle broke out in my mind. Because I loved Brac deeper and realer than a brother. I truly did, and the thought of losing him made me despair down to my bones.

But what had I done? Were Brac and I truly . . . engaged?

CHAPTER 49

BRAITH

"I NEVER EXPECTED IT TO END LIKE THIS." BRAITH SIGHED AND leaned her head back against the cool stone wall.

"Like what, my lady?" Cameria's words seemed to ping and echo around the whole cell.

The princess raised an eyebrow wryly. "I thought if I were ever to be executed, at least it would be for my own crimes." She ran her hand over the rough stones of the dungeon. "But perhaps I am as guilty as the king. That is, my fa—" Braith cut herself off.

She couldn't quite choke out the word *father*. And she knew now he had never really been king. "Truly, Cameria, I don't even know what to call him now. But whoever he is, I suppose I am complicit in his crimes."

"Complicit, my lady?" Cameria's voice was puzzled.

"Yes. Do you not think those who allow evil to continue and say nothing are as guilty as those who commit the evil acts in the first place?"

"I know not, my lady. But of this I'm sure." She looked straight at Braith and spoke each word distinctly. "You were not silent. You spoke out often. You tried to help those who needed it. You lived your conscience as best you were able. And you didn't know the whole truth." Her voice faltered. "But I—" Cameria broke off and looked away.

Braith tried to capture her friend's gaze. "You what? Please, Cameria. Let us speak plainly at last. At the end of all things when we have nothing to lose and no one left to protect."

Cameria looked at her again, eyes sorrowful. "I knew. Even as a child, I knew about the betrayal. That he murdered King Caradoc and those closest to him. I even helped with the failed uprising of Yestin Bo-Arthio. But when that fell apart, I retreated into silence. Accepted my reduced station. Accepted the enslavement of my people. If anyone is guilty of inaction—of allowing evil to continue and saying nothing—it is I."

Braith stared at Cameria as if a veil had been lifted off her friend. "You knew? But how . . . ?" All the times Cameria had been within touching distance of the king. All the times she had looked at his face, listened to him speak, swallowed his painful words.

And all the while, she had known he was a usurper of the worst kind.

Braith shook her head. "How could you stand it? Sitting at my father's table, a stone's throw away from the man who murdered your father and enslaved your people? Or sitting at the foot of my bed? Serving me. Waiting on me. Me, the daughter of the man who—" Braith couldn't force out the rest. Tears choked her breath. "Oh, Cameria. How you must despise me."

Cameria reached for Braith's hand. "No, my lady. I stayed close to protect you. You and . . ." She looked away again—distant, like she was adrift on some warm southern sea. "Others."

"Others?"

"Yes." Cameria gave a slight nod. "One other, anyway. He saved us from Dray in the throne room today. Do you remember the arrow?"

"Cameria, who are you talking about? One of the outlaw weavers?"

"No. Yestin Bo-Arthio. There's no sense keeping it quiet now. He is alive and has been living in the palace all these years."

Cameria leaned back against the stones. "I've helped him. Brought him food, ink for his journals, tried to keep his mind sound, though I'm not sure I've had success there. He was my father's closest friend in Tir. I needed to help him. I tried, at least." She sighed. "I don't suppose I'll get to see him again, but no matter. He'll find

Tanwen. She'll care for him now, and I believe they will find happiness together."

Words escaped Braith. Yestin Bo-Arthio—alive, just as her father had feared. And in the palace no less.

A sharp clang startled both women. They rose together and peered through the bars of their cell. The black-haired female soldier stood sentry by the door at the end of the line of cells, as she had since all the cell doors were locked and the other rebels left in search of the farmer boy's wife. But now there were more people in the hallway.

Braith stumbled away from the bars. She couldn't be seen. Not now. Not like this.

But it was too late. Tanwen's gaze locked directly onto the disgraced former princess. "Braith!"

CHAPTER 50
TANWEN

I SAW BRAITH TRY TO DUCK BACK INTO THE SHADOWS, BUT SHE couldn't hide from me. And stars' sake, why would she want to?

"Warmil!" I shot a look at him. "What are they doing in there?"

Warmil frowned into the cell that housed Braith and Cameria. "Everyone was to be locked up until we decide what to do with them. Everyone includes everyone."

I rolled my eyes and moved toward the bars. Braith stepped back even farther. I froze and cast a mystified glance through the iron barrier. Was she . . . angry? Ashamed?

I turned my irritation back to Warmil. "Blazing buttermints, War, they weren't part of Gareth's schemes. The princess always spoke up for us. And for Ifmere. You heard her yourself."

After a long moment of silence, Braith finally stepped out of the darkness, chin high but hands shaking. "I'm ready to accept whatever punishment is deemed appropriate."

"My lady." Cameria's voice was gentle but clear, her eyes insistent. "If that's true, then accept Tanwen's words—and what she offers."

Braith turned toward her friend. "And that is?"

I wanted to shout the word, but Cameria beat me to it.

"Mercy." Cameria smiled sadly. "You hardly recognize it, and no surprise. You're the only one around here who ever extends it."

Braith opened her mouth, but no words came out.

I turned back to my friends and addressed the captain again. "War, she has been my friend since the day I was brought here. You have to believe me. She wouldn't have been part of anything her father was doing. And Cameria . . ." My gaze shifted to the Meridioni woman. "If I'm not wrong, I think Cameria is a friend to my family. Or was once." I turned back to Warmil and threw my hands up. "You can't keep them in there like a couple of animals. It's not right!"

Mor put his hand on my shoulder. "Calm down, Tannie. War, you've seen enough of Braith to trust Tanwen's testimony, haven't you?" Then he turned to Braith. "If she tries anything, we'll put her straight back in. I'm sure she understands that."

I glared at him.

Braith maintained a dignified silence, though I could see a mix of shame and indignation churning on her face. As the daughter of Gareth Bo-Kelwyd, of course everyone would question her motives. Her very moral center, even. But it wasn't right.

Warmil nodded once. "Good enough."

Aeron put the key in the lock and opened the door. As Cameria and Braith passed by, she gave a nod of respect. "Ladies."

For a moment, we rebels, the former princess, and the maid stood in the hallway in awkward silence.

Braith finally broke it. "Thank you for releasing us. I can assure you we won't 'try anything,' as you say." She raised an eyebrow at Mor.

He bowed at the waist. "No disrespect meant, Lady Braith. You understand our position and our need for caution."

"Of course." She cleared her throat. "Might I ask a favor? Is . . . is my father nearby? May I see him?"

Aeron nodded. "He is, my lady." She looked at us. "Shall I escort her? I'll stay close."

"Very well," Warmil said. "Be careful."

Before following Aeron down the hall, Braith turned to me. Took my hand in hers. "Thank you, Tanwen."

I wanted to say something—to tell her what her kindness and moral stand had meant to me. But my heart was stuck in my throat. Instead, strands ribboned from my fingers. Warm light, shimmering silver mist, and a deep-green satin. Not green like Gareth's grass-colored strand, but rich like an evergreen tree.

The strands danced together. I thought her name—Braith—and the unexpressed gratitude crystallized. A flower with a deep-green stem, delicate white petals, and the silver sparkle that always signified Braith's presence in a story.

The flower dropped into my hand. I held it out to her. "Something for you, Braith. Something beautiful after so much pain."

She took it, tears glistening in her eyes. "Something new."

I grinned. "Aye. Something new."

CHAPTER 51

BRAITH

BRAITH HELD THE CRYSTAL FLOWER BETWEEN HER FINGERS AS she and Cameria followed the female soldier down a hallway lined with cells.

She forced herself not to look at the many guardsmen, former councilmen, and dignitaries of her father's court. The weavers had done quite a thorough job rounding them up, it seemed. There were some in there who oughtn't be—Braith was sure of it. Those who were loyal to Caradoc II in the old days but had grudgingly accepted her father's ascension. But if she could get the weavers to understand they could trust her, perhaps she could negotiate those nobles' releases.

"Here, Princess." The female soldier stopped several paces from the end of the hallway and gestured to the last cell. "He's in there. If you need me, I'll be just through that door."

"Wait." Braith put a hand on the soldier's arm. "What is your name?"

"Aeron, Your Highness."

"Thank you, Aeron. But why do you call me Highness? My father was never truly king. I'm not a princess."

Aeron paused. She glanced down at her boots, then turned her gray eyes back to Braith. "I like to call things as they are, my lady. Though you didn't inherit the throne through bloodline or fair conquest, I call you Princess Braith because I've only ever seen you behave in a manner worthy of the title. It's the same reason I never called Gareth king. If I'm to believe Tanwen's assessment of you, it only further supports my own observation—one that began many years ago when I was a young lass in Urian." She bowed. "I hope it doesn't bother you."

Braith's voice shook. "I only wish I had the same confidence in my virtue that you seem to. I didn't realize you'd grown up here. Did we know each other?"

"Not exactly. My father wasn't quite as important as all that. But that's a story for a different time." She nodded. "I'll be near, Highness, if you need me."

Cameria lingered for a moment. "I'll give you privacy, my lady." She gestured Braith toward the cell, then followed Aeron back down the hallway.

Braith paused then stepped forward.

"I did all you asked of me," a voice muttered from the darkness. Definitely her father. "Everything. Why did you let this happen? It was all supposed to be mine. Caradoc's life for my rule. Your systems, with those two fools at the helm, for my power."

Braith froze. Who was he talking to?

A roar from the former king ripped through the air. "Why won't you answer me?" A dull thud sounded, like something hard had been struck. The voice shriveled to a whimper. "Why have you left me?"

"Father?" Braith steeled her courage and stepped closer to the iron bars. She peered into the darkness of the cell. "Father?"

The deposed king sat on the straw-covered floor, hunched over, head down. Braith noticed his hand and stifled a gasp. Blood oozed down his knuckles, and several fingers splayed at unnatural angles. He must have punched the stone wall with his bare fist.

"Father, it's me." Braith stood close enough to the bars to touch them, but she folded her hands in front of her skirt. "Will you not speak to me?"

His gaze lifted to meet hers, and raw anger seethed there. He growled something in his throat, but Braith couldn't make it out.

"Father, who were you talking to?"

He squeezed a handful of filthy straw in his uninjured hand. "Left me."

Braith couldn't escape the feeling that her father's mind was splintering before her very eyes.

"Who has left you?"

But he didn't seem to be aware of her presence any longer. He grumbled and growled to himself, punctuating his ramblings with shouts every once in a while. Braith watched him in silence for a few moments. Tears snaked down her cheeks, and she gripped Tanwen's flower tighter.

Finally, she knelt so that she might see him face-to-face. "Father." Braith paused to allow her thoughts to collect. "I have often wished I were something different so I might have pleased you better. But I must always stand by what is right. Can you understand that?"

The disgraced man, mind disintegrating and hands covered in blood and straw, glared holes into his daughter. "Traitor."

Expected though it was, the word pierced Braith. She shored her heart against it and nodded. "Good-bye, Father."

He didn't acknowledge her.

Braith rose stiffly and strode toward the exit. But just as she passed by the last cell, a hand darted out from between the bars and clamped onto her wrist.

Braith tried to scream, but she was pulled toward the cell and another hand clamped over her mouth before any sound escaped.

CHAPTER 52

BRAITH

"SHH." THE SOOTHING HISS SOUNDED JUST BESIDE BRAITH'S EAR.

Familiar.

Then the expected voice followed. "I'm going to take my hand from your mouth. Don't scream." The hand dropped from Braith's face.

She inhaled deeply to settle the hammering of her heart. "Release my arm immediately, Sir Dray."

"Do you promise to stay?" A defeated note rang in his voice. He was utterly beaten and desperate. Braith had never seen Dray in such a state before.

Still . . .

"No. I make no such promises. Release me, just the same."

He did, and Braith turned to face him, but she stepped beyond his reach. In the dim light of the cell, his graying hair looked grayer. Braith had never seen a speck of dust on his clothing before—not a strand of hair out of place. Now he was positively bedraggled.

"Will—" He seemed to swallow with difficulty. "Will you please stay for a moment?"

Braith nodded. She hesitated for a few heartbeats, then stepped toward the cell bars. "What is it, Sir Dray?"

"Why do you call me that? Do you not realize it's over?"

Aeron's words flooded back to Braith—that she chose to call Braith a princess because the former guardswoman believed Braith worthy of the title.

Dray was no knight. Not as knights should be anyway. Nor was he noble in the true sense of the word.

"You're right, Dray." She took another step closer. "What is it you want to say?"

His arms reached through the bars. Braith recoiled, but she could see he didn't mean to grab her. Only—what? Reach out? Touch her?

Still too dangerous.

"I wanted to say that I—" Dray swallowed again. "I'm sorry. I didn't mean to hurt you the way I did in the throne room. It's only—" He broke off and looked down.

"It's only," Braith continued for him, "that you wanted to control me. You don't know how to manage something you can't control, except to crush it."

Dray's gaze lifted, and Braith couldn't conceal her surprise. Genuine hurt swam in his eyes—tears, even. "Don't you know I love you, Braith?"

Braith almost laughed—almost cried. Had to fight the urge to scream at him. But she kept her peace and said nothing for a moment. Then she looked him straight in the eyes. "I believe you do, in your own way." And it was true.

"What does that mean?"

"I think as much as you are able to love another person, and in the fashion after which you are accustomed, you might love me."

Dray pressed himself against the bars. Braith sucked in her breath at the hungry look in his eyes. "This from the ice princess," he said, bitterness hemming the words. "What does she know of love?"

Braith cringed under the judgment in that nickname she hated, often whispered behind her back. But she collected all the compassion she felt for Dray and spoke from that place instead. "I suppose you're right. I am an ice princess. I've built a wall of ice around my heart to protect it—to keep myself safe from those who would exploit me. But a heart still beats inside. A heart that can feel and love, if there is something in this world good enough to love. Today, I'm not sure there is."

The hunger in Dray's eyes settled into despair. "Like Princess Cariad," he said. "You're the Stone Princess, except your heart is walled with ice. Tell me, Braith. If your heart is surrounded by ice, what is mine? You speak as though you're better than I, so tell me. You're ice, and I am . . . ?"

Braith swallowed whatever emotion was rising in her throat. "You've compromised too much. You made your choices in life, and you've sold pieces of your heart along the way so you might better reach your ends. Your heart isn't protected by a wall of anything—it's been replaced a piece at a time. Flesh for stone."

Dray looked down. She was startled to see he was shaking. "Is there any coming back from that, Braith?" His voice sounded broken.

She stepped toward the exit. "I hope so, Dray. For all our sakes, I hope so."

CHAPTER 53
TANWEN

I COULD HAVE COLLAPSED ONTO MY BED AND STAYED THERE A fortnight, and it still wouldn't have been enough sleep. I also could have eaten an entire grazer, a field's worth of smashed watta root, a bushel of buttered sweet roots, and a mound of hathberries as big as the annual planting tax haul. Even then, I still might have been hungry.

But instead of any of that I shut the door to my chambers behind me, leaned against it, and let myself sob.

Wasn't sad, exactly. Everything was nearly as good as it could have been. Brac, my accidental betrothed, was laid up in the infirmary with Dylun, where everyone seemed confident they'd recover from their wounds. Gryfelle, Mor, and Karlith were settling a patched-up Zel into a vacant room in the palace. They'd found Ifmere in her cell. The baby had come already and was healthy as any wee one born of hearty Tirian stock I'd ever seen. A little lad with Zelyth's eyes and Ifmere's sweet-root hair. But Ifmere herself was exhausted to the point of death and half starved at that.

Karlith seemed to be making it her personal mission to see the lass and that ruddy, bouncing little boy recovered. So I knew they'd both be fine, and if they were, Zel's wound wouldn't trouble him much. He had his family, as he never thought he'd be able to, and I think if he could have stood toe-to-toe with the Creator, that would've been the only thing he would have asked for.

So I wasn't sad, even with the mess I'd made of things with Brac. Because at least he'd live. I was just utterly spent as a body could be.

Aeron and Warmil fairly exploded with strategies for how to proceed from here, though I could hardly think about that at all. What happened when a king was overthrown and there wasn't anyone to take his place? Couldn't exactly post the job opening in the town square, as was usual when looking to hire somebody for something. But I supposed I'd let someone else figure out that business. When it came to politicking, I was about ready to mind my own onions forevermore.

Seemed the former king was unraveling worse and in shorter order than I watched my father's mind unravel in his journals. Karlith was most troubled by his ramblings and thought we ought to have someone watch him—make note of the nonsense dribbling out of his mouth, though I couldn't see why. War said he, Mor, and Aeron could rotate shifts on that one, though no one was quite as needled about it as Karlith. Seemed to me Gareth just couldn't cope with defeat very well.

But, truly, when did I ever know what I was talking about?

Aeron had also been assigned to keep guard over Braith and Cameria. Didn't blame Warmil for being cautious about that, I supposed, but it still grated on me a little. Poor ladies had been through quite the ordeal, and being kept under lock and key—even if it wasn't in the dungeon—didn't seem entirely fair. But once they got to know Braith, they'd see she wasn't a threat. I knew it.

One question gnawed at me, and I wouldn't have satisfaction until I'd found a moment to ask Cameria. What had happened to my father? How long had she been able to keep him alive? How had . . . *it* finally happened?

Or had it happened at all?

I pushed away the tiny voice in my head that kept asking that question. It didn't seem possible he could be alive, so it was a fool waste of time to bother with wondering. But still . . .

I thought of Father's journals. I'd never had a chance to finish investigating. Where did the filled journals stop? Could it have been less than two days ago that I'd fallen asleep on one of those books? Seemed a moon, at least.

Why not check them now?

I found the secret key in its usual spot around my neck. Without thinking too hard about how tired and famished I was, I shuffled over to the trick bookshelf. The key slipped into its notch, and I felt a thrill shoot through me as the false rock clicked and loosed from its home. Then the lever came into view. A moment later, the panel creaked open.

I started. There was a man sitting in the middle of my secret passageway, a journal on his lap and a pen quiet in his hand. He covered his face to block the light, but I recognized him at once.

I gasped. "You!"

He lowered his hand and blinked several times, but he didn't speak.

"The wild bowman. What are you doing in here? Who—?"

But before my question could get all the way off my tongue, I froze, solid as grazer milk on a winter night. I glanced from the shelves of journals lining the wall to the one in his lap. The pen in his hand. The ink-stained fingers. The straggly gray hair.

This stranger, the wild bowman who had helped us in the throne room, was old enough to be my father.

I lifted one hand to my mouth. "Yestin . . ." I whispered. A lump formed in my throat. I took a halting step toward him. "Yestin Bo-Arthio?"

He didn't stir except for another blink. His muscles seemed coiled and ready to spring, but he kept still.

Before I had a chance to think about it, story strands poured from my fingers. Something in my mind wove the idea together. The strands coiled like wisps of smoke—fuchsia, gold, blue, purple, green. A knot like my secret key swirled in the middle of the colored smoke, except this one was gold instead of silver. I didn't know what it meant or where it came from, but all it needed was one command from me.

Finish it.

And the strands crystallized into a glass orb the size of a pebble with the golden knot and colored smoke still swirling inside. The orb dropped into my hand. I stared at it for a second, then held it out to the man on the floor.

His fingers—all callouses like I hadn't seen even on the oldest, craggiest Pembroni farmers—reached out, hesitated, then took the tiny ball from my palm. He stared at the thing like it was a ghost.

My heart fell. Could he speak anymore? Even if he could, it seemed clear he didn't recognize me—that his mind must have fully slipped away some years back. The reality of it was too unbearable to stomach. I'd finally found my father, my only family left. But would it make a difference if he didn't know me? Seemed his mind was lost long ago, so really I was only meeting yet another stranger. I was still alone—still an orphan.

I felt I was being sucked into a pit of despair that wanted to swallow me.

But then he spoke. The words came slowly. "She used to make this one." He stared at the glass marble.

My heart hammered at the sound of his voice. His throat sounded a size too small—I supposed out of lack of use. But his words were clear, understandable. Intelligent, like how he sounded in the old journal entries.

I just stared at him in dumb shock. Afraid he might disappear if I blinked.

"My Glain," he croaked. "Your mother. She told this story." His face creased into a smile and he held up the marble. "I don't remember the words."

I kept staring.

His gaze lifted from the glass orb to me. "Hello, my Tannie."

Finally, the spell broke. I rushed to him as he reached out for me. I dropped to my knees and burst into tears. We fell into a hug. A hug that'd been thirteen years in the making and left Yestin Bo-Arthio with a very wet shoulder and me with the fullest feeling inside I could ever remember.

"Daddy," I sobbed.

CHAPTER 54

TANWEN

"THANK YOU ALL FOR GATHERING TODAY," BRAITH SAID, SITTING uncomfortably in her seat. "I didn't expect such a swift or positive response to my request, in light of recent events." Braith's gaze dropped to her folded hands, and my heart flew out to her. Poor thing didn't know which way was up these last few days since her father fell.

But she held herself straight, like a lady of the palace ought, and managed to look dignified in a simple pine-green dress like a respectable merchant's daughter might wear. But not, I noticed, like a courtier or royal. Seemed she didn't think it was her place anymore.

Around a wooden table in some forgotten palace meeting room, a ragtag group had gathered at Braith's invitation. Most everyone from the Corsyth, including Dylun all wrapped in bandages around his middle; a few members of Gareth's court, who Braith seemed to trust on some level; some people I'd never seen before but who Father said were connected in some way to King Caradoc's court; and Cameria next to Braith.

My father paced in one corner of the room. He didn't like to sit in proper chairs, and all these people made him nervous, I knew. But he looked better by the day. His hair was groomed and pulled back into a tail, he wore clean clothes, and he'd trimmed his beard into something that looked proper. I'd made him take a real bath. Several of them, actually. He looked so improved, in fact, I could almost see a former First General in there somewhere.

And then there was me. I couldn't have belonged in the room any less if I'd tried. But Braith had asked me to come, so I had.

Braith cleared her throat. "I know I have no authority to call this meeting, but I beg your forgiveness and pray you will see I only do this to keep in mind what is best for Tir." Her voice faltered, and she paused a moment. After a visible swallow, she continued. "Something must be done about the state of things. Word of the king's fall is spreading quickly. Chaos is near at hand and, indeed, already reaches the palace doorstep. Riots, looting. Most of you know how it's been in Urian since my father—"

She paused again. Her eyes closed, like she was trying to keep from retching. Then she opened them again. "Since the end of Gareth's reign. As the trouble presses inward to the palace, it also presses outward. King's guardsmen all over Tir are abandoning their posts. Some are inciting riots. Others are simply waiting for someone to give them orders. It seems that Tir is in need of a leader."

One of Gareth's courtiers spoke up. "Has anyone heard from the queen?" He corrected himself quickly. "That is, Frenhin Ma-Gareth."

Braith's lips pressed together for a moment before she spoke. "It seems the former queen has fled. Several garments are missing from her closet, as are many of her items of personal and monetary value. Her closest servants are missing. The only logical conclusion is that she has retreated into hiding."

And left her only child in the palace to face the wrath of the Tirian people.

I felt sick on Braith's account.

"Forgive me, Lady Braith." Dylun looked directly into Braith's eyes. "But are you certain what Tir needs is another leader? How have we any guarantee this leader would not become a tyrant just like his predecessor?"

Mor plunked his elbows on the table and propped his chin on his fists. He shot a glance my direction. "Here we go."

Dylun lifted his chin but refused to acknowledge Mor. "Perhaps what we need is a stateless society. It could work, you know. Only then will there be true freedom, and not just for weavers and those of non–Tirian blood. But for *all* people."

Another of Gareth's courtiers, who I vaguely recognized from his seat at the council table, scoffed. "The Meridioni sure has novel ideas for Tir's future. But we have always had a king, dark one, and if you don't like it, I suggest you head south, back where you came from."

Warmil crashed his fist to the table. His fierce eyes shot daggers at the councilmember. I had to stifle a giggle. You would never guess that Warmil and Dylun had gone around and around about just this sort of thing. Reminded me of Brac and how he could tease and taunt and torment his wee siblings until the grazers wandered home, but if anyone else spoke a word against them, he'd level him to the ground in a flash.

I supposed Dylun and Warmil had become something like brothers in all those years crouching in that painted forest hideaway.

"Enough." My father's voice filled the room, the rasp of disuse framing his words. "Bo-Ino, isn't it?"

Dylun's eyes widened. "Yes, it is."

Father nodded. "I knew your family." Then he addressed the rest of the table, speaking slowly, each word an effort. "Bo Ino is not mad. I've seen much." He paused and looked down. "An age ago." His eyes clouded a moment, but then he was back. "Some peoples exist without rulers. But even were that not the case, all ideas must be listened to, respected, discussed. If you cannot do so, you should leave."

Thick silence enveloped the table.

Braith's gaze trained on Father. "What do you think about Bo-Ino's idea, General Bo-Arthio? Is a society without government—without leaders—possible for Tir?"

Father shook his head. "Too revolutionary now. Tyranny to anarchy will only make way for chaos. The Tirian Empire is too vast and has been oppressed too long." He swallowed visibly, then cleared his throat. "Perhaps revisit in a generation or two."

"Seems to me you wouldn't need to." The words flew out of my mouth unexpectedly.

Every head at the table swiveled toward me.

Braith nodded her encouragement. "Yes, Tanwen?"

"Well, meaning no offense, Dylun, but it seems if we had the right kind of leaders, we wouldn't need to do away with them altogether, would we? We're so used to a bad king, it doesn't take much brains to figure out why a country without leaders sounds nice." I glanced at Braith and felt a blush creep up my cheeks, but I went on. "Maybe if we found the right sort of people to lead Tir, we wouldn't want to shove them out after a couple generations."

One of the men I didn't recognize glanced around the table. "Fair point."

Phew.

I leaned back in my chair.

Discussion volleyed back and forth for a while after that. To tell the truth, I didn't understand a lot of it, and I don't think some of the others did either. Mor had to keep kicking Zelyth under the table, as the poor lad nodded off in his chair every few moments. Didn't suppose he was getting much sleep with the new wee one about. Plus, it's not like everything being discussed was riveting.

I did notice that whenever conversation got heated or two people couldn't seem to understand each other, all heads turned toward my father for help. Clear to see how he'd ended up leading every soldier in Tir under Caradoc II. Even rasping out his words in fits and starts, he was fair and reasoned and somehow managed to see all sides of an issue.

A movement caught my attention. One of Gareth's courtiers stared at Karlith. "What in the name of the goddesses are you doing?" he asked.

Karlith barely glanced up and continued curling her fingers around. She smiled. "Creating."

Another moment passed—dead silence all around—and Karlith had painted a throne that looked so real it seemed it might pop off the table. A vine wove about the intricately carved seat. And out of every inch of the vine bloomed shimmering white velvet-petals.

There was murmuring from those gathered at the table.

Braith held up a hand. "Please." She looked at Karlith. "I'd like to know what it means."

"It means," Karlith said with a smile, "it's high time we picked that right sort of ruler."

After a moment of quiet, an unexpected voice chimed in. "I have a nomination."

I knew the surprise was written all over my face as I turned toward Dylun. How had we gone from stateless whatcha-call-it to a nomination for the new ruler of Tir?

A lady of Gareth's court nodded. "I have a nomination too."

"As do I."

"So do I." It was the first thing Gryfelle had said all meeting. She looked pale, and I wondered how long her night had been. I hoped she hadn't been suffering.

I raised my hand, then immediately realized no one else had done so before speaking and dropped it. "I have a nomination."

Glances were shared all around the table.

But Father spoke first. "Lady Braith."

"Yes?" Braith looked at him, a question on her face.

"Braith, seconded." Dylun nodded to the former princess.

"I nominate Lady Braith."

"It has to be Braith."

"Lady Braith for Tir's new leader."

Braith started, her face stunned. "Pardon me?"

An old man, one of Caradoc's courtiers who sat next to Braith, leaned over and patted her hand. "If we're looking for the right sort of leader, my dear, how could we think of anyone else?"

Braith's eyes widened. "But I—" She shook her head. "I'm not anyone anymore. You understand, don't you? I'm not, nor have I ever been, a real princess. Why would . . . ?" But she couldn't finish her question through the tears trickling down her face.

Cameria was crying nearly as much, but she laughed. "You are right, my lady. Perhaps you were not a princess, but now you are queen. Your Majesty."

CHAPTER 55

TANWEN

I LEANED AGAINST THE TRUNK OF ONE OF THOSE TREES THAT grew along the river's edge—my favorite kind, where the branches seemed to be pouring their leaves out onto the ground. But this tree wasn't by the river's edge. It was in one of the palace gardens. This was the best garden because everything wasn't neatly manicured and trimmed just so. The flowers sprouted up here and there, the way they wanted to and not the way some royal gardener had planned. Felt natural. Peaceful. A bit like home somehow.

Though the sun had begun its slow dip toward the horizon, a warm breeze ruffled through the drooping branches of the waterfall tree, my skirts, and my hair. I closed my eyes against it—drank it in and let it wash over me.

It had been a couple weeks since Gareth was toppled, and I guessed we were already into the first moon of summer now. Hard to believe how the world had turned upside down and sideways since the last moon of spring.

"Care for company, Tannie?"

My eyes popped open with a start. "Mor?"

Blue eyes sparkled down at me. "Aye, that's what they call me. Leastways, to my face."

I didn't even try to hide my surprise. "Aye, but I thought you were dodging me."

His smile slipped and his gaze dropped. "I suppose I have been." He plunked down beside me and leaned against the trunk. "It's just been . . ."

He trailed off and silence settled between us.

After a moment, I offered a suggestion. "Awkward?"

"Aye." He looked away, out toward the banks of the river, though the buildings of Urian blocked them from our sight. "How's your . . . I mean, how's Brac?"

Now it was my turn to look away. "He's mending."

I let the subject evaporate like an errant story strand. What else was there to say? Should I insist I didn't mean to betroth myself to him?

Aye, that'd make the air between us less prickly.

"Mor?" I said.

"Yes?"

I kept on looking away so my gaze wouldn't unnerve him. "What did you do?"

"What, today?"

I laughed. His confusion sounded genuine. "No. In your past. The thing you're trying to erase by doing right. You never did tell me."

He let out his breath in a long, slow stream. "Promise you won't despise me?"

"No." I felt his gaze on me and I swiveled around to meet it. "What? For all I know, you pulled the legs off a passel of fluff-hoppers. Or dropped small children down a well on purpose. Or . . . something else unforgiveable."

He stared at me, then burst into laughter. "Pulled the legs off fluff-hoppers? Oh, Tannie." His laughter quieted, then he took to looking toward the river again. "It was nothing like that. My father, Lidere, was a fishing boat captain. I was raised on the Menfor Sea, working with him and his crew." He smiled at some fond remembrance. "I used to tell the men stories in the evenings. They loved that. Strands of magic and history and truth, swirling around a small lad barely old enough to tie a proper knot.

"We did well, my family. Well enough that Father hired a tutor, and I got a Urian education in the hull of my family's ship. It was a happy childhood, sailing and fishing and staying blissfully removed from all the unrest under Gareth. Father wanted it that way, I think. Knew I'd have a bull's-eye on my back because of my weaving gift. It was his way of trying to keep me safe.

"But the guard arrested him shortly after my sixteenth birthday, four years ago. The official story was something about unpaid taxes, but that's rubbish. Someone later told me it was because he'd refused to have me registered as a story peddler and he ought to have done by then, since I wasn't working under a registered mentor. In any case, they took him to the Urian dungeons. When they executed him—"

"Wait a minute," I cut in. "They killed him? For not registering you as a peddler?"

Mor smiled wryly at me. "No, they killed him for 'unpaid taxes.' But really they killed him because he wouldn't jump at the king's command." Mor paused.

"Mother was already ill, and when we got the news that Father was dead, it did her in. Lost both my parents in the space of a week. Then, a couple weeks later, the guard showed up again." His voice caught, and he had to collect himself before he could continue. "They took my father's ship and my little sister as payment for my father's supposed debt."

His words hung thick and heavy in the air for a long moment before I could form a response. "I didn't know you had a sister."

"I did. Once. They carried her off to become a servant in the palace, supposedly, but I'm sure they killed her too. She was thirteen. And I . . ." He swallowed. "Well, I just let them. Didn't fight for her or anything. Just let them take her away. I didn't go after her. They snatched her, left, and that was it." He picked up a pebble and chucked it at a cluster of wildflowers. "Instead of going after her, I took to the sea again. It was the only place anything made sense. Snagged an unflagged vessel—don't ask how—and started pirating to get by. Wasn't going to be able to live on the right side of Gareth anyway, so I didn't see wrong in pillaging and plundering his royal vessels or military outposts. And all the while, I left my only sister to her fate."

I sat quietly for a moment. It wasn't noble, what he'd done. No two ways about that. But he'd been a young lad, scrambling to make his way after his life had been uprooted. Just as I'd been a young lass, scrambling to make mine. I was certain I hadn't acted nobly every moment of the last moon.

"Mor?"

He turned to look at me.

"What was her name?"

"Digwyn." He smiled faintly. "Means 'little fish' in Old Tirian."

I smiled back. "I bet she'd understand. She'd understand that if you could do it over, you'd do it differently. And I—" I swallowed around the lump in my throat. "I understand too. Why you must stick by Gryfelle, even after she doesn't know you anymore."

I understood. Didn't mean I *liked* it.

"Aye," he said. "I made things worse for Gryfelle, in a way. She asked me to let her be and I wouldn't. I should've done as she asked, but I chose what was right for myself. Again. I was all moony over her, and I wouldn't let her alone."

He sighed. "But that's another story for another time. At least now you know the short of why I have to stop choosing myself. Why I have to think of Gryfelle above all else, even when it doesn't matter to her anymore. Right is right, whether Gryfelle can remember her own name or mine or nothing at all. And that matters to me. It will always matter to me. Or else I'm still that same selfish pirate who walked the other direction when his sister was stolen."

My heart seemed to press against the wall of my chest. But I knew there was truth in what he said, what he was trying to do, so I didn't fight it.

"I haven't seen Gryfelle in a while. How is she?"

Mor looked up toward the darkening sky. "Unwell, Tannie. She's quite unwell. She hasn't seen anything beyond the walls of the infirmary for the last two days. She . . . she doesn't know herself half the time."

My heart pressed harder. "Surely there's something that can be done." Seemed unfair that no answer, no solution, existed.

"That's actually why I came to find you." He pulled a piece of thick parchment from an inside pocket of his vest. I caught a glimpse of the royal seal as he opened it.

I peered over his shoulder and read the fancy script along the top. "'Vessel Ownership Registration.' What's that?"

"Queen Braith's given me a ship."

"Mor! Your own ship?"

Then an avalanche of uncertainty buried me. Did this mean Mor was leaving? Would he be gone in the new queen's service all the year round?

I tried to force my voice to sound as bright as it had three heartbeats earlier. "Does that mean you're setting sail soon? Captaining a merchant vessel under the new banner of Queen Braith or something?"

"Not exactly. The queen has granted me the favor of one of her vessels at my desperate request. I've heard rumors that there might be help for Gryfelle—hope for Gryfelle. We've heard word of an ancient cure, a relic whose pieces are scattered over the wide world. There's meant to be some kind of healing power in it. Maybe it's just a legend. Maybe the tales are rooted in truth. But I'll never know if I don't try. I have to try."

"Of course you do, Mor. If there's help out there for Gryfelle, I know you'll find it." And I meant it.

He nodded. "But I can't go alone. I'll need a crew. And friends about me." His gaze flicked up to mine. "The black-glass palaces of Minasimet, the sticky jungles of the Spice Islands, the windswept plains of Haribi, and anywhere else we can find port."

As he spoke, strands of story swirled into being between us, dipping and twisting and solidifying by the second. After a long breath, the strands blinked into a real form—a black tricorn hat like all the fishermen and sailors wore out on the seas. Except a silky white ribbon wrapped around the crown of this hat. And a fluffy white plume sprouted from the band, secured with a sparkling blue pin—a pin that, if I wasn't mistaken, was the exact color of my eyes.

The hat dropped into Mor's hands. He stared at it a moment,

then held it out to me. "What do you say, Tannie? Will you come with us?"

Could I pick up and leave Brac, leave Father, after I'd just been reunited with them?

But then I thought of Gryfelle. She lay dying up in the infirmary, and she was one of my kind—one of my own. If I had a chance to help her, I must take it.

I beamed at Mor but couldn't seem to form words.

He mirrored my grin and set the sailor's hat upon my head. It fitted perfectly.

Mor popped to his feet, then helped me up after him. He brushed a lock of hair back behind my ear, then settled the hat further onto my head. "All right, farm girl." His eyes twinkled with mischief and the promise of what tomorrow might bring. "You ready for a real adventure?"

EPILOGUE

"Dirty rotten liar." Gareth crushed a fistful of filthy straw in his good hand. "You promised me."

Had you done everything I required, this wouldn't be happening.

"I never failed you."

Then why has it all fallen apart?

Gareth smashed his good hand into the stone wall of his cell. "Goddesses' blood! Blazed if I know. You're supposed to be the one with all the answers. You tell me."

A pause. The Master didn't like to be questioned.

Perhaps I picked an inadequate representative.

"Then maybe it's time you found a new one." Gareth leaned his head back against the wall. "I'm finished."

Another pause.

As you wish.

A silky black strand slithered through the iron bars of his cell. The strand coiled up, raised as if to strike. Then the thing shot forward and clamped around Gareth's neck.

The strand tightened in a heartbeat. Gareth clawed at it.

But it was no use. Though it squeezed the breath from his lungs and cut the blood from his head, there was nothing solid to grab hold of. It was one of the very story strands Gareth had tried so hard to control—and at the Master's bidding.

And all along the Master was . . . a weaver?

Gareth collapsed to the ground, flailed in the straw for a moment. Then he stopped struggling.

As the last bit of air left his body, Gareth's mind went to the only good he had ever known. A terrifying final thought flickered through him.

What if the Master came after Braith next?

Continued in
The Weaver Trilogy: Book 2
The Story Mage

ACKNOWLEDGMENTS

Novel writing is a strange process—wholly solitary at most points, yet involving the support and skillful contributions of others at key junctures. I'm not sure I can adequately thank everyone who has poured into this story, but I'm going to try.

First, to Dave. Without your support and unwavering encouragement, I never could have pursued my passion for storytelling. You're my lobster.

To my children—Shane, Jared, and Keira—for mostly understanding when Mom is in the weird artist place and needs lots of space and silence. I love you all with the fire of a thousand suns. Now go clean your rooms.

To my mom, who was the first person to fall in love with Tanwen besides me. And to my dad, my favorite colormaster of all time. Thank you for the beautiful map of Tir featured in this book. My story strands are honored to keep company with your colormastery strands.

To my faithful agent, Rachel Kent. You saw something in me very early in my career, and you never lost confidence that I would realize my potential someday. You've been my professional lifeline in moments when I felt like giving up. Thank you.

To Kirk DouPonce, for the ridiculous cover. You're the literal best.

To my critique partners who helped me shape Tanwen's journey—fellow weavers Ashley Mays, Teddi Deppner, and Avily Jerome. I love you all. To the Smoking Gunns, who are the only reason I finished drafting *The Story Peddler* in the first place. To the mentors who supported, encouraged, and believed in me as a writer and this story, specifically—Randy Ingermanson, Robin Jones Gunn, and James Scott Bell. Thank you for your wisdom and for being nothing like Riwor.

And to Steve Laube, who gave me a chance. You took me and this story under your wing, and I'm forever grateful. You're a man of talent and integrity. I couldn't have asked for a better editor. Also . . . squirrel face!

And, of course, all glory goes to God, Giver of creativity and Weaver of all things.

Lindsay A. Franklin is a bestselling author, award-winning editor, and homeschooling mom of three. She would wear pajama pants all the time if it were socially acceptable. She lives in her native San Diego with her scruffy-looking nerf-herder of a husband, their precious geeklings, three demanding thunder pillows (a.k.a. cats), and a stuffed wombat with his own Instagram following.

Connect with Lindsay!

Website: *lindsayafranklin.com*
Facebook: *facebook.com/lindsayafranklin*
Twitter: *@LinzyAFranklin*
Instagram: *@linzyafranklin*
Pinterest: *@linzyafranklin*